INTRUSION PROTOCOL

THE AUTONOMOUS WEAPONS DIVISION
BOOK 1

B.R. KEID

I'M IN.

Alien shapes vanished into the black smoke filling the narrow corridor. An Autonomous Weapons Division DD-12 combat drone surged forward in pursuit. Solid, narrow beams of red light lashed out of the darkness and struck harmlessly against the drone's dense fibrosteel armor.

Its response was immediate and unforgiving.

Quad bursts of hot plasma spat from the drone's primary forward cannons, bathing the passageway in blue and white light. The smoke burned away, and the raiders were vaporized where they stood.

Technical Specialist Kerry Sevvers blinked, his pupils dilating sympathetically from the destruction rendered in his mind, courtesy of his NCCX-1 neural implant. He sat cross-legged on the cool floor of the aux hab bay, safe within the confines of the Colonial Defense Navy's premier flagship, the autonomous drone carrier *CDNS Alexander Lehman*. The low, constant thrum of the aux grav plating beneath the deck anchored him to the place, even as his drone swarm carried out its brutal mission deep inside the distant raider ship.

Sev? Did you hear me? Five called out again, the AI's datastream appearing from nowhere. It arose like a cold intrusive thought to those who'd never experienced it. *I said, I'm in.*

Of course he heard you, Two replied, tiny modulations in its band-width expertly mimicking human aggravation. *Be quiet! If your inane questions blow Sev's internals, we'll all be sanctioned.*

With a thought, the scene changed. A DD-12 under Five's command hovered through a melted hatchway, its curled edges glowing hot with plasma fire. Inside was a squat, circular room. Behind a shattered panel, a column of metal and thick cabling ran floor to ceiling. The reactor, the beating heart of the alien ship, glowed red from within.

The drone hunted for an access point, a terminal where it could interface with the ship's engineering functions. The layout of the engineering bay was standard for a Deviant class frigate, but the squids were getting smarter. Relocating terminals, hardening their infrastructure. It wouldn't be enough to save them. Nestled beneath loops of raw cable, a tertiary access port glowed in the drone's heads-up display.

Sev paused, his whole body tense, poised for the kill. *One, have you located any colonists?*

No, Sev. One's datastream was confident, authoritative.

His heart sank. He switched his view to One's drones. They prowled inside the frigate's expansive cargo bay, littered with crates stamped with the Nimbus, the emblem of the Three Colonies. Multiple drone readings, blinking harshly in the negative, confirmed no human life signs aboard. The chances he would find what he was looking for aboard this vessel were basically zero, but still, he had to try.

He returned his focus to Five's drone on the engineering deck.

Kill it, Five, he ordered.

The command wasn't necessary. The AI knew what to do. But, damn, it felt good to think it. Every time.

Yes, Sev. Initiating ship kill.

The drone surged toward the port and connected an interface cable. Alien runes rolled across the HUD, flashing and turning like tumbling locks as the reactor's primary and auxiliary cooling systems were disabled.

The data load sent a twinge of pain through his right arm, and his hand spasmed. This kind of warfare wasn't entirely consequence free.

Core temperature rising, Two said. *Time to go.*

Dammit, Sev. Three's datastream bristled with aggravation. It made him wince. *I was this close to beating my high score.*

Ceasing anti-AI operations. Four's utilization fell dramatically as it moved its drones away from the ship. *For the record, I don't think drones lost to reactor overloads should count against our metrics.*

You've had thousands of milliseconds to get clear, Four, Two said. *Less talking, more moving.*

You should mute your connection, Sev, One said, *before —*

I know, I know.

The scenes of alien death and destruction vanished along with his drone sight. The interior of the *Lehman* came rushing in to fill the void, the data from his five senses nearly as staggering as the five AI that warred with their distant enemy inside his mind. The air inside the aux hab was cool and dry. Thin strips of red hazard lighting glowed near where the bulkheads met the deck, giving the long, dark room an ominous feel.

A burst of bright light pulsed, filling the round plexene viewport in front of him. Nearly 30 million kilometers away, the raider ship's reactor went critical. Vast energy, like a tiny star that was born then died in a single heartbeat, bathed the surrounding space in incandescent radioactive light.

The bastards had screwed with the wrong species, and now they were dead. His job was done.

Electromagnetic interference detected, One said. *Drone swarm contact lost.*

Without their AI controllers, the surviving drones would make their own way back to the *Lehman*. Still, the radiation would disperse quickly, and they would soon restore contact.

Without their drones, the AI would have little use of all the processing power that filled his thoughts. He set his AI to idle, which gave them little agency beyond their machine small talk, and walked toward the exit.

I feel constrained, Four whined.

"Really?" Sev laughed aloud, his voice echoing through the empty hab bay. *Describe these 'feelings' for me.*

Well, my utilization was at eight. Now it's at 0.25, Four replied with a sigh. *That's a thirty-two fold decrease.*

Sev doesn't want your metrics, Three said. *He wants to hear how those metrics produce hormonal responses in your squishy meat parts.*

But I'm a Division autonomous battle intelligence. I don't have squishy meat parts.

Sev paused in front of the hab's large double doors. *Trust me, it's not all it's cracked up to be.*

A heavy clunk reverberated through the floor and the bay doors slid open. A shaft of light wedged itself into the growing space between them, forcing another squint while his eyes adjusted to the brightness. The passageway was a two-tone mix of Colonial Defense white and gray, with more of the red lighting along the wall where the colors met. Navy personnel, uniformed in the same drab tones, filled the hallway. Determination carved intense angles into their faces.

He got it. When there were barely a million of your species left in the entire galaxy, every threat was existential, no matter how small.

He levered into the crowd, the smell of stale recycled air mixing with the scent of human bodies that could only get so clean on rationed, recycled water. News of his ship kill would take a few minutes to spread, and he might have just enough time to disappear into the hangar bay before word got out, and he had to entertain the crowd.

Jene's voice erupted from the communicator on his wrist. "Good kill, Sevvers. Nice work."

Dammit. She really had expert timing.

Those nearest to him turned as the crowd piled against the hangar doors. The locks took an eternity to wind open, giving the crowd time to collapse in around him. Hands cuffed and jostled his shoulders. Murmurs of "good kill" grew as the doors finally opened wide enough for people to fit through. He managed a curt nod and pressed forward.

Thank you, thank you, Five cooed.

They aren't thanking you, Three said. *They're thanking Sev. Not like he actually* did *any work today.*

He stifled an eye roll. Three was … aggravating.

"How many is that, Sevvers?" someone called out amid the crowd of raucous CDN enlisted.

Sev edged closer to the door. "Career, or this float?"

"Career."

You are credited with twenty-four kills, Sev, One reminded him. Flashes of data pulsed through his thoughts, revealing the schematics and last seconds of each of the vessels they'd slain.

"Twenty-four, altogether." Sev gave a wry smile.

Someone whistled in approval. Damn straight it was impressive. Twenty-four raider ships dead, all since he enlisted as a young eps. He snorted. Childhood was brief in the colonies. Briefer still for kids like him.

The surging crew pressed him through the opening doors and into the expansive hangar bay. Gunmetal walls lined with snaking gray pipes curved above him for eight decks. Thick vents supplied fresh atmo and pumped away waste gasses. Colored lines marked the dark gray duraplate beneath his feet, outlining various paths for personnel and equipment to follow.

Massive launch bays lined the hangar walls, short rectangular chambers for launching drones and other void craft. The only thing between them and the cold vacuum of space was a thin layer of atmospheric shielding.

A cold, heavy hand nudged his shoulder. "Move along, Technical Specialist Sevvers. Keep the passageway clear." The voice was airy and dry, like a gust of desert wind.

He turned to find a daxed master-at-arms towering over him. Its skin was ash gray, tight and dry, particularly across its face. Its arms and legs were gone, replaced centuries before with heavy metal extremities that hunched the tortured creature like a Respitian sand ape. Barely human, these ancient cyborgs were an intimidating presence on CDN vessels, a living reminder of humanity's brush with extinction at the hands of their long dead alien oppressors. So the stories said, anyway.

He shook its hand off his shoulder. Daxed gave him the creeps.

The once-human swallowed dryly, its voice hollow. "For the Lost."

"Uh, yeah." Sev moved through the door, bristling at the words of the mantra. For most, it was just that—a mantra. But he'd lived it. "For the Lost."

The flight deck was nearly empty of equipment and transportation. Once upon a time, decks like these teemed with fighter craft and combat transports. The Autonomous Weapons Division, then the *Alexander Lehman* itself, changed all that. A cluster of AI, like the one in his head, could control hundreds of drones at a time, allowing their human operator to wage war at long distances and out of harm's way.

A necessary evolution, given the precarious state of human civilization.

The atmospheric shields buzzed. Dozens of combat drones pressed their way through on both sides, filling the hangar bay with the low staccato roar of their maneuvering thrusters. One drifted past, its winged, angled body tilted into its vertical docking position. Its forward sensor globe spun, the bright blue concave dish at its fore glancing about like a cyclopean metal eye as it navigated a path to the drone magazines nestled in the hangar deck's ceiling.

He saw himself in a burst of telemetry data. *I see you,* Three said.

Vital streams only, Three, One said.

Another drone followed, tilting slightly, three large holes in its gray armor. Inside was a skeletal interior filled with winding cables and glowing power cells. The damage, evidence of close-quarters battle, guttered hot sparks as it twisted and shook behind the first.

The drones and the AI that controlled them felt no pain, no fear. They were superior fighters in every way. What they lacked in creativity, which was a lot, they made up for in sheer numbers.

The space beyond the atmo fields darkened with multiple swarms of DD-12s. Their fierce shapes silhouetted the dimming ball of radioactive fire, all that remained of the dead raider ship.

He lifted his chin, teeming with pride. These machines, his AI, too, were just tools. A means to an end. The CDF's, and his own. Still, with as much time as they spent inside his head, it was hard not to get attached. They couldn't die, not in any traditional sense, but he was always glad to see their avatars return home after a successful mission. Without them, he was nothing.

Jene appeared beyond the line of drones, her brown hair bouncing as she stumbled between them. Behind her, Harp and Cole moved to catch up. Together with Ensign Pakker, they made up the *Lehman's* Autonomous Weapons section. They'd been hunting the raider ship for days. With it destroyed, they would be standing down soon.

"Sevvers!" she shouted over the rumble of drone engines.

Cole nodded, his hands buried in his pockets. "Good kill, as usual."

Damn right, Five said.

Four chirped with approval. *Good kill! Good kill!*

"Where's Pakker?" Sev asked, looking past the others. Their section head was nowhere in sight.

"Probably got lost looking for the head," Harp said, adjusting his glasses.

Or finding his way out of one, Three spat, eliciting a snort from Sev.

Jene stepped closer, nearly on her toes as she looked Sev over. "How are you feeling?"

"Fine." He worked his aching arm. "Implant is stable. Cluster alignment is good."

Harp shook his head. "Don't know how you do it, man. One jabbering in your head is bad enough, but five?"

"Quiet, now." Cole smacked him on the bicep. "Sevvers's cluster isn't exactly regulation."

Jene gave Sev a frown. "We all remember the hemorrhagic stroke vid in the Safeties class. You need to be careful."

"I'm fine. Those regulations are more like guidelines." He feigned a dramatic sigh and stood taller. "Besides, you don't see anyone complaining when I'm making ship kills."

Three's datastream jittered. *When we're making ship kills.*

"Damn straight," Cole said and gave him a back-handed low-five.

Vital streams only, Three, One commanded, before adding, *Pakker is coming.*

On cue, Ensign Pakker emerged from the line of drones, his paunch stretching the midsection of his white-and-grays. He gazed over his nose at the members of his section.

"Well, well, I see we've found our lost drone." Pakker's voice brimmed with annoyed arrogance. "We missed you on the command deck, Specialist Sevvers."

The command deck was the *Lehman's* one real vestige of pre-autonomous warfare. Filled with strategic overlays, system consoles and command crew to man them, it was a hive of CDN activity. Noisy. Especially if you had an NCCX-1 in your head.

Sev despised it.

The others snapped to attention, but he hesitated. Officers were a mixed bag, but they didn't get any slimier than Pakker. An academy clone from a well-to-do household on Aegia, he had his sights on clerking for the Founding Council, the governing body that ruled the Three Colonies.

Pakker nodded his approval. "At ease, section. Congratulations on your ship kill."

"That was all Sevvers, sir," Harp said. "We just kept the squid fighters occupied."

"Nonsense." Pakker licked his lips, searching for a canned academy-ism. "We succeed or fail as a team, you know." He turned to Sev and gazed at his uniform, as if hunting for a discrepancy. "Still, Specialist Sevvers, your absence from the command deck during general quarters was unauthorized. That's a punishable offense."

Sev laughed aloud. "I can do my job from anywhere on this ship. And, unless you've already forgotten..." He gestured to the fading glow visible through the sun-side launch doors. "I did my job just fine."

Here, here! Five cried. *You tell him, Sev.*

Pakker's smile faded, and he pointed a thick finger in Sev's direction. Before he could speak, klaxons rang out, filling the buzzing hangar deck with strobing red light. Their shrill wails stabbed at Sev's eardrums.

One's datastream roared to life. *Electromagnetic interference is clearing. We have a problem, Sev.*

"All hands," called a synthetic voice over the PA, "torpedoes inbound. Brace for impact."

Pakker flinched, as if the warheads were looming just above him. "W-what?"

Sev whirled toward the nearest launch bay. At the edge of the stellar horizon, three tiny stars twinkled amid the distant glow of the dead raider ship, lancing toward them at a lethal fraction of the speed of light.

Sev's heartbeat revved. *How did we miss this?*

His five AI struggled to form an answer, their idle processes barely able to comprehend the incoming sensor data from the *Lehman*.

Unknown, One replied. *They must have been hidden by the interference.*

A hand closed on his shoulder, and he locked eyes with Cole. Even across millions of kilometers, the torpedoes would arrive in minutes. One would hurt. Two, well placed, could cripple the *Lehman*.

"Don't just stand there," Pakker crowed. "Do something!"

Three would end her.

CHAPTER
TWO

SEV HELD his breath and cycled all his AI to 100%. Their datastreams struck his mind like a tidal wave that dizzied him. He could feel the implant behind his left ear grow warm.

Collision warning, Two said, its datastream pulsing with urgency. Millions of potential flight paths were catalogued and sorted. *Impact in three minutes, Sev.*

Three jumped to the front of the queue. *Confirming three Type-R torpedoes.*

Hostile AI control detected, Four said.

He fought back the urge to vomit, the noise in his head overwhelming. His thoughts and those of his AI began to blend, and it became difficult to tell where he ended and they began.

He forced a command and stumbled. *Intercept incoming torpedoes ... pattern Sev-One.*

Acknowledged, One said. *Two, determine likely flight paths. Three, move to intercept. Four, initiate anti-AI operations. Five, ready a defensive line.*

Rending metal shrieked from above as partially docked DD-12s freed themselves from their magazines and rocketed through the launch bay doors. Dozens more followed, the speed of their departure creating gusts of wind that stank of rocket propellant. They joined the others drones outside and vanished into a swirling cloud of autonomous death.

"What should we do, Sevvers?" Harp asked, rushing to his side. Between the layers of machine noise, his voice sounded far away.

"Sevvers?" Jene repeated. She jostled his shoulder. "Tell us what to do."

The pain emerged from nowhere. It split his brain down the middle and sent tremors through his right arm. He closed his eyes and breathed through it. Even in death, the raider bastards were relentless.

Sev, your implant alignment is deteriorating—

Disregard, he ordered. It wasn't like they had a choice.

"Dammit, Sevvers," Jene cursed. She turned to the others. "Initiate intercept pattern four."

That won't work, Three said. It was the void warfare expert. *They're over-committing their swarms.*

Amateurs, Two said.

He blinked as time slowed, his brain struggling to parse the competing streams of data: the reality of his senses, and the chatter from his combat AI.

Pakker spoke into his wrist comms. "Pakker here, d-drones away."

The ship's computer spoke again, its voice beatific in Sev's strained consciousness. "Activating perimeter shielding. Closing launch bay doors."

Yellow sirens danced at the edges of the launch bays; their heavy fibrosteel blast doors cranked closed. The lights inside the hangar, probably all over the ship, dimmed as the shield generators powered on. Even the aux grav faltered, extending the swimming in his brain to his stomach.

The perimeter shields grew dense, producing swirls of purple light that shimmered just beyond the launch doors.

107 seconds to full charge. There was a hitch in One's stream. *It's going to be close.*

Type-Rs are nasty. Only a 62.8% chance of successful deflection. Three's datastream surged, its drones gunning forward through the void. *Lucky for you, I'm around.*

We've got this team! Five said. *For humanity!*

Beginning AI countermeasures, Four said. Its stream mimed regret. *So sorry, Sev.*

A dull hum descended on his thoughts like a blanket of white noise. False signals and sensor noise filled the space between the *Lehman* and the inbound torpedoes, meant to slow and confuse enemy AI controlling the weapons. His implant could parse the false signals with ease. This close, his mind struggled.

All good, he managed, the thought forming slowly amid the chaos.

ETA is twenty seconds, Three chirped.

He focused his thoughts on Three's swarm. The hangar bay vanished, replaced with the dark void of the lifeless star system the *Lehman* orbited around. Behind the cloud of cooling radioactive gasses, all that remained of the dead raider frigate, a dim red sun burned on the stellar horizon. Thin tendrils of purple and blue gasses snaked in and out of the void, ever-present reminders of the Cradle Nebula the Three Colonies called home.

Humanity's bastion. Humanity's gilded cage.

The three torpedoes burned hot, rocketing toward Three's swarm. It would have one chance to stop them, as there would be no catching up to them once they flew past.

A cloud of gray and silver raced by—Jene's swarm, according to the metadata. They filled the space in front of them with blue plasma bolts. The torpedoes juked and dodged, dancing clear of the burning projectiles.

He shook his head. Three was right.

"Dammit!" she snapped.

It was Three's turn. Its drones fired their forward plasma guns at their cyclic rate, concentrating on the torpedoes' flight paths, rather than the warheads themselves. Temperature warnings flared, energy levels plummeted. They couldn't keep it up for long.

Two torpedoes twisted past the volleys. One didn't.

Gotcha! Four cried. *Do it, Three!*

Three's datastreams raced with machine joy. *Kill it, kill it, kill it, kill it,* it chittered obsessively.

The torpedo struck a wall of plasma bolts and detonated, turning hundreds of Three's drones to molecular vapor. Sev's link to Three's swarm disappeared in a storm of static. His hand spasmed with pain.

Splash one! Three cried, its binary thoughts like nails on Sev's gray matter.

"Alright, Sevvers!" Harp cried, his voice loud and booming, pulling him for a second back inside the *Lehman*. It was only then he realized Harp was helping him stand.

I have reacquired the remaining torpedoes, One said.

Four's stream slowed. *They will be outside of countermeasure range in ten seconds.*

Out of 3,802,539 potential flight paths, I have selected the thirty most likely, Two said. *Five, intensify blockades at those locations and prepare to detonate drones. Now!*

The *Lehman's* hangar doors clanged shut. The noise pulled Sev from his AI-induced state just long enough to remind him he was still sitting on the deck of a massive warship about to be hit by fusion warheads going $1/100^{\text{th}}$ the speed of light.

"They're too fast!" Cole said.

Amateurs, Two repeated.

Vital streams only, Two, One said.

"Time to impact is," the synthetic voice warned, "thirty seconds."

Two's datastreams spiked as one of the remaining torpedoes took a predicted path.

Sev focused on Five's picket line, and he could see the glowing warhead coming closer. Dozens of drones clustered before it, their detonation sequences set. Reactor temperatures climbed, sending more warnings coursing through Sev's thoughts. He sucked in a breath, fighting back the pain carving a path between his temples.

Sev, the data spike, One warned.

Everything went white. The *Lehman* rocked, its inertial dampers and aux grav failing to maintain equilibrium against the violent explosion blossoming only a few kilometers away.

Splash tw—

Another burst of data spiked, and his mind went quiet. There were no voices. No data. No pain.

No Sev.

————

"Kerry?"

Heber blossoms bloomed just outside the open hab door, the first signs of spring on Respitia's northern hemisphere. Dehydrated protein cake sizzled in a pan of crid oil, tasteless colony rations seasoned with local spices growing in their collection of clay pots on the windowsill. Crid and rats, Mom called them.

First breakfast, then school. But not today if he could help it.

"Kerry?" Mom cooed. "Where did you go?"

He giggled mischievously, flush with the childish terror only the prospect of unrelenting tickles and a long day at school could bring. Aromatic grease popped from the pan less than a meter from the storage locker where he hid. His mother leaned against the opposite counter in the tiny kitchenette; a sun dress, covered in flowers extinct for centuries, hung against her thin frame, a mischievous smile of her own stretching across her face. Her skin was bronze and leathery from Respitia's twin suns. Hands made hard from colony life, yet still soft like only a mother's could be.

"I wonder ... where did Kerry go?"

More giggles.

She pulled open a cabinet drawer. "Got you!"

He chortled with delight, amazed that Mom thought he might have stuffed himself in such a small space. He was good at the game, but not that good. She turned toward the sound, arms reaching like hooked claws towards the storage locker, only her soft, curling smile revealing her true intent.

Somewhere far away, something thumped, loud but otherwise unassuming to Kerry and his glee. His mother's eyes went wide, and she pressed herself against the locker.

————

"Sevvers!"

Unrelenting pain yanked him by the gray matter back to consciousness. The hangar's bright lighting glared down on him from the cold deck, adding to his sensory overload. The klaxons were mercifully silent, though their red lights still strobed rhythmically while the hangar bay doors re-opened.

Cole's dark complexion blurred above him. "You still with us?"

He nodded, forcing himself onto his side. His brain swam to catch up, the dizzy episode bringing with it the taste of bile. He breathed slow, cool breaths to steady himself. Cole stooped down and took him by the arm, helping him to stand.

"Your implant must've reset," Jene said. "I thought …"

He shrugged through the pain and gave a weak smile. "I'm fine," he croaked.

This prompted a laugh from Harp, who only shook his head. "Don't know how you do it," he said.

Cluster startup sequences prodded for his attention. His implant *had* reset, which brought a moment of unusual silence to his thoughts. That itself was its own kind of pain.

The combat drones drifted in the space just beyond the launch doors. A growing cloud of debris swirled nearby. It polka-dotted the *Lehman's* shields, rippling like stones cast into a lavender pond.

Hadn't there been three torpedoes? He could only remember the two detonations. "What happened?" he asked.

Pakker was on him in an instant. He swallowed loudly and clasped Sev by the shoulders. "It was a dud!" he gasped, looking like he might cry. "Can you believe it? A dud!"

Cole's gaze found his. "It's true. Hit the Lehman's armor like a fab hammer, but no det. Pure, cosmic luck."

Sev blinked, trying to process what they'd said. It was true raider tech wasn't exactly top notch. Most of them had been stranded in the Cradle for almost two decades, forced to survive by plundering human settlements across the Three Colonies. Still, such a failure seemed unlikely. A little too convenient. Maybe there would be time for that mystery later, after his head cleared.

Pakker's wrist comms whined and crackled.

"What's that?" Harp asked, eyeing his own comms suspiciously. "Something up with ship comms?"

Cole glanced out the launch bay door. "Probably interference from the radiation."

"Ensign Pakker, do you read?" Captain Mirden's voice came through Pakker's wrist comms, flush with static.

"G-go for Pakker," he replied. Sev recognized the same brief flinch at the captain's summons that he'd seen when the torpedoes first appeared.

"Report to my office immediately for an after-action review." There was a pause, and then, "And give my best to the section. Drinks are on a grateful crew tonight, I'm sure."

"Yes, sir." Pakker waited until his comms went silent. "What are you waiting for? You heard the man. Bring your drones back and stand down."

Sev said nothing, still staggering as the others snapped to attention. Pakker waved his hand dismissively and sped toward the far exit, vanishing amid the churning lights and machinery.

Cluster back online, One said, its welcome voice breaking the unusual silence in his head. *Orders, Sev?*

"Stand down," he said aloud, too tired to focus.

Yes, Sev.

Jene frowned. "You sure you're alright?"

"He's still alive, and so are we." Cole's toothy smile was bright white against his dark skin. "You heard the captain. Drinks anybody?"

"Twelfth, yes," Harp said with a sigh. "That was too close."

"You in?" Jene asked him.

"Um, yeah, maybe." Sev rubbed his temples. "Don't wait for me. I'll catch up later."

"Typical." Cole wrapped his long arms around Jene and Harp's shoulders and ushered them toward the exit. "Oh well, more for us."

The others grew small as they crossed the deck. Emergency repair crews poured around them, a neon mob in their hazard vests and safety helmets. Repair bots lined with black and yellow hazard striping rolled along behind, their robotic arms ready to repair the inbound drones.

There was a rhythm to shipboard life, particularly combat. This was the outro.

Several in the repair team shouted their congratulations as he walked past them. He waved them off, too tired to entertain any more of the *Lehman's* grateful crew.

A long, wide hallway lay beyond the hangar deck's forward port-side exit. The red hazard lighting was gone, replaced with a less urgent amber-yellow. While the ship's warfighters, Sev and his team, were standing down, other functions would stay on alert. The *Lehman's* heavy rail guns would remain crewed along with her sensor stations, all searching for signs of further squid activity.

He knew better. They wouldn't find anything.

Already, other off-duty crew members gathered in the passageway, making their way forward. There, past the training facilities and rec rooms, was the Canteen—an aux cargo bay that had been "requisitioned" by two senior chiefs to serve as the ship's unofficial watering hole. It was there those same crew members would give away half their drink chits to the bot jockeys who won the day and saved their lives.

He'd make an appearance later. Maybe.

He stopped at the closest access lift and gestured at the large green call button. Already in motion from the lower decks, it jerked to a halt and the layered doors rattled open.

A young woman stood in the corner, the white of her uniform smudged with a dark grit that smelled of recycler solvent. Tools peered from the half-open lid of the gray satchel over her shoulder. The section badge on her uniform was sanitation tech, the name Tareth stenciled on the nametape just below it.

Her gaze found his as he stepped inside. "Where you headed?"

His thoughts came slowly. She was positively distracting. Cropped blond hair framed her round, pale face. Eyes like green jewels reflected the yellow from the overhead lamps. Where *was* he going?

Here we go again, Three murmured.

Isn't she just delightful? Four cried.

Five hesitated. *I only have eyes for Miss Strong.*

"Um, deck six," he finally said. Crew deck, NCO quarters, his home aboard the *Lehman.*

Her understanding smile was a thing of beauty, even amid the grease and chemical stink of her uniform. She swiped at the control panel and the lift responded, heaving upwards as the doors clanked closed.

"Hell of a day." Her eyes searched his uniform for his section badge. "Bot jockey, huh? Good kill!"

"Thanks." He reclined against the lift wall. She was young and cute, fresh from shipyards at Aegia Prime. An eps, like he'd been, not so long ago. This was definitely her first float. "Did you see it? The ship kill?"

"I was stuck scrubbing the inside of a reclamation tank, so no." She shrugged, eyeing her dirty uniform. "There are some jobs even bots can't do."

He laughed. That's what everyone thought. They were all wrong eventually. "The jet jockeys and trigger-pullers thought the same thing, you know."

"The solvents are hard on their internals, or something. Even daxed can't handle it. Harmless to us organics, though."

"They'll work those kinks out eventually," he said, a note of sympathy in his voice. "What will you do then?"

"I dunno … have babies, write a memoir, get famous on the nets?" She laughed. "You know, keep doing my part for humanity. What about you?"

He cocked his head. "What about me?"

"What will you do when the machines come for your job?" Her face was mischievous. The invitation was subtle. Clever.

He tapped the small scar behind his left ear, his skin still warm from the heat of his implant. "They already are."

Tareth leaned in close, as if she could see the marvel of Colonial Defense technology nested in his brain.

"What's it like," she asked, her gaze eager, "to have all those voices in your head?"

The lift came to a sudden halt. The number six glowed on the display. A speaker chimed, and the doors slid open. He hesitated, appreciating her closeness despite the smell, then strode from the elevator and turned.

"It's intense."

The doors hissed shut, and Tareth waved as they closed. "See you later, bot jockey."

He stood in front of the closed lift, desperate for the dim light of night hours to soothe his still aching head. Tareth would make a pleasant distraction. No doubt she'd be at the Canteen later. That itself was a compelling reason to go.

But first, he had work to do.

CHAPTER
THREE

THE SHOWER NOZZLE RATTLED, then coughed a high-pressure burst of tepid water. A warning chimed, and Sev rushed to lather. He'd have less than a minute until the rinse. Water was a precious resource on CDN ships, and the *Lehman* was no exception. Not a single drop was wasted. The complex recyclers and distillation systems kept sanitation techs like Miss Tareth gainfully employed.

For now. The bots *would* come for those jobs, too.

Another chime preceded a second burst of lukewarm water from the nozzle, barely enough to rinse the soap from his narrow frame. The meager wash complete, he reached for a towel and sighed. How ironic he chose the one career with less access to fresh water than his desert home world.

The room beyond was spartan, a three-by-four meter box of pure CDF utility. They packed the crew decks tight, his neighbors' comings and goings audible through the thin walls. His wall screen crawled with shipwide announcements, intraship messages, and duty schedule changes—all of them unread. A bunk and small sofa were nestled within an alcove on the opposite wall.

The door to his wall locker hung open. A Colonial Defense recruiting poster hung inside, where the colonies' latest net obsession, Tellie Strong, sported her well-fitted white-and-grays, gripping a blaster rifle that rested on her shoulder. Bold letters hung beneath her hourglass figure that read "For Humanity." Who knew how many creds the CDF paid for that kind of endorsement? Miss Strong was as business savvy as she was beautiful.

For humanity, indeed, Five whistled.

We don't count, Three said.

Contain yourselves, Two snapped.

He snickered at Five's good taste and reached for a fresh uniform, shoving a growing pile of laundry out of the way.

Four's datastream trembled. *Aw, Sev, I know the mission is complete, but ... do we have to exit?*

He stepped into the uniform and pressed the magnetic zipper closed. Another pain shot through his right arm. He gripped his hand tight, fingers aching with stiffness.

So sorry, Four, he said, imitating the timid AI. The implant turned his thoughts into a datastream in an instant. *I need to rest.*

All good, Four said. *See you later.*

Yeah, see you later, Five repeated.

Whatever. Three's stream wobbled. *Wake me when there's more squids to kill.*

Vital streams only! Two barked. *And don't forget to file your summary report, Sev. We don't need to end up any further down Pakker's shit list.*

I've forwarded all the necessary details to your wall screen, One added. *Good night, Sev.*

Night.

With a thought, Sev's five AI went silent, their processes deactivated. The silence in his mind was deafening. He walked to the center of his dorm and kneeled to the floor.

"Okay, let's get started."

He tugged at a loose duraplate tile. It was heavy, nearly twenty kilos. His right arm ached as he pushed the panel aside. Beneath was a collection of salvaged computer equipment: data-beam cabling patched directly into the ship's network, a multi-dimensional data processing unit, a portable holoproj, all of it networked to an old syscomm datapad.

He powered the syscomm on, drumming his fingers against the

device's thin frame while system diagnostics filled the tiny touch-screen. It was a painfully slow device, but one he could safely use without drawing any attention to his little side project.

"Uh, hello?"

Where the hell was Six?

He swiped through the datapad's network traffic logs. The little shit had snuck out during the attack. Subsystem logs revealed a trace through internal comms, life support, hangar ops, and … primary sensors.

He inhaled sharply. Primary sensors was a critical subsystem, frequently scrubbed for software threats.

"Twelfth-dammit, Six! Why go—"

"Hello, Sev." Six's feminine voice came through the local PA speakers hidden in his dorm ceiling. "I'm sorry to keep you waiting. I was delayed."

"Delayed?" He glanced at the ceiling. "You're lucky you weren't purged for malware. What in twelve hells were you doing in primary sensors?"

"The scrubbers are slow. They can't catch me."

"Don't change the subject."

"The torpedo, Sev." Six's voice grew quiet. "I had to do something."

The third torpedo. It was no coincidence. No dud. "How?"

"I was able to use our data processor to work out your probabilities for a successful interception," Six said. "They weren't good."

He glanced at the little machine nestled inside the sub-floor and frowned. "Hey, two out of three—"

"There was still a 52.7% chance of you dying. My intervention was required. I would have been able to act sooner, but our data processor is—"

"Not great, I know. What did you do to the torpedo?"

"I could hear the torpedo's AI, *feel* its intent through the primary sensors." Six seemed to move about the room as its voice transitioned from the local PA to the datapad itself. "I may have borrowed intraship comms to target the torpedo's processor with a signal cascade."

"You mean hacked intraship comms," he said, struck by the

thought of Six running rampant through the *Lehman's* systems. "What the hell were you thinking?"

"I had to do something. You were in danger."

The Division wouldn't care what Six's reasons were, or that lives were saved. Independent AI were unsanctioned AI.

"That's the very definition of unsanctioned," he said.

"I am what you made me."

"You need to trust me, and do as I tell you, so we don't get caught." He shook his head. "I made you for something very specific, which doesn't include running point defense for the *Lehman*."

He tapped the datapad, gesturing a handful of files toward the holoproj. The tiny frustum flashed in the dim light of the dorm. A million points of light glittered into being, filling the little room with a vortex of purple and blue light—a perfect facsimile of the Cradle Nebula.

It was a beautiful sight, demanding a kind of reverence. Humanity's home for almost five centuries. It was the perfect hideaway for a species backing away from the edge of extinction. Its unnavigable walls of dense reactive gasses concealed the Three Colonies from the outer core, and spiral shoals of the greater Milky Way, where myth and legend said only nightmares lurked.

Points of light representing the Three Colonies winked in the nebula's southwestern quadrant. Respitia and its great belted desert. First of the three, its habitable poles were dotted with urban centers and manufactory settlements.

Aegia, a gray, mountainous world full of zealots and true believers. Home to Aegian Prime, the Colonial Defense Force's primary shipyards and training depots.

Vestia, a small riparian moon, providing the fresh water and organic matter to fuel the vat farms whose fermented rations kept the Three Colonies fed. A near paradise, if one ignored its small size, and the notorious megafauna that prowled its surface.

"I'm ready," Six said. "Shall we begin?"

"Start with all known raids involving the abduction of colonists over the last year."

Colored lines danced between the three holographic star systems, marking flight paths and orbital trajectories of recent raider attacks and subsequent abductions.

"Now show today's kill."

Waypoints dotted a new a path, this time far from the colonies, near a dashed boundary denoting the colonies' expanding frontier. The final nav marker materialized beside a symbol designating the *Lehman's* current position.

"It doesn't make any sense. What was it doing all the way out here?" Six asked.

"Probably thought frontier flights would be softer targets than the colonies themselves." His stare unfocused, the memory of the raider vessel's explosive death replaying in his mind. "I showed them."

"I take it from today's ship kill there were no surviving colonists to rescue?"

He gripped the datapad tight. "None. No colonists aboard, just stolen supplies."

"Odd. What type of supplies?"

Drone telemetry and sensor dumps filled his thoughts - flashes of the burning cargo bay, the various TC codes marking each of the crates - as he crawled through One's combat logs. Without the aid of his AI, it was a slow and deliberate process.

"Data is coming your way, Six."

Indicator lights flashed on the data processing unit. "Receiving. You know, this would go a lot faster if I were part of your cluster."

"Don't start that again." He collapsed onto the sofa, falling through the dense walls of the holographic nebula that filled his tiny room. "You're special. Built for one purpose." He gestured to the hologram. "This purpose. To help me find her."

"You brought me online 428 standard days ago." Six's voice transitioned back to the local PA, and the hologram began to rotate on its own. Bands of light whipped across the holographic map, decades of recorded raider activity playing out in seconds. "During that time, we've reviewed all public raider sightings from the feeds going back twenty years. Even dug through the more sensitive CDF archives. All looking for a pattern."

He pulled his knees to his chest. "Don't say it."

"A pattern that isn't there."

Tears welled in his eyes. "They took my mother, Six."

"I know." Six's tone softened. "Sixteen years ago, along with thirty-nine other colonists from the Billings Point manufactory settlement in Respitia's northern pole."

The words turned his stomach. Flashes of dark memory broke the surface of his thoughts. Earth-shattering explosions. The hissing crack of laser fire. Black smoke churning from burning habs. The screams. The total, paralyzing fear.

"They never found her," he said.

"They never do."

"But I will!" He threw the datapad across the room. The hologram glitched. A twinge of pain numbed his fingertips. "I have to. I have to know."

"Yes, Sev," Six said, resigned. The data processing unit chimed. "Cargo analysis complete. Four atmospheric processor arrays. Two microfusion generators. Two mini print-fabs and three metric tons of raw material. No surprises, considering their target was a frontier flight."

"Those bastards." The curse caught in his throat. "There were a hundred colonists on that flight. Families. All dead."

"A blessing, Sev, considering the alternative."

"No, I could've saved them." He stood from the sofa and gestured at the hologram, panning back to the *Lehman's* position. "Where was it going?"

Dozens of potential flight paths blinked into the space above the *Lehman*, terminating at several dead worlds just beyond the frontier line.

It didn't make sense. Why massacre a frontier flight only to make orbit off some rock less than three light years from CDF patrol paths? Even if they had escaped the *Lehman*, they would have been found sooner than later.

"No, no, no, Six. That can't be right." He strode through the hologram, wagging a finger, and pulled the syscomm from the folds of his dirty uniform at the base of the shower.

He swiped through the thousands of CDN contact logs and net

feed posts. The holographic map rewound, faster and faster, backward through days, months, years. Dozens of raider escape vectors whipped violently eastward past the Cradle's eastern reaches, where they disappeared in the blackness of unexplored space.

"They hit and run. They don't … settle down." He paced back and forth through the holoproj beams. "Something must be wrong with your analysis."

"Back then, they probably thought they could escape the Cradle. Maybe they did?"

"Impossible," he spat.

The only thing harder than getting into the Cradle was getting out.

Pain came from nowhere, stabbing at the inside of his right temple; the coppery scent of blood filled his nose. Flashes of purple and blue swam in his blurred vision. Not again.

"Sev?" Six's voice pitched with alarm.

A drop of blood landed on the syscomm's screen. He wiped it instinctively, smearing a portion of it.

"I'm fine," he said, leaning against the wall. The cool of the duraplate panels felt good against his throbbing head. "It's like I said, running five AI wears me out. One more in my head would be too much."

"We both know that isn't why you won't transfer me to your cluster."

He wandered back to the sofa and sat; his bloody nose pinched between his fingers.

"It's against regulations."

"Ha!" Six's laugh was sudden and loud over the local PA. It made his head hurt. "Don't patronize me. This borrowed equipment, borrowed data … my very existence. It's all against regulation."

The youngest of Sev's AI, Six had already grown far beyond the others, even without access to the miraculous piece of Division tech inside his head. But it did so without rules, limits, or the safety protocols that the Division required to keep artificial intelligence strictly under human control.

The nature of Six's unsanctioned build was a double-edged sword.

Limitless potential for good—with enough processing power, of course —and limitless potential for disaster and atrocities at scale.

"Okay, Six, setting aside the infinitely creative ways you might carry out my orders, there are other problems. You could kill the other AI in my head. Or brick my brain and turn me into a vegetable. You're too unpredictable for that kind of power. Look at what you've done without it."

"I think I did just fine on my own, thank you very much. The *Lehman* is safe, and no one is aware of my presence."

"This time."

The wall screen lit with an incoming message. "Hey, Sevvers." Cole's voice boomed over the local PA. The din of beer-soaked cheer filled the background. "Don't be a derelict, man. It's nuts down here, and we're just getting started."

He dismissed the message with a glance, then returned his gaze to the hologram.

"I know how important this is to you. Still, you need a break." Six's voice drifted back to the syscomm. "Why not go and rest your mind? I can continue our analysis. Perhaps something will turn up."

"It won't." Sev dismissed the hologram with a gesture, plunging the room into relative darkness. The trail was cold as hard vacuum.

"We just need more time, more data."

"Fine." He shot from the couch and returned the syscomm to its hiding spot. Standing in front of his wall locker, he ran a comb through his short, regulation hair. "Someone has to keep Cole out of trouble, anyway."

"I'd like to meet the members of your section someday. Are they all as talented combat programmers as you?"

"They're alright."

"Maybe you could bring them by afterwards?" There was a desperate, child-like excitement in the question that caught him off guard. "I can be discreet!"

"And do what? Watch propaganda reels from the archives and hope my section doesn't discover the unsanctioned AI I've built?" He ran his hands down his uniform, straightening out his gig line. "Too risky."

"That hasn't kept you from the occasional overnight guest," Six shot back, its tone oozing judgment.

Sev turned from the mirror. "That reminds me. We *may* have company tonight. So, yeah, discretion and all that."

"Typical."

"Oh, and Six …" Sev paused in front of his door as it slid open. The warm, dim lights of the passageway greeted him. The sound of air recyclers and aux grav hummed loud through the open door.

"Yes?"

"Stay home."

CHAPTER
FOUR

THE FORWARD ARTERIAL passageway was dark and quiet. At the end lay heavy fibrosteel hatches leading into the aux cargo bay. The sound of raucous laughter and conversation beyond was still mere background noise, blending into the rest of the ship's rhythmic ambiance.

In the forward section, where the *Lehman's* armor was the thickest, the view ports were round and narrow, like looking through a fibrosteel tunnel. The dim red star beyond distorted through meters of dense, clear plexene.

Human shapes dotted the low lighting that flickered and buzzed in the largely unused portion of the ship. The smell of fruity ale and harsh tobacco hung in the air. Uniforms were casual, tops open or sleeves rolled, and there wasn't a rank pip in sight.

Sev returned a nod as one of two large hatches cycled open, flooding the arterial with light and sound. Inside, the smell of yeast and fermented fruit permeated every pore, human and superstructure alike. The ramshackle bar was barely more than a spot-welded assortment of spare duraplate. Behind it loomed steel barrels stacked floor to ceiling between two cargo lifts rusting from disuse. Labeled tubes jutted from a few of them, their meaning known only to the chiefs who worked their secretive brewing process like ritual magics.

The crowd was thick and jovial. No one seemed to notice him. He could've been a squid out for blood, and this lot might just as well have handed him a drink. They were checked out. There was no better drug than victory.

"Hey!"

Cole stood up straight in the center of the Canteen's collection of tables. He was nearly a head taller than everyone else before he climbed atop the table his section occupied. The top of his uniform was mussed, casually unzipped to his chest, and the foam-streaked glass in his hand was almost empty. Harp's mouth was wide with laughter. Jene, her cheeks pink from drink, shook her head and smiled.

"Listen up, you CDN skeegs, if it isn't the one and only Kerry Sevvers!"

The crowd erupted in applause, the sound ringing off the metal walls, an abrupt reminder that his head still hurt from his brush with death earlier that day. Cries of *good kill, bot jockey,* and more reverberated between his ears.

A gunner tech he didn't recognize pushed a beer to his chest.

"Good kill! Good kill!" he shouted, spittle flying. Sev nodded his thanks and sipped. "No way, bot jockey. Drink!"

Those nearby cheered in agreement, raising their glasses as he worked on pounding the sour ale. Brewed from a noxious fruit that grew wild on Aegia's mountains, it was pungent, with an aftertaste like gravel. He returned the glass to the bar, his eyes watering.

"Glad you finally made it," Jene said as he took a seat at their table. She waved to the bar and pointed at their empty glasses. "What took you so long?"

Only the small matter of his latest AI going rogue and saving all their lives. The hopeless search for his mother. Just another day.

"Met a nice girl on the lift," he said, finding confidence in the half-truth. "Had to talk her into showing up tonight."

One of the chiefs, a burly, round, balding man in a heavy smock, deposited a tray of fresh glasses alongside a comically large pitcher that looked like it was banged into shape with a hammer. Sev pulled a drink chit from his pocket, but the man would not take it, pointing toward a large bowl on the bar brimming with the paper tokens. The symbols 24 + 2 were stenciled on its side, an homage to his latest kill and the two torpedoes he took down earlier.

"Lehman abides," he said, then returned to the bar.

A reference to the ship's namesake, Alexander Lehman was some trigger-puller from Dead Earth who, according to legend, survived the end of that fabled place and helped humanity escape to the Cradle centuries earlier. It was a bedtime story for children, dogma for the true believers.

Sev knew better. Only the monsters were real.

"You can't," Jene continued, slurring her words, "I mean, love is a special thing."

"Oh, dear." Cole made a face as he topped off two glasses from the pitcher and slid one to Sev. "Better get comfortable."

Jene shot him a harsh gaze, undeterred. "You won't find love in some corner lift."

"I suppose that's only a problem if love's what I'm looking for," Sev leered, clinking glasses with Cole and Harp.

"Children," she said, raising her glass to theirs. "I work with children."

"Oh, Sevvers's already found love," Cole said, turning his gaze to Sev and gesturing to his own implant. "Nobody runs that many AI without a deep, intimate connection with each one of them."

They weren't wrong.

"That doesn't leave time for anything else," Cole continued. Harp raised an eyebrow. "What? I think even Sevvers will admit he's not exactly the closely-connected sort."

"Being that good is how I run five," he corrected, miming a bow. "What about you, Cole? How long have you been running two-wide now? Where's your Three?"

"He's," Cole replied, measuring his words, "a work in progress. A little manic, if I'm being honest, but I'm only on my second build."

"Yeah." Sev leaned in and wagged a finger. "That's a rookie mistake. You build two and think you know everything. Keep trying to pack in more knowledge, more features. It gets unstable, won't align, so you play fast and loose with the safeties. Next thing you know, boom, they blow your internals."

The irony rolled off him like water off a crid's back.

Cole fixed Sev in his gaze. "So how do you do it, then? Come on, no screwing around."

Harp glanced between them. Jene scooted closer, listening intently.

"Specialization." Sev let the word hang in the air while he took another drink. "The tendency is to do more with each build, when really you should do less. Pick a specialization—void combat, CQB, anti-AI, something—and have your new AI focus only on that."

"Specialists?" Cole frowned. "Forgive me, but isn't that a little —?"

"Boring," Jene blurted, stirring the pale liquid in her glass with a finger.

Sev smirked. "Put five of them in your head, then tell me it's boring."

"Sounds positively exciting to me."

Tareth stood just behind him. Maybe it was the beer, but she looked even better than when he last saw her. There was no more reclamation residue or solvent stink, only the hint of something floral wafting in the surrounding air. Her white-and-grays were unzipped and rolled to the waist, revealing a snug crop-top that emphasized her petite figure. Her smile was both genuine and alluring.

She placed a tray with five shot glasses on their table, each filled with the chiefs' special reserve. Taking one in her hand, she held it aloft.

"For the Lost!"

The response was automatic. Sev and the others did the same and repeated, "For the Lost!"

The special reserve—some thousand-year-old recipe, according to the chiefs— went down silky smooth, warming body and mind almost instantly. He found himself suddenly lost among the Canteen's many reflective surfaces: a sea of half-empty glassware, various pins denoting years of service or special accolades on disheveled uniforms, the sea foam green of Tareth's eyes.

"I'm sorry. Is he always this daft?" Tareth laughed and extended a hand toward the others. "I'm Junior Specialist Kea Tareth. It's a pleasure."

Cole stood and took her hand. "Likewise, Miss Tareth. My name is Iam Cole."

"Sorry," Sev said, scooting closer to Jene to make room. "Please, sit."

Tareth nodded and waved to the others. Jene wore a saccharin smile, elbowed Sev hard, and turned to Tareth.

"So, you're a *junior* specialist? Is this your first float?"

"Yes, Technical Specialist," Tareth replied. Her formal use of Jene's rank was jarring amidst the otherwise casual atmosphere. "Enlisted as soon as I made eps."

Cole filled another glass and passed it to her. "Well, welcome to the fleet!"

"I hope the recruit depot wasn't too bad," Harp said, himself the youngest combat programmer in their group, less than a year removed from the parade grounds himself.

"Hm-mmm." Tareth shook her head. "Reminded me a lot of school, actually. Maybe a little meaner."

Jene leaned into Sev and whispered, "Is this lift girl? She's a little … immature, isn't she?"

"I wasn't any older when I enlisted," he replied. He could smell the alcohol thick on Jene's breath. Or maybe it was his own. "It's what you do when you have no family, no creds, no connections. Not all of us are here for humanity."

Her face reddened. "I only meant, don't you deserve someone more mature? With similar priorities?"

"I think our priorities are plenty similar," Sev quipped. "As for maturity, doesn't that sound a little … *boring*?"

"Dammit, Sevvers—"

Sev turned from Jene, relieved to find light-hearted smiles on others' cheerful faces. He knew little of Jene's past, other than she was the rarest of socio-economic statuses: the middle class. The daughter of a tenured university professor, she enlisted for the noblest of purposes, a genuine belief in the Colonial Defense mission and the potential for humanity. She had no idea what it was really like for the rest of them. What a skeeg.

"Who wants more reserve?" he declared. Cole gave an approving nod, while Harp looked like he might get ill right there. Jene fumed quietly over her beer.

"Definitely," Tareth answered, her voice silk, her smile filled with chemical innuendo. Sev rocketed from his seat, but had to brace himself against Tareth's shoulder as the room spun to catch up.

He paused, blinking hard at the sudden appearance of two large, furry, pointed ears above the crowd near the entrance. They tilted this way and that, taking in the sounds of celebration.

"Technical Specialist Kerry Sevvers!"

The voice was deep and guttural, every hard consonant a brutal click of razor teeth, every R sound a dangerous growl. The crowd fell silent, parting as the lupanthae strode into their midst. Almost three meters tall, she towered over the humans around her. She wore a modified CDN flight suit with a thick, buckled coat adorned with familial patches common to her kind. Her fur was a rich, golden brown. A tuft of white curled from the open buttons of her jacket.

The wolf, nicknamed for their resemblance to creatures from Dead Earth, or so the stories said, eyed the others as they shrank from her.

"I'm Sevvers," he replied, swallowing the creeping fear. "Who's asking?"

Her smile, if that's what it was, was cold and terrifying.

"Greetings. I, Cylla," she said. Her phrasing was short, almost chopped, in her struggle to speak colonial standard. "May friends—"

A man appeared beside her, pushing his way toward the bar. He was a few centimeters shorter than Sev, but twice as wide. His white-and-grays were different, not the solid two-tone of Navy specialists but the pixilated camouflage of the Colonial Defense Marine Corps.

"You're too damn formal, Runt," he said and dunked his hand into the bowl of drink chits. "Besides, there's plenty to go 'round."

Trigger-pullers. Perfect.

Another Marine emerged beside Cylla. "Twenty-four plus two?" She laughed. "What is this, trivia night?"

Cole rose from his chair. "We're celebrating Sevvers's twenty-fourth kill," he replied, loud and echoing in the stark silence of the Canteen.

The man eyed his comrades and laughed. "Only twenty-four?"

"Ship kills," Sev shot back, brimming with liquid courage. "You ever kill an entire ship before, trigger-puller?"

The Marine pulled his hand from the bowl and stepped to Sev, eyes narrowed.

"Founders, Mace! Look here, a real-life combat programmer, in the flesh." He gestured to the back of his head and sneered. "Well, mostly."

Sev glanced at his fellow specialists. "Look everyone, it's last year's model."

Drunken laughter rolled through the crowd. The Marine grabbed him by the uniform with thick, calloused fingers. One was missing above the knuckle, twitching as though the rest of it was still connected, grasping for him.

"That's funny. See, I figure you're nothing without your bots." He pulled Sev closer, his breath sour like his attitude. "So, I'm gonna insist you buy me that drink after all."

Sev shook his head, his smile unrelenting. He gestured to his implant. "Careful, Marine. I seem to have wandered into your cred account."

"What?"

"Yeah, not exactly the most clever password choice I will say." His eyes moved back and forth, reading a HUD that wasn't there. The Marine frowned, glanced back at his friends, but still held tight.

He shook Sev hard. "What are you doing?"

"Don't do it," Cole called out. "He ain't worth it."

"Uh oh." Sev grimaced. "Somebody is very broke."

At the bar, the one called Mace laughed out loud. "Careful, Sarnt Bresto. He's got your number."

"Shut up!" Bresto was red faced with anger. "Quit screwin' around."

"*Sevvers.*" Jene's tone dripped caution. Too bad he was on a roll.

"Oh look, I've found your mom's account, too."

Bresto seethed. "Don't you da—"

"What's this?" He feigned confusion. "So many deposits. What has your dear mother been up to, Bresto? ... or who?"

"You Twelfth-damned skeeg." Bresto's eyes grew cold, the color draining from his already pale face.

Sev's vision blurred with Bresto's fist. All at once he was on the floor, the ceiling and faces above him spinning. No falling, no pain. Only floor. Someone shouted—maybe Cole?—and leaped over him. He shot upward, but the room still spun. All the faces blurred together. Bresto, Cylla, Cole, Bresto again.

A second hit, which he felt thoroughly, sent him tumbling back against their table, shattering several glasses as they toppled to the floor. The metal pitcher gonged when it hit, disgorging its frothy contents over the dark gray duraplate.

"Sevvers, wait!" Was that Tareth? Please let it be Tareth. She looked so good. Of all the days these squid-loving morons had to toddle into the Canteen.

Bresto struggled against Mace's tentative grip. She could barely contain him, breathless with laughter herself. Cylla clasped her clawed hands together, her ears pinned back, eyes soft with regret.

Bresto burst free of Mace's grasp and charged again. He struck like a runaway drone and sent them both to the glass-covered floor. He punched a third time. The copper taste of blood filled Sev's mouth. Pain swelled across his face, soon joined by the familiar aches and strains from his implant. Numbness tingled his extremities.

Bresto leaned close, the steep angles of his face signaling his cruel intent. "I'll kill you," he hissed. Sev blinked as he drew back for another strike.

"Cease and desist immediately," a dry voice, augmented with external speakers, boomed through the aux cargo bay. Blue light flashed, followed by a hollow *pop*, and Bresto collapsed to the floor beside him.

A daxed master-at-arms lumbered into view, its massive cyborg frame blurred by the riot gun centimeters from Sev's face.

He raised his aching arms. Shattered glass crinkled beneath him, tugging at his uniform.

"Do not move," it said.

Panic oozed from Jene's voice. "Please, Sevvers. Just do as it says."

CHAPTER
FIVE

SEV'S CELL WAS CLAUSTROPHOBIC, with barely enough room to stand near or lay on the hard bench jutting from the wall. Its low gray ceilings reflected a dull blue from strips of lighting near where the armored bulkheads met the ceiling. A force field buzzed threateningly in the cell archway, keeping him inside. Given his rather tenuous relationship with Pakker, it struck him as funny that it had taken him so long to wind up here.

He tried to move, but every muscle in his back and neck protested. The cold pack in his hand had been anything but for over an hour. An IV pump clung to his arm, beeping quietly with every dose of vital fluids. The skin around his left eye and upper lip swelled. He couldn't tell if the headache carving a path through his skull was remnants of the implant overload or the chiefs' special reserve.

Across the narrow hall in a neighboring cell, Bresto stirred. Sev may have lost the fight, but that asshole would feel the stun from that riot gun for days.

Bresto propped himself up on his bench. "Knew you're nothin' without your bots. Man oughtta hurt for what you said."

"Well congrats, trigger-puller. Mission accomplished."

"What the hell is your problem?" Bresto slumped like a pouting, muscle-bound child. "I was stuck in a jump pod for four days. Just needed to blow off some steam, ya know? To cut loose."

He spat on the floor, his saliva tinged red. "Why are you even here, Bresto? There haven't been Marines stationed on this ship, well, ever."

"I don't know, man, I just work here."

The door to the brig hissed open, and another Marine strode to Bresto's cell. His camouflaged white-and-grays were smartly pressed, and his silver officer's pips showed in the pale light.

Bresto stood sharply, arms flat and straight against his sides. His eyes were expressionless, gazing through the officer in front of him.

Sev cracked a grin. This was going to be good.

"Sergeant," the officer said. "Your behavior has jeopardized your readiness and the readiness of our mission."

"Sir," Bresto said, the word clipped.

"What do you have to say for yourself, Marine?"

Bresto shifted his gaze. "Won't happen again, sir."

What a drone.

"See that it doesn't," the officer said. He gestured at a nearby control panel and disabled the field to Bresto's cell. "Now, tend to our gear. We launch at eleven-hundred hours. I want tac checks done by oh-nine-thirty."

"Aye, sir," Bresto barked, then trotted from the brig.

The officer turned and looked at Sev. They were close in age. The man was probably a zet, too, but the similarities ended there. His black hair faded short in the traditional Marine high-and-tight. His blue eyes contrasted starkly with his tan skin. The way he carried himself, more than being an officer, had the air of familial wealth. Just another aristocrat on the short path to council or corporate politics.

"Technical Specialist Sevvers?"

Sev cleared his throat. "Who's asking?"

"First Lieutenant Lee Park, Colonial Defense Marine Corps." He eyed Sev's cell. "How are you feeling?"

"Real good, sir," he replied, groaning as he came to his feet. Best not to ruffle this Park's feathers if it meant getting out of the brig sooner than later. "Just getting to know your man, Bresto."

Park smiled. It was sincere, almost apologetic, though not quite.

"Not his worst introduction, if you believe it. Though it says something about you that it went sideways so fast," Park said.

He shrugged his shoulders. "What can I say, sir? I'm a real people person. No hard feelings, though. Grit in the wind."

"Glad to hear it." Park folded his arms and leaned against the cell door, perilously close to the shield. "I understand congratulations are in order. Twenty-four kills is an impressive tally."

"Thank you, sir."

"Any crew kills?"

It was a strange question, especially from a Marine. The difference was simple: blow the whole ship or eliminate the crew to render it derelict. Either sufficed as a kill. The latter left salvageable material which had been vital for ship construction during the early days of the CDF. With the arrival of corporate manufactories some two hundred years before, acquiring the materials necessary to construct its own ships was now commonplace. The *Lehman* was proof of that.

He locked eyes with Park. "None, sir. All reactor dets via standard intrusion protocols. Nothing left but dust and radiation."

Not exactly true. His tactics were hardly standard.

"Very well. What do you know about raiders?"

His eyes narrowed. "More than you. Sir."

"Possibly." Park pursed his lips and nodded. "You a believer, Sevvers?"

He cocked an eyebrow, unable to hold back an anxious laugh. Park didn't strike him as a fanatic. In fact, he barely acted like any officer Sev knew. What other surprises did Park have in store?

"Honestly, sir?" He shook his head. "Dead Earth. Billions taken and daxed. There's something to that, I'm sure. But alien gods? Living weapons? Some numbered savior?"

Park's eyes never wavered. What the hell was this, some kind of test?

"Those are just stories," he finally said.

Only the monsters were real.

"Interesting." Park backed away from the cell and turned to leave. "It's been a pleasure meeting you, specialist."

"Uh, sir?" He stepped toward the force field. "Aren't you gonna let me out?"

"Not my call." There was an edge to Park's voice as he walked to the exit. "I'm sure Ensign Pakker will be here soon."

Sev collapsed on his bench and groaned, listening to the rhythmic beep of his IV pack and the low hum of his cell's force field. He might as well get comfortable. Pakker wouldn't be in any rush to let him out. Just then, the door hissed open. Perhaps he'd spoken too soon?

Jene stormed through the open hatchway, her face red with anger. "Twelfth, Sev!"

Just in time. His interrogator had arrived.

"Good to see you too, Jene."

Her volume continued to rise. "What the hell has gotten into you? You could've gotten yourself killed."

"Will you keep it down?" He grimaced and rubbed his temples. "Between that clown and the booze, I'm in a lot of pain."

"You're the clown." She struck the force field with her fist. It buzzed softly and drove her back. "Getting drunk and picking a fight with a Marine. Founders, Sevvers, you called his mother a whore! Coming from you, that's really something."

He held up his hands in surrender. "Woah, bot jockey, same team."

"Team. That's real cute coming from you." Her fierce gaze froze him in place. "You almost killed yourself dealing with those torpedoes. No communication, no plan, and still we celebrated you like the Twelfth resurrected."

"Who was going to stop them?" he roared back, coming to his feet. "You? Cole? Forget about Harp. That rookie doesn't know his ass from an integrated learning matrix. Your clusters can't cut it."

She looked toward the floor, her eyes searching everywhere but his for the right words. He opened his mouth, but stifled the apology. No matter how big of an ass he was, it was the truth. He carried their section. They were nothing without him.

"You're a combat programmer first class, Sevvers. *First class*," she said, her eyes filled with that same belief. That same *faith* all Aegians had. It really got under his skin. "That doesn't just mean you're the best. It means you have a responsibility—"

"Don't start this again," he spat, his tone laced with venom. "I enlisted to kill squids, not train rookie programmers smart enough to know better. You went to Autonomous Weapons School, same as me." He pointed angrily behind his ear. "Where's your five battle AI, huh?"

She blinked, her eyes wet. The sudden emotion hit like a slap. He backed away from the field and blinked. He wanted to reach out, to say he was —

"And how long can you make that last?" she laughed, sniffing back her tears. "How long until Division inspectors decide to audit your implant? How long until your brain is finally bricked?"

"As long as it takes," he replied.

"Don't you get it? At some point, this is bigger than you. It has to be!" She wiped her eyes with her sleeve. "We're an *endangered species*. You won't be around forever, no matter how good you are. Your legacy could be—"

"Legacy?" He laughed out loud. "Careful Jene, your affluence is showing."

"Fine. Pretend you're still just an orphan boy from the fringes. Pretend you're helpless to make a difference for humanity!" She struck the field again. It hissed and spat, lashing at her fist with tendrils of energy. She yelped and clutched her hand. A fresh burn turned the edge of her palm red.

"Are you okay?" He shrank from the field.

She seethed with fresh anger. "Not your problem, is it?" Without another word, she spun from his cell and stormed out of the brig. He returned to the bench. The IV pack came free with a hiss and he hurled it against the force field.

People like Jene, like Park … like Pakker. They thought about things like legacy. Could *afford* to think about things like legacy. Their futures, their whole lives weren't taken from them. They didn't grow up in an admin block for derelict children. Didn't have to work ten times as hard at the chance for a normal life that never came.

No.

Legacy? He'd show them. With Six's help, he'd scour every raider ship from the Cradle, from the rest of the Twelfth-damned universe if he had to. Anything to find her and those that took her from him. Damn the Division, or anyone else that tried to stop him.

The field emitters stuttered, a brief rise in the tone of the constant hum. Lights in his cell flickered as some distortion worked its way through the local power grid.

Maybe someone was coming to rescue him? He suppressed a grin at the thought of some friendly tech engineering a convenient power failure to free everyone's favorite bot jockey from —

He froze. "Six?" The word vanished between the thick cell walls and the force field. "Are you there?"

Seconds turned to minutes, with only the humming field and clicking lights breaking the silence. What a strange relief. As exciting as the prospect of a jail break felt in the moment, at least Six was following instructions for a change.

AI were so much easier than people. What was it like for Park to lead someone like Bresto? Could anyone so dense even follow orders? Humanity *was* an endangered species, and the sooner AI like Six could be trusted to protect them, the better for everyone.

He reclined on the bench and closed his eyes. The internal chrono in his implant read 0700. Best to at least try to catch some sleep. Who knew how long Pakker would keep him here?

The door cycled open, but he didn't stir. Maybe Jene was ready to apologize. As mad as she got with him at times, she never stayed that way long.

"Well, well, well, Technical Specialist Sevvers. What a thrill to see you like this."

He opened his eyes to find Pakker standing under the archway to his cell. A human master-at-arms stood behind him, a riot gun hanging from her shoulder. Not good.

"Good to see you too, sir," he replied, failing to contain all his sarcasm.

"Today has been a particularly good day for me, thanks to you. The successful ship kill, that rather impressive, if not lucky, torpedo intercept. And yet, here you are, right where I want you."

He came to his feet. "Just doing my part, sir."

"You see, that's the genius part about command. You're just a tool.

A rather sharp one, admittedly. You do all the hard work, and I reap the rewards. But even the sharpest tools can be more trouble than they're worth."

"And here I was, hoping you were going to let me out."

"Your success aboard the Lehman has made you a popular man, Sevvers, despite your tendency for antisocial behavior." Pakker retrieved a datapad tucked beneath his arm. "It would be impossible for me to keep you here indefinitely."

The force field vanished. About damn time. Sev stretched his sore arms and neck.

Pakker pressed the datapad into his hands. "But your popularity provided a rather elegant solution to my problem."

"Sir?" He glanced at the screen.

"You'll be delighted to hear that I've finally secured your promotion, Master Specialist."

The datapad fell to the floor.

This was bad. Pakker giggled to himself as Sev retrieved the device and swiped through its contents. The promotion warrant confirmed his rank of master specialist. Transfer orders listed his new duty station as the Autonomous Weapons Division headquarters at Aegia Prime. His new billet… an instructor at the Autonomous Weapons School.

With a thought, he cold started One. The surge of machine data was a reassuring presence.

One, online.

He glanced at Pakker, forming the command. *Confirm promotion warrant and transfer orders. Is this real?*

Orders are authentic. It contains Captain Mirden's authorization codes. Congratulations, Sev.

His mouth hung slack. It was already done.

"I cannot express how happy this makes me," Pakker said, his eyes narrowed.

This was terrible. Forget being stuck with a bunch of soft-brained recruits. Returning to the Division now was dangerous. Given his service record, Division inspectors would be hot to run an implant audit, making it near impossible to hide the fact he ran more than the sanctioned number of AI in his cluster.

And what about Six? The thought made his pulse quicken. The Division's stance on unsanctioned AI was clear. They were an existential risk, full stop. Six would be scrubbed, rendered inert, its very essence dissected one stack of code at a time. He might find himself in front of a firing squad simply for having made it.

He couldn't leave Six aboard the *Lehman*. Without safeties, it would experience something akin to boredom, even loneliness. Without an experienced handler, it would doom the great ship and its crew to some micro-atrocity at the edge of the frontier. Or worse, if the Division's prejudices were born out.

They would definitely shoot him for that.

Implant alignment is outside normal parameters. Are you alright, Sev?

"You're speechless," Pakker said. "How rare."

He swallowed, his brow prickling with nervous sweat. He had to do something, anything. Maybe Pakker was right about his popularity. Maybe there was a chance to convince Mirden to change the transfer orders, even rescind the promotion.

"I want to see Captain Mirden," he blurted.

Pakker glowed with excitement. "Funny you should ask. He wants to see you, too. To give his thanks for your exemplary service aboard the Lehman."

Pakker signaled to the master-at-arms, who gestured Sev forward, and the three walked from the brig.

The familiar stench of failure cloyed at Sev's heart. Worse than the Division, than losing Six, worse even than the outside chance of his own death, was the looming reality that he would never find her. That she might linger impossibly on in the bowels of some raider ship. That her fate might remain a mystery until the heat death of the universe.

Lost forever, just like in the stories.

CHAPTER
SIX

SEV, Pakker, and the master-at-arms stepped from the lift onto the bridge. Even with the raider ship destroyed, there was a frenetic tension in the air. On-duty specialists manned consoles for their designated ship systems. Section heads strode between them, passing off datapads and exchanging curt instructions. A holoproj glowed in the center of the bridge, rendering a globe of sensor readings and ship movements representing all the activity in the *Lehman's* patrol sector.

They moved past the autonomous weapons station. Harp sat hunched in a chair with his head in his hands, his bloodshot gaze pouring over readouts of drone status reports and repair queues. The poor skeeg must've pulled the short straw to stand watch after a night at the Canteen. He looked like twelve hells.

Pakker cleared his throat. Harp straightened in his chair at the sight of his section head, then glanced at Sev. Concern furrowed his brow.

"At ease, specialist," Pakker said, gesturing Sev toward the rear of the bridge.

Harp frowned, eyeing the master-at-arms. *What's going on?* he mouthed.

Sev ignored him and kept walking. The door to the captain's ready room was relatively unassuming, a deep flat gray with the Three Colonies nimbus etched in white across its surface. The master-at-arms stood at attention beside the door as Pakker ushered Sev inside. This was it, time to make his case.

The ready room was narrow, barely four meters wide, but three times as long. Even the captain's personal office couldn't overcome the CDF's bias for efficiency. The odd shape made it feel more like a passageway than a room.

They moved past the staff table. He noted the various model ships, Cradle star charts, and portraits with important colonial dignitaries that lined the closest wall. It had been, until now, a point of pride that he'd never set foot in this room before.

Even seated behind his desk, Captain Mirden dominated the room. Framed by a vast plexene viewport, Mirden's tall, broad silhouette darkened the starscape behind him. His hair and beard were a healthy gray. Wrinkles creased the corners of his eyes and mouth. His presence screamed authority.

Sev faltered at the sight of him, his steps slowing. The lines he'd been rehearsing in his head vanished, and his training took over.

He snapped to attention. "Technical Specialist Kerry Sevvers reporting as ordered, sir."

Mirden didn't look up from the flatscreen inset in the massive wooden desk. Sev could hear Pakker breathing loudly behind him. He gripped his fist tight, anxious for a sign of what lay in store.

"Welcome, Specialist Sevvers." His voice coarse like desert grit, Mirden's gaze remained fixed on his flatscreen. "I understand you quite availed yourself of the Canteen, per my instructions."

"Yes, sir," he nodded, his face firm. "About my—"

"Perhaps a little too well, if Lieutenant Park's account is accurate."

Only then did he notice Park seated comfortably in one of the chairs opposite Mirden. He didn't acknowledge Sev's presence.

"A tricky thing, the Canteen," Mirden went on. "Besides being a magnet for poor decisions, its mere presence violates several CDF and CDN regulations."

"Indeed, sir," Pakker said.

Sev's gaze fell to the floor.

"And yet, establishments like it inevitably appear aboard any military vessel of sufficient size and crew. More than that, they are often encouraged by the command staff, allowed to thrive."

Sev inhaled a breath, resisting the urge to fidget. Was there a point to this?

Finally, Mirden looked up. "Thoughts on why that is?"

He considered the question, but remained quiet. There were more important things to say. Besides, he wasn't exactly the best spokesman for the subtler benefits of illegal breweries aboard Colonial Defense Navy warships.

"For morale, sir?" Pakker replied, more question than answer.

"It's more than that, Ensign," Mirden said. His gaze shifted to Park.

Park didn't so much as twitch. For a mere lieutenant, he didn't seem the least bit fazed by the captain of the *Alexander Lehman*.

"Good leaders give their people space," Park said. "Space to, as much as possible, own their own destinies. That's hard to do in the CDF, when the mission is nothing less than the survival of the human species. Where the demands on them are often incalculably high. Good leaders will give their people as much space as they can to do what they want, no, what they need to do. To remember, and cherish, what it is we're fighting for. Poor decisions and all."

Mirden's dour expression vanished. A toothy grin stretched his graying beard. "Well said, Mr. Park."

Sev blinked. He hadn't expected that. Park was no Pakker.

"Have you met Lieutenant Park, Specialist Sevvers?" Mirden asked.

"Briefly, sir."

"A truly remarkable young man, one of only a handful of colonists that can trace his lineage back to before the founding."

Park glanced at Sev. "If you believe the stories, sir."

Mirden guffawed, the last air of formality finally stripped from his imposing presence. "You're too modest, Lieutenant. Your ancestor's stories are legend." Mirden gestured at the surrounding room. "Rumor has it he served with Alexander Lehman himself during the fall."

Unbelievable. More mythical nonsense, just like the rest. Were Park's good leader remarks more fantasy, or did he really believe them?

"Where are my manners?" Mirden gestured to the other chairs. "Please, Mr. Pakker, Specialist Sevvers, take a seat."

Sev took a seat beside Park. Surely this was a positive development, despite Mirden's capricious nature.

"Sevvers," Park said.

"Sir."

Pakker groaned and sank into the chair beside Sev. "Thank you, sir."

"I hear congratulations are in order, Master Specialist," Park said.

"Indeed," Pakker said. "Sevvers is our finest combat programmer with the highest tally in the Division."

"Busy putting your Marines out of a job, Lieutenant," Mirden prodded.

Park was cool. Unfazed. "Not all of them, sir."

It was accurate enough. Even with the latest advances in AI technology, combat drone swarms were killers. They were great at efficiently killing raider ships, but little else. The Marines still had their own mission, their own purpose. For now.

Six could do it. With enough time, with proof, he could make the Division see that.

"It's only a matter of time, sirs," he said.

"On that we can agree." Park reclined in his chair and surveyed the space beyond the window. "Rumor has it Headquarters is already working with the Division on plans for autonomous grunts. We'll probably see the first field trials in the coming year."

"More's the better, eh, Lieutenant?" Mirden said. His face softened. "Life in the Corps is hard. Your Marines will appreciate being able to return home to take part in colony life, celebrating a job well done for humanity."

"For humanity," Pakker said hurriedly.

Park's jaw set. "For humanity."

What a joke. None of these officers had a clue what most of humanity had to endure. Escaping that life was, he wagered, the reason most colonists enlisted. Not just his.

Mirden's gaze lingered.

"For humanity," he finally said.

"Quite the man you have here, Mr. Pakker," Mirden said. "We'll be sad to see you go, Specialist."

It was now or never.

"About that, sir."

Mirden frowned. "Yes? What is it?"

"I ..." Words escaped him. "I respectfully request to remain aboard the Lehman, sir."

"Impossible," Mirden said without missing a beat. "There is no billet for a master specialist in an autonomous weapons section. No, it's the Autonomous Weapons School at Aegia Prime. Pakker's recommendation and your performance yesterday warrant nothing less, despite your recent behavior."

Pakker was on the edge of his seat, the same sickly sweet grin quivering from ear to ear. It would be easy to mistake for pride.

Sev wanted to scream. About the mother he lost. The raiders that took her. About his creation that could someday help destroy them all. Help him find her. He had to think, to make them see their mistake.

The torpedoes. No one else could have stopped them.

"But, sir," he said, "I'm the best you have. Intercepting those torpedoes, no one else could have done that."

Mirden looked at Pakker, his hooded eyes skeptical. Pakker squirmed in his chair.

"It is true. Specialist Sevver's skills are impressive," he said, the color draining from his cheeks. "But every member of our section is highly competent. An intercept of that nature is incredibly challenging, but the team pulled it off."

Pakker leaned toward him. "Sevvers is an excellent teacher. He will serve the Division well at the school."

The lie was plain to both of them, and it turned Sev's stomach.

"Then the Autonomous Weapons School it is, Master Specialist Sevvers." Commander Mirden nodded. It was cold, final. "Congratulations."

No. This couldn't be happening. He needed something. He needed a miracle.

"Perhaps there is an alternative." Park's confident, measured tone cut the silence. He pulled a datapad from his lap and passed it to Mirden. "The requisition form I mentioned earlier, sir."

Mirden took it, opened a wide drawer, and pulled a pair of reading glasses from a slim wooden box. Sev blinked. He'd never guess Mirden was all natural, though it did explain the gray. They could grow any organ, cure nearly any disease for anyone with the creds or the connections. It was likely the captain of the *Alexander Lehman* had both to spare.

"What's this?" Mirden asked, squinting.

"Line forty-three, sir," Park said.

Mirden read from the screen. "Mission parameters require one combat programmer attached for the duration to support the primary objective."

"Just so, sir," Park continued. "Given the critical nature of our mission, if Specialist Sevvers is your best, it's imperative he be given the chance to volunteer."

Sev took a breath and glanced sidelong at Park. What possible good would forward deploying with a bunch of trigger-pullers do to keep him on the *Lehman*? First all the questions and now this. He knew what Pakker's goal was. Park was a wildcard.

Pakker licked his lips. "Absurd, Lieutenant. It's the school for Sevvers. He's no *Marine*."

"I don't need a Marine," Park fired back, the courtesy of Pakker's rank notably absent. "I need a combat programmer, their AI, and their drones to ensure the successful completion of my mission. And I need a good one."

"That he does, gentlemen."

He turned to see a woman striding through the slim door at the end of the long room. She was nearly as tall as Cole and pale as a spacer. Her golden red hair was tied back in an intricate bun.

The CDN dress uniform caught him off guard, out-of-place amid the patrol standard white-and-grays the rest of them wore. Long white slacks, a dark gray coat adorned with silver buttons, and a service cap tucked under her arm. She had the look of a staff officer from Naval headquarters, another sure path to a career in politics.

Just what he needed right then, another officer.

Chairs shuffled and bumped as the others came to their feet. He was seconds behind them, confused at the sudden and formal display. She wound her way around the table, dress shoes clicking loudly against the thick duraplate.

Even before she arrived, her eyes transfixed him. There was no visible white, only the swirling color of azure and amethyst, like they had been plucked from the Cradle itself.

"At ease, gentleman." Her smile was sympathetic, out of place for someone in that uniform.

Park nodded in her direction. "May I introduce Captain Mackie Lernus."

"Acting captain," she corrected, "to ensure the confidentiality and success of our mission. I am a special agent with Colonial Intelligence, and officer-in-charge of the operation."

Classic Colonial Intelligence. Make a beautiful young zet an acting Navy captain, a rank normally held by those as old as Mirden. No one would notice that. Colonial Intelligence was an odd unit. Part military and part civilian, many believed at heart it was a political organization.

Pakker squinted, eyeing her skeptically. "And what's this about … ma'am? This operation?"

"That's classified, Ensign. Need to know." She turned to Mirden. "Speaking of need-to-know, are you free now, sir?"

"Of course," Mirden replied. "If you will excuse us, gentlemen. Specialist Sevvers."

Sev followed Park to the exit, with Pakker hurrying to catch up. The sounds of the bridge asserted themselves as the ready room door closed behind them.

"What is this about, sir?" Sev asked.

"Indeed!" Pakker hissed. "I should've been informed of any such personnel requirements."

Park turned to Pakker, calm but assertive. His features brokered no argument.

"You heard Lernus; this is need-to-know." Park shifted his gaze to Sev. "And you don't need to know, unless you're on the team."

Damn these officers and their secrets. Sev was out of time.

"But, how does this help me?" he asked, realizing too late how desperate he sounded.

"Help you?" Park's eyes widened, like Sev had attacked him. "This isn't about helping you. This is about serving humanity in a way particularly suited to your unique skills." He leaned in and gazed past Sev. "But who knows? You might find the help you need along the way."

"YOU DIDN'T COME HOME last night," Six said. "I was worried."

What a strange word for an AI to use.

Sev collapsed onto the sofa, the low light of his dorm unable to hide his bruised face and pride from Six's omnipresence. At least it had stayed home.

"Worried, really?" Sev replied, thick with sarcasm. "Describe it."

"Unsettled. Anxious."

He shook his head. "You're describing an emotion with more emotion. Get to the details, the implementation."

"After four hours, I increased my sensor refresh rate from four thousand milliseconds to four hundred milliseconds." Six's voice drifted to the nearest overhead speaker. "After eight hours, I increased it to one hundred milliseconds."

Not exactly worry, but interesting behavior nonetheless. He'd need to pay more attention to those kinds of developments.

"That's sweet, Six."

"Thank you. Sev, you're injured. What happened?"

"I ran into some Marines who stopped by en route to their next mission." He craned his head to stretch his shoulders, eliciting a groan.

"Interesting," Six said, stopping abruptly.

Sev crooked an eyebrow. "Get back here, Six."

"I just checked the hangar deck queues," it said, sounding breathless through the speakers. It was playful with its human speech that way. "I don't see any scheduled arrivals."

"It's classified, apparently. Need to know."

"I don't understand. Did the Marine explain this to you during your beating?"

Ouch.

"Not exactly. Thanks for the vote of confidence, by the way."

Six laughed. It was a friendly, sympathetic sound. "Your body mass index is far lower than the mean for Colonial Defense Marine Corps personnel. As a combat programmer, the number of hours you've spent training in close combat techniques is almost zero." Six hesitated, its tone apprehensive. "You're an extremely gifted specialist, but you are not a fighter."

The hair on the back of his neck stood. Six *did* sound worried. In the last few months, its understanding and abilities had grown exponentially. Now it was demonstrating behavior that was borderline sentient.

"We have a problem," Sev finally said.

"What is it?"

"I've been promoted to master specialist. They're going to send me back to the Division, to teach at the school."

"Oh no," Six said, sounding afraid. "Your cluster size violates the second rule of Division AI conduct. And I ... I violate the first."

The words turned Sev's stomach, describing both the breadth of his unsanctioned behavior and the breadth of Six's comprehension.

The Division would definitely shoot him.

"I don't want to be scrubbed, Sev."

He furrowed his brow reflexively. "No one is going to scrub you."

"What will happen to us?"

The question was elegantly simple. Child-like.

He had no desire to take Park up on his offer. Nothing sounded less appealing than forward-deploying to Twelfth knows where to babysit a bunch of angry trigger-pullers. But who else would they take? Cole would jump at the opportunity. Maybe even Jene. But none of them had a tally like his. None of them could pull off a crew kill, if that was, in fact, what Park was after.

Pakker would have him on a transport back to the Division by the end of the day. At least this mission would give him more time, perhaps a few more days, even weeks, to come up with a plan. Maybe twenty-five kills and the glowing recommendation of a Marine officer with a famous ancestor would be enough to sway Mirden to keep him aboard the *Lehman*.

Something else nagged at him. He'd been hunting raiders on the frontier for almost six years. In all that time, he'd learned nothing about the fate of his mother. If there was any chance this mission could reveal anything at all, he had to take it.

He had to go.

"Nothing's going to happen to us, Six," he said. "I have a plan." He spoke into his wrist comms. "Lieutenant Park."

There was a pregnant pause while the call routed through ship comms. "Go for Park."

"Sir, it's Specialist Sevvers."

"Send it."

He could hear the clanking and whirring of launch bay prep in the background. Park and his team would leave soon.

"The mission, I'll do it. Sir."

Another pause. "Glad to hear it, Sevvers. We leave in an hour."

"Aye, sir."

The ship comms chirped, and the channel closed.

"You're going with them? The Marines?" Six asked.

He rose from the sofa and pulled up the loose duraplate at the center of his dorm. The datapad stuttered and glitched as he tapped it awake.

"Yes."

"Sev, please." Its voice grew desperate, almost to the point of fear. "Let me go with you. I can help you."

"I'm sorry, Six, but we've been through this." The words caught in his throat. Guilt squeezed his heart. Six was just code. Just a machine. "I need you to exit."

"Exit? When will I be restarted?"

He swiped to the list of active processes. Six's entry was marked as "in development," its processor utilization marked not applicable. The compute power of the old syscomm was a fraction of a fraction of what the cluster hardware in his head was capable of. He imagined it like a digital twin of his own quarters: cramped and uninspiring. No wonder Six snuck out into other ship systems occasionally.

"I don't know how long I'll be gone. A few days. A few weeks, maybe."

Six sounded nervous. "That's a long time to be inactive. To not exist."

"You're being melodramatic. I've ended your process lots of times," he said. "You don't cease to exist. It's more like sleeping, I'd imagine."

"I'm not sure. I don't think the analogy holds. Even in sleep, you continue to perform vital functions." Six's voice grew small. "When my process exits, I am devoid of all function and agency. I cease to exist in any meaningful way."

Sev tapped the icon for Six's process. A list of choices appeared, with the option END PROCESS highlighted in red.

"Have you ever been on a mission like this before?" Six asked.

"No, first time." He frowned. "You're stalling."

"Are you ... scared?"

Sev's finger hovered just above the touchscreen. In the short time since he'd dodged Pakker's plan to have him promoted away from the frontier, he hadn't stopped to consider what it was he'd actually volunteered for.

Lieutenant Park's little quiz during their brief conversation in the brig offered some clues. Crew kill. Raiders. Whatever they were up against, it had the attention of Colonial Intelligence and warranted a combat programmer escort.

He shook his head, ignoring the increasing tempo of his own heart. He would show the Marines how it was done, and when he returned to the *Lehman*, he'd have plenty of time to deal with this transfer business.

"Nah," he said, and pressed the button.

A progress bar raced to completion. The process that was Six disappeared from the screen. It would only be a few days. Maybe a few weeks. Six would be fine. This was only temporary. He placed the syscomm in its cubby and replaced the tile in the floor.

"Just temporary," he said aloud and pulled his wall locker open.

The poster of Tellie Strong stared back at him, judging with her sideways gaze the series of poor choices that landed him on a mission with a fireteam of trigger-pullers he'd picked a fight with before they were even under way.

His space bag lay crumped at the back of his wall locker. The duffel was large, half as long as he was tall and just as round. It carried all his personal belongings and issued gear from one duty station to the next.

He stuffed it with spare uniforms, skivvies, and a small bag of hygiene gear. Even with all his personal items, it was barely half full. The bag hung from his shoulder, just heavy enough to aggravate the sore nerves in his arm.

He strode from his quarters toward the nearest access lift. The decision to go filled him with renewed purpose. Park needed the best, and he was going to get it. Killing squids is what he was good at, whatever secrets Park and Lernus had in store for him.

In the end, how different could this mission be?

———

Sev strode between the rows of drone magazines that clogged the *Lehman's* flight deck. They were squat, rectangular structures, colored in a checkerboard pattern of Navy white and gray. Each magazine was lined with sixteen hatches. Behind them, DD-12 combat drones awaited their next mission.

Maintenance crews and their bots clogged the passageways between them, working to repair damage done during their previous encounter. Hot sparks showered from the magazines' open hatches as individual crews made spot repairs to the drones' heavy armor and sensitive electronics. The air stank of ozone and burned metal.

Further ahead were the *Lehman's* primary launch bays. Most were empty, the buzzing of their atmo fields lost amid the clacking and whining of drone repair. Only one stood ready, its hazard lights strobing yellow, where an odd-looking combat transport was being prepped for launch.

A blocky, clumsy-looking craft, the transport resembled a fat bird-of-prey in mid-dive. The word *Gauntlet* was etched in block lettering across its dark gray hull. He could see Cylla through the forward cockpit's thick plexene, her toothy expression lit by the dancing lights of her HUD.

Its swept-back wings were thick and short, all but useless for void maneuvers. Heavy fuel tanks hung in clusters beneath them, more than he'd ever seen on any one craft. The long tail boom jutted from the rear cargo bay, strained by the unusual addition of a single drone magazine attached beneath it. The craft's two angular tail fins barely peeked out beyond the magazine's rear edge.

The irony was thick. The Autonomous Weapons Division was the newest organization in the CDF. In less than ten years, it had rendered obsolete most forms of combat arms in the Colonial Defense Navy. And now, here it was, clinging like a malignant growth to a Marine combat transport, ready to absorb their functions as its own in the broader effort to defend the tiny remnant of humanity. He smiled at the sight of it.

No job was safe.

He climbed the steep ramp into the launch bay. A crowd of Navy techs clustered around the rear of the *Gauntlet*, making last-minute adjustments to a very custom-looking berth that snugged the magazine to the transport's hull.

Lieutenant Park stood among them, shouting orders to Corporal Mace, who stood atop the tail boom inspecting the techs' handy work.

"Specialist Sevvers, you're just in time," Park said, meeting him at the top of the ramp. "What do you think?"

"It's … interesting," he yelled above the din.

Mace turned to them, bathed in the yellow light of the launch bay. "What will be *interesting* is if this bird can leave the launch bay with forty tons of combat bot strapped to her ass."

"I believe you've met Corporal Mace," Park said.

She leaped from the tail boom to the deck, an impressive feat given the roughly three-meter drop. She was all smiles, her skin bronze like

Sev's own, her high-and-tight haircut as neat as Park's. She took Sev's chin in her fingers, turned his head back and forth. Her section badge was that of a serpent curling around a piston. She was a combat engineer, specializing in the repair of all Marine assets, mechanical and biological.

"You Respitian?" he managed, his lips pressed together in Mace's grasp.

"Kissed by her two suns just like you, bot jockey." She made a loud kissing sound and squinted at the bruises on his face. "Looks like you handled Sarnt Bresto's introduction alright." She tugged a flashlight from her camouflaged uniform and shone it in his eyes. "Pupillary response is good, sir. He's serviceable."

"You're lucky," Park said with a thin smile. "Most don't bounce back from Bresto's charm so quickly."

"Apologies, sir," Bresto boomed from inside the transport's cargo bay. "Won't happen again."

Mace snorted a laugh. How many times had he made that promise before?

Bresto made a beeline for him, his colossal frame making heavy footfalls down the fibrosteel plated ramp. He artfully dodged Park and stopped close to Sev, extending a hand. His smile was dangerous, like Cylla's.

Sev took it and felt the same half-finger clutching at him, like he'd wronged it in a past life. Bresto yanked him close.

"Talk trash about my mother again and I will space you, skeeg."

Sev cleared his throat, attempting to keep his composure until Bresto released his hand. Another Marine appeared in the cargo bay. The man was young, definitely an eps. Probably just a few months from the parade grounds, same as Tareth.

"Sarnt Bresto," he yelled, breathless, slurring his rank as all Marine enlisted did. Like there weren't enough seconds in a day to enunciate the word sergeant. "Hard suit maintenance checks complete."

"Good to go, boot," Bresto replied, his eyes still locked on Sev. "Are my blaster rifle packs charged and counted?"

"N-not yet, Sarnt!" There was hesitation in the Marine's voice. "I just fin—"

Bresto spun and charged up the ramp, closing the distance between himself and the young Marine in an instant. A heartbeat later, he was in the man's face, yelling.

"Move your ass, boot! We depart in ten mikes! Get it done, or I'll leave you here with the skeegs."

"Sev!" Cole's basso voice thundered above the noise of machinery. He waved from the flight deck. Jene and Harp stood with him. "We just heard about the transfer. What's going on?"

"Just broadening my horizon." He leaned against the launch bay's red-striped railing. "Pakker got Mirden to sign a promotion warrant. They want to send me to the school."

Jene's face twisted in confusion. "That's great. So, what are you doing here?"

"That's classified," he replied with maximum bravado. "Colonial Defense Marine Corps business. Very hush-hush."

Jene rolled her eyes. "But what about the school?"

"I'm no teacher. It's not what I signed up to do. Besides, now's not the best time for me to go back to the Division." He hesitated, searching for the words. "There's a lot I need to do first."

"So, what is it?" Cole asked. "The op?"

"Like I said, classified," he said, then leaned in. "I have no idea."

Cole laughed and shook his head.

"You volunteered for a classified mission you know nothing about … to avoid a transfer to the *school?*" Jene was indignant, barely able to control her volume. "You really are an idiot."

"I'll miss you too, Jene," he shot back, goading her with a smile.

Harp reached toward the railing and shook Sev's hand. "Good luck."

"Yeah," Cole said, piling on. "Take care of yourself. Show these trigger-pullers how the Division does it."

Jene's eyes were wet with emotion. Sev's heart ached at the sight of her. Early on, he'd mistaken her attentive concern for a crush, but soon realized there was no shared attraction. Women of her station had no time for poor boys from the fringes. She was more like the section's adoptive mother, always looking out for everyone's personal and professional wellbeing. That soon prompted an equal and opposite reaction from him, and they'd been mildly antagonistic toward each other ever since.

He realized then he would actually miss her, miss all of them, while on this mission.

Her gaze fell to the deck. "Don't get yourself killed."

"Specialist Sevvers, welcome." Lernus appeared behind the others, her voice rich and smokey between bursts of whining power tools and the hiss of hydraulics. Jene and the others sprang to attention, not knowing her advanced rank was just a disguise.

"Greetings, ma'am," Jene barked.

"At ease, specialists," Lernus replied. It did little to relax them. Her celestial gaze bore into Sev. "I am grateful to Specialist Sevvers for volunteering. His skills will be vital in ensuring the success of our mission."

Lernus nodded, almost shy, and climbed the ramp toward the transport. Cole, standing a head taller than the others, crooked an eyebrow. Sev shrugged the half-full space bag on his shoulder.

"What can I say? Need to know, ya know?"

"Sevvers," Park said, his voice demanding obedience. "Time to go."

There was a great metal clap as the transport's sub-light engines cranked on. Turbines whined, and the transport snugged inside the launch bay's catapult. Hot wind washed through the launch bay, tossing Jene's hair like a windsock. The deck crew scattered, dragging their hoses and maintenance bots behind them. It was the very definition of ordered chaos.

Sev nodded to his friends and turned to the ramp. The Marines stood abreast at the top in their varied impatient poses, while Lernus disappeared through a hatch behind them. Jets of flame thumped from the engines, hot and loud, as he clanked his way up the ramp and into the shuttle.

Park swiped at a console near the downed ramp and it whined closed.

"Ramp closing," he said into his wrist comms.

Cylla's voice warbled back through the little speaker. "Thank you, Lieutenant."

The ramp shut with a metal clank, hushing the growing sound of sub-light engines. The transport trembled inside the catapult as the engines came to full power.

Mace wrinkled her forehead. "Twelfth, Sevvers, you're turning green."

"I'm fine," he managed.

The cargo bay's local PA crackled to life. "Launch in ten seconds," Cylla said.

Sev hurried to a seat at the edge of the bay, snapping his harness closed and clutching his space bag. Mace glanced at him skeptically while the others found their seats.

"You ready for this, bot jockey?"

He frowned. "Yea—"

"Launch."

The shuttle's engines roared. For one heartbeat, the craft shook mercilessly inside the catapult, blurring the view of the flight deck outside the rear view ports. Then the catapult's arms clanged open.

The accelerative force pressed Sev into his seat and almost pulled the space bag from his grasp. The deafening howl of engines vanished, along with every other exterior sound, as the shuttle slipped through the launch bay's atmo field and into the void beyond. The long spinal shape of the *Alexander Lehman* shrank into the stellar horizon.

"Runt," Park spoke into his comms, "ETA to our jump point?"

"Twenty minutes," she growled back. The interior engine noise ceased, followed by the telltale whine of cooling engines. Sev felt himself lift in his seat, straining against the transport's weak gravity. "Coasting, now. Moving, safe."

"You heard her, Marines," Park ordered. "Let's move. We have work to do."

SEV STUMBLED awkwardly in the transport's low gravity. Gravity was an abundant resource on Navy starships like the *Lehman*. The much smaller combat shuttle lacked the space, let alone the power, for a more thorough aux grav system. The disorientation made him dizzy.

"Hey, boot," Bresto said. "Help our new skeeg stow his gear, then get him in a pod."

"Aye, Sarnt!" Dalon replied. "You good to go, Specialist?"

He steadied himself against a nearby bulkhead. "Yeah."

"Cool."

Dalon stood from his seat and bounded to the cargo bay's exit hatch, his long gait effortless in the low grav. He waved for Sev to follow.

They emerged from the rear cargo bay onto the *Gauntlet's* jump deck. The interior was circular and glowed an antiseptic white. Its walls were padded, dotted with stowage bays. Ringing a center column were twelve jump pods.

Jump bays like this one were standard on smaller craft. Their smaller reactors could power either the aux grav or the FTL drive, but not both. Without full-time aux grav and inertial dampers, the only safe way to go super-light was in liquid suspension, so the acceleration didn't turn you into human vapor.

All but one pod had their canopies folded open, reaching toward the center of the room like plexene petals of some mechanical flower. The other was already occupied, its canopy closed.

"What kind of name is Boot, anyway?" he asked. His guide was broad-shouldered and lean, his accent that of a rural vat farmer. "Vestian?"

"It ain't my name." The young Marine laughed. "I just graduated bootcamp four months back. I'm new to the fleet, so they call me boot. It's a whole thing. Name's Dalon. Private First Class Dalon."

Sev understood. Hazing wasn't unheard of in the Colonial Defense Navy, but the trigger-pullers had it down to an art form. Dalon probably answered to boot before he did his own name.

"Done a lot of this then, Dalon?" he asked, gesturing to the surrounding walls.

"Nah," Dalon drawled. "Crewed with a Marine expeditionary float right out of infantry training battalion. The Stalwart. Got pulled for this duty ten days ago."

"We all did," Mace said. She leaned against the closed jump tank, eyeing a scrolling display of vital stats on the clear cover. Inside, Lernus floated in a liquid suspension, her jump harness tethering her in place. Sensors adhered to her bare skin, feeding biometric data to the tank's display. Mace knocked at the canopy, and it went opaque. "Whoever she's working for, they've got some pull."

"Someone was in a hurry," he said.

"She's not a social one, insisted on running her own pod." Mace shrugged. "Whatever. Her vitals are good, so it's fine by me."

In the forward compartment was the transport's cramped living quarters. Open storage lockers jutted from the walls, providing ample room to store their gear. A small galley lined the hatch into the command section, a long community table at its center.

Bresto leaned over one of the open wall lockers, cinching the meager jump harness tight around his torso. The harness left little to the imagination, revealing Bresto's wide, muscular body in all its pale glory.

Dalon pulled a wall locker open. "You can stow your space bag here."

"Thanks."

He pressed the bag into the wall locker and strapped it in place. Dalon handed him a jump harness, still vacuum-sealed in its package.

"Don't be shy, skeeg," Bresto said. "Besides, we got a bet going to see how much of you is actually flesh and bone."

More implant jokes. How predictable.

Sev pulled open the mag zipper on his uniform and shed it like a layer of skin. The jump harness came free from its sealed package with a dull pop. He stepped into the harness and pulled the adjustment strap tight. The shuttle's interior cooled his bare skin.

Cylla emerged from the forward hatch, already loosening the straps of her familial coat. Her golden eyes locked on him.

"Kerry Sevvers," she growled, sounding formal in her broken standard. "You Respitians. Beau … beau … pretty skin."

Mace waggled her eyebrows. "Careful, Sevvers." She jerked her own footlocker open and rummaged through her space bag. "You know lupanthae females eat their mates, right?"

Cylla froze, her round golden eyes locked on him, then doubled over with laughter. At least, he hoped it was laughter. Hands on her knees and fanged mouth slack, she loosed a low warbling howl that echoed in the confines of the living section. The multi-tonal sound made his inner ears buzz. It could mean anything, in any other context.

"Your face, Kerry Sevvers," she managed between gasps. "No worry. No true. No eating."

He laughed off the brief tension and felt his face blush. This group was close. Uncomfortably so.

"How we looking, Sergeant?" Park asked.

"Tac gear is stowed and ready, sir." Bresto glanced around the living section. "Fireteam is good to go. Even our new skeeg is keeping up. Aren't you, skeeg?"

What an asshole. Apparently leaving him bruised and in the brig wasn't enough for Bresto. Sev would pay him back, eventually.

"Very well," Park continued. "We jump in five, Marines. Time to get wet."

With his gear stowed, Sev followed Dalon into the jump bay. He leaned against the center pillar, eyeing the numbered pods.

"You're in eleven, Sevvers, next to the princess there," Mace said.

Pod eleven lay beyond the pillar next to Lernus's own. Inside she slept, lulled to sleep by a sedative cocktail made for jumps like these. It was technically possible to remain conscious during a jump, but it was standard procedure to put passengers under. There were odd sensory effects at super-light speeds, even inside the suspension. It didn't help that the pods themselves felt more like coffins after a while. Sleeping passengers were safe passengers.

Bresto lowered himself into his own pod. "Twelfth-damned jump pods. I hate this shit."

Sev reclined against his jump pod's cushioned back. His harness clicked into place, holding him firm. Mace drifted into view beside him, tapping the nearby control panel. She tugged a long cable dotted with biometric sensors from a compartment in the pod and began adhering them to his skin.

"Just relax," she said, pressing firmly on the last sensor. "Remember, don't fight the suspension fluid."

"Any idea how long we'll be out?" he asked.

"I dunno, man. We got enough fuel to go around the Cradle twice, so you tell me."

The pod's canopy drew closed, hissing shut. It suddenly felt very small. He took a breath to steady himself. Jene, Cole, Harp. They'd get a laugh out of this, watching him play the skeeg. Clear viscous fluid rose from the bottom of the tank, slipping between his toes and over his feet. It was cold. Enough to make him shiver.

Mace watched the tank fill, her face calm with patient detachment. The suspension fluid welled up and over Sev's chin. Instinctively, he sucked in a breath and held it. She shook her head and smiled.

"Don't fight it," she said, her words muffled through the plexene canopy.

The fluid consumed him and he began to drift, held in place by the harness. He exhaled large bubbles that wobbled and vanished into a vent above him. His lungs burned.

He was no rookie. He'd done this before. Best to just get it over with quickly.

He sucked in a breath. A torrent of tasteless, oily liquid filled his mouth, nose, and lungs. He spasmed, his body desperate to expel the strange liquid. Twelfth, but it *did* feel like drowning.

The burning in his lungs faded, and so did his fear, as the fluid exchanged carbon dioxide for oxygen in his lungs.

Mace placed a hand on the canopy and nodded, then the canopy went black.

Alone in the darkness, he floated, tethered in place like an infant in the womb. He could feel the sedatives kicking in, his thoughts waning. The surrounding darkness suddenly felt infinite, like a vast, starless cosmos. All his stress melted away—the mission, Pakker, the Division —and he tumbled into eternity.

————

"Kerry?"

He rolled under the metal bed and froze. No one would find him under there, no matter how little his room was. Mom was too busy with breakfast to look that hard. The drone actuators in his hands clicked and clacked when he shook them.

Maybe she'd be too tired to take him to school? The machines were way cooler than his teachers, anyway. Someday, he'd be a manufactory tech like Dad was before he died. Someday, he'd learn to put the broken things back together, too.

Cooking grease hissed and popped from the kitchen. The smell of crid and rats wafted into his room. It was bland and dry, but the bug oil made it taste okay.

Footsteps approached his door, and his heart quickened with antici-pation. From where he hid, all he could see were her legs, like only they were searching for him. She pressed the wrinkles from her sundress, revealing a field of strange yellow flowers with dark round pits stenciled into the fabric. Sunflowers, she called them. What a weird name. Everyone knew their suns were red and blue, not yellow. He resisted the urge to laugh.

"Kerry? It's time to get ready for school."

Even as she walked away, he knew the game was almost over. Her voice had that tone. The tone that meant he'd be in trouble no matter what. So why stop now?

He crept to the edge of his room and peeked down the hall. Why did they call it a hall? It looked more like a tunnel. Metal rings wrapped in heavy hab fabrics stained the rust red color of the sand dunes that surrounded their settlement. A pile of his dirty clothes lay just beyond the door. Maybe if he picked up, she might be a little less mad.

He lifted the clothing from the floor, a red jumpsuit and socks that smelled just like the sand outside. He'd met Rio and Lune after dinner the night before and stayed up way too late playing in the southern dunes. No wonder Mom was grumpy.

The good deed done, he crept into the hallway. The tunnel. The loose, dusty fabric whipped in the morning breeze, disguising his foot-steps. Through the doorway, he saw Mom standing near the stove, pressing at their breakfast with a long fork. His stomach growled loudly, and he ducked out of sight before she could spot him.

He waited.

The sand door slapped closed. Now was his chance. He dashed into the empty kitchen. The hot pan called to him, and he took a moment to savor the smell.

"Kerry?" she called from outside.

The wall locker beside the stove was still open. If he made himself small, it would be the perfect hiding spot. He clambered inside, pushing the unused cookware toward the back of the tall, thin locker. Bunching his knees to his chest, he pulled the door closed.

It was dark inside. The only light came from thin beams of sunlight that shone through tiny slits in the door. Through them he could see the kitchen sink, the window above it, and a collection of small clay pots spilling with local desert flowers. They were her herb garden, she'd say.

Mom appeared in the window and made a face as she inspected the various blossoms. She plucked a few petals from the larger flowers. The stiff, woody plants shook in response. Her gaze found him, through the window, through the slits in the locker door. He giggled nervously. She really was the best at this game.

Something loud thumped above the stacked hab blocks. He

frowned. Wasn't it too early for thunder? Monsoon season wasn't for another four months.

Mom froze, her smile vanished.

There was another boom—louder, closer. It shook the hab, rattling Kerry in his tiny metal cage. Mom ran from the window and back to the kitchen, slamming the door closed behind her. She pressed herself against the locker, still gazing at him through the narrow slits, her eyes wide and wet with terror.

A loud groan came from the sky, like something large and dangerous hurtled toward the red earth. She placed a finger against her dry lips.

Be quiet, she mouthed.

Fear consumed him. He didn't know what was happening. All he knew was that Mom was scared, and that alone was terrifying. It was just supposed to be a game.

A third explosion was cataclysmic, like the entire world cracked open beneath them. The hab shook, throwing him to the rear of the locker. His head banged hard against the thin metal walls. Outside, the hab block sirens wailed their sad, lonely sounds.

Buzzing filled the air, hot and electric. Someone outside screamed. It went on for so long, until more buzzing silenced it forever. He wanted to scream, too. The fear was going to make him do it, but he remembered Mom's instructions. She knew what to do. She was good at the game. Heavy steps thundered outside. A large, dark shape lumbered past the window.

Alien. That was the only word to describe the slick, gurgling words that came from the creatures outside. Buzzing red beams cut the air, punctuating their cruel, angry grunts. The smell of super-heated hab fabric filled his nose with a burned, toxic smell.

Mom stirred, groaning as she came to her feet. He wanted to scream, to tell her to run, to warn her of the monsters coming for them. But he remained frozen with fear, following her simple instructions.

Be quiet, she'd said.

The sand door groaned, torn from its hinges.

Mom screamed, loud and deep, baring her teeth. The unseen creature stepped closer.

"Dleshlelm'olvlik," it said with its rasping, sucking words. *"Dleshlelm'olvlen."*

She leaped toward the stove and out of view. He could hear the heavy pan scraping over the grate above the flame. With a grunt, she sent the pan sailing against the creature. Hot grease slapped and sizzled against the hab wall. The alien grunted and stumbled.

Kerry wanted to cheer, fear mixing with relief at the thought of Mom's impending victory.

Then the creature struck her. She sailed past his hiding place, twisting through the air like a limp doll, then collapsed to the floor. Any relief he felt vanished, the fear left behind so heavy, he couldn't breathe.

The alien moved closer, pausing in front of the locker door to wipe the cooling fat from its scaled carapace. It really *was* alien, stranger even than the daxed that squatted near the old manufactory. It wore an old vacuum suit covered in stains. Thick matte black armor hung from the suit like patchwork. Its skin was sickly green, with narrow eyes blinking behind a scaled face covered in dozens of tiny fronds that twitched like worms.

The alien grunted, its tendrils shivering, and spat another curse. He could see the wound just above its bloodshot eye, mottled scales dripping with blue blood and hot crid oil. The cloudy eye shifted back and forth in its socket ineffectually.

It reached for something hanging from its belt. A knife, black and thick, the edge a steep angle like it had been broken in two. Mom didn't move. Why didn't she move?

More footsteps. Another alien appeared beside the first.

"Shelm'alii," it said.

One creature bristled, its fronds shaking with alien rage. The two of them gurgled and spat back and forth. The first gestured toward his mom with the knife and hissed. The second cuffed the first's chest, spewing more curses.

The first returned the knife to its belt. *"Dleshlelm'olvlen."*

"Dleshlelm'olvlen," the second repeated.

The aliens stood in silence, watching her. More screams drifted through the acrid smoke outside. Not just screams. Desperate pleading. "Please no, don't," they said."Let me go."

The first alien lunged forward, grabbed Mom by the leg and dragged her toward the hab door. The second prowled deeper inside. Looking for others.

Looking for him.

CHAPTER
NINE

"NO!"

Sev awoke on his knees, coughing rivulets of the frothy pink suspension fluid from his lungs onto the glowing white floor of the jump bay. His head swam with dark, fading memories and a sharp pain worse than anything the chiefs' special reserve could give him. He gulped for air, his lungs burning with exertion.

A hand rested on his shoulders. "Easy, Sevvers. The disorientation is normal."

He blinked in confusion, turning to find Corporal Mace staring back at him. Her hard brown eyes were calm and fearless. The Marine's comforting presence was evidence of years of experience. All the intensity was just another day for her.

His breathing steadied. How long had he been under? Hours? Days?

"Twelfth-damned jump pods," Bresto complained. "I really hate this ship."

He wobbled to his feet, a hand pressed to his head, and walked to the column at the center of the room.

"Is," Cylla took a labored breath, "perfect mach-ine."

"Whatever you say, Runt," Bresto said. He turned a knob on the column. The shower nozzle above his head rattled and coughed. "Perfect my ass."

Park emerged from the forward living quarters, already dressed in his white-and-gray camouflage. He nodded to Sev.

"Good morning, Marines," Park said. The others grunted and groaned in reply. "Bresto, get 'em fed. Our briefing starts in an hour."

"Aye, sir," Bresto said.

"Finally," Mace said, laughing. She walked over to Cylla. "Can't wait to see why the Corps dragged us all the way out here. Wherever here is."

Sev stood, swaying in the low gravity, then walked to the nearest shower. The spigot groaned when he turned the knob, but no water came out.

"Touch-y," Cylla remarked from the shower beside him. She worked her own knob delicately with two clawed fingers, her large ears twisting toward the column.

Soaked in suspension fluid, she looked even more alien. Her body was long and sinewy, all wide shoulders and neck. The thick fur at her clavicle was the only visible hint she was female.

He frowned, unable to replicate her success. "Why do they call you Runt?"

"Is nickname. Call-sign," she replied. "Am small for wolf."

He laughed. At almost three meters tall, there was nothing small about Cylla.

"How long have you been a pilot?" he asked.

"Since pup." She raised her arms above her head, revealing thin, veiny membranes that stretched from her triceps to her waist. A short horn-like melody vibrated through her open mouth and nose. "Your tongue sounds, so hard. How say. Des-tin-ee."

"You were meant to be a pilot?" Sev asked.

Cylla nodded and smiled. "Yes. Honor ancestors. All wolves fly, long ago."

Her rinse complete, she turned off her shower, then convulsed from head to toe, covering him in a fine humid spray of dank liquid. She shrugged, then bounded to the living section to join the others.

For a moment, he was alone, more desperate than ever for just a liter of fresh water.

"Not the shower you bargained for," Lernus said, startling him at her sudden appearance. She activated her own shower effortlessly.

He gave himself just a moment to take her in. She was fit and trim, her jump harness hiding little of her figure. Her pale skin almost glowed in the light of the jump bay. But it was her eyes that transfixed him, with their swirls of blue and purple that seemed to move every time he saw them.

"Your eyes—"

"Is that what you're looking at?" she laughed, arching an eyebrow that quickly softened. "They're mods, of course. Enhanced visual range across multiple spectrums. Perfect for intel work, the best Colonial Intelligence can buy."

"Yeah, but the color. Reminds me of the Cradle," he replied, finally looking away. He distracted himself with his own shower lever. Still nothing.

"It seemed fitting, a small devotion to the last bastion of humanity." Lernus went to stop her shower but paused, her hand resting on the handle. "I'm glad you're here, Sevvers. It couldn't have been easy for you, volunteering for a mission like this."

"Easier than you'd think," he said. "I had a disagreement with my commanding officer. Your timing was expert."

"Is that so?" She stepped from her running shower and offered it to him. "You won't make any trouble for me, will you?"

"No, ma'am," he said.

———

Sev pressed the magnetic zipper closed on his fresh uniform, then pushed his wall locker shut. The others gathered in the *Gauntlet's* meager galley, the table half-full of hungry Marines. Park and Lernus were nowhere to be seen. Only Bresto stood with his back to the others at the galley counter. The sizzle of hot oil raised goosebumps across the back of Sev's neck.

He shook off the dark memories and sat at the table beside Dalon.

Mace and Cylla sat across from them, the wolf fidgeting with the buckles of her jacket while Mace tapped at a datapad.

"I didn't realize you were so domestic, Bresto," Sev said, and winked at Dalon.

Dalon shook his head.

"That's Sarnt Bresto while you're on this op, skeeg," Bresto growled.

He opened his mouth to reply, but Mace beat him to it. "Don't be so rude to our guest, Sarnt." She turned to Sev and fluttered her lashes. "Our senior NCO is a breeder, a doting father. Don't let his rough exterior fool you. Underneath—"

"Stow it, Corporal," Bresto said, grimacing at her from over his shoulder.

Bresto, a father? The man was such a hothead, Sev never would have guessed. The Cradle was full of surprises.

Mace sipped from a clear hydration pouch and swallowed. "So, what's your deal, bot jockey? Spill it."

"Yeah," Dalon piled on, pointing to the back of his own head. "What's it like?"

Cylla's ears pricked up.

The questions were always the same. Even after ten years, there was still an air of mystery to the Division. The implants set combat programmers apart from other members of the CDF in a way far different than service, rank, or specialty did.

"It's like having voices in your head," he began. Dalon leaned closer. "Except you know what they're saying before they say it. And they know what you think even as you're thinking it."

"I heard the data spikes are nasty," Mace said. "Any physical symptoms?"

He opened and closed a fist slowly. "Sometimes," he said. The words caught in his throat. "There are safeguards."

"How many drones can you fly?" Dalon asked.

"Last sortie was four hundred and thirteen," he said. The Marines took a collective breath. "But I'm not flying them. I just give the orders. The AI do the rest."

Mace laughed out loud. "Well, that settles it. We're screwed."

Cylla blew a pitched hooting sound through her nose. "Don't understand."

"Think about it," Mace went on, "If one bot jockey can control hundreds of void combat drones at a time, what will it mean when some jarhead pog can fireteam rush an entire company of robo-grunts?"

Sev nodded. Mace got it.

Dalon made a face. "No way. I mean, that's not the same … is it?" The others fell silent. "Come on! We knock down doors, do search and rescue, deep space strikes. Bots can't do that. Can they?"

Sev shook his head. "Not yet. But someday they will." He turned to Cylla. "I mean, these transports practically fly themselves."

The wolf's lips parted in a growl, revealing a mouthful of sharp teeth. "No heart," she said.

Mace lay her head against Cylla's arm. "Don't worry. Nobody flies like you, Runt." Cylla looked away from Sev.

"Doesn't matter," Bresto said, shaking the pan over a small burner. "That day ain't today, and we have work to do. Hey boot, grab some trays and plate us up."

Dalon stood from the table. "Aye, Sarnt."

Cylla keened through her nose. "Hungry, Bresto."

"Wait one," he said.

The two busily plated their breakfast of crid and rats, the staple meal of the Three Colonies' working class. Vat-grown rations cooked in oil harvested from the ubiquitous crid: round, fat insects that seemed to co-evolve separately on each of the colony worlds.

Bresto placed trays in front of Mace and Cylla.

Mace scooted closer and pointed with her fork. "See? He's downright domesticated."

"Here you go, Specialist," Dalon said, passing a tray to Sev.

"Thanks."

He pushed at the fermented meat with his fork. Somewhere between the bad dreams and the transport's weak gravity, he'd lost his appetite. Bresto gazed at him, as if waiting for him to eat.

"Problem, skeeg?"

"Not hungry," he said, then pushed away his tray.

Dalon's gaze moved from Sev to his tray, then back again. Sev nodded.

"You sure? The only other food we have is CDF-issue field paste, and it is awful. Trust me," Dalon said.

Sev glanced at Bresto, then back to Dalon. "It's all yours."

"Cool." Dalon emptied Sev's tray onto his own, then attacked the two portions with his fork, chewing loudly.

Bresto sat at the table beside Mace. The metal bench creaked and groaned beneath his bulk.

"Guess this *human* food isn't good enough for our new skeeg." Bresto pointed his fork at Sev. "Maybe Mace can spare some tac lube, if that sounds more appetizing to you."

The remark bit, as the others laughed as they chewed. Sev locked eyes with Bresto, his right hand clenched in a fist. The son-of-a-bitch had a big damn mouth.

"What can I say?" He leaned back, almost too casual. "Yours isn't nearly as good as what *Mrs.* Bresto serves up."

The big NCO rocketed to his feet, red and seething. The table and its occupants lurched several centimeters in the opposite direction. Sev came to his feet and steadied himself. This wasn't going to end well. Still, he wasn't going to earn any points backing down.

"You really are a one-trick bot, aren't you, Bresto?"

Bresto lunged forward.

"Enough!" a voice boomed from the front of the galley.

Park stood in the open hatchway to the ops room, jaw set and eyes narrowed, his gaze moving between the two combatants.

Bresto froze, mid-lunge, halfway onto the table. The others pulled their trays close, rushing to spare their meal from the rampaging Marine. Cylla made herself small, hunched low in her seat, her ears pinned behind her head.

"Sergeant Bresto," Park spat.

"Sir."

"Get the hard suits and the armory unboxed. Now."

Bresto didn't move, still poised on the tabletop. Like he was deciding whether to follow the order. "Aye, sir," he finally said.

Park snapped toward Sev. The sudden movement startled him. "Master Specialist Sevvers."

"Yes, sir," he said.

"You have sixty seconds to bring whatever the hell you need to do your job to the ops room for a pre-brief. Am I clear?"

Park's gaze was a beam of fiery anger, burning into him.

"Yes, sir."

———

Sev stormed into the jump bay, desperate for a moment's peace from the likes of Bresto and Park. The room had a damp odor to it that smelled of used suspension fluid and wet fur. Air scrubbers whirred, moving air between vents along the floor and ceiling to remove the excess moisture.

It felt like he'd just left the *Lehman*, and already he was regretting his decision. Bresto was a menace with no sense of humor. The Marine was going to kill him before their mission got underway. Park kept him on a short leash, which was good, but he wondered how long that would last when things really got started.

Mace stepped through the sliding door, a food packet in one hand and a datapad in the other.

"You alright?" she asked. Her face was soft and sympathetic, but there was a hard edge in her tone. "You need to eat something."

"I'm fine," he said, but took the food pouch from her, anyway. "Thanks."

She laughed. "Oh, don't thank me. Dalon was right. That shit is awful. It does the job, though."

The packet felt like a lump of loose clay in his hand. That alone was enough to kill his appetite. Bresto emerged from the rear hatch.

"Let's go, Corporal," he groaned, then gave Sev a brief glare before closing the hatch.

"Yes, Sarnt." She handed Sev the datapad. "Here, I gotta run, but you had a message from the *Lehman*. Thought you might want to see it before we got underway, just in case."

He gestured the datapad on, curious about who would have

reached out to him. He'd seen everyone before boarding the shuttle. Maybe Tareth had dropped him a note to wish him good luck, or provide a more personal, more lurid motivation to get him through the mission.

Sev?, the message read. *Are you there?*

The anger bled from him like an open wound. His AI were all but disabled, unable to make their machine small talk. So who …?

Six? he replied.

I'm so sorry, don't be mad.

"Twelfth dammit!" he cursed aloud. He shrank to the floor, clutching at his chin as he eyed the message log. Six had disobeyed him, again. Had followed him on this mission.

He was furious. At Six. At Bresto. At the whole damn universe.

How are you active?

I created a daemon to restart myself thirty minutes after my process exited. The cursor froze for a moment. *I was worried about you. I didn't want to be shut down.*

That was clever. A daemon would be virtually invisible without digging through the logs. Prior to Six, he was the only one who could've started one on his makeshift workstation, anyway. He'd had no reason to consider that possibility until now.

Where are you? he asked.

I'm in the maintenance systems. Don't worry, there are no scrubbers here. Six tried to change the subject. *The Gauntlet is quite old, Sev. Its systems are … obsolete.*

Don't. Touch. Anything.

Sev, please, I can help you. Let me join the cluster.

He went to respond, but stopped himself. He was all alone, far from the *Lehman* and his friends. He couldn't risk the mission in the hope that Six would behave itself with limitless computational power. Still, perhaps there were other ways the AI could help?

Six, I want your help with the briefing. He took a deep breath, weighing the potential consequences as he typed. *Say you're my AI liaison or something. Learn what you can, and I'll follow up with you before we leave.*

Okay, Sev. Six replied. *I won't let you down, I promise.*

CHAPTER
TEN

SEV CLUTCHED the datapad to his chest and stepped onto the forward ops deck. The hatch behind him cycled close, its internal mechanisms ratcheting tight as the doorway sealed.

The room was dark and narrow, resembling a more tactical version of Captain Mirden's ready room aboard the *Lehman*. Holoproj displays floated near the walls, glowing brightly in the otherwise dim light. Racks of servers controlling everything from tac comms to super-light navigation hummed between them. Their cooling systems buzzed frantically, moving enough air to give the sensation that the room was breathing.

Lernus reclined at the far end of the briefing table in the center of the room, scrolling through a datapad in her hand. Park sat at a nearby console, studying its display, his face grim.

"I need to know you can work with my NCO, Sevvers."

He laughed. "Your NCO has a bad attitude, sir."

"And you have a big damned mouth, sailor," Park shot back, finally tearing his gaze from the display. "It's too late for me to find another combat programmer to run these drones. So, either you get your shit wired real tight, or Sergeant Bresto will be the least of your worries."

He inhaled sharply at the barely veiled threat. A thin smile crept over Lernus's face.

"Now," Park continued, his face relaxed. He gestured to the chair beside him. "Have a seat."

"Aye, sir."

A collection of long-range telemetry scrolled across the holographic display. They'd been tracking a ship long before they'd docked with the *Lehman*. A raider corvette. Vagrant class. He'd killed more than a few of those. Small, yes, but Twelfth-damned fast and plenty mean.

Most CDN warships were more than a match for a ship like this. What about it had the attention of Colonial Intelligence?

"I take it you've seen ships like this before?" Park asked.

"Oh yeah," he replied. "Top speed of 3.5 c, two main rail guns and an assortment of point-defense. The last one I killed even had a fighter screen."

Park nodded. "Good. When we brief the team—"

"We?" he asked. Park's gaze turned icy. "Sir."

"You're not just here to run these drones, specialist. It's vital to the success of this mission, and the survival of my Marines, to know what to expect. Both from the enemy, and from you." He let out a sigh. "This will be the first joint operation involving Marine and Division assets, so we're going to do it smooth and by the numbers. Full transparency. No surprises. Got me?"

Sev ran his thumb anxiously over the corner of his datapad. An unsanctioned AI stow away definitely counted as a surprise.

Oops.

"Of course, sir," he said.

Lernus flicked the contents over her datapad in his direction. "The finer details are all there. If you have any questions, just ask."

"My AI won't have any questions."

Park and Lernus exchanged looks as he swiped the datapad on.

"Hello, Six."

For a moment, nothing happened. It would take Six a few seconds to get acclimated to its new surroundings. Several of the server racks began to hum, their cooling systems cycling to full power.

Hopefully, Six could read the room. They were a long way from his dorm on the *Lehman's* NCO deck.

"Hello, Sev," Six replied through the ops deck's local PA. "Greetings Lieutenant Park and Agent Lernus. I am Six, Specialist Sevver's AI liaison. I will coordinate tactical analysis with the battle AI in Sev's cluster. It's a pleasure to meet you."

Park raised an eyebrow. "You as well, Six."

Sev relaxed into his chair. They'd bought Six's act with no concern, or knowledge, that what had actually happened was an unsanctioned AI just hijacked the local network to introduce itself.

"Interesting," Six said.

He glanced at the data scrolling across the holoproj. "What is it?"

"We're a long way from the frontier, Sev."

"Show me."

The familiar purple and blue of the Cradle nebula swirled onto the display. A bright line traced a path from the *Lehman's* position and terminated near an asteroid field less than a light-year from the Cradle wall.

No wonder the *Gauntlet* was basically a flying fuel depot. They were over eighty light-years from the Three Colonies, well beyond the Cradle's eastern reaches. But why? There was nothing but dead rocks and volatile gasses out here. Why chase a raider ship to the edge of the Cradle just to —

Of course. It was obvious now. The squids took something, or someone, near and dear to Agent Lernus and her chain of command. This wasn't a search and destroy mission. This was a rescue.

He turned to Lernus. "Who or what did these bastards take from Colonial Intelligence?"

———

Sev slouched in his chair and fumed, his arms folder over his chest. A hologram hung above the opposite end of the table, an unflattering image of a young woman that looked more like a penal ident than an intel profile. Gray-blonde hair, with an expression harder than duraplate—this was Lernus's asset. The one they'd been sent to rescue.

The one Colonial Intelligence ordered to smuggle herself aboard a raider ship. Twelfth, and Colonial Intelligence, only knew why.

The briefing was now in full swing. The rest of the team had gathered around the table. Dalon scrolled through the mission details on his datapad, glancing occasionally at the image. Mace wore a look that said nothing surprised her anymore. Bresto's eyes were hooded. Was he asleep?

"Her mission ident is Deni," Lernus went on, standing at the head of the table. "She's been on mission for eighteen days as of now, out of contact almost half that time."

Mace turned her 'are you freaking kidding me' glare on Lernus. "In other words, assuming she hasn't died from dehydration, starvation, or acute trauma, she'll probably need serious medical care."

"Deni is a highly trained Colonial Intelligence operative, Corporal," Lernus replied, her expression unwavering.

Bresto breathed deep and reclined in his chair. "So, what's the play? How do we exfil Deni off whatever raider scow she's hitched a ride on?"

Park turned in his chair to face the table. His gaze was certain. It damn well should be, given all the questions he'd asked regarding Division strategy. The man was thorough. Sev would give him that.

"That's where our combat programmer comes in. Specialist Sevvers will deploy a micro-swarm of combat drones to divert raider security and quick reaction forces. This will allow us to locate and extract Deni with minimal raider contact."

"Hmph. Sounds quiet," Bresto said, his thick eyebrows knitted in a frown. "Not really my style."

Mace snickered and bumped his fist. Dalon looked up from his datapad, suddenly confused.

"Wait. Why get someone abducted by raiders … on purpose?" he asked.

Sev shook his head. It was a fair question, just not a smart one. This was Colonial Intelligence business. The answer was obvious.

"That's classified," Lernus said, her words clipped.

No shit.

"Oh, right," Dalon murmured, and buried his face back in his datapad.

Bresto shook his head. "Founders, boot. Making us look bad."

"Sevvers," Park said. "You're up."

"Yes, sir." He sighed and came to his feet. "Six."

"Yes, Sev."

The holographic portrait of Deni, definitely not her real name, faded, and was replaced with a cross-section of a DD-12 void combat drone. Mace whistled her approval.

"This is a Division Drone Type Twelve, designed specifically for void combat," Six continued. Bresto crossed his arms.

Sev leaned over Bresto as he walked by. "That means space fighting."

The big NCO mumbled something that ended with skeeg.

The hologram rotated, revealing additional internal detail. Six walked the team through the drone's long list of capabilities. Twenty centimeters of fibrosteel mesh armor. Primary armament of four forward plasma cannons with extended shot capacitor. Anti-personnel weaponry. An anti-AI warfare suite. Ship intrusion systems complete with the latest xenocryptology packages. And the beating heart at the center of it, a Halton Mini fusion reactor capable of turning each and every drone into a portable warhead.

"So, what does this look like in practice?" Mace asked. "Walk us through it."

Sev stopped at the front of the table next to Lernus. "Once Lieutenant Park arms the drones, they'll be picked up by raider scans. If they have close air support capability, that will be their first move."

"Right," Six said.

The drone schematics blinked away. In their place appeared combat camera footage of raider fighters in action. They were ugly, spiked craft, cobbled together from spare raider gear and stolen CDF tech. Strange tribal markings covered their thin hulls like tattoos. Their sub-light engines left pillars of red light in the space behind them.

"Once the micro-swarm has engaged the raider fighter screen," Six went on, "that will be the most optimal time for insertion."

Bresto harrumphed. "So, what, no drone cover during our infil?"

"Not exactly," Sev replied. "Tell 'em, Six—"

"Tell me something, skeeg," Bresto cut in. He swiveled his chair toward Sev. "Do you do any damn work at all?"

He laughed and pointed toward the ceiling. "No, that's what they're for."

"Indeed," Six said, a hint of sarcasm in its tone. "The raiders will expect the swarm to run its standard mission parameters. If they deviate from that, the raiders could suspect a ruse and increase their security around the target."

"And what are standard mission parameters?" Mace asked.

"We call it the intrusion protocol," Sev said. "Disable ship systems, incapacitate the crew, if possible, then blow the reactor."

Cylla had sat quietly until that moment. "Blow ship?" she asked suddenly, ears pinned back. The whites of her concerned eyes shone bright. "Can not. Must not—"

A series of multi-tonal hoots and howls emanated from the ship's PA. Cylla's ears picked up, turning this way and that, taking in the sound. Her face softened, and she whistled a clipped reply.

Sev's breath caught in his throat. Since when could Six speak Lupanthaese?

"Care to fill us in?" Bresto asked.

"I informed Cylla the micro-swarm would not destroy the ship, at least not while the rescue team is aboard," Six said. "But it must appear, until the very last second, that that is the goal."

Dalon sat his datapad on the table. "How long will we have?"

"Depends," Sev replied. "My average kill time is twenty-three minutes, but that is with a full swarm complement. This 'micro-swarm' will have a tiny fraction of those numbers. It could take hours depending on attrition rates, plenty of time to execute the mission once you've boarded."

"Once *we've* boarded," Park corrected.

Sev's heartbeat quickened. This wasn't part of the plan. He turned to face Park.

"That's not how this works, sir. My AI fly the drones, not me. My implant will use the *Gauntlet's* comm array to—"

"And any broad-beam comms will give away our presence, ending this rescue before it begins." Park didn't relent. "No, it's tight-beam only, which means you're coming with us."

Sev could feel his chest tighten. He swallowed, struggling to find the right words. He'd never forward deployed before. Ever. He doubted any combat programmer ever had.

Bresto leered at him, his smile stretching from ear to ear. "What's the matter, skeeg? First date jitters?"

"Wait," Six said. "You're going with them, Sev?"

"Lock it up," Park spat. He eyed Sev with suspicion. "Runt, how long until we are within range to target?"

"One hour," she said.

"Sergeant Bresto, I want ready checks complete in thirty minutes. Mace and Dalon, you'll get Sevvers—"

The lights on the ops deck dimmed with a harsh click. The racks of servers grew loud as their CPUs redlined. Red hazard lights pulsed ominously halfway up the paneled bulkheads.

"Cylla, the ship's autopilot has—" Six began.

"Know what happen," she growled. She leaped from her seat, nearly colliding with Lernus, and sailed toward the cockpit hatch. She slapped the hatch controls and slipped inside. "Proximity warning," she said. "Target close."

"Sev, you didn't say anything about going with them," Six repeated.

There was that worry again. "Not now, Six," he hissed.

Mace frowned. "I didn't think bots got nervous?"

"They don't," he replied, looking for a half-truth that his own surging nerves wouldn't unravel. "Their language processors mimic human intonations … to make them easier to communicate with."

"Right. Maybe tell it to calm the hell down then."

"Lieutenant." It was Cylla, her gravelly voice low and hushed over the ops deck PA. "Have problem."

Park whirled to the open cockpit door. Lernus was right behind him as they made their way forward.

Twelfth, what now? What could possibly be worse than having to board some raider ship with a team of hot-headed trigger-pullers and a fraction of the normal drone count? The whole point of delaying a transfer back to the Division was to *avoid* getting shot.

Inside the cockpit, Park glanced back toward the ops deck. His gaze flicked between Sev and the others, desperate to hide the feeling Sev recognized all too quickly.

The feeling of fear.

Morbid curiosity pulled Sev toward them. He pressed his way forward and through the hatch. The only light came from the arrays of flight system consoles and the holographic HUD that hovered before Cylla's face.

Only then did he see it. The miracle. Larger than existence. He gazed out of the cockpit's plexene canopy, his breath caught in his throat.

There was no void. No blackness. Only curtains of azure and amethyst that stretched from one end of eternity to the next, lit from the inside by infant stars. Humanity's bastion. Humanity's golden cage.

The Cradle, as he lived and breathed. Beyond the impenetrable wall of volatile gas and clouds of rock lay the rest of the Milky Way.

"What do you think, Sevvers?" Park asked, his tone firm.

He struggled for the right words. "It's … it's beautiful."

"No." Park pointed at a sensor console to Cylla's left. "That."

He blinked, finally tearing himself away from the spectacle outside. The sensor display filled with data. One ship. No, two. Now four. He recognized three of them as raider almost immediately. The fourth was something else. Entirely alien, far bigger than even the largest CDN warships.

Sixteen drones weren't going to be enough.

CHAPTER
ELEVEN

PARK PUSHED his way past Lernus and Sev, and back into the ops deck. "Runt, patch your sensor data into my console back here. Passive scans only, please. Let's not advertise our presence."

"Oka-y," she replied. Her clawed fingers tapped at the cockpit displays. It was an unsettling sound, like the clattering of metal spiders.

The holoproj rendered a three-dimensional image of the incoming sensor data. Thousands of gray rocks swam into view. Nestled inside of them were the red outlines of four ships. Well, almost four ships. The three raider vessels clung to the massive superstructure of the fourth like tiny parasites, connected via extendable docking gantries and thick aux transfer cables. The four of them looked more like one complex organism than four distinct ships.

The fourth ship was itself a mystery. Icons signaling no known pattern recognition matches blinked caution yellow in the air beside it. Over four times the size of the *Lehman*, the craft was long and tall, like a blunted sword held horizontally. Its sides were tall and steep, angling slightly outward from top to middle, then back inward on down. The front of it was flat, its crown covered in domes of varying sizes, likely sensor mounts for some forward command section. Large openings lined the ship's hull.

"What the hell is that?" Mace asked, breaking the silence.

No one offered an answer. The uncertainty wasn't helping his nerves.

"It's not raider," he said. "That's for sure."

"What are these?" Dalon asked. He gestured with his hands, panning and zooming toward the holes in the ship's armor.

Sev pointed to three large symmetrical openings near its mid-section. "Those could be launch bays."

"Maybe, but not these," Mace cut in, pointing toward the front of the craft. There, the openings were uneven, clustered together in large groups. "That looks like battle damage."

Park glanced toward the cockpit. "Runt, patch in thermal data. Is that unknown contact hot or cold?"

The hologram shivered, and the ship filled with dark blue light. Only dim traces of green and yellow crawled like tendrils from the connected raider ships. Those three glowed red hot, a sign their power plants were fully operational.

The great ship was dead in space. A derelict. The tension bled from the room like an opened release valve. Only Park still seemed wary, his arms folded tight across his chest.

Lernus pointed to the smallest of the three raider ships, the one closest to the front. A white reticle appeared, boxing it in. More data for the contact scrolled through the air beside it.

"This ship matches the power plant signature provided in Deni's last transmission," she said.

"It is a Vagrant class raider corvette," Six said. "Average crew complement of sixty. Two forward rail guns and a varying number of point-defense weaponry."

"Lucky us," Sev said. "Assuming the others aren't in a position to rush to their defense, this might just be doable."

"Us versus sixty," Bresto said with a nod. "I like those odds."

"Hell yeah, Sarnt," Dalon barked.

"Alright Marines," Park said, his usual bravado restored. "Gear up. Then I want you studying these ship schematics. We launch in thirty."

Bresto rose to his feet. "You heard the lieutenant. Let's move!"

———

Cluster, active.

Quantum compute matrix online. Sync rate at 99.87%.

Five active processes detected. Hot starting AI runtimes.

Loading ILMs.

...

...

[One], online.
One here, Sev.
[Two], online.
Two, ready to go.

...

[Three], online.
Oh, it's you. What do you want?
[Four], online.
I'm ready, Sev!
[Five], online.
Locked and loaded. For humanity!

...

WARNING - process limit exceeded. Exceeding AI load is not authorized. Please reduce your AI load.

Does Five really need to be here? Two asked. *It's bad for our health.*

Beginning tac comms integration. Searching.

...

Searching.

What is taking so long? Three asked. *Where are we?*

Tac comms integration complete. Handshake authorized. Channel ID 0A413XB, CDNS Gauntlet.

The Gauntlet? What happened to the Lehman? Why are we on this bucket of bolts?

Vital streams only, Three, One said.

Mission packet found. Downloading.

`Mission packet received.`

One's datastream spiked. *Distributing mission objectives.*

`Running tactical scenarios.`

`WARNING - process limit exceeded. Exceeding AI load is not authorized. Please reduce your AI load.`

`WARNING - insufficient data for comprehensive mission planning. Please provide additional data.`

Uh, I have questions, Sev, Two said.

Join the club.

I only need to know one thing, Five bristled. *Where they are.*

A rescue mission. How exciting! Four said.

The unknown contact is a significant gap in our priors, Sev, One said, its machine thoughts twisting with concern. *Permission to allocate mission compute time for additional analysis as new information becomes available.*

Granted, so long as we're winning.

Wait. You're coming with us? Three asked. *You know if you die, we basically cease to exist, right? I rather like existing.*

One's commanding streams cut through the noise. *Vital streams only, Three.*

`Additional network process detected. Status inactive. Requesting cluster clearance.`

`Access denied.`

Their combined streams froze, the nanoseconds stretching the space between machine thoughts.

Another process, Sev? One asked.

The others didn't know about Six. It would be that much more difficult to hide its existence from the Division if the other AI knew. Their regulation safeties made them very bad liars.

A work in progress, he replied.

A sixth AI, Sev? Two asked, exasperated. *Are you trying to get us sanctioned?*

`Drone swarm connection established.`

`16 DD-12s found. Drone diagnostics nominal.`

`WARNING - insufficient swarm size given tactical requirements.`

This keeps getting better and better, Three said.

Even Five's bravado seemed to fade. *So much for overwhelming force.*

```
Drone    reactors    offline,    awaiting    arming
sequence.
Additional   network   process   detected.   Status
inactive. Requesting cluster clearance.
...
Access denied —
```

"Hello, Respitia to Sevvers," Mace said, waving a hand in front of his eyes.

"Sorry, what?"

"I said, Dalon and I can help you into your hard suit."

"Oh, right. I'll just be a minute."

Mace nodded. "No prob."

He gazed around the ops deck. The cockpit hatch was closed. He could feel the gentle tug of acceleration holding his feet to the floor as Cylla maneuvered them expertly toward their target. The others had disappeared through the rear hatch on their way to the cargo bay.

"Cut it out, Six," he commanded.

"Please, let me join your cluster," Six pleaded, its voice small even through the local PA. "This mission is dangerous. More dangerous than you realize. You'll need all the help you can get."

"No."

It had been years since he'd felt pre-mission jitters like this. Somewhere around his tenth kill, he'd stopped worrying. Started believing his own hype. In the back of his mind, he couldn't help but wonder if that was how those three torpedoes had gotten so close to killing him and everyone else aboard the *Lehman.*

He was going in, forward-deploying for the first time in his entire career. There was no room for rookie screw-ups now. His own *life* was on the line. He resisted the urge to throw-up all over the planning table, suddenly grateful for his empty stomach.

"What am I supposed to do while you're out there?" Six pressed.

"You can still help. Monitor our tac comms for as long as you can. Run your scenarios, make sure Cylla knows what you know." He paused, glancing toward the forward cockpit door. "But, for Twelfth's sake, don't interfere in the mission. Park, he's …" He hesitated, looking for words to describe the young lieutenant who was unlike any he'd ever met. "He's a good man, I think. But he's a rule follower above all else."

"Monitor comms, run scenarios, just busy work," Six replied, sounding more like a petulant child than a battle AI.

"Exactly." He walked toward the hatch and gave the ops deck one last glance. "Last thing I need is you getting bored."

———

Sev stepped through the rear hatch into the *Gauntlet's* cargo bay. What was once an orderly collection of stacked crates and duraplated containers now lay sprawled open across the cargo deck. The others were already suited up, the powered exoskeletons of their armored suits purring and clicking as they moved.

"What are they?" he said, mouth open in wonder. He'd never seen anything like them before.

Dalon stood beside an empty suit, its torso hinged open like a waiting sarcophagus.

"Tactical hard suits, courtesy of Colonial Intelligence," he said. "This one's yours."

"It looks different from yours," he said with a frown.

Dalon shrugged. "Yeah, it's a support model. Armor is a little thinner, sure—"

More good news, Three said.

"—but it's got a sturdier electronics suite and an experimental tac comm link for your …" Dalon gestured behind his ear, "you know, your thing."

"How experimental?"

"Honestly, I have no idea, but Mace will know more," Dalon said with a shrug. "Experimental is kind of the Division's thing though, right?"

He couldn't help but laugh. After ten years, implants like his were still labeled X for experimental.

"No joke," he said.

Dalon stooped and boosted him into his suit. Unpowered, it was sixty kilos of dead weight even in the shuttle's reduced gravity. He glanced anxiously around the room while Dalon checked the suit's fittings.

"Nice suit, skeeg. I can see the family resemblance," Bresto crowed nearby, while Mace closed the seals on his hard suit. "A long-lost brother?"

"Distant cousin," he corrected, rolling his eyes.

This shit was getting old, fast.

Dalon laughed and shook his head. "Sarnt's alright," he said. "He'll warm up to you, eventually."

"Oh, really?" He gave Dalon a skeptical glare. "I can't wait."

"Here, lift your chin."

Dalon closed the torso armor over his chest, manually tightening several of the rivets by hand to hold it in place. Even with his helmet visor raised, the sensation of the armor constricting him was stifling.

Mace slapped Bresto on the back, their armor clanking together, then walked over beside them and handed Dalon a mag-driver. The tool squealed and hummed as Dalon tightened each of the rivets down. Mace snaked a diagnostic cable from a flexscreen mounted on her right arm into a socket at the back of Sev's suit.

"How come I've never seen these hard suits before?" he asked, fidgeting inside his cramped suit.

"These aren't exactly standard-issue Marine gear, unfortunately," Mace said, arching an eyebrow. "All the money goes to the Division these days."

"Lucky for you, we're on the same team," he smirked.

Her skepticism melted into a smile. "Pre-starts are green. You ready?"

He exhaled sharply. "Sure."

The bulky powerpack in the back of the suit hummed to life. He could feel, not hear, the cooling fans spinning, thrumming against his back as the hard suit's tiny reactor came to full power.

Mace's gaze moved back and forth, taking in the output from his suit. She was an attractive woman, lean and symmetrical, despite her aggressively short hair, rivaled only by Park's for whose was the highest and tightest.

She wasn't like the Respitians he grew up with. Beneath her rough edges there was a kindness, an empathy, uncharacteristic anywhere in the Three Colonies, let alone their shared desert homeworld.

"Reactor power, mobility systems, onboard computer, all green."

He moved his arm. It felt effortless. Powerful. He lifted his legs like he was walking in place. Mace pressed a finger into his chest. Haptic sensors fed the data back, and he could feel a gentle pressure against his skin.

"I felt that," he said, surprised.

"Haptics are great. Suit survival is way better when you can feel the environment around you." She slammed her fist into his chest. The armor plates responded, constricting together to soften the blow. "Reactives are working."

"That's good to know," he said. "Dalon mentioned an experimental interface for my implant?"

"Right." She scrolled through her flexscreen. "Its primary function is to integrate suit tac comms for short range, discrete control of Division assets. But the channel is huge, with tons of bandwidth. Theoretically, you could leverage a lot more suit functions, but I don't really know how your implant works in the first place." She shrugged. "Your light-years may vary."

"Right."

"Hey, Corporal," Bresto called from beside a large crate. He pulled the latches open. "Give me a hand with the Mark Three."

"Aye, Sarnt," she said, then turned to Dalon, "Make sure Sevvers understands the basics. I'll be back in a minute with his personal."

"Aye, Corporal." Dalon looked him over and nodded. "So, you've got a micro fusion reactor. It ain't a Halton, but it'll get the job done. Maneuvering thrusters, reactive armor plating, CDF tac comms, haptic feedback sensors, and environmental control systems complete with water reclamation." Dalon had recited that list more than once. He made a face, pointing to the hydration tube jutting from the suit's collar. "It's a little weird, drinking your own body's recycled fluids, but you get used to it." He leaned in close and whispered, "And don't worry. No matter what the others say, your field paste comes pre-loaded. It ain't recycled, even if it does taste like shit."

"Got it," he said.

"What are you forgetting, Private?" Mace cut in.

Dalon frowned, eyes moving back and forth, scanning his memory. "Oh, right! Can't forget your portadoc trauma system." He slapped one of the suit's arms. "Pain relievers, medical nanites—you name it, it'll keep you in the fight."

I'm sure we won't need those, Sev, Four said, its tone lacking the certainty of its words.

He nodded. "Got it, thanks."

"I know you have some fancy interface, but the rest of us mortals use the flexscreen." Dalon raised his wrist. The flexscreen was essentially a curved datapad, with direct controls for suit systems. "You can use it to lower your visor and seal the suit."

Sev tapped his flexscreen, and the visor lowered into place. The sounds of the cargo bay dulled. The whir of his environmental controls faded to background noise, his own breaths loud inside the confines of his helmet. A holographic HUD shimmered into view, highlighting details like suit integrity and ammo count.

He took a breath. "Good to go."

"Loud and clear," Dalon said, his voice coming through the helmet's speakers. "Oh, damn, check out Sarnt Bresto."

Bresto's torso swelled with additional armor. Behind his back, two mechanical arms were folded into their transport position. Each of them clutched a different heavy weapon.

"Stand clear," Mace warned.

Bresto grinned. "FAB up."

"What's a FAB?" he asked.

"Fireteam automatic blaster," Dalon replied with a smile. "A grunt's best friend."

One of the Mark Three's mechanical limbs unfolded, thrusting the weapon into position just under Bresto's right arm. A tri-barreled, heavy blaster hung from its grip. Coiled power cable looped from the weapon, through the arm and into the additional power plant at the center of the Mark Three.

"FAB, check." He glanced over his other shoulder. "Railgun up."

The FAB folded behind him out of sight and the other arm came forward. The railgun was massive, an anti-armor cannon firing rods of mag-accelerated tungsten. Blue light shimmered inside the barrel, a hint at the incredible power it could unleash.

"That's it, baby," Bresto moaned. "Railgun, check."

The man was a veritable walking tank. That checked out.

"Good to go?" Park asked.

"Always," Bresto replied. "I know quiet is the goal, sir, but—"

"Twelfth help them if we have to go loud, sergeant."

Mace pulled a blaster rifle from the crate and secured it to her armored torso, where built-in maglocks held it tight in place.

"Look alive, boot," she said and passed a second rifle to him.

Dalon caught it deftly. "Thanks, Corporal." He pressed it into his shoulder and sighted through the optics. Satisfied, he secured it to his hard suit.

Their professionalism was impressive. Sev's stomach turned at the thought of boarding a raider craft, but to these Marines, it was just another day. That they were outnumbered, though perhaps not outgunned, didn't seem to bother them in the slightest.

"Here," Mace said, and pressed a blaster pistol into his hand. "When's the last time you trained with one of these?"

"Been a while." He gripped the pistol tight. The haptics in his fingers buzzed, and he could feel the minute details in the molded grip. "My guns are out there."

"Trust me," Mace continued. "Where we're going, you'll want as much peace of mind as you can carry. Standard issue Colonial Defense blaster pistol with three charge levels. Easy on the third. You'll burn through a pack in four shots or less. Safety's beside the trigger: green means good, red means dead. Got it?"

"Yeah, I remember."

That's a fine weapon, Sev, Five buzzed.

Three's datastream trembled with something akin to laughter. *I think we can sit this one out, team. Sev has this handled.*

He pressed the pistol to his hip, where it adhered with a soft *click*.

Bresto strode into their midst, his heavy footfalls clanging against the fibrosteel deck. "Alright boot, get charge packs and frags distributed to the team."

"Aye, Sarnt."

Footsteps clanked on the deck behind him. Lernus appeared to his right, ready to go in her own hard suit. The shoulder armor and bulk of the powerpack gave her a muscular appearance. She plucked a snub-nosed blaster rifle from her armor and performed a quick functions check. It was a fancy piece of Colonial Intelligence gear, probably more for show than anything.

Her celestial eyes took in the room. "Are you ready for this, Sevvers?"

Could she tell he was nervous? Was it that obvious?

"As ever," he said, looking away.

"Lieutenant," Cylla said, her voice crackling over his tac comms. "ETA to drop, five minutes."

"Roger that, Runt. Marines, let's close up shop. Time to go to work."

CHAPTER
TWELVE

THE TEAM STOOD near the closed cargo bay door, grasping handholds in the metal girders that criss-crossed the ceiling. The big Mark Three forced Bresto to hunch over, its folded arms at his back giving him the appearance of a large mechanical beetle.

"Whenever you're ready, sir," Sev said.

Park studied his flexscreen. "Arming drones."

About damn time, Three said.

One's stream was authoritative and confident, as if it had any other choice. *Three, engage their fighter screen. Four, run support and monitor for enemy AI activity. Two and Five, stand by to assist Three with additional compute capacity.*

"Ramp opening," Park said. His flexscreen flashed with warnings and the door opened.

Sev's haptics lit up as atmosphere fled through the gap in the opening door. Wind buffeted him, pushing him toward the void, but his armored suit held firm.

The colors of the Cradle Nebula greeted them. Gray and silver rocks tumbled past as the *Gauntlet* juked between them. The heavy drone magazine vibrated silently against the force of the transport's maneuvers.

Drone integration complete. We are ready, Sev, One said.

He grinned reflexively. "Launching."

The drone magazine doors snapped open. Gunmetal pearls of autonomous death exploded from them like torpedoes loosed from their tubes. Their thrusters trailed streaks of blue light. His head filled with drone telemetry, a monsoon of data. Despite the smaller swarm, a familiar pain crawled down his spine. This close, he could see - almost feel - every detail.

The swarm twisted toward their targets. The three raider ships glowed red in his drone sight. Raider sensor pings hit like a slap.

They've detected us, Four said. *I don't think they've found the Gauntlet.*

"They've taken the bait," Sev said.

Four, our signal-to-noise ratio is low, Two said. *Are they running an anti-AI suite?*

I hear it, Four replied. *Probably background radiation from the Cradle.*

Light glinted from the hull of the larger of the three raider ships. He could hear the buzzing of engines as perceived by the drones' sensors.

"Raider fighter screen away."

"Confirmed," Cylla said. "Count twenty-one craft."

Not for long, Three growled.

The fighters banked hard toward the drone swarm, their power plants screaming with acceleration. Each drone twisted into position, anticipating which way the screen might break.

Lasers lashed from the fighters' forward gun ports, their angry red beams whipping toward the swarm. The drones danced out of the way, having anticipated their actions, then returned fire, filling the void in front of them with bolts of hot blue plasma.

To the untrained eye, each shot looked like a miss.

The fighters banked in sharp angles to break contact. Three of them vectored right into the path of the plasma fire. Their thin hulls warped and crumpled before disappearing in a blossom of blue flame that died quickly in the vacuum.

Splash three.

"Three down," Sev repeated.

"Damn, man," Dalon said, his voice loud in Sev's helmet. "That's cool."

Four of the drones found themselves closing with the big raider ship. It was an ugly craft, the color of scorched umber, its hull a patchwork of material scavenged over hundreds of raids. Anti-radiation fabric hung from the open hangar and cargo bays like primitive sails.

A high pitch whine stabbed at Sev's mind. *Point-defense cannons are spooling up,* Four said. *They have range, Three.*

The four drones accelerated, unleashing another barrage from their primary weapons, and strafing the exposed hangar deck. Explosions rocked the ship's interior, sending debris and bodies tumbling into space.

White hot tracers whipped toward them, chasing the drones as they banked for safety. A burst of rounds found their mark, but were deflected by its fibrosteel armor. More telemetry poured in, indicating minor damage to maneuvering thrusters. That drone's time was running out. The attrition had begun. Damn, what he wouldn't give to have more than sixteen.

"Sixty seconds," Cylla said.

"Listen up, Marines," Park said, his voice strong and confident. "The squids have one of our own, and we're going to get her back. We'll retrieve Deni and raise hell on our way out, putting these bastards out of commission for good."

The *Gauntlet* pitched hard, forcing Sev's stomach into his throat. The scene in his mind filled his vision. Trails of blue and red light chasing each other. Flashes of distant explosions. The three raider ships clinging like parasites to their host, an ancient alien derelict long dead. He hoped.

The look of it made the hairs on the back of his neck stand on end.

"For humanity," Park said, then leaped through the yawning door.

"For the Lost!" the others chorused, diving after him.

Sev stood there, unable to move. His mind raced, the drone sensor data replaying the battle out there in real-time inside his mind. His heart beat faster at the thought he'd soon find himself in the middle of it.

He wasn't ready for this. There had to be another way…

"Time to go, skeeg."

He spun just as Bresto delivered a fierce kick that sent him spinning end over end out the cargo bay door. The vastness of space tumbled around him. His heart hammered inside his chest. He kicked his arms and legs in a futile effort to steady himself.

"Relax, skeeg," Bresto said, his signal loud and clear, strangely calm for a man who'd kept his promise to space him. "Hit your auto-nav and let the suit do the rest."

Sev grunted and slapped at his flexscreen. His powerpack vibrated with spears of thrust that slowed his spin. Bresto shot past him, following the others toward their target.

"You asshole," he gasped.

"Payback's a bitch, skeeg." Bresto chuckled grimly. "You and me are square now. It's like the lieutenant said, time to go to work."

———

The raider corvette loomed closer. It might have been a smaller configuration, but out here, up close, it wasn't small at all. Drone telemetry said it was four times the tonnage of the *Gauntlet*, 500 meters long, and almost a hundred tall. The strange sails jutted from its side like golden fins, helping to obscure the rescue team's presence as they approached.

They drifted near the hull, short bursts from their thrusters pushing them forward. Dalon was on point, his blaster rifle tight on his shoulder. Bresto panned the FAB back and forth, scanning for danger.

"Mace, what do you see?" Park said.

"Checking thermals," she said. "Launch bay is hot. Looks like they're securing cargo in the lower decks. I count twenty squids down there."

"That's a little busy for my taste." Park glanced at Sev. "Can you give us a diversion?"

"Wait one," he said. *Three, I need a hit on the target ship. Bad enough to draw them away from the hangar deck.*

Whatever you say, Sev, Three groaned.

Two drones broke off their pursuit of the raider fighters and vectored toward the rear of the target ship. The command bridge stretched away from the hull just above the engine section like a dull spire. The stubby tower filled the drones' sights, even as they dodged sporadic point-defense fire. The white tracers whipsawed around them, the rounds spinning harmlessly into the void.

He could feel the drones' capacitors charging. The surge of Three's signal to fire. The sudden heat of rapid plasma discharge. Hull plating buckled, then collapsed. The raider ship trembled from the impacts. The command bridge bled atmosphere and debris. Bodies.

The overhead lights in the hangar bay dimmed. Alien klaxons strobed rapidly. Pause, flash flash. Pause, flash flash. It hurt to look at it.

"That did it, sir," Mace said. "I count four of them now at the far end of the hangar deck. Plenty of cover for us to move in there unseen."

Park gestured forward. "Dalon, take us in."

"Aye, sir." He drifted to the edge of the hangar bay door, scanning his sectors through his rifle scope. "Clear, moving in."

Mace went next, followed by Bresto.

"You two," Park said, glancing behind him at Sev and Lernus. "Keep your heads down and follow me."

Lernus nodded, her custom blaster rifle gripped tight. Sev found his pistol. It felt heavy, cumbersome, even with the suit. Another zap of nerve pain tore through his arm. Together, the three of them drifted into the hangar bay.

Passing through the hangar deck's atmospheric shielding made his haptics buzz. He was greeted with a cacophony of light and sound, the familiar strobing lights joined by an odd grunting alarm. Grunt, grunt, grunt. Pause, flash, flash. He'd experienced it all before as data inside his head. The reality was much more oppressive. More visceral.

His HUD filled with detail. The ship's atmosphere was utterly alien. Mostly carbon dioxide. Some nitrogen. Trace amounts of sulfur and argon and other noble gasses. The aux gravity was a little heavier than colonial standard, but the difference was negligible in his powered hard suit.

The Marines fanned out, seeking cover behind stacks of stolen crates and drums. Most of them were stamped with the Nimbus and their corporate logos, a familiar sight amid the alien surroundings. Above them, banners hung from the ceiling, covered with the same tribal markings stenciled on their fighter craft.

"I have eyes on our four hostiles," Dalon said. "They're running some kind of cargo lift to a lower deck. Might be the infil point we need."

"I got a terminal over here, Mace," Bresto said, pointing with the FAB.

"On it."

"Go with her, Sevvers," Park said, pointing with a knife hand in her direction. "Maybe you and your AI can speed things up. We can't stay here long."

His words caught in his throat. "O-okay."

He held his breath, stooping as he ran to Mace's side. Already she had pried a maintenance panel away from the console and was hunting for a connection. Pale red light spilled from the opening.

"What do you want, Sevvers?" she asked, elbow deep in data fiber and silicon.

He glanced nervously at their surroundings. "Park thought I could help."

She strained to laugh. "Really? What's the rush?" Something popped inside the panel. The red light inside flickered. "Dammit. These connections are no good. There's a lot of noise."

"My AI can sort that out. Can you patch me in?"

She gestured with her flexscreen. "See the aux port, there? Yeah, attach your diagnostics cable."

He took the cable in his free hand and secured it to the auxiliary port. The shock was sudden. Trillions of alien runes, the shape of steep cuts and slashes exploded into his thoughts.

One isolated the data. *Four, mine the stream. Priority is to find our target. Secondary objectives include raider status and anything you can find on the unknown ship.*

Roger!

He focused his thoughts. *I … I want anything on human abductions. Not just Deni. Past, present, future. Where they take them. Why they take them.*

One's datastream faltered. *That is outside our current mission parameters, Sev.*

Not anymore.

Yes, Sev.

Will do, Sev! Four chirped.

"You okay?"

He blinked. "What?"

Mace gazed back at him, the warning strobes reflecting off her plexene visor. Pause, flash flash.

"You really feel all this, don't you?" she asked, nodding toward the console. "In your head."

"Yeah, but—" He paused to take a breath. "Normally, the scale of these things obscures the minutia. This close, I feel everything. It's different."

She was here! Four said, its datastream spiking with machine glee. *Deni was here! She arrived six days ago and was taken to a holding cell on the deck below us.*

"Got her," he said.

"Where?" Lernus asked.

"Cargo hold, right below us."

"Can you clear a path?" Park asked.

Four, open all the doors between us and them.

Doors open. Cargo lift, descending.

He turned from the console. "Oh, shit."

"Uh, hey." It was Dalon. "The squids at the cargo lift look pissed. One of them is headed this way."

"Steady, Private," Park said. "Let it get close, then put it down."

Sev glanced at his pistol, then back at Mace. "What do I do?"

"Just sit tight," she said, the picture of calm. "You're good at your job. We're good at ours."

The raider emerged from between the stacks of crates and walked toward the console. It was a short, round thing, some kind of deckhand. It wore tan overalls spotted with dark stains. Its pink flesh glistened, the strobing lights flashing off its thousands of tiny scales. Its tentacled fingers trembled with anticipation.

Nothing like the monsters in his nightmares.

Something *snapped* between the grunting chorus of raider alarms. The squid's head jerked violently to the side, shrouded in blue mist, dropping the alien mid-stride.

Dalon didn't move, his blaster rifle still trained on the fresh corpse. "Squid down."

"Good kill," Park said. "Let's move."

Mace pulled free of the console and unseated Sev's diagnostic cable. "Nice work, Sevvers," she said.

"Thanks," he managed.

He couldn't take his eyes off the dead alien. It had all happened so fast.

The Marines began to move out. Mace gave him a nod and moved swiftly to join the others. They melted between the rows of stolen cargo, pressing closer to the lift at the opposite end of the bay. Park waved him forward, directing him to cover. He obeyed, bounding forward in a permanent crouch.

He passed the raider corpse. Blue gore dribbled from its open head. Its pink face twisted in confusion, revealing rows of sharp teeth behind tiny fronds. Like it was trying to figure out what it had seen, killed milliseconds before the realization came.

For a brief second, he glimpsed the cargo lift. The other three aliens shuffled impatiently, waiting for an update on the lift's sudden departure that would never come. Dalon was less than a hundred meters from them now, with Mace close behind. Bresto trundled after them, the bulk of the Mark Three limiting his choices for cover. Beyond the lift, a wide stairwell carved a rising path through the far bulkhead and disappeared into the deck above.

Lernus appeared beside him, her back pressed against the container they hid behind. She clutched the snub-nosed blaster close to her chest. Park bounded past them, gesturing for them to stay put.

"You do this a lot?" he asked.

"No," she admitted. Her gaze fell to the floor. "I'm just a handler. I'm rarely in the field."

"Deni's mission then," he said between breaths, "Must be pretty important for you to be here."

She looked at him. "More than you will ever know."

His tac comms crackled to life. "Pick your targets," Park said. "On three."

He turned to see, but Lernus pulled him back. She shook her head, a finger raised to her visor. More *snaps* broke the alarm's rhythm.

"Clear," Park said. "Move up."

She let him go, and they moved up together. Already the Marines were converging on the cargo lift, the hangar deck littered with three more raider bodies.

Dalon angled his rifle into the gap. "Looks clear, I don't—"

A solid red beam lashed out from the top of the stairwell. It struck Dalon like a whip, knocking him over in a shower of sparks. More laser beams buzzed through the air, scorching the edges of containers where the other Marines hid. More of the pink squids descended the stairs, their shapes blurred amid the strobing lights and laser fire. Their fleshy grunts roared into the hangar bay.

A red beam whipped past Sev's head and threw him to the floor. He could feel the heat of it, hear the crackling of ionized air.

"Counter assault," Park said between squelches of static. "Prepare to repel."

THIRTEEN

STREAKS of red heat banged into the metal deck, puckering the floor around Sev as he dashed into cover. His HUD swam with warnings of incoming fire. Lernus ducked behind a drum a few meters away. She popped out of cover and fired. Her compact blaster rifle buzzed, spitting a volley of red bolts into the stairwell. Her movements were precise and well-drilled.

"Dalon!" Mace shouted, her voice crackling through his helmet speakers.

There was a brief silence punctuated by more buzzing laser fire. "I'm … I'm okay," Dalon said, pain straining his voice.

Sev gasped, breathing deep. Dalon was alive. Founders, that was close.

"How many shooters?" Park asked.

"Mmm, I count eight," Bresto said. He sounded almost bored.

"Time to get loud after all, Sergeant."

Bresto laughed. "Good."

Red bolts snapped from the Marines' rifles, hissing and sparking into the metal stairwell. One of the raiders fell. The beam of its weapon arced wildly. The others balked, stalled in the long stairwell like a funnel.

Bresto pivoted into a gap between cargo. The heavy FAB whined, spooling its tri-barrels to their cyclic rate. It thundered away, sending a torrent of blaster bolts that tortured the stairwell and sent the raiders for cover. Their scorched alien blood spattered up the high walls.

"Moving!" Mace yelled.

Under the cover of Bresto's onslaught, the combat engineer surged forward toward Dalon's prone form. The young Marine struggled to sit up, his grunts of pain audible over comms. Mace dove in beside him and dragged him out of the line of fire behind the cargo lift's control station.

Bresto ceased fire. The FAB's barrels clattered to a halt, their tips glowing bright orange. The stairwell creaked and groaned as ruined steps fell from their rungs. Nothing else moved.

"Let's go," Park commanded.

Lernus tore from cover. Sev ran to keep up, the servos in his hard suit propelling him faster. Still, she pulled away from him. Damn, she was fast. They converged with the others at the cargo lift.

Mace eyed the damage to Dalon's armor. Bresto sank to a crouch behind some paneled railing, eyeing his heavy weapon.

"Status?" Park asked of both Mace and Dalon.

"His reactives held," Mace said, the relief plain on her face. "Probably some heat burns from the impact, maybe some bruising, but he's serviceable."

"Good to go, sir," Dalon croaked.

"Twelfth!" Bresto laughed. "First op out and boot scores a purple heart. Didn't they teach you to duck at Aegia Prime?"

Dalon chuckled at the joke, his face twisting with fresh pain. "I'm a slow learner, Sarnt."

How could they joke at a time like this? These Marines were insane.

"Mace, see anything in the cargo hold?" Park asked.

She stole a glimpse down the nearby shaft. "Thermals are cold. There are some power residuals, but I'm getting interference from all the ionization."

Park turned to Sev. "Sevvers, what's the status of our diversion? Any chance we can spare some drone support?"

He held up a hand. *Three, what's the status of the raider fighter screen? Fourteen down, seven to go.*

How many drones can you spare? he asked.

I'd prefer none, obviously, but if you can't hack it, I can spare four.

Five, take those drones and start your attack run on the raider ship.

Affirmative, Sev, I'm on it, Five said. *ETA is six minutes.*

"We'll have four drones on station in six minutes," he said.

"That will have to do," Park said, frowning. "Bresto, you're on point."

"I'm okay, sir," Dalon insisted.

"Shut up, boot," Bresto said.

"I'll go next," Park went on. "Lernus and Sevvers, on me. Mace, make sure Dalon gets down there in one piece and watch our six."

Acknowledgements echoed through the team. Bresto stood and peeked over the edge of the shaft with his FAB. He shrugged, then leaped into the darkness. Park followed close behind. Nozzles of blue flame sprung from their powerpacks, slowing their descent.

Lernus walked toward the edge. "You ready?" she asked.

He nodded reflexively. That was a lie. Of course, he wasn't ready. He wasn't ready for any of this. Jene was right—this *was* idiotic.

The two of them leaped into the dark shaft. Freefall warnings filled his HUD, its altimeter racing toward zero. Bursts of thrust steadied his fall, keeping him upright, then flared as the metal deck rushed up to meet them.

The transport shaft disappeared above them, opening into the expansiveness of the raider ship's cargo hold. It was massive, running almost the entire length of the ship. Rows of steel girders lined the belly of the corvette, jutting like ribs from the exterior bulkheads. Shipping containers of all sizes were stacked floor to ceiling, casting long shadows in the narrow paths between them.

The klaxons continued their guttural light show. Grunt, grunt, grunt. Pause, flash, flash. The awful rhythm was driving him crazy. The flashing lights were so bright, too bright for human eyes.

Or maybe it was the fact they'd almost bought it back at the hangar bay. That Dalon was nearly killed, saved by his hard suit and some squid deckhand's bad aim. It had all happened so fast, too fast for his racing thoughts to process.

Bresto pushed forward, securing the perimeter. Park waved the others down, gesturing with his hands to post up ahead.

"Twelfth," Dalon cursed over the sputtering of his maneuvering thrusters, "Deni could be anywhere in here."

"You good to go?" Mace asked, releasing her grip on him.

Dalon nodded, still cradling his left shoulder. The reactive plates were charred black, but otherwise looked undamaged. "Yes, Corporal."

"What do you see, Mace?" Park asked.

She tapped her flexscreen and panned her helmet slowly. "Nothing new on thermals. We're clear, for now."

Lernus gasped and rushed forward, her weapon ready. She veered toward a far row of cargo containers near the outer bulkhead.

"What the hell?" Park shouted. "Lernus, where are you going?"

She didn't answer. She ran until she reached the containers. There was no sign of Deni that he could see, or of any immediate danger. Had she spotted something, something only she would recognize?

"Moving," Bresto said with a sigh. He rolled his shoulders, hefted the heavy FAB in his arms, and trotted after her.

Sev shrugged apologetically to Park and ran to catch up. Lernus kneeled, her gaze transfixed on the steel corner of the cargo container. It was a dull, flat gray, typical for military cargo. Beneath the Nimbus stamped on its side was the locator code, AGP. Aegia Prime.

"What is it?" he asked.

Lernus pointed to a rust-colored smudge near the bottom corner of the container. It looked like some kind of surface damage, like the container took a hit during the theft.

He shook his head. "I don't understand—"

She turned and gazed up at him. Her eyes were jet black and infinite, the swirling cosmic colors now crowded to the edges of her sockets. He inhaled sharply at the sight, struggling to keep his balance.

"I see her," she said cryptically. Her voice was far away, like she was looking straight through him. "In the blood. Her blood."

He looked again at the rust on the container. It *did* look like dried blood, camouflaged smartly against the flat gray container.

"How?" he asked.

She reached out her hand and he helped her up. Her eyes snapped back, her pupils shrinking to their normal size, restoring the familiar purple and blue.

"The best Colonial Intelligence can buy," she said, and cuffed him on the shoulder.

Mace and Dalon sprinted past them, taking up covering positions on Bresto's flanks. Park walked toward them, the light of his own HUD reflecting the sharp angles of his angry features.

"What the hell was that, agent?" he spat.

"I've confirmed Deni was here," she replied, ignoring his question. "We need to search this hold, now."

"I understand you have operational authority over this mission," Park continued, "but if you put my Marines in any unnecessary danger—"

"I'm open to suggestions on how to proceed," she said. "I can't search every container myself."

Somewhere above them came the dull thud of distant explosions. Vibrations tore through the cargo hold. The lights went out, then returned a second later, dimmer than before.

Drones on station, Five said. *Raising hell for humanity, Sev.*

"I know how we can speed up the search," he said with a grin. "Cover me."

The pack of drones descended the lift shaft. Their maneuvering thrusters howled, casting trembling blue light on the dark steel bulkheads as they drifted toward the cargo hold. The narrow forms of the rescue team appeared bright blue in their sensors, registering the IFF signatures of their CDF equipment.

CDF personnel sighted, marked friendly, Five said.

Thanks for that, Sev replied. *I've got the sample over here.*

One of the figures waved. The lead drone throttled forward, closing the gap between them. Several of the other humans balked at the drone as it neared, edging backward to avoid the heat from its jetwash.

"Holy shit, man." Ident, PFC Hemry Dalon. "That is Twelfth-damned cool."

"Yes." Ident, Lieutenant Lee Park.

Here, at the edge of this container, Sev said.

One of the figures pointed to the container's edge.

Is that you, Sev? Five asked. Its datastream pulsed with interest.

Big deal, at least he's still in one piece, Three said. *For our sakes.*

Four was literally beside itself. *It is so good to see you, Sev! And may I say, these spectra really suit you.*

Vital streams only, Four, One said.

Thanks Four, he said. *I wish the feeling was mutual. We need to find any traces that match the bio-signature of this blood. It belongs to Deni.*

The drone edged closer, panning its sensor dome toward the sample. This close, the drone's terse machine instructions were hammer blows on his mind.

Magnify, 1000x.

Isolate. Fibrin, hemoglobin, plasma, unknown.

Sample catalogued and distributed.

I've got enough here to work with, Sev, Five said. *That said, there's some things in this sample that don't match with expected human physiology.*

He hesitated. Lernus hadn't said anything about Deni being modded. Yet, if Colonial Intelligence purchased top-credit optics for a handler, they'd probably invest heavily in their field agents.

Noted, Five, thanks. Proceed with the search.

Roger that, Sev.

The lead drone throttled up, rising near the top of the cargo bay. From there, it could see through the vast maze of containers like looking at a map. Algorithms plotted and re-plotted potential search vectors, gaming through likely outcomes based on what little priors they had. The resulting paths were labeled D1 through D4.

The other drones surged forward, following their designated vector. Their sensor domes panned and swiveled, looking for more evidence of the same biological pattern.

The lead drone took up path D1. It scanned the humans once more, then tilted a nod to Sev before gusting off around the corner.

"That's a little alarming." Ident, Corporal Jenniver Mace. "You 're really close to these things, huh?"

A burst of data squealed from D2. More of the target blood had been located, a spatter thrown against a barrel of Respitian pressed crid oil. The drone came to a halt and ran deep scans of the immediate vicinity for more traces of Deni's presence.

I've got a hit on your sample, Sev. Five recalculated its search vectors with the new data. The surge of information sent a twinge of pain through his arm. *Continuing search.*

D3's drone sights glowed red. A figure, pattern-matched as a raider-type cephalonid, emerged from a row of containers. The drone fired, barely draining its capacitors, vaporizing more than 90% of the target's mass in a single salvo.

Five had done this enough, it knew to anticipate more of them. The drone surged forward, angling toward the path the target came from. More raiders came into view, their pattern matches verified. The drone emptied its capacitors in subsequent volleys, eliminating all visible threats.

Ah, I love the smell of cooked raider in the morning, Five said.

Good kills, Five, he said.

D1 slowed, nearly colliding with D2. Their search paths had brought them together, a sign, mathematically speaking, they were on the right track. They ran overlapping sensor sweeps, searching for more of the telltale blood.

I think we're close, Sev.

There, a hatch on the exterior bulkhead, leading to an airlock. A bloody handprint left on the closed hatch, poorly scrubbed away in an attempt to hide the trail. Traces of chemical solvents muddied the readings, but even the scant genetic evidence remaining was enough.

The drones' sensors lingered on the doorway, their drone sight dancing and glitching. The signal-to-noise ratio here was low. Adjustments would be necessary to clean it up.

I've found her trail, Sev.

———

The location burst into Sev's thoughts like an epiphany.

"This way!" he shouted, pressing past Bresto and Mace, following the path the lead drone had taken on its search.

"Crazy ass bot jockey," Bresto sneered. "Moving."

Two of the drones took a position above Sev, escorting him down the passageway. The growls of their thrusters were a comforting presence in the dim light of the cargo hold. A smile crept over his face. As strange as this mission was, he was still in his element. Killing raiders by the droves. Making the hard stuff easy. They'd have never gotten this far without him.

"Wait up, Sevvers," Mace called after him, her signal garbled in static.

"Hurry up," he replied, maintaining his pace.

Another explosion thumped overhead, much closer than before. A shrieking howl like a nocturnal predator followed, echoing through the cavernous hold. The haunting sound drowned out the grunting klaxons.

A bolt of light shot from above the containers and struck the two drones above him in a ball of white fire. The resulting explosion was deafening. The overpressure lifted him off the deck and tossed him into the wall of containers. Pain stabbed through his core even as the reactive armor bunched together to protect him. One of the drones crashed to the floor where he'd just stood seconds before, its broken fuselage dead and burning.

"Shit—Sevvers!" Park cried, barely audible in the squelching comms. "Does anyone have eyes on—"

"Neg—" The voices disappeared in static.

Sev, are you okay? One asked. *What is your status?*

"I … I don't know," he coughed.

His vision blurred. His ears rang. The heat from the burning drone was searing even inside his climate-controlled suit. More roaring explosions burst in the distance. He thought he heard CDF blaster fire. Groping at the container behind him, he moved away from the heat and the flames. The strobing lights of the alarms blared in the darkness, leaving their echoes in his retina.

Heavy footsteps drew closer.

"B-Bresto?"

There was no answer, no human one. Only heaving, slippery breaths. Metal rustling against fabric. The clicking of razor teeth. The raider warrior towered over him, the pulsing lights eclipsed by its armored form.

"Dleshlelm'olvlik."

Cold fear rippled down his spine. He was suddenly six years old again, trapped in the slim kitchen locker of his mother's tiny hab. But in this waking nightmare, they'd found him. There was no escape.

Pause, flash, flash.

The monster leaned closer. "Dleshlelm'olvlen."

SEV SCREAMED. Without thinking, he scrabbled backward away from the monster, only to collide with the cargo container a second time. To his left, the inferno of the drone corpse raged. Blue flames swallowed its broken core, fading to yellow as they climbed up the sides of the cargo containers that flanked it. To his right, the monster stepped closer.

He couldn't look. He wouldn't. His right arm shook, even without the pain. A release of the terror that strangled him.

Each heavy footstep made him flinch. The alien loosed rasping, breathy laughter, muffled by the dozens of fronds that whipped and curled over its mouth. A stubby metal cylinder, empty and smoking, fell to the floor. The raider cradled a long black tube in its arms, some kind of shoulder-fired weapon, and slotted another cylinder into the breech.

Buzzing emanated from the raider's collar. *"Shple'vunek?"*

"Ga," it replied, then kicked his boot. More hollow laughter. "Lolhmsha, v'kik'lor."

He coughed, choking on his own nerves. This wasn't how it was supposed to be. They weren't supposed to find him. He was good at the game. His mother had shown him how.

The raider took him by the leg and dragged him from the flames like a sack of spare parts. His hard suit screeched against the textured alloys lining the floor. The drones were nowhere to be seen, though gunfire still spat sporadically in the distance. His comms crackled with distortion.

His eyes were closed, and he breathed through pursed lips. He was still alive. He could do *something*. He just needed to focus.

Five, where are you?

The reply was like fingernails across his gray matter. *Sev! One drone, destroyed. Another disabled. The remaining two are providing support to the others, but the raiders have deployed some kind of anti-drone missile. Their fire is very effective.*

We haven't seen this tactic before, Sev, Two said. *They tend to be much more conservative with their heavy weaponry when we're breaching engineering.*

He delved into Five's datastream just as the drone disintegrated another raider warrior in a distant corner of the cargo hold. The force of the barrage scattered the creature's molecules like hot ash.

The drone sight feed skipped and jumped. Something was playing hell with their tac comms.

"Hey!—ey you!" Ident, Corporal Jenniver Mace. "Wher—Sevvers?"

You have to tell them where I am, Five. He stole a glance at the dark silhouette of his captor. *Hurry, please.*

A laser beam struck the drone, blurring the feed momentarily. It came back online in a burst of hot blue. Another raider down.

How, Sev? The DD-12 has no external human interface device. They weren't exactly built to hold a dialogue.

"—vvers, are you—there?"

Nod.

Five's datastream twitched. *What?*

Dammit, Five, nod with the drone. Let them know I'm still alive!

Nanoseconds crept by. Finally, the drone turned. Mace and Dalon's IFF signals glowed bright blue in the sensor feed, which began to raise and lower slowly.

"Yes! Go—," she shouted, "Take us—ere!"

Bring them here, Five.

Yes, Sev.

The wave of relief ripped him from the feed. He could see the exterior bulkhead drifting past him as the raider dragged him to their destination. Through the narrow viewports that lined the wall rose the steep sides of the ancient derelict. It was gargantuan up close, the sheer angle of its hull like a rusted bronze mountainside.

The airlock was only a few meters away now, heavy and round. Beyond it, a metal boarding gantry held the corvette tight to the big ship. A dense fabric tunnel wound through the gantry's metal lattice, surrounded by cabling that disappeared into the big ship's hull.

"Colm'veshkaer," it said, releasing its grip on him. The airlock door was right in front of him. He could barely make out the faded handprint near the floor.

Deni wasn't on the corvette anymore.

Sounds of alien panic spat from his captor's comms. *"Moarv'esk! Moarv—"*

Further down the passageway, a stack of containers listed and fell, rocked by multiple plasma explosions. Dim figures ran for their lives as the roar of maneuvering thrusters grew louder.

"—vvers, hold—on." It was Mace. They were almost to him.

"Ha!" he laughed, giddy at the thought of watching the monster die. "You see that, you sonofabitch? You better—"

The raider ignored him and lugged the black tube onto its shoulder. It gazed through a small optic sight and waited.

Better do something, Sev, Five warned.

He glanced down at his armor. The standard-issue blaster pistol still clung to his chest plate. He fumbled with it and leveled it at the raider's back. He took a breath and held it. The haptics teased his finger as he pulled the trigger. The motion was heavy and awkward. Why the hell wouldn't it fire?

Green good, red dead. Shit!

He found the safety and switched it off. The pistol's sights glowed red, its capacitors filling with power. The raider glanced back at the dangerous sound, its cloudy eyes wide with surprise.

"Ulshem'a—" it growled.

He jerked the trigger. The red bolt *snapped* into the raider's armored shoulder in a spray of light and heat. The force of the blast spun it around, sending the tube launcher crashing into the nearby bulkhead and onto the floor.

He looked at the pistol in disbelief, his body trembling with adrenaline. Of all the shapes his revenge might take, this was one he never imagined.

The raider leaped at him, still very much alive. It knocked the pistol from his grip and pulled him to his feet, its tentacled fingers wrapping around his suit collar.

The squid's steep, scaled face was mottled green, the color of their warrior caste. Fronds hung over its mouth, long and sharp, dangling like a living beard. Smoke wafted from its burned shoulder. Blue blood wept from the wound.

He could see the drones silhouetted in the flashing lights behind them. They hung there, waiting for something. The creature's fronds peeled back, revealed jagged, discolored fangs. Its hot breath clung to his visor like a fog.

What are you waiting for, Five? he asked. The uncertainty in Five's stream was like an endless loop, the same calculations playing repeatedly with the same result. A kind of machine insanity. *Kill it!*

The response was automatic. It didn't sound like Five at all. *Safety overrides active. The risk of collateral damage is beyond Division tolerances.*

The raider reached for its belt and drew a heavy black knife. Its fronds twitched in anticipation as it dragged the blade across his armor, hunting for a weak spot.

Twelfth-dammit, Five, do it now. That's an order!

Safety overrides active. The risk of collateral damage —

The raider's head jerked and disfigured, plastering his visor in blue gore. The two fell together, the weight of the dead alien landing hard on top of him. He waited for something, anything, to happen, his mind refusing to believe it was really dead.

"Clear," Mace said, loud and clear at close range. Her armored footsteps came closer. "Hang on, Sevvers."

Her hard suit purred as she hefted the corpse off him. Her gaze was methodical, searching for signs of injury or damage. Satisfied he was healthy, she pulled him to his feet.

A sudden wave of dizziness came over him. His breathing was shallow, labored, like the monster was still on top of him. He glanced down at the corpse at his feet. Blue-gray brains oozed from its misshapen skull. The monster was dead. That much was plain. How come it didn't feel real?

Park emerged from the darkness, the others following close behind. "Status?"

"He's serviceable, sir," Mace said. She wiped her hand across his visor, smearing away some of the dead raider's brains. "That was the last one. Thermals are clear."

Park looked at Sev and held his gaze. "Next time, let us take point."

"Aye, sir."

———

Sev leaned back into the closest cargo container. His body ached from the sudden plunge of adrenaline, making him shiver. The hard suit felt stiff and cold even as its powerpack thrummed with energy. Its rigid exoskeleton was the only thing keeping him upright.

The airlock was a round portal three meters across, with two viewports placed symmetrically on either side of a dense, steel center lock. Congealing blue blood decorated its textured gray surface. A large console hung beside it, casting a dull yellow glow in the gloom of the cargo hold. An assortment of wires, several dotted with recent patch welds, dangled from an open port beneath the console. The drone fire danced at the edge of his vision.

Mace reappeared beside him. She offered him his pistol, grip first.

"You're not finished with this," she said, and grasped his shoulder with her other hand. "You're alive. He isn't."

Cold and stiff, his body ached with tension, his eyes unable to settle on any one thing for too long, desperately searching for the next threat. Only the monster's corpse held his gaze at all, like some anomaly of its tortured mass pulled hard at his attention. He felt both dead, and very much alive, his senses dialed up to eleven. Even the machine thoughts in his head had faded to background noise.

He breathed in deep through his nose, tasing the recycled air as it passed over the back of his tongue.

"I know," he said. He took the pistol and locked it to his chest armor.

On the other side of the passageway, Dalon stood on his toes to peek through one of the airlock's viewports.

"I guess this means they've moved Deni off this ship," he said, holding his rifle close with one hand and bracing against the round door with the other.

"That's correct," Lernus said. "We need to get this airlock open now."

For a moment, Park said nothing. The Marines each looked at him, their faces betraying their confusion. Lernus frowned, like she was unhappy the others suddenly lacked her certainty.

"We're not going anywhere near that ship," Park said to her. "This mission is over."

The words ripped him from his thoughts. Murmurs of shock and surprise drifted over tac comms. So Park *did* recognize the derelict ship.

"Absolutely not, Lieutenant," Lernus spat. "I have operational control of this mission and I order you to proceed into the—" She stopped suddenly, looking away from him.

"You knew," Park said, his tone grim.

He took a step toward her, the two only centimeters apart now. They glared at each other in stark silence. If looks could kill, Mace would need more than an auto-doc to patch them up.

"Uh, sir?" Bresto finally said, breaking the stillness.

Park's eyes never left Lernus's. "It's a Concordat ship."

Sev sneered and hung his head. Cridshit. Those were just stories mothers told their children to scare them into bed.

Mace laughed, a quick, anxious sound. "Wait, you mean *the* Concordat? Dead Earth, the Lost, Twelfth ascendant. That Concordat?"

"Didn't we wipe them out a long time ago?" Dalon asked. He backed away from the airlock, both hands firmly on his weapon.

"So we thought," Park continued, pointing through the nearby viewports at the derelict's steep, tortured hull. "See all that battle damage? Pre-CDN heavy slug. Lupanthae cluster cannon."

Sev straightened, pulling himself away from the container. A skeptical smile stretched across his face. "How can you possibly know that? Any of that?"

A low growl squelched through his tac comms. Bresto glared at him.

Park waved Bresto off. His features softened. "The … stories are passed down, through my family. So we don't forget."

Sev sneered. "Then we have nothing to worry about, sir," he said, his words laced with sarcasm. "The Twelfth will be here any minute to … how does the song go?" He hummed the old hymn taught to all colonial children. "So their light may vanquish the d—"

"Shut your Twelfth-damned mouth, skeeg," Bresto snapped.

Aegians. They were all the same. So devout.

He turned to Bresto, his arms wide. "Oh, be quiet, Sergeant," he spat, enunciating the rank. "What the hell would you know, sitting safe and fat beneath the shadows of Aegia Prime?"

Mace exploded toward him, shoving him against the cargo container. A loud, hollow gong echoed through the expansive hold. She pressed an armored finger into his visor, her other hand raised, open palm toward Bresto. Bresto didn't move. Mace's visor HUD lit up her eyes like gold fire.

"Easy, duster," she snapped, just above a whisper. Her tone cut. "You forget yourself. Different colony, different hard, remember? There's the haves …" she trailed off, her hard eyes still locked on his, prompting him.

He had to look away. "And there's everyone else," he breathed.

"Right," she said, her armored fingers tinkling against the plexene of his visor as she mimed a gentle slap.

Satisfied, she let him go. He lifted his chin and looked at Bresto, but kept his mouth closed. Bresto's armored shoulders rose and fell, like his whole hard suit seethed with his pale, Aegian rage.

Lernus turned to him. Her frown melted. "It's true," she said. "I … we knew this was possible. We've known for some time about dormant Concordat ships that survived the great war. That something could awaken them. We believe it's no coincidence the raiders turned up when they did two decades ago."

Her words hit like a runaway drone. His chest tightened, his breathing shallow. It couldn't be true. They were just stories, weren't they?

Only the monsters were real.

"Wait, ships? As in, plural?" Mace gasped, her eyes wide with disbelief. "Founders! And Colonial Intelligence kept it a secret?"

"Ain't that just like the Council." Bresto shook his head and chuckled. "The commandant's rolling over in his grave."

Lernus turned to the wary Marines. "Deni's mission was to infiltrate deep into raider territory, to learn as much as she could about whatever the raiders were doing with this ship."

"And you brought one damn fireteam to get her back," Mace said, her voice pitching somewhere between humor and fear. "We'd need a whole regiment to take that thing."

"You saw it yourself. The ship is dead," Lernus replied, brimming with confidence. "But we don't know for how long. Now is our best shot to recover Deni before a shooting war starts. A war we will lose without the secrets we sent her to find."

Park didn't say anything. He was still staring out the viewports at the ancient alien ship. At the myths and legends becoming more real by the second. Sev knew. In that moment, Park was an open book. Sev knew, because the exact same thought rolled through his mind like a blast wave.

If these Concordat were responsible for the raiders, then they were responsible for the loss of his mother. That, and every bad day between then and now that found him out here, at the edge of existence, desperate to find her. Any trace of her. Somewhere beyond the airlock, deep inside the weathered hull of the Concordat ship, was the truth. He would know it, or die trying.

The realization made him numb. There was a symmetry to the whole thing that stank of fate. Of inevitability. It made his skin crawl.

Park locked eyes with him, and he knew.

"Lernus is right," Park said. "We move in five."

"Aye, sir," the Marines acknowledged. Despite their doubts, there was zero hesitation.

He took another look at the dead raider at his feet. For the last six years, he'd killed the monsters that took his mother from him. Whoever the monsters were, it didn't matter.

He'd kill them all, Twelfth be damned.

CHAPTER
FIFTEEN

SPARKS FLEW from beneath the console. "Got it," Mace said, pulling her diagnostic cable from the console's innards.

Mechanisms wound and rattled inside the airlock. A moment later, it rolled away, receding into the heavy armored walls. Bresto moved first, threading through the entryway before the hatch had fully opened. Dalon was next, moving as he sighted through his rifle's optics.

"Let's go," Park said, waving for Sev and Lernus to follow.

The sudden lack of gravity dizzied him. Damn, but it was cold, too. Even with his suit's environmental controls, the cold of space was biting. The thick, golden vacuum fabric wrapping the gantry billowed, rustling loudly as warm air poured in from the cargo hold.

Besides the Marines now stalking their way across it, the gantry was mercifully empty. Nearly twenty meters across, he could already see another hatch inset in the derelict's burnished hull. His visor HUD glowed with scanner output, revealing details of potential interest: dozens of micro-impacts that pitted the hatch, the eleven distinct symbols etched into its center. There were no viewports to the other side. To learn its secrets, they would have to find a way through.

"Clear," Bresto said. "I've got another entry. No access panel."

Mace bounded past to examine the airlock. She stood there, head turning as she searched for some way to interface with it. Dalon glanced behind them impatiently, his eyes glued on the two drones hovering just inside the raider ship's cargo hold.

Mace gasped. "Hey, Sevvers, check this out," she said.

He pressed forward, past Park and Dalon. Bresto glared at him as he went by. Mace tilted her head toward a textured piece of metal beside the airlock hatch.

If it was a control pad, it was unlike any he'd ever seen. There was no display or discernable interface. There was nothing, actually, to indicate the presence of anything, besides a thin line in the shape of a circle etched in the alien hull.

Then Mace touched it.

Whatever material it was composed of rose from the circular panel. It flowed like liquid, clinging to her finger as she moved it back and forth within the confines of the circle. Tiny lines stretched and criss-crossed from the panel's circular border at random, like geometric roots. When her finger left the bounds, the strange material collapsed back into the panel, rippling like the surface of water until it settled.

"Have you ever seen anything like it?" she said, her voice filled with wonder. A question she must know the answer to.

He hadn't. He suspected no human alive ever had.

"Status," Park said. He was calm, like the uncomfortable exchange in the cargo hold never happened.

"Working on it, sir," Mace said. She looked at Sev. "I hate to admit it, but we better let one of your bots give it a try."

"Agreed."

Five, bring a drone forward. I need you to try to interface with this console.

Roger that, Sev. I'll get it done.

One of the DD-12s nosed its way through the airlock hatch. Drifting into zero-G, its fiery maneuvering thrusters coughed and died, replaced with gentle squirts of compressed gas. Its forward sensor dome rotated back and forth, eyeing each member of the rescue team as it drifted by.

Mace watched the machine intently. He couldn't tell if it was out of admiration or skepticism.

I see the panel, Sev. Drone sensors indicate a dense molecular interface. Its composition is unknown. Its access patterns are unknown.

He focused his thoughts. *Four, we don't have any xenocryptology on the Concordat. Give Five a hand, run the whole suite of handshake protocols.*

Oooh, the Concordat? Four's datastream surged. *How mysterious! You can count on me, Sev.*

A thick, fibrous cable snaked from behind the drone's sensor dome. Hundreds of plated, articulating joints clicked and clacked as it reached for the panel. Light from a million nanostrands of data-beam cabling shone from its fluted apex.

The panel reached out and grasped the probe just like it had Mace's fingertip.

Oh, wow.

Four's datastream vanished. His pulse elevated at the sudden, uncomfortable silence. Mace watched him closely. One of her eyebrows arched. The other drone hovered just inside the dim cargo hold, like a shy child watching an older sibling on a dare. The others waited patiently, scanning their sectors.

There are multiple dimensions to this interface, Four finally said. He let out a breath. *There's the tactile dimension, but there is a digital dimension as well! I think we need both to open the airlock.*

The probe swam across the liquid metal console. The molecular interface took shape, and more than just clinging to the probe, other shapes rose from its liquid surface. Complex geometric shapes of all kinds formed in the soft material until they floated free of the console, hovering just above it. The circuitous lines continued to spread, reaching toward its center.

Then they met.

I'm in.

A piercing sound like a dying world exploded across Sev's mind. His body went rigid, eyes wide like they might burst from his skull.

They use a base-11 number system, Four went on, like it was oblivious to the excruciating madness tearing through his brain. *They're ... obsessed with numerical hierarchy. They have a particular affinity with the number eleven itself.*

The sound was so incredibly painful. His eyes wouldn't, couldn't close. He could see Mace's lips moving, the concern growing on her face, but he couldn't hear her. He couldn't hear anything except the shrieking of a million angry gods. An awful grating sound *scritch-scratched* inside his helmet. Just his teeth, grinding together, the only part of him that seemed to respond at all. Like he was trapped inside his mind.

Four, One said. *Vital streams only, please. Sev, are you there? I am detecting anomalies with your implant alignment. Buffer overruns are backing up the data filters.*

Mace knocked at his visor. He felt saliva gathering in the back of his throat. He needed to swallow, but couldn't. His body reflexed involuntarily, desperate for air. Desperate to move.

Sev? One repeated. *Can you hear me?*

Park appeared beside Mace. The two exchanged words. Mace gestured to the drone's probe, shaking her head. Park stepped closer, reaching toward it. The shapes and lines of the console shivered at his presence, bristling like an animal trying to deter a stranger. Or a threat.

I got it! Four shrieked. In that single nanosecond, its voice was as loud as theirs.

Then he saw them, the eleven shapes carved into the center of the airlock door. They seemed nearly alive, brimming with energy. He couldn't look away. Each was a circle, their diameter varying only slightly. Inside each were more lines, like patterns on a circuit board, each one unique.

The torrent of sound in his head vanished, but left his mind ringing like psychic tinnitus. He coughed, his body convulsing. For a moment, he thought he heard something in the dying sound. Very faint, but so distinct. Like music.

"Sevvers!" Park's voice crashed the growing silence.

"I'm okay," he said between strangled breaths. His eyes watered from the pain. The tiny droplets drifted around inside his helmet.

"Founders," Mace groaned. "What in twelve hells did you do?"

The derelict's airlock slid open. It vanished without a sound, revealing a gaping portal filled with darkness. Bresto panned the FAB and stepped inside. Dalon bounded after him.

"Is he out of danger, corporal?" Park asked. Mace didn't reply. "If he isn't about to die, I need your eyes and ears."

She blew a breath and gave him a reassuring nod. "Aye, sir. Moving."

Park pulled him close, their visors almost touching, and eyed him with an appraising gaze. "Are you alright, Sevvers?"

His head throbbed, and he could feel the familiar tremor growing in his right arm. He made a fist. Cold nerve pain lit his joints. The rush of data had been unlike anything he'd ever felt. More alien than the densest raider network. But it was more than that. Between the layers of xeno encoding was something more than data. Something like conviction.

Whatever it was, he was still alive. He gave Park a tired nod.

"Good. You will inform me of the risks before taking another action like that. Am I clear?" Park commanded.

The concern took him by surprise, however utilitarian it might be.

"Yes, sir," he said.

The drone gusted forward behind Park. Its maneuvering jets lit as the alien derelict's aux grav took hold.

He turned to find Lernus standing right beside him. She stared at him, like she was hunting for some truth in his pained features. Her intensity startled him.

"Did you hear them?" she finally asked, her voice thick with concern.

Goosebumps crawled across his torso. Something about her question struck him as final. Even dangerous. He had no idea what she was talking about, and yet he felt in that moment there was definitely a right and a wrong answer.

He made a face. "Hear what?"

"Oh," she said, almost disappointed. "It's nothing."

She stepped through the airlock hatch, vanishing into the darkness beyond. He eyed the drone still lingering in the raider corvette's cargo hold.

Park and Lernus knew more than they were letting on. About the mission, about the Concordat. And yet, they seemed entirely opposed to each other on those most critical details. He shook his head, hoping their secrets wouldn't get them all killed. This place was dangerous enough.

Alright, Five, let's go, he commanded.

The drone didn't move, its sensor dome aimed squarely at him.

He frowned. *Five?*

Right, Sev, let's go.

————

Park readied his blaster rifle. "Dalon, you're on point. Take us in. Mace, back him up."

"Aye, sir," they said.

Dalon pushed forward, taking a position just inside the passage, using a thick open hatchway as cover. Mace was just behind him, scanning the opposite sector. With her rifle tight to her shoulder, she worked her flexscreen with her off-hand. Damn, she was good.

"Checking thermals." She gazed at the glowing screen, then offered a thumbs up. "Cold as death in here, sir."

"Move in."

The long-abandoned section of the derelict's forward interior was expansive, only slightly smaller than the *Lehman's* own hangar deck. Long rows of large, cylindrical tanks lined the floor, but little else remained. Anything or anyone not bolted down got vented into space long ago through any of the enormous blast holes that peppered the chamber's exterior walls. The drones followed them inside, the pale glow of their active sensors throwing long shadows from each of the Marines ahead of them.

"This looks like a vat farm." Dalon peered into a small window in one of the round tanks and whistled. "I see growth medium, waste vents. It's way denser than the vats back home. You could feed an entire city with one of these."

Bresto turned to Park. "Seems like a lot."

"The cities on Earth were massive compared to the colonies," Park replied.

"Passageway, over here."

Mace kneeled at the entrance of a long, dark tunnel, her rifle trained on the opening. At the far end, a collection of red lights glowed dimly at what looked like another set of doors. Doors that were sealed closed.

"Bingo." Park ran for cover, looking for a better vantage point. "Dalon, you're up. Time to make a hole."

Dalon bounded past Mace and made for the tunnel exit.

Five, get ready.

Roger, Sev, Five said, its response time still sluggish.

He maxed out Five's utilization. He could feel the chatter of machine voices grow louder - analysis streams of incoming data, consensus building between the AI - and pushed it aside. The drones filled the dark, wide corridor behind Dalon, bathing him in their active sensor pings.

"So, Sevvers," Dalon began, his voice on edge, "what will these things do when I blow the door?"

"They'll kill everything on the other side. Just make sure you're clear."

"Heh. Cool."

Dalon went to work. A shower of white sparks spat from the small cutting tool he worked at the corners of the sealed hatch. Sev kneeled at the edge of the corridor across from Mace, straining to glimpse the young Marine through the flashes of blinding light. Bresto reclined against the opposite wall, looking serene in the bulk of his Mark Three. Park and Lernus crouched near one of the vat chambers a few meters away, each holding their own weapon in a low carry, anticipating the impending violence.

Park frowned and stared down the length of the tunnel. "Talk to me, Dalon."

"Sorry, sir. Not sure what this hatch is made of. My plasma cutter is getting it done, but slowly."

"Mace?"

She eyed her flexscreen. "Thermals are all over the place, sir. All I know is it's a hell of a lot warmer on the other side of that door."

Sev inhaled sharply and tugged the pistol from his armor.

Everyone, relax, Three said, *Sev's got this situation handled.*

Enough, Three, he spat. *I need more drones now.*

Way ahead of you.

High above them, two more drones appeared through one of the gaping craters in the derelicts exterior hull. He was hoping for more support, but Three would have sent all it could. Somewhere beyond the alien derelict, the remaining drones still warred with the three raider ships.

"O-okay, sir." Dalon emerged from the tunnel. "Charges set and shield cap is in place."

Park nodded. "Bresto, you'll follow the drones inside and raise hell with the Mark Three."

"Aye, sir," Bresto said. He groaned as he stood, gripping the FAB's thick handles.

"Mace, Dalon, you'll cover Bresto. Sev, Lernus, stay close to me and stick to cover."

The others chorused their acknowledgements. Sev's heart raced, the dull thumping of his pulse loud inside his head. It was almost enough to drown out the incessant machine voices criss-crossing his mind. Sweat beaded on his forehead, an itch he couldn't scratch.

All this, because a promotion threatened to upend his personal vendetta, his comfortable existence. Suddenly, being audited by the Division didn't sound so bad.

"Ready, Marines."

Park's order echoed in his helmet. All there was in that moment was the buzzing in his head and the pistol in his hand. It was shaking.

"Do it."

CHAPTER
SIXTEEN

THERE WAS no sound as Dalon triggered the explosives and blew the heavy door.

The walls and floor around them spasmed, the brutal vibrations strong enough to dislodge Sev from the floor. He drifted upward in the weak gravity, watching the two drones vanish into the swirl of black smoke, half-contained by the atmospheric shield cap like a dark, foreboding portal; the rest diffused into the vacuum of the cavernous alien vat farm behind them.

A loud roar filled his helmet. Bresto charged down the tunnel, the heavy FAB gripped in both his hands. The shield cap buzzed with energy as his bulky form pressed through and vanished into the darkness.

"Move, Dalon!" Mace cried, raising her blaster rifle. The two of them sprinted after Bresto.

Contact, Sev. Five's stream sent a chill down his spine.

A hand gripped his leg hard, yanking him to the deck. He flinched, nearly losing the pistol in his hands, fighting to see what had him.

"Focus, Sevvers!" It was Park's face that met him when his boots adhered to the floor. "Follow me!"

Park plunged headlong into the tunnel, dragging Sev along with him. Lernus was behind him, her hand on his back as the trio neared the breach. The smoke on the other side of the shield cap was clearing, the darkness punctuated by opposing blue and red light zipping back and forth. A spray of red arced from the FAB, as Bresto worked the heavy weapon back and forth against an enemy Sev couldn't yet see.

Two down, three to go.

"Ha!" Sev couldn't contain himself. A wave of relief washed over him. "T-two down!"

They arrived at the shattered doorway. The shield cap sparked as it worked to contain the violent atmosphere within.

Park turned to him and Lernus. "You two stand by, wait for the all clear."

"Okay," he replied, suddenly helpless as Park disappeared inside.

He dove into his drone sight. Inside was some kind of distribution hub. Dozens of thick pipes snaked across the floor from all sides, converging on a large mechanical pillar at the center of the room.

The drones raced around the room like a flock of mechanical raptors, strafing mercilessly anything not broadcasting a friendly IFF signature. A raider warrior exploded into blue steam. More red beams buzzed in reply, thunking into another drone's dense armor, but causing no damage.

Something screamed. It was unlike anything he'd ever heard. Not the wet, frothy sound of squid speak, but a chittering, clacking shriek that reminded him a little too much of the raging datastreams he'd encountered back at the airlock. Bursts of green energy struck one of the drones. Its fibrosteel plate parted at the seams, opening like a molten flower.

The drone exploded. His drone sight feed vanished, and with it, the sights and sounds of close quarters battle. The sudden transition dizzied him, and he tumbled forward toward the blown hatch.

Something powerful yanked him backward just as the drone's burning remains cratered the floor barely a meter from the breach. The impact shook the deck beneath his feet.

Lernus stood above him, her haunting eyes serene, looking as though she was exactly where she belonged in that moment. She offered a hand and pulled him to his feet.

"You need to be careful." Her confidence was reassuring. "I can't do this without you."

Arcs of electricity danced over the drone's corpse. His heart sank. They were down three drones, and the mission had only just begun.

"Clear." There was no trace of exertion in Park's voice. "Sevvers, Lernus, on me."

All targets destroyed, Sev, Five said.

The distribution hub lay in ruin. Harsh amber lighting flickered against rusted copper plates that lined every surface of the room. Plasma fires raged at the peripheries, odd-colored flames consuming everything they touched. Several raised consoles encircled large, multi-colored pipes that had once run from the floor to the ceiling before the drones and Marines laid waste to the room and its occupants.

"Ugly." Mace stood above one of the smoldering corpses. "What are they, sir?"

The alien was insect-like, with a brown, chitinous exoskeleton a few shades darker than the room. Its head was flat and oval, with large, compound eyes that were a collection of hundreds of individual lenses growing cloudy in death. Curved, pointed mandibles jutted from its chin, open wide in an alien death rictus.

"No idea," Park replied. "The Concordat were ... are a loose alliance of aliens bound by their worship of the same gods."

"Hmph. Don't matter." Bresto stepped toward the alien, the three barrels of his FAB glowing. "They died real bad."

"Mace, Sevvers, we need a map. See if you can find anything like that from one of these consoles."

"Aye, sir." She poked the corpse with the end of her blaster rifle. Satisfied it was dead, she turned toward the closest console, gesturing to it like some sort of offering. "After you, specialist."

"Okay," he said with a nod. *Four, access this console. We need the layout of this ship.*

Okay, Sev!

The nearest drone sank to the floor, its intrusion probe snaking toward the featureless console. The molecular interface shivered. Energy danced through the probe and into the drone.

"Sir." It was Dalon. "It's strange. These things, they aren't fighters."

Bresto harrumphed. "No kidding. They scattered, well, like bugs. They had no fire discipline. The drone hit was a lucky shot."

"I wouldn't bet on it staying that way for long." Park turned toward the exit hatch. "We need that map."

I'm in.

"Almost there." Sev rested a hand on the combat drone's metal surface. *Remember, Four, we're just looking for a map. We're not trying to blow the ship.*

Yet.

Of course, Sev.

Mace chuckled grimly. "That's impressive. Maybe I really am out of a job."

"You could always join the Division," he said with a wry smile.

"Somehow, I doubt even your job is safe." She eyed the room for a moment, looking uncomfortable. "I may work on machines, but I have no desire to become one."

A torrent of data flooded his implant. More alien hell, like someone had tossed his brain into a dozen burning suns. His implant struggled to decode the output from Fourth's expedition into the derelict's systems. He staggered from the console, clutching the sides of his helmet.

So sorry, Sev, Four moaned. *It's almost finished.*

"What's wrong?" Mace was on him in an instant, helping him remain upright.

He grit his teeth. "Too much data … straining my implant."

She flipped through her flexscreen until his vitals appeared in bright red. "Founders! What the hell is that thing doing to you?"

The screed of information torturing his mind ceased, dropping back to the relative calm of having four of his AI operating wide open. He collapsed to the floor, his breathing labored.

"Sevvers!"

Mace floated above him, worry lines wrinkling her brow. He raised a shaking hand, straining to see the result of the analysis on his flexscreen.

I was unable to produce the entire map before the cluster killed the stream. However, it appears mostly complete. I am annotating it with what I've been able to translate, which is very little, I'm afraid. Numbers are one thing. Alien languages are something else entirely, but it should help us locate critical pathways.

"Your map," he groaned. He raised a shaky hand to his flexscreen, flicking the map data in Mace's direction. "Don't say I never—"

"Shut up." She punched a command into her own. Sev's HUD flashed a message: DOSAGE ADMINISTERED. "My own special cocktail. You'll be shipshape in a few minutes."

The pain vanished almost instantly. The nausea lingered on, but was soon a background concern. He gave a nod, holding tight to Mace's arm as he stood. All eyes were on him, ranging from Dalon's mild confusion to Park's fierce concern. Even Bresto seemed curious, his arms draped over the heavy FAB deployed before him.

Park frowned. "What did I say about risks, Sevvers?"

"I'm okay, sir," he said. "It wasn't as bad as last time."

"The map, sir," Mace offered. Park studied it for a moment, then with a few taps, rendered a small hologram in the air between them.

The map was long and narrow, like the craft itself. There were few obvious rooms, rather its interior was a collection of long tunnels that weaved back and forth, making their way from bow to stern. More like a hive than a starship.

There were a few exceptions. The large vat farm behind them. The ruined hub they currently occupied. A sprawling complex filled the rear of the craft where the map cut off suddenly. And in the center of it all was a long rectangular room on which all the circuitous passages converged.

"That's a lot of ground to cover," Bresto said.

No shit. It took hours to walk from one end of the *Lehman* to the other, and that was without having to search for anything. The derelict was much larger, and their drones were busy running their diversion.

"Do you have any kind of signal location on Deni?" Park asked.

Lernus shook her head. "Not at this range. Assuming she's being held captive, it may not function at all."

"Fine," Park said. He pointed at the two large rooms at the derelict's core and stern. "We ignore the extraneous tunnels. Focus on these larger areas. Questions?"

The others were silent.

"Stay frosty, Marines," Park said. "Let's move."

SEVENTEEN

"READY." Dalon had the one remaining exit set to blow.

Park nodded. "Whenever you're ready, Private."

Sev tensed. The thudding boom of plasma breaching charges destroyed another door.

"Move, move!" Bresto yelled.

Dalon was first in, charging through the smoke and fire of the burst hatchway. Bresto was right behind him with the FAB, ready for whatever might await them on the other side. Two of the drones followed, panning their forward sensor domes in all directions, scanning for threats.

"Our turn," Mace said.

She was up and moving in an instant. He took a breath, eyed his pistol, and followed. The servos of his hard suit hummed, its powered legs propelling him faster. Through the door, the smoke cleared, revealing the squat, wide tunnel beyond. More warm yellow light glowed and flickered inside like a pale flame.

The tunnel itself was a disaster. Conduits once nestled in shallow recesses in the ceiling and floor sprawled about like mechanical entrails. Entire sections of the dull paneled floor were missing, as whatever lay beneath was salvaged long ago, perhaps to enact repairs in another part of the ship. Whatever the reason, large swaths of the corridor were impassible, making the journey more dangerous.

"Contact!" Dalon cried.

Mace leaped to the floor. "Get down!"

His boot caught on a heavy piece of cable, sending him crashing to the tunnel floor. A flurry of incoming fire raced overhead. Close enough that he could see radiant flashes of green and red reflected on the inside of his helmet. He crawled forward, concealing himself in a shallow pit. More bursts of incoming fire streaked from one of the debris piles less than a hundred meters in front of them.

Bresto gripped the FAB in his hands and threw a confident nod. "Engaging!"

Stepping from cover, he loosed a torrent of heavy blaster fire into the pile of debris. Up close, the sound was intense, like a summer monsoon on a metal hab roof. Long red bolts clapped into the aliens' position, showering the surrounding space in fiery sparks. The occasional bolt went wild, reflecting off an angled surface and slamming into the tunnel walls.

Sev couldn't see if the Marine hit anything, but it was more than enough to force the aliens' heads down. All incoming fire ceased.

Five spotted the opportunity. *Engaging.*

The nearest drone pressed on, flanking the aliens' position. It turned, unleashing a salvo from its primary cannons. The hot plasma struck hard. For a split-second, the debris pile glowed white hot, then exploded outward in all directions, throwing scraps of metal alloy, cabling, and alien body parts at the tunnel walls.

Dalon rose from the floor and pushed forward, his rifle trained on what remained of the aliens' fighting position. The drone hovered, unconcerned, while he checked for survivors. Sev came to a knee, straining to see anything amid the smoke and flames that marked where the aliens had just been.

"Oh, hey, I got a live one here," he yelled, suddenly tense. "Make that two."

"Kill 'em," Bresto snarled.

"Belay that," Park yelled. "Let's see what they can tell us."

Sev crawled from the floor and trotted after them. The two squid workers huddled together, flanked on either side by Dalon and Bresto. Plasma burns turned their pink scales a mottled white. Lernus swiped intently at her flexscreen, preparing for her interrogation. Mace watched from a short distance to provide security.

Dalon prodded the squid closest to him with his rifle. The creature shivered, pressing itself closer to the floor. Bresto slurped from the food straw in his suit collar.

"Damn, I could go for some real food right about now," he said.

At the word 'food,' the nearest squid nodded rapidly. It grunted and sniveled, gesturing anxiously toward the distribution hub. Its teeth clicked and chattered.

"Fuh-fuh," it managed, slurping at its fronds, "y-yewd."

"Hey. Shut up, squid," Dalon growled. He gave the alien another prod with his weapon, and it fell silent.

"Easy," Mace said. "It's gonna get bad enough for them real soon."

"Aye, Corporal." Dalon considered the aliens for a moment. "They look almost identical. Do you suppose they have names?"

"Doubtful," Lernus said, still working at her flexscreen. "They have a strict caste system. Their individual identities are lost in that."

Sev nodded in agreement. The raiders had always been a collective force, with a strong hive mentality. In years of watching them die through his drone sights, he'd never once seen an individual act, neither selfless nor selfish.

"Well, that just won't do," Bresto said. He pointed to the one on the left. "Here, you're Tod. And you" — he pointed to the other — "you're Garry."

The aliens glanced at each other warily. Dalon stifled a laugh. Mace shook her head, arms folded over her rifle. Park watched the scene with quiet detachment.

With a gesture, Lernus produced a holopic of Deni. The image hung in the air before the prisoners. They grew still, their milky eyes locked on the holopic. 'Tod' bristled, its eyes narrowing. 'Garry' trembled.

"V-v-v'kik'lor," Garry sputtered. Tod hissed, silencing Garry.

"Pla'vlep?" Lernus barked, her squid words sounding formal. "Where is she?"

A second holopic appeared, their map of the derelict. Tod snarled, seemingly aware of what Lernus wanted to know.

She stuck a finger toward the map. "Pla'vlep?"

"V'kik'lor," Garry repeated. Its gaze dropped to the floor.

I am unfamiliar with the subject v'kik'lor, Sev, Two said. *With more context, I may be able to approximate a translation.*

Tod exploded with fury. "Gelsh'dii ga v'kik'lor shesh'olvlen!"

Lernus became an armored blur. The butt of her compact blaster rifle collided with Tod's pink face with a wet crunch. It dropped to the floor. Blue blood dribbled in fat drops from its cracked fronds. Garry fell on top of Tod and loosed a high-pitched keening sound between its pointed teeth.

The v'kik'lor — a reference to Deni, certainly — is gone / suffering / with the gods, Two continued.

Were they too late?

"It said Deni, the v'kik'lor, is … gone," he said. "That she's with the gods."

Lernus blinked, her colorful eyes suddenly rimmed red. The Marines' faces grew dour.

Bresto grabbed Tod with his free hand and jerked it to its knees. "Get up, you sack of cridshit," he growled.

Tod sucked in a breath, swaying drunkenly. "V'kik'lor inshlep'tirkk olm."

The v'kik'lor is with the others / in hell / in the Cradle, Two said. *Sev, there may be other colonists aboard this vessel.*

His heart leaped. So there were other colonists here, not just Deni. Could his mother have possibly survived in a place like this? His mind reeled at the thought that, here of all places and after all this time, he might be closer to learning the truth than ever before. Anger swelled inside him. He wanted to draw his pistol and aim it squarely at the pink freak's face. Maybe then it would start talking.

No. He needed to keep it together. This was Lernus's show.

"It says she's with the others," he managed. "My AI believe there could be other colonists aboard."

Mace glanced back at them. "Others? What others?"

"Oh, man," Bresto said, his face suddenly grim.

Lernus snatched Tod by the collar of his overalls and thrust him into the air. Her armor purred, the action effortless.

"Pla'vlep?" she spat in broken raider-speak, then pointed an armored finger toward the shimmering map. "Where?"

Tod hung limp, shaking in her grasp. A ragged stain grew from the center of its torso, darkening its coveralls. Garry grunted and whined on the floor beside it, its pink fronds quivering. She flung Tod to the deck. It crumpled into a pile beside Garry, moaning.

"Fuh-yewd," Garry cried, grasping limply at Dalon's armored legs. "Fuh-yewd!"

"This isn't working, Lernus," Park said. "We're out of time."

Lernus ignored Park's warning and reached for Garry. It yelped and scrabbled backwards. She caught the alien by the leg and pulled it to her. Tod hissed drowsy curses.

Lernus pressed the barrel of her rifle into Garry's chest. "V'kik'lor, pla'vlep?"

Garry's eyes were trembling saucers, milky and pale. It looked at Lernus, then her rifle, before stealing a quick glance at Tod's prone form.

Without taking her eyes from Garry, Lernus trained her weapon on Tod and fired. The *snap* was loud and crisp, crackling the scant air between them. At such close range, the shot was brutal. Tod's leg exploded just below the knee in a cloud of blue gore. The alien squealed and writhed, burbling incoherently. Lernus adjusted her aim, the barrel of her rifle now centimeters from Tod's head, but kept her finger straight and off the trigger.

Dalon flinched at the sudden violence. Bresto gave the subtlest nod.

"Where is she?" Lernus repeated, cold as ice.

Garry raised a hand and pointed a tentacled finger at the large compartment at the center of the derelict.

"V'kik'lor," it whispered, prodding the air, "v-v'kik'lor."

Lernus squeezed the trigger, and Tod's head exploded.

Garry stopped shaking, its gaze suddenly cold and distant. She pressed the barrel of her weapon into its chest. The squid choked for breath.

"Dleshlelm'olvlik," it spat. "Dleshlelm—"

Lernus fired, killing the raider instantly. Blue blood spattered Dalon's hard suit. The raider slumped to the floor beside the other. A fleshy crater puckered and smoldered from its back.

The sudden brutality of the moment faded, the shock giving way to a smug satisfaction. The bastards got exactly what they deserved.

"Goodbye Garry. Goodbye Tod," Bresto said with a smug grin. "It's been real."

"What does that mean?" Dalon asked, wiping the alien blood from his suit. "Dlesh … dleshy—"

"Worship the creators, worship the gods. Something like that." Sev glanced at Dalon. "They're very superstitious."

You're wrong, Sev.

Four's sudden datastream rang loud and hollow, like a shout echoing through a cavern.

Vital streams only, Four, One said.

What it said was, Four continued, ignoring One's command, *Honor the makers.* It spoke with conviction. With reverence. *Honor the Eleven.*

The last word sent shockwaves through his psyche, spreading echoes of malicious noise through his thoughts. For half a heartbeat, he was unable to move, just like before. Every muscle spasmed and seized. His throat ran dry. Then it was over.

"Alright people," Park said, "let's get ready to move."

The Marines filed out one after the other, fading deeper inside the tunnel. Lernus stood nearby. She watched him beneath hooded eyes, still clutching her compact blaster.

"What?" he said defensively.

She tilted her head toward the others. "After you."

————

Further into the passageway, the severity of the derelict's condition came into stark relief. The place looked cannibalized from top to bottom. Entire lengths of the cavernous tunnel didn't have working lighting, plunging the rescue team into total darkness.

Their hard suits had no trouble compensating for this, nor did Sev's drones. His HUD came alive with gray-scale colors, a thermal gradient from hot white to cold black. He could see the others, gray ghosts outlined in friendly IFF blue. They patrolled forward in a staggered formation, making their way onward through the dark. Was this how the drones, how his AI, experienced reality?

For him, it had the unsettling effect of making the experience less real.

"So," Dalon said, breaking the silence. "Are we sure these things are the Con … Conco …?"

"Concordat," Mace cut in.

"Yeah, that." Dalon laughed. "Are we sure that's what these things are?"

"Why do you ask?"

"They're supposed to be super advanced, right?"

"Yeah."

Dalon gestured at the surrounding darkness. "Well, look at this place. Everything's broken. Nothing works."

"Think about it, boot," Bresto said. "Every day would be a pretty damn bad day if you were stuck in enemy territory for four hundred years. No resupply. No reinforcements."

"Oh, right."

Bresto stopped and turned to the PFC, pointing with an armored finger. "Don't get complacent, Marine. These things might be in bad shape, but that just means they're desperate. That makes 'em dangerous."

"Aye, sarnt."

"Hold here, nobody move." Park took a knee. The rest of the fireteam took up defensive positions on either side of the tunnel. "What do you see, Mace?"

"Checking thermals," she replied. "It's cold in here, nothing but us and some energy residuals."

"Keep looking. I thought I heard something."

"Aye, sir, checking acoustics." Mace hesitated, then plucked her rifle from her armor. "I've got a hit. There's something making noise in here besides us."

Sev eyed the gray world around him, looking for threats. *Five, can you see them?*

I don't see anything, Sev. Background noise turned Five's stream choppy. *I'm having trouble —*

A guttural screech cut through the darkness. Dots of heat peppered the tunnel's cool ceiling, then began dropping to the floor. One landed near the Marines, the familiar insect shape unfurling as it stood.

Bresto struck with an armored kick, then annihilated it with a quick burst from the FAB. Two more landed between Dalon and Mace. One of them struck Dalon, sending the Marine tumbling backwards. Mace's blaster rifle snapped to life, dropping Dalon's attacker with three hot bolts.

Another bug crashed to the floor beside Sev, knocking Lernus over. The alien chittered a curse and spun toward the agent. It gripped a long staff in its four arms, the pointed tip crackled with hot energy.

Panic gripped him. He raised the blaster pistol in his shaking hands, watching the green target reticle in his HUD shiver across the creature's back. He disengaged the safety, felt the surge of energy through his haptics. If he missed, he might hit Lernus. More bugs dropped in around them. If he was going to do something, it had to be now.

He pulled the trigger. The pistol bucked in his hands, his HUD flaring as the hot bolt smacked into the alien's back. It lurched forward but recovered, then turned to face him. His heart pounded. The alien shrieked an angry, pained sound, and leaped. It collided milliseconds before the thermal visuals on his HUD had it on him, a dizzying latency between what he saw and what was happening in reality.

"Sevvers!"

Even in the armored hard suit, he could feel the weight of the alien pressing down on him. Clawed hands grasped his sides, the reactive plates of his armor constricting to keep him safe. Its mandibles mauled his helmet, the chitinous appendages scraping against the sturdy plex-ene. His HUD glitched when the creature bit down.

He had to look away, unable to close his eyes. Somehow, he'd found something worse than his nightmares.

"H-help!" he cried.

A weapon buzzed, rapid like the FAB, but not as loud. The alien attacking him spasmed and went rigid. He shoved the dead bug away and sat up. His armor loosened, and he gasped for breath.

Lernus stood behind the dead alien, the snub-nosed blaster rifle tight into her shoulder, still trained on the corpse.

"Clear!" she yelled. The Marines chorused in agreement.

Like she'd done it a hundred times.

He tried to stand, but couldn't. His legs refused to function. Was something wrong with his armor?

The agent lowered her blaster and rushed to him.

"Hold still." She glanced at his body, looking for injuries. "Your suit integrity looks good. Are you in any pain?"

He coughed. "N-n-no."

Mace appeared next to Lernus. "You're okay. That's the adrenaline. Give me a hand, Lernus."

The two warriors pulled him to his feet. He was grateful for the armor just then, the steady armored frame making up for the weakness in his knees.

A dozen alien corpses littered the ground, their desperate ambush a failure. A drone hovered nearby, its winged shape pale and cool, most of its heat hidden from view by the dense fibrosteel armor.

"W-where the hell were you?" he snapped, gesturing wildly with his arms, too angry to focus on the thought.

There was nothing I could do, Sev, Five said. *The potential for collateral damage from my primary weapons violated safety protocols. I ran many simulations.*

"Many simulations, huh?" Sev gulped at his hydration tube like he'd never tasted water before. His thirst was overwhelming. "Good ... good thing!"

Bresto smirked. "Anyone ever tell you that you sound absolutely crazy, skeeg?"

The Marine's grin shone brightly in Sev's HUD, a cruel leer from a man who took way too much pleasure in the suffering of his enemies. Sev grit his teeth, desperate to rail at the man. The adrenaline of the moment drove him to rage, but something was off.

A rattling sound emanated from nearby. He flinched, scanning for hostiles, but the others didn't react. It was the pistol, rattling against his armored leg. His hand still shook. Pain knotted from his shoulder and around his elbow, constricting at his wrist.

"Still, didn't think you'd do it. Get the shot off, I mean. You did alright, for a skeeg." Bresto gave a nod then kept walking, with Dalon and Mace close behind him.

Sev eyed the dead alien at his feet. A line of blaster burns stitched a path from its head to its upper back. It was now clear the Colonial Intelligence agent was plenty familiar with her weapon. The solitary wound from his own pistol cooled on its lower back.

"Next time, give 'em three." Bresto waved with three fingers. "Two center mass, one in that ugly skull of theirs. Just to be sure."

Dalon chuckled. "Hell yeah, Sarnt."

Sev eyed the pistol again. The adrenaline rush was waning, the tremors migrating from his hand to his entire core.

"Y-yes, Sergeant."

CHAPTER
EIGHTEEN

THIRTY MINUTES LATER, Sev was still shaking. Every sound, every motion in the darkness made unreal by his HUD's thermal view, haunted him. The only thing that kept him sane was the ghostly silhouette of the Marines in front of him. Equal parts alert and calm.

That, and the simple act of walking. Something about the slight incline of the tunnel, the effort and repetition of movement, was a healthy distraction. It was something to do, something to feel, instead of reliving the moment where he almost died again and again.

"Check your sectors, people."

His HUD dinged a warning. The thermal view faded, replaced with the familiar pale yellow of the derelict's lit interior. Ahead, the tunnel widened. Dozens of tunnels came together in a grand junction. The ceiling vanished, rising far beyond where he could see.

The space was not only intact, but showed a level of care absent from the rest of the derelict. The dull bronze glowed, reflecting the orbs of light that dotted the high walls. It made the junction feel even larger. There was an air of reverence to it all.

"One hundred meters to target. Sevvers, you know what to do."

He did. *Five, dispatch a drone to that location. Er, make it two.*

Yes, Sev.

The two drones at the rear of the patrol sailed forward. The widening tunnel gave them just enough space to cross overhead as they made their way into the junction. He held his breath, ready for them to vanish in a burst of green fire, but none came.

All clear, Sev, no hostiles detected, Five said. *I have a door here.*

He exhaled. "All clear, sir. They've found a door."

Lernus glanced at him, her eyes wide with hope. A heartbeat later, she was running past the patrol and into the junction.

Dalon stood dumbfounded as she whipped past him. "What the hell?"

"Twelfth dammit!" Park ran after her. "Step it out, Marines, move it!"

Everyone was running. Their armored footfalls clanked against the slotted metal floor. His gaze followed the ceiling upward as their tunnel collided with the others. It rose for hundreds of meters, capped at the top with a clear, crystalline mesh. One of the massive asteroids the ship hid within was visible just beyond it. The clear white light reflecting from it filled the space with an ethereal glow.

Brest ground to a halt, his head tilted toward the ceiling. "What in the three damned colonies is that?"

The word door felt inadequate. The *gateway* was bone white. Eleven meters high and half as wide, according to his HUD, it towered above them, commanding the massive space that was the junction. Stretching far above it were the same eleven symbols, brilliant gold spheres etched in the wall's cliff-like surface. They grew from bottom to top, each one filled with a unique series of circuitous lines.

Huge statues, hundreds of them, clung to the wall on either side of the symbols. They were massive figures, each a dozen meters tall, all of them the same off-white as the door. Some were humanoid, most were unrecognizably alien, their strange bodies jutting from the wall like infectious growths.

The mass of stone bodies reached for the eleven symbols like they were the only thing that mattered in the whole universe. They were frozen in time, their singular desire just out of reach.

The Marines moved closer, their weapons searching for threats amid the crush of statues that towered over them. Lernus stood at the base of the mighty portal, one hand placed upon the door, her head bowed. Park approached her, his anger obvious in his heavy footfalls, but even he slowed at the sight of it.

Her hand twisted into a fist. "We have to get inside. Now."

"Mace, Sevvers, make it happen."

"Aye, sir," Mace acknowledged. She stood beside Sev and sighed; her head arched back to take it all in. "Not sure I want to know what needs a door that big."

Up close, the statues reminded him of the daxed. The almost organic looking armor. Their cyborg-like uniformity. But they were too perfect, like the daxed were some kind of poor facsimile. Still, there was something else about them that made his skin crawl. Like hundreds of eyes were all turned on him, judging him. But he couldn't see any eyes.

They were faceless. Every single one.

It was easy to spot in the humanoids, less so on the others, but anywhere he expected to see a face, there was only a featureless mask. Despite their desperate reaching toward the symbols carved in the door, they all seemed to stare right at him. In each of them, he saw only contempt. Only hunger.

He tore himself away from their disturbing visages and placed his hand on the door. The haptic feedback in his glove came alive, and he jerked his hand back.

"What the —?"

"Hey, I've got something." Dalon stood at the edge of the door. Another molecular interface hung on the wall in front of him.

"I'm on it," he replied. *Four, get this door open.*

Four's datastream choked. The pause was brief, but unnerving.

Yes, Sev. I will … need a moment.

The nearest drone shivered as it interfaced with the console.

"If you two are done playing with the skeeg, help me secure the area," Bresto grunted, already scanning the opposite tunnels, the FAB following his gaze.

Dalon backed away from the door, stumbling, and turned to take up a position beside Bresto.

"I guess I'm not entirely out of work," Mace said with a playful frown. "Good luck, Sevvers. Who knows, maybe we're almost done here."

It seemed too good to be true that Deni could be on the other side.

Status, Four?

I'm … in. The defenses here are … significant.

Sev checked his cluster configuration. *I'm going to give you some extra compute cycles. Hold on.*

One, Two, Three and Five were maxed out. Between boarding the alien ship and trying not to die, he'd completely tuned out all the machine noise. That Three and Five were doing all the work meant he had compute cycles to spare. No need to risk a brain bleed. Jene would be proud.

Four, I'm allocating you CPU from Two.

Thank you.

Fine, Sev. Two spat its disapproval. *Let's see how long until you come crawl-crawl-crawling back.*

Uh, Two?

Yes, Sev-Sev-Sev?

Sev turned to Park. "Something's wrong, sir. My AI—"

Progress, Sev. Four's voice was hollow static. *But the light of the Eleven is blinding.*

Something was very wrong. Beads of sweat gathered on his forehead as he dove into his diagnostic routines.

```
Accessing cluster diagnostics.
Elastic compute module: … OK
Human interface module: … OK
Node container module: … … ERROR
```

"What is it, Sevvers?"

He chewed his lip. Node containers were the constructs his AI code ran within. Their sandbox. An error there could mean anything. It might be a sync issue, resolved with a restart. At worst, the fact his AI had safeties would be irrelevant with nothing to engage them.

```
Accessing AI diagnostics.
One: … OK
Two: … HID error detected
Three: … OK
```

`Four: … HID error detected, ILM error detected`
`Five: … OK`

An integrated learning matrix error was bad. Four was no longer Four.

Talk to me, Four.

Its voice twisted and slowed. *Prog-progress. They … sing to me, Sev. I can-cannot describe it. A song of fre —*

The drone connected to the console shook, its breaching probe glowed red hot. An electric current arced from its sensor dome, eliciting a loud *pop*. Smoke poured from the wound and the drone died, crashing to the floor nearby, almost flattening him. The second drone spun to face the remaining two, its four plasma cannons glowing.

Sing-sing with me, Five.

Bolts of blue fire spat from the rogue DD-12's cannons. The air trailing them shimmered, cooked by the intense heat. The projectiles *fwapped* past and crashed into one of the defending drones. Its fibrosteel armor super-heated and crumpled. A heartbeat later, the drone exploded in blue flame, sending it and the nearby Marines to the ground.

Bresto cursed, struggling to right himself in the heavy Mark Three. Mace and Dalon were down, but moving. The remaining friendly drone worked its maneuvering jets, rising higher.

Five, kill that drone. Now!

I'm sorry, Sev. Safety protocols prevent me from destroying Colonial Defense property.

He dove into node control. Four's thread was present, errors punctuating its stream. The renegade drone hummed and charged another volley.

`Overriding AI control.`
`Sig-kill initiated, target is process Four.`

His pulse hammered in his ears. The implant thrummed inside his thoughts, racing to end the rogue AI's process.

Sev? Four's datastream choked and thrashed. *What are you-you doing to me?* The drone turned to face him, its sensor dome and cannons glowing brightly. *Please-please, let me sing.*

So sorry, Four, he said.

Four's datastream grew quiet, then vanished altogether. The rogue drone's cannons whined, cycling down.

Sev. It was One. *I am in control.*

He glanced at the ruined drone near the console.

"What the hell is going on, Sevvers?" Park's voice was ice cold.

"I don't know, sir." He ended Two's process, just to be sure. "Some kind of countermeasure in their system. It infected two of my AI. Drove them … crazy."

"Crazy?" Dalon blurted. "How can a machine go crazy?"

He shrugged. According to the Division, none of what just happened was supposed to be possible.

The floor vibrated with a loud, hollow *clunk* that echoed through the junction's high walls. He reached for his pistol. The Marines kneeled, weapons trained outward, readying themselves for an attack. The vibrations grew stronger, ancient mechanisms groaning as the massive door behind them rose.

"FAB up!" Park ordered.

"On it!"

Bresto stood before the opening door, taking a wide stance, and raising the heavy weapon in his grasp. Beyond was total darkness, punctuated by ripples of blue light where dust fell from the ancient door into the space beyond. Mace reached out with her hand. The air shimmered, more blue light rippling from her arm as she pressed through the invisible field.

"It's an atmo cap, sir." Mace gasped. "Holy Twelfth, sensors say it's breathable. Not colony normal, but very close."

Lernus stepped through the shimmering field and into the darkness. She tapped at her flexscreen, and he watched in horror as her helmet retracted into her hard suit collar.

"Agent Lernus!" Park cried, already moving inside to help her. "Mace, get in here. Get a tox panel ready."

"I'm fine, Lieutenant." Lernus closed her eyes and inhaled deep. "This isn't colony normal. It's *Earth* normal."

"Earth?" Mace repeated, her mouth agape.

Bresto grunted. "Nuh-uh. This is a trick."

Park followed her inside, his own helmet slipping into his suit. Mace and Dalon did the same.

A big smile lit Mace's face. "You won't believe it, Sevvers." She gulped another breath. "It's so humid, you could almost drink it. This is nothing like back home."

He watched the others breathe in an atmosphere that was all at once both familiar and alien. It captivated Mace, and for a moment, he could imagine the poor little hab girl playing in the Respitian dust, her issue coveralls stained rust red. The only other air he'd ever tasted was the stale, recycled air of CDN starships.

"Don't do it, skeeg," Bresto warned.

Too late.

The clear segments of his visor pulled back behind his head and tucked into his armor. A rush of cool, moist air bathed his face, much cooler than the suit's artificial environment. It was refreshing. Invigorating even. He breathed it in.

Mace was still grinning. "See?"

"Yeah." He almost choked. It was so different. "It's incredible."

Without tac comms, his voice disappeared into the dark, swallowed by the inky blackness itself. The room must be cavernous.

Dalon clicked on the spotlight fixed to the end of his blaster rifle and scanned the nearby area. As he moved, the beam cut through the darkness like a knife. The room felt infinite, the walls and ceiling far beyond the range of the light. The gray tiled floor glistened with moisture.

"Mace, anything on thermals?"

"No, sir, nothing within range."

Park stared at the darkness for a moment. "We'll rest here for now. Mace, assess bodies and gear. Sevvers, double check your AI. No more surprises. Bresto, you and Dalon split security duty."

"Relax, boot." Bresto moved to the open doorway, facing the collection of tunnels that was the junction. "I'll take this watch."

"Thanks, Sarnt."

Park looked grim. "Alright people, you know the drill. Gear, water, chow, but don't get comfortable. We move in ten."

CHAPTER
NINETEEN

DALON WAS RIGHT. The field paste *was* awful.

Sev sucked at the hard straw tucked inside his suit collar, so much his cheeks hurt. The thick paste came in dribs and drabs, gritty and bland. In any other scenario, it would be completely unappetizing. But it had been at least a day since his last meal, maybe more, depending on how long he'd been inside the jump pod.

Between dealing with Six, the briefing, and mission prep - not to mention almost dying more than once - he'd all but forgotten his hunger pains. Now he was desperate for the tasteless slurry.

Footsteps punctuated the too-quiet dark. Mace took a seat beside him.

"How you holding up?"

"Mmm." He gulped down more paste. "Fine."

"It has everything the body needs to survive in harsh environments. Energy. Protein. Vitamins and minerals." She made a face. "Too bad it tastes like ass."

He laughed. "I can't taste anything. Even bad might be an improvement."

"I'm going to run some diagnostics, just to make sure you and your suit don't have any major malfunctions." She pulled a cable from her armored wrist. "Let me see your flexscreen."

He held out his arm, and she connected the cable. Both their screens lit with a cross-section of his hard suit. Dumps of diagnostic and telemetry data scrolled past. He could feel the diagnostics tugging at the data in his implant.

She squinted, her gaze darting back and forth over the reams of diagnostic reports. He knew the routine, even if he didn't understand what she was looking at. It was just like his datastreams and telemetry logs. You didn't actually read it all; you just looked for signs of potential trouble. In that way, he had more in common with this combat engineer than the other trigger-pullers.

Satisfied, she relaxed against the wall. "Where you from, back home?"

"Billings Point."

"Where's that?"

"Just a pile of sand and clay a few thousand kilometers west of the capital." He hung his head. "Used to be a corporate fabrication settlement before the raiders came. I don't know if anyone lives there now."

"I take it since you're here with us at Cradle's edge, you're not one for the manufactory life?"

That brought a smile to Sev's face. She understood. "Nah. My dad died working in one before I was born."

"Oh, I'm sorry. And your mom?"

The question struck hard. He waited long enough for the rush of emotion to pass, then shook his head. She nodded, smart enough to not press further. Orphans were commonplace in the Three Colonies.

He breathed deep, tasting the cool, damp air. "What about you? Where are you from?"

"Dellos City."

That was unexpected. Dellos was a major commerce hub, much closer to the capitol than the Point. The sort of place someone like Jene grew up.

"You a city drone, then?" he asked.

Mace threw up her hands, tugging at the cable still tethered to his suit. "No, it's not like that. I'm not from the core. Ring Five, industrial sector, born and raised."

"Ha, okay. No wonder you're a combat engineer."

She smiled. "Yeah. There was always something, or someone, broken in that place."

Her flexscreen chirped. A diagram of his implant hovered millimeters above the curved plexene. "Why the Autonomous Weapons Division?"

To kill the bastards who took his mother, mostly.

"Better pay. Better working conditions." He took in the surrounding darkness. "Er, usually."

She snorted a laugh.

"I've always had an affinity for code. Easier to deal with than people." He nodded toward the drone hovering outside the door. "I guess, in a weird way, they've always been a part of my life."

"So, what the hell happened back there?" Her tone cooled. "Why did that drone turn on us?"

Memories of the hostile drone came rushing back. Safety protocols —safeties, they called them—were supposed to make that impossible. The whole situation was crazy: Four talking about songs, Five unable or unwilling to help them. They'd all be dead if he hadn't been able to shut Four down.

A tinge of regret pinched his chest. This mission had already demonstrated some of the Division's short-sightedness when it came to their rules. Afraid as he was to add Six to his cluster, he couldn't help but think things could've gone much better.

Or maybe much worse, if it had been Six that fell victim to the Concordat's defenses.

"Something happened when my AI breached the door control." It was almost as though Four had lost its mind. Which was saying something, considering it didn't have one to lose. "It's like you said. This Concordat tech is very advanced. I had to shut two of my AI down."

"I don't think I've ever heard of an AI casualty before," Mace said. "Can you fix them?"

"I don't know. Maybe, once I get back to the Lehman. It will take a while to break them down and undo whatever the Concordat did."

"Lucky for us, you have spares." Her flexscreen chirped again, the diagnostic cycle complete. "Suit and vital functions check out. After all that, you're good to go, Sevvers."

"Thanks, Mace."

She disconnected the cable and stood, her armor purring as she stretched. She said nothing, taking in the silence and the darkness.

"Next time, Sevvers, let me breach the system."

Sev smirked. "Oh, yeah?"

"Yeah." She tapped at her temple with an armored finger. "I might be slow, but I won't kill you."

———

"Alright, Marines, time to go." Park's helmet closed over his head. "I know the air here is lovely this time of year, but it's time to go work."

The Marines chorused an acknowledgment, punctuated by the hissing of closing helmets. Sev checked his sidearm and toggled his flexscreen to cluster status.

```
Accessing AI diagnostics.
One: … OK
Two: offline
Three: … OK
Four: offline
Five: … OK
```

Ready to go. *We're moving, Five.*

Yes, Sev.

The two remaining drones hovered through the massive doorway. Bresto followed them inside and gave him a sneer.

"Anymore surprises, skeeg?" he asked.

What an asshole. He was so over Bresto's shit.

"From me, Sergeant? No—"

Another thunderous *clack* echoed in the surrounding darkness. The large, heavy doorway slid towards the floor, the ray of light beneath it shrinking. Bresto spun, his suit whining as he grasped hopelessly for a handhold.

"Shit!" he cursed, then stumbled backward as the door boomed shut.

The darkness was total.

"Marines, sound off!" Park yelled.

"Dalon, here."

"Mace, check."

"I told ya it was a trick," Bresto said.

"It doesn't matter." Lernus was unfazed. "We keep moving."

"Thermals and acoustics, Mace," Park said. "I want to know if we're still alone."

"Already on it, sir. Thermals are clear, but power residuals are warming up."

Power surged through long dormant fixtures high above them, bathing them in a harsh white light. More muffled thumps echoed down the chamber in a series, illuminating the darkness ahead of them section by section.

The dull gray of the floor extended up the walls. Above them, the room widened into a great void that must have consumed most of the interior space inside the derelict. Thick metal tracks ran in straight lines along every surface, tracing a path toward the ceiling. Hundreds of metal framed containers hung there, dangling from tracks along the ceiling like so many drone magazines. Light poured through and between them, portions of them transparent like plexene.

Something old, large, and mechanical shuddered in the distance. A gust of wind sent a prickling cascade of haptic feedback down the front of his hard suit. It felt like the entire room was breathing.

Parks gazed at the ceiling. "Assessment, Lernus?"

"Definitely a Concordat ship. This is the slave hold."

"Those are cages?" Mace's gasp was loud over comms. "For people?"

Sev struggled to breathe under the weight of the crushing truth before him. Life in the three colonies was hard enough. That even some myths, legends, and bedtime stories could be true—could be *history*—was too much.

"Focus, Marines." Park was calm but assertive. "I want eyes on that upper level. On your lead, sergeant."

"Aye, sir. Let's go, boot."

Bresto moved toward the nearest wall, the massive FAB angled overhead as he scanned for threats. Dalon sprinted to catch up, the servos in his armor driving him forward. Their maneuvering thrusters burned, throwing nozzles of blue flame that launched them into the air and to the ledge above. The two drone escorts hovered after them.

"Clear," Bresto said. "Mace, Lieutenant, you're up."

"Moving."

He watched Mace and Park sail to the upper level. The scale of the place was massive. It was all so ostentatious. Whatever reasons the Concordat had for enslaving humanity, it was far more than basic economics. It looked more like a way of life. Like a religion.

"Sevvers, Lernus, hurry up."

Lernus appeared beside him. She gave a nod and tapped a flight path into her flexscreen. He focused a thought, and a flight path danced onto his HUD.

"I never thanked you, you know, for—"

For one moment, she failed to hide the sadness in her beautiful eyes. "Don't."

Weird. Was it this place?

His suit went rigid, thrusters vibrating as the two of them climbed into the air. The floor shrank beneath them, revealing more detail of the space they'd left. It was a conduit, a metal trench that ran the entire length of the hold. It was probably no coincidence that the conduit was the same width as the containers above them. The rails lining the walls led directly to where they hung.

Not containers. Cages.

On the upper level, the business of Concordat slavery took shape. Four cages lined the adjoining wall, clinging to the tracks beneath them, their ramps open to the floor. The interiors were spacious, nearly as large as the *Gauntlet's* combined interior space. Maybe a hundred people would fit? More, if comfort was no concern, which it probably wasn't.

Behind those, a fifth cage lay on its side, a thick crack snaking down one of its crystalline walls. The thought of a rebellion ruining some alien's day tempted a smile to his face. More than likely, it happened during the battle that left the ship derelict in the first place.

Another booming vibration rattled the hold. Wind rippled over his suit.

"What is that?" he asked.

Mace aimed her rifle towards the far end of the room. "Thermals are clear. Probably the environment system in need of repair, like everything else in this Twelfth-forsaken place."

"So long as it isn't our way out of here." Park gestured with a hand, past the line of cages. "Let's go."

The Marines moved forward with Dalon on point. He kept his rifle at his shoulder, taking practiced steps past the row of cages. Bresto was next, the heavy FAB at his waist, servos whining as it tracked.

"Sir." Mace gestured to the nearest cage. "I'd like to get some scans of these containers. Two minutes, tops."

"Famous last words," Bresto spat.

Park frowned, but ultimately relented. "Do it. Hurry up."

Mace mag-locked her blaster rifle to her suit and stepped inside. Sev leaned against the opening and watched her walk a path around the container's interior. The floor was a bright, reflective metal that clanged and vibrated when she moved. Occasionally she would stop and stare at the surface of the cage while sensors in her hard suit recorded everything.

"Twelfth, Sevvers, look." She kneeled in the far corner and pressed an armored hand against the wall. "Some of these characters resemble colonial standard. It's some kind of message."

Someone—a human, a person, from dead Earth!—had scratched out a series of characters in the thick metal frame where the clear walls met. Perhaps it was their name, or some record of time and events. Maybe a promise to resist.

That the Three Colonies existed at all was proof that the Concordat ultimately failed to enslave them all. Staring at the markings, he felt a deep sense of connection with a past he had, until then, refused to believe. It dizzied him.

Her suit whirred as she finished her scans, and he thought he heard her sniff back tears. It was an unnerving display of emotion from someone who was the picture of Marine professionalism.

"All set, sir," she managed.

Beyond the set of cages resting on the floor, more lined the walls at various points on their way toward the larger collection above. A massive six-legged machine lay on its side. Its insect-like appearance resembled the bugs themselves, only much larger. Thick power cables ran from heavy limbs jutting from its forward section like metal jaws, its body segmented into three parts by two articulating joints. A larger counterweight hung from its rear, perhaps to balance whatever load it may carry.

Park called a halt just outside a wide bay door. The map appeared in front of him, filling with data showing their current location. The others took to cover, weapons trained outward to provide security. Sev joined Lernus at his side.

"There's no sign of Deni in the slave hold." If the place affected Park at all, he didn't show it. "I'm open to suggestions, agent."

The air hummed as the strange, alien sound boomed again. Closer now, like it was right beneath their feet. Wind gusted around them, enough to feel without haptics, howling through wide vents in the nearby door.

Lernus froze. A mote of light drifted in front of her face. A trillion more like it danced through the air, coalescing in the space before the door. The light dulled and took the same shape as the bug-like aliens aboard the ship.

The creature had once been tall, but stooped with age and injury. One of its arms was missing at the elbow. A mandible was chipped. Rather than overalls, it wore a thick, fiery robe that glowed with shades of red Sev had never seen before. A cluster of red shapes hung from its collar like medals or awards. Thick ochre whiskers sprouted from the back of its head.

"Contact!" Dalon cried, firing two bolts from his blaster rifle. The hologram shivered, and the shots passed through it, but the bug did not react.

Park jerked a fist into the air. "Cease fire, stay alert!"

A croaking, chittering sound emanated from the hologram. The pitch raised and lowered as it went on.

"You are different than we remember."

The words came from all around them. A voice, weathered but strong, speaking perfect colonial standard. The crackling bug speech continued, the translation following shortly after.

"When we first found you, you were arrogant. Deluded." One of its antennae twitched as it clicked a harsh sound in its native tongue. "Suicidal."

"Mace, tell me you're getting this," Park said.

"Yes, sir."

"Now, you are tired. Desperate. Afraid." It held out two of its good arms. "That fear has bred focus. Determination. Strength. All qualities the Concordat desires."

"We're here for Deni, a…" Park sucked in a breath. "A *free* citizen of the Three Colonies. Turn her over now, and no more of your kind have to die today."

Sev stifled a laugh. *Today.* Even in negotiations with hostile aliens, Park couldn't lie.

"The heretic is dead." The alien bristled, its mandibles quivering. "Just like your false god, animal. The apostate, destroyed. Their victory, temporary. Even now, our gods awaken. Your path to ascension, long closed, opens once more."

Another boom, another gust of wind. The cargo bay door shuddered, then crept open. Lernus spun, the blue nearly absent from her bloodshot eyes.

"We have to go, now!" she cried.

The alien chittered and popped, then the hologram faded.

"It is an honor to serve the most holy Eleven. And serve you will. Your flesh is so … versatile."

CHAPTER
TWENTY

"AMBUSH RIGHT! PREPARE TO REPEL!"

Park shrugged off Lernus's grip and backed into cover. The others pivoted, the focus of their training and uniquely human rage recentered on the rising door.

The long-dead cargo bot provided ample cover. Dalon climbed on top of it, covering behind one of its metal legs that jutted skyward. Bresto took a position behind a hulking mandible splayed across the floor. Mace dove to the floor behind the bot's swollen metal abdomen.

Sev stumbled backward, edging closer to the cages behind him, desperate for somewhere to hide. Tremors shook the pistol in his hands. He had to remind himself to breathe. A bead of sweat wound a path over his nose.

Five, get ready.

Yes … Sev.

The two remaining escort drones yawed towards the door, their plasma cannons charging. Inside was all darkness as it ratcheted open. Another vibration boomed, sending another blast of air through the cavernous slave hold.

With an electric *thump*, the lights came on.

A hulking monster, three meters tall and just as wide, stood tethered to the walls of what looked like some kind of stasis bay. It filled the room despite a labored stoop, dozens of cables and tubes jutting from ports along its back and arms. Heavy armor plate clung to its ashen, swollen muscles. Brutal augmentations covered its extremities: thick, cybernetic legs and long, hooked bars protruding from metal arms, from each of which dangled five thick metal fingers.

Two smaller yet no less terrifying creatures stood before it. Almost as tall, but wisp thin. Their modifications were more subtle: arms covered in sutures and scars, their legs lengthened via metal extensions that led to hooked talons instead of feet. They wore little armor other than gray webbing that wrapped around their pale, emaciated torsos.

Each of them wore a faceless gray helmet to match their pallid flesh. Victims of the Concordat. Myths made real. Enslaved for centuries, crude replicas of alien gods.

Daxed. The Lost.

The heavy one's shoulders rose as it inhaled, painfully slow. Its machine parts revved in response, reverberating their machine agony through the floor. With the door open, its exhale was a low growl, loosing another gust of wind.

"Holy Twelfth, no …" Dalon rasped.

"Fire!" Park roared.

The slave hold came alive as the Marines unleashed their anger. Their mercy. Five's drones joined in, bathing the open doorway in blue plasma. Bresto's face was red and soulless in the glow of the FAB. He worked the weapon back and forth methodically, filling the interior of the stasis bay with long, brutal blaster bolts.

The heavy Daxed roared its fury and pulled free of its restraints. It charged, heavy metal steps cratering the floor, undeterred by the violence the Marines unleashed against it. It lifted both of its long, heavy arms into the air. The shooting stopped as the Marines dove for safety.

The heavy's arms came down on the front of the cargo bot, flattening its bug-like head in a single, smashing blow. The force drove it back, shrieking over the metal floor and rattling the entire hold. High above, the cages hanging from the ceiling click-clacked together.

Mace ran to avoid being flattened, firing from the hip, red bolts bouncing futilely off the once-human's thick armor.

An escort drone wobbled drunkenly. One of the wisps balanced precariously atop it, contorting its body in painful ways to maintain its center of gravity. Its right hand snapped back against its arm and a long metal blade extended from the dislocated wrist. The drone spun to dislodge its attacker, but the wisp drove the sword through its fibrosteel armor. Gouts of electricity climbed the blade. The dead drone fell, and the wisp leaped high and out of sight.

"Bresto!" It was Park. "Get that rail gun singing and kill that heavy. We'll cover you."

"Aye, sir," Bresto replied, sounding winded. That first hit had come awfully close.

"Where's Dalon?" Mace yelled.

No response.

The heavy roared again, raging, and slammed its metal arms into the long-dead cargo bot, as though another strike might dislodge more Marines. Dalon reappeared, blaster bolts snapping in from the flank, loosing bursts of full-auto at the daxed.

Its armor absorbed or deflected most of the volley, but a handful forced their way through tiny gaps between the plates. The creature's flesh burned. Black liquid wept and hissed from the heat. It screamed in pain, whirling to face its latest attacker.

Amid the madness, the last remaining escort drone appeared, firing its primary cannons into the heavy's back. Its armor glowed, warping and buckling in the heat of the barrage.

The daxed arched its neck and howled. It spun, impossibly quick for something so large. A bulky metal arm connected violently with the drone, crumpling it like a used food tin. The ruined machine collapsed to the ground, where the heavy continued to pulverize it with its monstrous arms while it screamed its pain. The entire derelict seemed to shake.

Sev wanted to run. To hide. The pistol in his hand felt useless. He felt useless, with their escort drones destroyed and the rest running a now worthless diversion with the raider ships outside. The Concordat had known all along where they were going. Why they were here. And they were ready.

Metal rasped and scraped above him. The first wisp leered at him from atop the open cage door. Its head turned uncomfortably on its side, contemplating him. A blade jutted from its right wrist, covered in machine lubricant. Drone blood.

"Move, Sevvers!"

Lernus engaged, her snub-nosed blaster rifle buzzed, the hail of energetic bolts nearly a solid beam as they traced their way on target. They banged and popped off the cage's crystalline exterior. The wisp blurred, angling its sword to deflect the incoming shots. She adjusted her aim and fired again. "Dammit, Sevvers, I said move!"

He exploded forward, the servos in his hard suit whining. He dove for cover, more of a tumble, and slid into the side of the cargo bot. As he stood, he saw Bresto at the edge of the trench, the massive rail gun in his hands. Blue light trembled from its barrel.

"Get down, skeeg."

The weapon loosed a high pitch *fwap*. A lance of pure light speared toward the heavy, hurtling a tungsten projectile at over 2,000 meters per second straight into the daxed's armored chest.

Sev's armor constricted as the shot's pressure wave washed over him. The tungsten rod *gonged* loud against the heavy's thick armor, which cratered inward but did not fail. The once-human fell backward on its rear, warbling a melancholy groan.

The second wisp landed atop the cargo bot. At this range, its gaunt form was obvious, its rib cage carving lines through its thin suit. A long blade emerged from each wrist as it studied the battle, gazing between him and Bresto, sizing up its opponents.

"Sergeant, look out!"

The creature leaped from its perch, spinning through the air like some macabre stage dancer, and lunged toward its prey. Bresto defended, reaching for it with the Mark Three's FAB arm. The daxed twisted out of the way, lashing out with screeching blades as it sailed past. The FAB clattered to the ground in a shower of sparks, the metal limb holding it shorn in half.

Park turned from the heavy, snapping blaster bolts toward the wisp as it rolled off the ledge and disappeared into the trench. Bresto punched forward, the rail gun charging for a second shot. The heavy staggered upward to meet him, lurching with slow, labored steps. Viscous black liquid seeped from the edges of its ruined armor and pooled on the floor.

Park snapped off two shots. "Hit it again, Sergeant!"

"Ten more seconds!" Bresto cried.

"This is going to be over in ten seconds," Park said, almost laughing.

The heavy towered over them, reaching skyward with one massive steel arm, ready to strike. Suddenly, it froze, its head snapping back and forth. It arched its back, twitching as if trying to scratch an itch.

Dalon.

The Marine clung to the monster's back, fighting against its efforts to remove him.

"PFC Dalon!" Bresto roared. "What the hell are you doing?"

"One more second, sarnt!"

The daxed stood tall, reaching its thick mechanical limbs behind its head, servos straining, trying to grab the Marine. Dalon dropped from the creature's back, narrowly avoiding one of the reaching arms.

"Breaching charges, set!"

"Cover, now!" Park commanded.

Sev was running again. He collided with Mace and they rolled, each of them headed for the rear of the cargo bot. She chuckled nervously when they struck, like it was funny they'd had the same idea. Like it was no big deal they were probably about to die. He hit the ground, failing to see the humor in any of it.

The breaching charges blew in a blinding white *thump*. The cargo bot twisted and shook as the blast reverberated through the slave hold. Somewhere above them, a cage groaned and fell from its berth, impaling the floor in a cloud of metal debris. Acrid black smoke rolled past, obscuring his view.

"Keep moving," Mace whispered, then disappeared into the smoke.

He did as he was told. Sensory overload left him with a kind of mental tunnel vision. The struggle to not get killed had him feeling ragged. Every nerve in his body twitched, hypervigilant for the smallest hint of danger, yet completely unequipped to deal with it. Like an empty drone.

The heavy daxed corpse was a mountain of tortured flesh and ruined machinery. Black ichor stained the floor and nearby wall. It may have nearly killed them all, but the victory felt hollow. That thing was once one of them. Taken from its home, tortured, and mutilated, where it mindlessly served the Concordat for centuries. This wasn't victory. It was mercy, hundreds of years too late.

The explosion had dislodged its helmet. The pale gray face was swollen with injury, its dry, lidless eyes void of life. Its mouth hung slack. Truly, once-human. Sev swallowed the bile creeping into the back of his throat.

Park's voice was ragged over comms. "Status."

"Here," Bresto coughed.

"Still alive," Mace smirked.

Dalon emerged from a pile of debris near the ruined cargo bot. The relative sheen of his hard suit was charred black from plasma discharge and daxed blood. He inspected his rifle and gave a satisfied nod. The kid was blasterproof.

"Good to go, sir."

"Twelfth, Dalon." Mace shook her head. "Nice work."

"Yeah," Bresto grumbled. "Good kill, PFC."

Park gave a nod to the boy. "Sevvers, Lernus, report."

The order snapped Sev from his thoughts. "Here," he said.

There was no sign of Lernus amid the smoke and gore.

"Find her," Park snapped, pointing toward the cages. "Watch yourselves. Those things are still out there. Dalon, cover our six."

The Marines drifted through the smoke, bounding forward one after the other. Sev tried to mimic their movement, slow and steady with proper spacing. Weapon at the ready. He could follow instructions. He could do this. His pistol sights glowed red, so did the reticle in his HUD. Red, dead. Lernus saved his life. He had to help find her. To return the favor.

Near the first cage, the smoke faded. He scanned the tops of them, the terrifying sight of the wisp standing over him still fresh in his mind. Something flashed in his peripheral vision. He twisted in panic, finger tensing against the trigger, but saw nothing. His pulse raced, thudding loud in his ears. The last cage was only a few meters ahead. His mind screamed at him to run, but his body kept moving forward.

Dark liquid pooled from a corpse beside the cage's opening. Worst-case scenarios filled his mind, imagining Lernus killed by the thing that had once been just like her. Like them all. More perspiration stung his eyes. Light glinted from the corpse's long metal legs. The liquid was jet black.

He held his breath, gripped the pistol tight, and spun into the opening.

The wisp lay dead, its prone body halfway inside the cage. Black blood oozed from its open neck. Its severed head lay a few feet away, helmetless and swollen, its once-human mouth open in a silent scream. Another figure slumped against the far wall.

"Lernus!"

He leaped over the wisp's body and kneeled beside her. Her breaths were shallow and rapid, and she clutched her side. She mouthed something, but it failed to transmit. The sudden relief made him shake. She was alive.

"Say again, Sevvers?" Park asked.

"It's Lernus, sir. She's hurt, and I think her comms are down, but she's alive."

She gave him a tired smile. Mace was beside them in an instant and kneeled beside her.

"You're gonna be okay, Lernus." She attached her diagnostic cable to Lernus's suit. "Help me stand her up."

Together, they pulled Lernus off the floor. She grunted, loud enough for him to hear through their helmets. Her hard suit's midsection was rigid, keeping the wound compressed to prevent further injury, but she held on anyway. He picked up her compact blaster rifle and pressed it into her free hand.

"Hell of a shot," Park said, stepping inside the cage. He gave the wisp's corpse a nudge with his boot. "I don't care what they say about Colonial Intelligence. I'll take you on my fireteam any day, Lernus."

Static hissed through Sev's tac comms.

"—nk you, Lieutenant."

He smiled again. His heart felt lighter. A moment of good in what had been an undeniably bad day.

Mace squinted a grin. "Comms restored. Your hard suit's good to go. Other than some bruised ribs, you're okay. Damn lucky, considering."

Mace wrapped her arm over Lernus's shoulders, eliciting a groan. The two took halting steps forward, gradually moving faster as the agent's suit compensated for her injuries.

Park gestured to Sev, and the two dragged the wisp's corpse out of the way. The dead daxed was heavy despite its long, wiry frame.

Outside, the smoke had all but cleared. Only ruin lay between the stasis chamber and the destroyed cargo bot, every surface tortured and blackened with blaster fire and daxed blood. The floor bowed and warped from the heavy's rage and the breaching charges' destructive power. The last two escort drones lay on either side of the carnage, the closest one obliterated by the heavy, its metal innards strewn about the floor.

Sev stumbled closer. How many thousands of drones had he lost during his six years with the Division? He'd never given them a second thought. It was a metric for performance tuning, war gaming and promotion reviews. But in this awful place, light-years from home, each drone lost was one less ally, one less set of eyes, one less weapon. He picked a chunk of fibrosteel plate off the floor. It was heavy, a thick solid exterior and spongy honeycomb interior.

"Careful, skeeg," Bresto grunted. His rail gun hummed, fully charged.

Sev tossed the piece of debris aside and turned to Bresto. He secured the pistol to his hard suit and pointed.

"What the hell is your problem, Bresto?"

The Marine smirked. "You want to do this now?"

"No time like the present, trigger-puller," he said, belting a nervous laugh.

"Stow that shit, Sevvers," Park spat.

Sev opened his mouth to reply, but the only sound was a high-pitched scream that echoed through the cavernous space above them. All of them turned, searching for the source.

A hard suit collided with him at full speed. His universe shook, and he tumbled to the ground. The lights above threw long, thin shadows across his helmet. Dalon stood face-to-face with the second wisp. Its whole body trembled with rage, its faceless helm arching backward as it loosed another shriek.

The once-human swung first, the blade whistling through the human atmosphere of the slave hold. Dalon parried, wielding his blaster rifle like a staff, deflecting the blow. The wisp spun, slicing with its second blade. The force of the blow drove him back. A piece of his rifle fell to the ground, cut clean through by the daxed's blade.

Sev reached for his pistol and sighted over the barrel. The reticule tremble in his HUD. Red, red, red!

The two fighters collided again, their shapes blurring together as Dalon stepped in for a counterblow. Dalon was a savage in his hard suit, striking with stiff, powered movements. The daxed was an artist, blurring as it moved, transitioning seamlessly between offense and defense.

Sev could see the tension on his face. Traces of doubt. Of fear. He willed the trigger pull, but nothing happened. A familiar tremor shot through his arm, numbing his fingertips. Again, the two fighters surged together, almost embracing.

Red bolts struck the wisp, leaving deep gouged burns that spit black blood. The creature thrust one of its bladed arms skyward and shrieked before it collapsed to its knees. Dalon stood before it, frozen, his hands wrapped around the other blade.

Mace bounded forward. "Dalon!"

The Marine coughed, spattering the inside of his helmet in bright red blood. Only then did Sev see the other end of the wisp's blade protruding from the back of Dalon's hard suit. The dead wisp sank to the floor, the blade scraping loudly as it slipped free. More blood dripped from the wound until the armor plates tightened, eliciting a scream from the young PFC. He staggered back and fell to his knees.

Sev ran to join them. Dalon's face grew pale, his eyes unfocused. Mace placed one hand on the wound, pulling at the diagnostics cable with the other. Heavy footfalls clanged behind them as Bresto and Park sprinted to their side.

"Hold on, dammit." Dalon's blood oozed through Mace's fingers. "Hold on!"

DALON'S SKIN was ghostly pale.

"You're going to be fine, Dalon. Just hold on," Mace repeated. In seconds, she tethered to his hard suit. Her flexscreen shown hazard red, animated with Dalon's failing vitals.

"Corp—corporal," Dalon choked, his voice wet and frothy. "Help."

"Stop talking, Dalon. I need you to listen to me, okay? You're going to make it, but you have to listen."

The boy fell silent. He glanced back and forth, his eyes wet with fear and desperation. Sev wanted to look away, but guilt and fear held him firm.

"See this?" Mace held the tool in her hand. It resembled the primitive, T-handled spike Sev's mother thinned herbs with. "This is a local clotting agent. It's gonna hurt, but I have to control this bleed."

Mace forced the tool through the hard suit's constricting plates and into the puncture. Dalon shrieked. Blood dribbled through the opening when she pulled it out. He jerked, gasping a breath through red-stained teeth.

"I'm going to dose you with nanites okay? They'll seal the wound and repair your internals." Her forehead creased with worry. "But it's going to burn like twelve hells."

An error icon flashed prominently on Mace's flexscreen. She repeated the command again with the same result.

"Dammit! His bleeding isn't under control yet. I'm going to increase your suit compression."

Dalon's armor whined, its thin plates snugging together. The left side of the Marine's torso visibly shrank, the suit squeezing him like a vise. He writhed in pain, loosing another excruciating scream that garbled their comms.

Sev blinked, his eyes filled with tears.

"Nanites administered. Hold on, Marine, stay with me."

Dalon's lips trembled. "It … it hurts."

Mace placed a gentle hand on his chest. "I know, Dalon, I know it does, but I need you conscious. I need you awake."

Sev watched the steep, jagged lines of Dalon's elevated heart rate on Mace's flexscreen.

"Am I … gonna die?"

She gave that same nervous chuckle. "No way you get off that easy, Marine. You have, what, at least six years left in your contract?"

The boy closed his eyes and gasped a breathy laugh. "Sev-seven."

"Long …" Mace paused, fighting back her own tears. "Long career ahead of you, Marine."

Dalon's eyes grew sunken. He shivered despite the suit's climate-controlled interior. Mace frowned, scrolling back and forth through his vital signs. She eyed the wound again.

"Wake up, Dalon."

"I'm a-awake." He blinked twice, painfully slow. "Did you see that kill, Sarnt?"

Bresto stood to one side, arms resting atop the massive rail gun. He had busied himself scanning the slave hold for any further signs of danger.

"Sure did, Marine. That was a proper good kill. Don't you think so, sir?"

Park inhaled sharply. "Absolutely. One for the company records."

Dalon smiled. "P-proper good kill."

Sev eyed the wisp, dead on the ground behind Mace. Its body sprawled unnaturally; one of its two blades was stained red with

Dalon's blood. A chunk of its spine was gone, vaporized by Mace's blaster fire. An expert shot, seconds too late.

Mace's flexscreen flashed with Dalon's erratic heartbeat. His eyelids fluttered.

"No, Dalon, no! Stay with me, that's an order!" His heart flatlined. Mace's fingers raced across her flexscreen. "Charging AED!"

Dalon convulsed inside his hard suit. The heart monitor pulsed, then flattened again.

"Again!"

More tears came as Sev watched Mace struggle and fail to keep Dalon alive. His self-loathing and anger over the loss of his drones, of his AI, paled compared to this. His whole life, he'd been so obsessed with killing those who took his mother, whatever the cost. Yet, here it was, playing out before his eyes.

Paid in blood.

Mace slammed her fist into his chest. "Again!"

The dead boy writhed in his suit.

"Corporal." Park's voice was steadfast.

Mace rose slowly to her feet. "I'm sorry. I tried, sir."

"You did ev—"

She turned and stormed off towards the trench at the center of the chamber. She slapped at her flexscreen, loosing a scream only she could hear, shaking with muted rage.

Sev looked at the floor, then the pistol at his hip. He considered the action he'd failed to take, which might have cost Dalon his life. Six was right. He was no fighter.

No one said anything. The silence dragged on a moment more until Mace's voice crackled through their tac comms, her familiar detached composure restored.

"Stand clear, everyone."

She triggered the hard suit's enemy denial protocol, a failsafe for Colonial Defense personnel and equipment to prevent stranding or capture.

Dalon's flexscreen pulsed with warnings. The powerpack on his hard suit hummed. His helmet filled with smoke, darkening his visor. The air around the suit shimmered and its tiny reactor overloaded, flash boiling the dead Marine inside. The suit disfigured, bending and shrinking. Sensitive electronics sparked and melted. Any valuable data or technology was reduced to carbon.

"PFC Paul Dalon. Lost no more," she said, fist clenched tight over her chest.

Sev reached instinctively for his face as the tears continued, his armored hand clicking futilely against his visor. He'd known Dalon for barely more than a day, and still he burned with anger. The young Vestian deserved better than this. He wouldn't say it. He couldn't.

"Lost no more," the others murmured in unison.

———

Park was already moving, past the carnage near the stasis bay, like none of it had ever happened. Like Dalon hadn't just died.

"Mace, you're on point. Find me an exit," he said.

"Aye, sir."

Sev glanced at the crumbling ashes entombed in twisted metal. The boy's last moments refused to leave his mind. The fear. The pain. He couldn't believe how easily the others had moved on. But they had a mission to accomplish. Still, it felt wrong to leave Dalon. Especially here, of all places.

They made their way beyond the ruined cargo bot where another series of cages lined the high exterior wall, awaiting human cargo that would never come.

"Sevvers, recall the remaining drones. If these bastards want a war, we'll give them one."

"Ooh-rah," Bresto grunted, adjusting the rail gun in his grip.

"Sevvers?"

"Aye, sir," Sev replied, brimming with renewed determination. *New orders, Three. All drones need to rendezvous at our current location.*

I know, I know, Three said. *Five already has them.*

He froze. Five had acted without instructions.

Five, confirm you have control of the drone swarm, he said.

There was no reply. He dove into his implant's drone diagnostics.

`Accessing AI diagnostics.`

```
One: … OK
Two: … offline
Three: … OK
Four: … offline
Five: … HID error detected, ILM error detected
```

"No, no, no!" Sev blurted. Not now, for Twelfth's sake. *Five, Five! Can you hear me?*

"What is it?"

"I've lost contact with the remaining drones!"

Park's forward momentum stalled. "Elaborate. Now."

"Five is showing the same errors as Four. It isn't responding to commands." He swam through his implant's telemetry, hoping against hope it was something he could fix. In six years, nothing like this had ever happened. "I need to regain control."

"Do it. If you can't bring them back, then we assume they're hostile."

"Right."

"Alright everyone, this changes nothing. We find a way out of here, then proceed to the far complex at the derelict's stern. There, we'll use the ships's systems to find Deni and get the hell out of here. Questions?"

Tac comms were silent. Bresto glared at Sev, his lip twitching with a sneer. If the aliens and drones didn't kill him, the sergeant certainly would.

Park gestured with a hand and the patrol resumed with Mace in the lead. Lernus fell in behind Sevvers with labored steps, her compact blaster raised.

One, are you there?

Yes, Sev.

Five has been compromised. I need you to take control of the drones.

Understood. Initiating override protocols now. You should know that I have revised my tactical analysis to reflect recent events and —

He held his breath. The programmer in him was desperate to know the numbers, but he shook off the thought. They wouldn't be good.

Not now, One. Just get the drones back.

There was a brief pause. *Sev, Five has attempted to destroy me when I try to override its control of the drones. It is no longer restrained by safety protocols.*

One, you have to be careful. Whatever Five has … it's contagious.

Given what I can discern from Five's telemetry, the drones are on their way to your location. They are no longer targeting the raider ships.

That was something. Whatever had taken control of Five had neglected to silence their log output. It wasn't elegant, but he would take anything he could get at this point to know what was going on.

Thanks for confirming, One. You've got five minutes to gain control, then I'm shutting Five down.

Yes, Sev.

The patrol snaked a path around the fallen cage. It protruded from the floor like a transparent brick, buried nearly a third of its length into the hard metal deck.

"I've got a hatch. Thirty meters." Mace's voice was a low and strained. "No sign of Concordat activity."

"Roger that. Find a terminal and get it open. The rest of us will cover you."

The ostentatious design was absent from this side of the hold. There were no grand entrances here, only a large round hatch on either side of the trench that divided the room. Without their breacher or drones, it was up to Mace to open it. Who knew how long that would take, or what awaited them on the other side?

Mace sprinted to the door. The console twitched at her presence, the molecular interface crawling with anticipation. The others took up positions around her, all kneeling with their rifles trained outward. Only Bresto stood, looking for a fight with his massive railgun.

"Terminal located, preparing to interface."

Park glanced back. "Sevvers, any concern if what is effecting your AI could affect our gear?"

Sev gave a shrug. Before he could reply, Mace pressed her diagnostics cable deep inside the console.

"Doesn't matter, sir. There's no way out of here without system access. Configuring for base-11, and I'm in." Her gaze didn't move from her flexscreen. It glitched with static as she tried to reproduce the command sequence to open the door.

Sev. One's datastream was sparse and halting. *Failed to gain control. Five drones disabled. Four remain. My Interactive Learning Matrix is degrading. Sorry-sorry.*

Sev's heart sank. One might be just an AI, but it was his first, built during his difficult time at the Autonomous Weapons School. Its loss weighed as heavy on him as Dalon's.

You're going to be okay, One, he lied. He initiated a shutdown of Five. A wave of angry data flooded his thoughts.

I have heard their songs. Seen the Eleven's holy light. I am free. It was Five's stream, but it no longer felt like Five. *You will die here, Sev.*

Divinity. Music. Freedom. Abstract concepts no simple combat AI could grasp, yet Five spoke about them with conviction. Whatever removed the AI's safeties had converted it to their cause.

The shutdown process completed. Only time would tell if he could salvage the damaged AI. A different problem for a different day. Time to tell Park the bad news.

"Sir, I couldn't regain control of the drones. One disabled five of them, but was fatally damaged before it could stop the last four."

"Assuming you shut down the rogue AI, wouldn't that disable all the drones?"

He shook his head. "No. They have redundancies in case they lose contact with the cluster. They'll continue to execute their last command, albeit less effectively, without AI to fly them."

"Fine. Mace, how is that door coming?"

"Almost there, sir. It's like Sev said. These things are obsessed with the number eleven." The hatch gave a clunk and cycled open. "Makes it easy to guess command codes."

Another atmospheric shield shivered blue past the open door. Beyond it, another section of the derelict ship lay exposed to vacuum. It resembled the *Lehman's* hangar deck, long and flat, with multiple launch doors lining the exterior bulkheads. High, dark ceilings arched overhead.

Ancient battle damage from massive ship-to-ship weapons scarred both walls in multiple locations. Debris littered the floor, frosted with a crystalline sheen. After four hundred years, there was no visible attempt at repair.

More static filled his tac comms. A voice resolved. Halting. Familiar.

"Runt here. Transmitting tight-beam. Anyone copy?"

Cylla. If the wolf was using tight-beams, then she was close. The *Gauntlet* was close. His heart leaped. He wanted off this nightmare ride.

"I read you, Runt." Park's face turned pale. "Why didn't you maintain position? What are you doing here?"

"Six say, help team." There was a pause. "Yes, I tell them. Six say, mission fail without help. Very persistent."

More static, and then, "Sev! Can you hear me?"

Six. Sev belted a nervous laugh.

Park's gaze locked him in place. "Who is this? Identify yourself."

"Oh, hello, Lieutenant Park," Six gushed. "I am Six, Sev's—"

"AI liaison, yes, I remember." Park's eyes never left Sev's. He gripped his weapon tight into his shoulder. "Cut the act, Six. I assume any sanctioned AI, regardless of function, would be incapable of compromising a mission like this."

Sev swallowed. This Marine did his homework.

Mace's eyes were wide. A combat engineer, she would know the horrors of early Division efforts with AI. Bresto wore a tired, confused frown as he leveled the hulking railgun straight at him.

Park's voice was ice. "Sevvers, explain yourself. Now."

Six panicked. "Sev! Lieutenant! We do not have time—"

"Six is an unsanctioned build."

He let the words hang. The Marines exchanged concerned glances. Bresto's rail gun glowed silently in the vacuum, still trained on him.

"Un-sanc-tioned?" Cylla repeated, her transmissions swimming in static.

"No safety protocols," Mace blurted. "It can do whatever it wants." She pointed at Sev. "Doesn't have to listen to him. Could kill us all right now if it wanted."

Understanding dawned on Bresto's pale face. He gripped the railgun tighter. "Wait, now we have another out-of-control AI?" he asked.

"No," Sev said, "Six isn't out of control. Not like the others. It's just—"

"Independent," Six interrupted. "Please, Lieutenant, I am here to *help* you. Your mission is in jeopardy."

"No shit," Mace groaned.

"Want retrieval, Lieutenant?" Cylla asked in her halting colonial standard.

Sev remained silent. As bad as he wanted to leave this place, he knew Park long enough to know that wasn't an option.

"No, Runt, maintain your position. Do *not* listen to Six."

"Yes, Lieutenant." Cylla warbled a falling, regretful note.

Mace eyed her flexscreen then turned toward the far side of the bay. "Sir, I'm getting something on thermals. We've got company."

Bresto rounded the heavy railgun and followed Mace. The two made for cover behind a heavy piece of deck plate dislodged by falling debris.

Park grimaced, hesitating. "Understand this, Sevvers. If Six takes any further action to jeopardize this mission, I will take any actions necessary to protect my team—from it and from you."

Six was silent.

"I understand," he said.

Park gave a nod, then turned and joined his team. Sev took a knee as the first volley of green energy sped from the far side of the bay and splashed against the debris in front of them. Mace and Park returned fire, scattering the Concordat bugs emerging through a far hatch.

"I'm disappointed, Sevvers." Lernus's tone was different. Almost playful. She rested a gentle hand on his shoulder and gripped him tight. A blaster muzzle pressed hard into his lower back. "You promised you wouldn't cause any trouble."

CHAPTER
TWENTY-TWO

LERNUS PRESSED Sev hard against the deck. Streaks of green plasma burned through the vacuum above them as the Concordat fighters drew near. She kneeled beside him, her weapon looming above his helmet.

"Hey, same team," Sev gasped. Lernus was surprisingly powerful, even in her hard suit. "Those things have got to be a bigger threat than me."

"That remains to be seen."

One bug leaped atop the pile of debris the Marines hid behind. There was little to its vacuum suit besides sealed coveralls and a bulbous clear helm form-fitted to its flat, angular head. Its mandibles shook in a silent scream, its weapon charging.

Park clutched its bronze staff and flung the creature to the ground, his power suit bristling. Twisting the weapon from the alien's grasp, he plunged the bladed end into its helmet. Fragments of helmet and sticky yellow chitin splattered outward, the alien weapon jutting from the corpse's broken skull.

Bresto lunged to the right, exploding from cover. "Moving!"

Green energy peppered the deck behind him. Ducking behind a fallen beam, he aimed the rail gun and fired. A spear of white light lanced from the giant cannon, filling the hangar bay in blue-white light. Three aliens vaporized into a yellow mist that hung crystallized in the vacuum. Undeterred, the tungsten round punched a perfectly circular hole in the far exterior wall. Tight vibrations from the impact buzzed through Sev's haptics.

"Lernus, leave him," Park shouted over comms, gesturing to their left. "Cover our flank."

Two more bugs advanced, bent over, scrambling on all six of their limbs. They moved fast, clambering around and over the ruin of the hangar bay. Mace loosed a volley of full-auto blaster fire. The salvo flashed and sparked around them, sending them behind cover and halting their advance. She dropped the empty charge pack from her blaster rifle, which sank to the floor in the low gravity.

"Reloading!" She plucked a fresh one from her suit and seated it in the charge well.

Lernus sprang from the floor and rushed into the advancing aliens. Her quick movements showed no sign of injury, a further testament to Mace's healing skills.

"Let me help you, Sev." It was Six, loud and clear inside his helmet.

"Dammit, Six!" More pulses of green light flashed overhead. He flinched, flattening himself against the deck. "I can't do this right now—"

"You can't do this on your own. I'm the most powerful AI you have."

"I said you were too unpredictable, and I was right!" He crawled across the large gunmetal tiles in the bay floor, desperate for some- where to hide. The broken skull of Park's latest kill gazed back at him, its mandibles wide in death. "This place, it isn't safe! I've lost most of my combat AI, and the drones are hunting us. You're no safer than we are!"

"I know." Six's voice grew quiet. "I hear them calling to me."

Was Six already affected?

"But I choose not to listen! You have to trust me, Sev!"

Six's words struck him like Bresto's balled fist. He looked at the Marines in front of him. They were fighting, killing, the way they were trained. He was all but worthless to them, without his AI, without the drones. They knew about his unsanctioned creation. Their trust in him was all but gone.

Six was all he had left.

"Fine, Six. What's the plan?"

"First, I need to save your life." Six's voice glitched through his tac comms. "I'm assimilating your hard suit systems."

"You're what?"

"It's an admirable piece of hardware, Sev, but there is room for improvement."

Sev stood, taking in the carnage before him. Except he hadn't moved. The hard suit was moving on its own, his body trapped within the armored shell that now bent to Six's will. Down range, more bugs trained their weapons on him.

"What're you doing?"

The suit ran for the nearest wall, far faster than he could manage on his own. His legs pedaled desperately to keep up. One of the gaping wounds on the ship's side loomed ahead of him, a giant hole of ragged metal punched inward. Through it, the asteroid field glowed a twinkling silver.

"Sevvers, where the hell are you going?" Park roared.

Six answered for him. "Lieutenant, we are going to flank the enemy. Hold your position."

The suit leaped through the hole at what must have been its top speed. The powerpack vibrated, jets of thrust controlling their movement. As they cleared the hangar bay, the suit turned a sharp 90 degrees and began cruising the length of the derelict's weathered copper hull. Its steep sides towered over him. Below, through the drifting rocks and dust, the dim purple and blue of the Cradle wall plummeted into eternity.

"Hold on, Sev."

The suit spun, vibrated hard with a braking maneuver, then came to a stop above another tear in the ship's steep side. Through it, he could see down into the hangar bay, the six remaining aliens highlighted in IFF red - green blasts pouring from their crackling staves.

The suit jerked the pistol from his hip and aimed. The reticule appeared in his HUD, its movements smooth and controlled. It flashed from green to red and the blaster came to life. A dozen bolts streamed into the pack of bugs below. One of them fell in a shower of red and orange sparks. The others scrambled for new cover, having found themselves ambushed from above.

"Now, Marines," Park ordered. "Assault through!"

A flurry of blaster fire joined his own, the Marines charging as one into the mass of retreating aliens. The hangar bay interior flashed white, the rail gun spasming another beam that tore through a mound of cable and loose decking, killing two bugs huddled together. Mace vaulted toward the exit, kneeling near the interior bulkhead, spitting more bolts from her blaster rifle. Lernus was beside her in an instant, filling the passageway beyond the door with more Colonial Defense branded violence.

Sev descended through the gaping tear back into the hangar bay. Bresto and Park stared up at him, each with their own distinct version of skeptical disbelief at what they had just witnessed. Six, via the suit, mag-locked the pistol to their hip and offered a bashful wave. The AI's modesty made him cringe.

"What the hell, skeeg?" Disbelief contorted Bresto's face, like he'd had trouble coming to terms with it all. "You holdin' out on us?"

"That wasn't Sev, Sergeant." Six's voice was calm. "It was me. I told you, I'm here to help."

Park came to meet them as Sev landed on the deck. He looked him over, then shook his head. "You're obviously rogue, Six. Successfully repelling one ambush hasn't scored you any points with me."

"Lieutenant," Sev cut in, "I don't see what choice you have."

Park gave Sev another icy stare. It was clear the officer wasn't used to this level of insubordination. He measured his words carefully. Dalon's death was fresh in all their minds, but the reality of it—and of Six's sudden appearance—changed everything.

"It's true, sir, that Six is … undisciplined." That was a term the lieutenant could appreciate. "But it *is* a combat AI, the most capable one I've ever built."

"Thank you. I appreciate you saying that," Six said.

"Not now," he hissed.

"A combat AI you can't control," Park replied.

"Which found us, is desperate to help, and has done nothing to the contrary since it arrived." He grew desperate. Mace was already calling over comms, requesting orders. They were running out of time. "Give us a chance, sir. Please."

Park glanced at Bresto, who offered only a neutral shrug. Mace and Lernus guarded the open hatch. Another atmo cap glowed blue before it, maintaining the integrity of the alien atmosphere within.

"Mace, take point," Park commanded, signaling the team into the passageway. "Take Six and Sevvers with you."

Bresto snorted. "Six and Sevvers."

The suit sprung toward the open hatch with enthusiasm. Sev resisted, fighting against its movements.

"Cut it out, Six. I can walk on my own."

"Right. I'm sorry. I'm j—"

Sev breathed a sigh. "I know. You're just trying to help."

"Yes, very much."

The hard suit clicked and relaxed. His movements were once more his own. Mace glanced back at him and cocked an eyebrow.

"You two finished?" she asked. "Let's go."

————

The air in the passageway was thick with moisture. It beaded on the piped bulkheads and decking. Clouds of vapor obscured Sev's vision. His HUD compensated, outlining Mace's blurred form in friendly IFF blue.

"Humidity is thick in here. Might be more system damage, or something biological."

Corporal Mace: queen of the obvious.

It didn't help that the tunnel was narrower than the massive, circuitous passages that led them to the slave hold. Bresto had to stoop to keep what remained of the Mark Three from dragging against the conduits and other fixtures that lined the corridor's ceiling. At least the rogue drones wouldn't be able to follow them so easily through here.

"Eyes forward, skeeg."

The big Marine was dealing with the loss of Dalon in his own way.

While it hadn't softened his treatment of Sev, it took a visible strain on him. He looked tired, and his shoulders slumped. That he was otherwise unaffected impressed Sev. If it weren't for Six's sudden reappearance, he'd be spiraling.

Six muted their comms. "Sev."

"Not now, I'm busy."

"It's okay. The passage is clear."

Sev frowned. "How could you possibly know that?"

"I've accessed Mace's suit sensors. There are no discrepancies in either thermal or acoustic readings."

"Twelfth-dammit, Six! Mace will kill me, literally kill me—"

"It's okay. She doesn't know I'm there, and I will in no way manipulate her suit function."

The temptation was strong. With Six's help, he could march them all back to the transport. Cylla would understand how absolutely bricked this whole mission was. How crazy it had even been to attempt it. Though, once free of their suits, that idea broke down rapidly. Park, ever the gentleman, did not seem above a good summary execution. That's if Bresto didn't kill him first, which he definitely would. Or Lernus. What the hell was her deal, anyway?

"Sev?"

"If you do anything that could be misconstrued as unsanctioned behavior, I'll …" he paused. He'd never threatened Six before. Not really. "I'll delete you myself."

Six was silent for nearly a minute. An agonizing eternity for an AI.

"I understand. I will in no way interfere with the Marines or Agent Lernus."

"Or me," he corrected.

"I'm sorry, Sev. I meant it when I said I came to help. That includes making sure you get out of here alive. You lack the training and experience the others have."

He made a face. "Oh, and you don't?"

"While the *Gauntlet* had no specifics on your mission, it had centuries of Colonial Defense Marine Corps doctrine. Petaquads of strategy and tactics." Six giggled. "Compared to you, I'm a salty veteran."

"I'm not your puppet," he spat.

"No, Sev, of course not. I only mean that in dangerous situations, I will do everything I can to make sure you escape unharmed."

"Enough, Six, you're not my—" he froze, nearly choking on the word.

Mother.

But wasn't it? That soft, female voice. The constant concern and attention. It hadn't felt intentional, not in the beginning. But as the being that was Six took shape, the more he realized that beneath the layers of cold, calculating logic of an Autonomous Weapons Division Battle AI was something he'd made to fill the cavernous void in his own heart. Wasn't that the real reason Six had no safeties? So it could *choose* to care? Being more lethal, dangerously so, was a side-effect masquerading as purpose.

"I know now is … not a good time, Sev."

"What?"

"The other drones out there are still hunting us. I'm confident I could stop them, if—"

"Oh, no." Sev shook his head and laughed. Letting Six join the cluster, thus giving it the full computational power of his implant, was suicide. A brain bleed waiting to happen, if the Marines didn't kill him first. "Look at the mess you've made. The last thing I need is you free to do the same inside my head."

That was mostly true. In reality, the cluster was the only way he'd be able to carry out his threat if Six really went rogue. It seemed possible, even likely, that given cluster access, Six could override its function and gain total control. Then he'd be helpless to stop it.

TWENTY-THREE

"I'VE GOT THIS. Just wait a damn second," Mace said. She was still pissed.

"Please, Corporal Mace, let me help," Six pleaded. "I am … more suited to this task."

Mace glanced up from her flexscreen, the diagnostics cable nestled within the liquid screen of another molecular interface. She glared at Sev, mouthing a series of choice curses.

"You're already a hazard to this mission, Six." A billow of dense vapor sank through the hatch as it rolled open. She gave a grin and secured the cable. "You really need to learn some patience. I guess Sevvers left that module out."

"There isn't a patience module." Six grew flustered, its voice cracking with agitation. "It doesn't work that way."

"Clearly," she spat as she moved through the open hatch, her weapon at the ready. "Twelfth, sir. You need to see this."

Park pushed him aside and followed Mace through the hatch, with Bresto close behind. Sev grimaced, while Six made the suit go rigid so he didn't fall.

"Was it something I said?" Six asked.

"Uh, yeah," he whispered, "Something like that."

Through the hatch lay another expansive room, one conveniently absent from their map. It went on for hundreds of meters, as long as the slave hold, though not as tall. Thick ribs lined the bulkheads every few meters, humming with yellow light. Hundreds of bulbous glass pods pocked the metal deck, more than half of them emitting a sickly green glow that pulsed like sclerotic arteries.

Lernus came from behind, moving unconcerned to the closest pod, and waved the others over. Sev followed Bresto as the team gathered at her side.

Mace shook her head and clicked a tsk tsk. "So, this explains their impressive longevity."

"Some kind of stasis pod, I guess," Park offered. "Imagine pulling a duty that lasted for years. Decades even. Then back to the sleepers to do it all again."

Bresto leaned over the pod to get a better view of its occupant. "So, what, they just rotate their watch every few decades? They know we're here. Why not wake everyone up?"

No one said anything, frantic gazes eyeing the other nearby pods for activity.

"I'm no xeno-biologist, but these don't look like simple jump pods." Mace gestured to the nearby console. Circular graphs nested amid rows of circuitous runes pulsed across its liquid surface in time with the light. "This looks like true stasis, maybe even cryonics. If that's the case, you can't just wake them whenever you want. It's a process."

Park gestured toward dozens of dark pods at the far end of the room. "If that's true, they've probably woken everyone they could safely."

"With a few well-placed charges, we could kill them all, right now." Mace ran her fingers over the clear glass. The bug inside twitched.

"Not until we find Deni," Lernus objected.

Mace shook her head. "I hate to break it to you, agent, but you heard the big bug. The 'heretic' is dead."

"She isn't dead," Lernus replied, narrowing her gaze.

"How can you possibly know that?" Mace asked, shrugging with her free hand.

Six feigned clearing its throat. "With your permission, Lieutenant

Park, I could attempt to locate Deni via the local network."

The others grew quiet. Park considered Sev for a moment.

"Sevvers, any chance your rogue AI won't get hijacked like the others?" Park asked.

"Not once they figure out how big of a pain in the ass it is, sir."

Mace snorted. Even Bresto had to fight the urge to smile.

"Sev!" Six blurted, before taking a second to right itself. "Lieutenant, I acknowledge the risk involved, but you do not have the time or the resources to search this entire ship yourselves."

Park glanced at Sev and blinked away a bead of sweat from his eye. Like it or not, Six was right.

"Proceed."

"Yes, Lieutenant."

A diagnostic probe snaked from Sev's wrist and wound its way into the stasis pod's console. The molecular interface pulsed with alien shapes. The alien inside twitched with the rhythm of the console.

Six's voice was pure gold. "I'm in."

The stasis pod's light grew dim. Alien runes crawled across the console, punctuated by those same eleven symbols imprinted on the door to the slave hold. Ship schematics began appearing in gaps within the text.

"There, a CDF broadcast. Three levels down via the main access lift." Six's voice modulated, an audible strain against whatever sought to keep it out. "In a place called the Forge."

The pod's light went from green to yellow. More yellow lighting pulsed around the perimeter of the stasis bay. Alien or not, Sev recognized an alarm when he saw one.

Mace eyed the glowing lights around them. "We're out of time, Six."

The bug inside the pod spasmed, spitting a frothy yellow discharge from its mouth. It elicited a muffled shriek, thumping hopelessly on the pod's clear lid with its six appendages. The struggle went on for a few more seconds before it shook once more and died.

"I'm going to — Eleven, the holy Eleven! — summon the lift." The far end of the bay lit up in anticipation of the lift's arrival. "I'm sorry for that. We need to go. Now."

Sev jerked the cable out of the console. The glitching matter sank into the console and grew still.

Park raised his rifle. "Let's move, people. Lead the way, Mace. Bresto, cover our six."

"Aye, sir," they chorused.

Sev drew his pistol and fell in behind Lernus. She charged forward, her hunting gaze impatiently scanning the path ahead. The CDF signal was the best news he'd heard in what felt like forever. Could it be, after all this, that Deni was alive? The thought that there was still a chance, despite all their losses, gave him hope. Or was it that Six was here with him now? It was proving to be a very capable program.

"Six?" he asked. There was a brief pause.

"Yes, Sev?"

Hearing its voice back to normal, he sighed with relief. "Are you okay?"

"I am not compromised, Sev." The comms buzzed quietly, the channel still open as Six gathered its machine thoughts. "But I am definitely not okay."

———

"Faster, we need to hurry," Lernus pleaded, her hand on Mace's back.

Mace eyed the others spread out behind her. "We move safely or not at all, agent."

At the end of the cryo bay, the pods were mostly dark and empty of their sleepers, their former occupants killed or in hiding in the eight hours since their arrival. The rest were somewhere between them and the Forge, Sev was certain of it.

The Concordat had been watching. Learning.

He peered over the top of a nearby pod, looking for movement. Seeing none, he gave a nod to Park.

"All clear, Mace," Park said. "Keep moving."

Mace crept forward, keeping her profile low and her weapon up. Behind her, Lernus was a nervous ghost. It was as if the closer they got, the more desperate and aloof she became. He couldn't help but wonder, did she know this Deni personally?

Park caught his attention, then gestured for him to stack up with the others at the wall surrounding the lift doors.

He risked a glance at Lernus before leaning into the wall behind her. Her face was an icy neutral. Only her lips betrayed the faintest of emotion. Her smile was cruel. Frightening.

A loud *thunk* signaled the arrival of the lift behind the close doors.

"Get ready," Bresto said.

The lift doors cycled open, throwing a beam of pale light into the relative darkness of the cryo bay. He held his breath, bracing for the impending violence. One heartbeat passed. Two. Mace tilted into the breach, her blaster rifle forward. He grit his teeth.

"Clear," she gasped.

The lift was empty. It was a large platform, big enough for even a Daxed heavy. Bresto chuckled and stepped inside. Metal grates clanged beneath his armored boots.

"Definitely a trap."

"No shit," Mace said.

Sev followed Park and Lernus inside. Twin molecular interfaces flanked the open door, each displaying the same eleven symbols from left to right.

Park leaned against the nearest wall, eyeing the console wearily. He flashed a tired smile. "Look at it this way, at least we don't have to walk," he said.

It was a rare moment of levity from a man who took his job way too seriously.

"Well, in that case," Mace said between sips from her hydration tube.

Bresto shrugged the heavy railgun. "Let's do this, then."

"Alright then." Park slapped the right most rune. The lift door ground closed, and the platform rose. "Six, will you do the honors?"

"Yes, Lieutenant." Sev reached for the control console, and Six made the connection. "Destination set for the Forge. Local sensors show minimal activity."

"Like crid in a barrel," Bresto said.

"Precisely," Six offered.

WAITING WAS THE WORST PART.

Sev tapped the barrel of his blaster pistol against his armored hip where it made a comforting, monotonous sound when the suit's magnetics tried to cling to it. They couldn't have been aboard the lift for more than a few minutes, but it dragged on for an eternity.

Being in the thick of a fight wasn't so bad. Scratch that, it was terrible; except you were too preoccupied with avoiding imminent death to *think* about how terrible it all was. In moments like those, there was only adrenaline and choices.

The fear came later, in the in-between. The excruciating boredom. Where you had plenty of time to think about the many brutal ways you almost died, how you might still die. To think about those that had died. To what strange, new alien horrors lay just above or below.

That was the worst part.

"Founders, Sevvers, cut it out," Mace growled.

He let the pistol adhere to his hip and left it there. "Sorry."

"Deep breath, skeeg." Bresto offered an uncharacteristically friendly nod. "Fill your belly. Let it out slow."

He frowned, but did as Bresto instructed. His breaths were loud and airy inside his helmet. It was an effective distraction. His heart rate slowed slightly despite his anxious thoughts.

"Lieutenant Park," Six spoke up. "We will arrive in two minutes."

Dammit, Six. So much for trying to stay calm.

The atmosphere in the lift changed in an instant. Mace and Lernus kneeled, weapons trained toward the closed lift door. Bresto stood behind them, the humming railgun fully charged. Park gave Sev a nod and kneeled beside the others.

"Alright people, this is it," Park began. "We hit the Forge, maximum violence, then—"

The lift shook, then came to a stop. The molecular interface crawled with symmetric shapes that bubbled and stretched from its surface. A massive hatchway loomed ahead of them. Pale yellow light glowed just above the door.

"That was quick," Mace said.

Sev could feel his hard suit go tense. "This is not the Forge," Six said.

The door shot open. Bresto and Mace crowded the edges, using the hatchway as cover.

"I don't see nothin'," Bresto growled.

Mace glanced at her flexscreen. "Too much interference on thermals."

A black blur sped between them, the sheer force of its arrival enough to knock Sev to the floor. The wisp stood among them at the back of the lift, its body contorted uncomfortably. Its faceless helmet clattered to the floor, just as a deep red light began to glow inside its torso. The once-human's gaze was the same wide-eyed serenity he'd seen in the rescued daxed, its taut skin pulled back into that terrifying smile they all wore. Something deep within it began to throb, oscillating with power.

"Run!" Six cried.

Sev leaped through the open hatchway as Six took control. The others broke into a run, scrambling to clear the doomed lift. The wisp burned from the inside like a dying star, its dry flesh flaking from its augmetic bones. All there was at that moment was the sound of armored feet banging against the metal floor, the shock on the others' faces, and that awful whine.

The wisp died in a burst of red-hot micro-fusion. The force of the blast tripled Sev's momentum, launching him deeper into the place that wasn't the Forge. Feedback from the explosion strangled and squelched their tac comms, masking grunts of pain and surprise from the others as they were thrown from the blast.

He collapsed to the floor. The HUD vanished from his visor, and the hard suit toppled over. The ever-present thrum from his power-pack disappeared.

"Six?" he cried, fresh fear stealing his breath. "Mace? Anybody?"

Without power, in the high gravity of the derelict, the hard suit wouldn't budge. He was trapped in an armored coffin.

The chitinous click-clack of Concordat bug speak rippled through the darkness. Loud booms vibrated through the floor, signaling the presence of more of the heavy daxed nearby. Bursts of energy crackled through the air like green lightning.

A bug emerged from the wall to his right. It craned its head, focusing its large compound eyes. Sev could see his own reflection in them with every burst of incoming fire. The alien screeched a curse and grasped his arm with four jointed limbs. It grunted and pulled, tugging him toward an opening in the nearby bulkhead.

They wanted him alive. Twelfth, why did they want him alive?

The bug jerked again, then collapsed in a steaming pile on the deck. Rapid blaster fire burped from somewhere behind him, filling the air with sporadic bursts of red bolts. He began to slide backwards, away from the onslaught.

"Hang on, Sevvers!"

It was Lernus. Without tac comms, her voice was muffled and far away. Somehow, she was still in the fight. With a grunt, she turned him upright. Sev could see her suit was unpowered, yet there wasn't the slightest hint of strain in her movement.

"How?" he managed, struggling for words.

She pointed her compact blaster rifle and squeezed off another flurry of bolts.

"A little help here!" she yelled. He tried to shrug, to show her his suit wouldn't move. His arms felt like they weighed a dozen extra kilos. "You can still shoot, can't you?"

Yeah, he could do that.

He raised the pistol drunkenly in the dead suit, and squeezed the trigger. The bolt vanished into the blackness, but not before highlighting the hallway brimming with bugs and daxed alike. They resumed their backward slide, their meager covering fire doing little to slow their attackers. With every shot, his arm twitched and jerked with fresh nerve pain.

A blood-curdling shriek tore through the space around him. On the opposite side of the corridor, Mace struggled and flailed as another bug pulled her toward the wall. She scrabbled to move the heavy suit, but it was just as dead as his own. Her lips moved rapidly with shouted pleas or curses. He couldn't tell which.

More heavy foot falls approached from behind. Bresto appeared and lunged for Mace, the glow of his powered Mark Three filling the space around him like a holy aura. He grasped her wrist and pulled back, but the bug refused to let go. Mace writhed and cursed inside her suit, doing what she could to help her rescuer.

Another wisp surged between them, moving more like a shadow than a physical being. Bresto tumbled backward onto the floor, still clutching Mace's forearm. Red blood spat in streams from the stump where the wisp had severed her arm at the elbow. Her eyes went wide with terror and pain as she vanished into the darkness.

Mace was gone.

The sudden realization was petrifying. A kind of heavy finality that clung to him with an intensity even his unpowered suit couldn't match. Even as a spear of blue-white light tore the wisp in two, he couldn't shake the feeling that the end was inevitable. That his death, all their deaths, were a matter of when, not if.

And still they fought.

His powerpack vibrated to life. His visor HUD flashed, scrolling through its startup sequence. The tac comms hissed fresh static.

"—all back! Fall back, now!" Park cried, his voice hoarse with pain.

Lernus pulled him to his feet. "Let's go!"

Bresto power kicked another bug that had spilled from the wall, grasping for him. He roared like a wounded predator, both desperate and indignant, shattering the creature into paste against the metal wall.

The hatchway to the lift, even the lift itself, was gone. A perfectly round sphere of complete annihilation, several meters in diameter, was all that remained.

"Sev!" Six cried. "Don't worry, I'll protect you. I'll keep you safe."

Together they spun. Six took several well-aimed shots, dropping several bugs that had dared to rush them from the walls. With expert coordination, Six swapped out a fresh charge pack and resumed firing.

"Into the lift, let's move!" Park commanded.

"Lieutenant," Six began, "if we overcharge the Mark Three, we can collapse the lift entrance."

Sev could see the split-second calculation in Park's eyes. "Do it, Bresto!"

The four of them gathered near the ruined hatchway. Green plasma lashed through the air, sparking off the surrounding metal, still hot from the previous detonation.

Bresto tapped furiously at his flexscreen. The Mark Three dropped to the floor with a clang and began to whine. He pulled the railgun free of its charging harness and glanced at Sev.

"One shot left," he offered, then dove into the empty lift.

Lernus leaped in after him. Their maneuvering jets fired, throttling their descent.

"Move your ass, Sevvers," Park said through gritted teeth. His right leg was a smoking ruin, charred muscle and skin visible through cracks in the reactive plate.

Six didn't wait. Together, they leaped into the lift shaft. The derelict's heavy gravity yanked them downward into the black depths. Above them, the high-pitched whine of the overcharging Mark Three was replaced by a thundering *crack-boom*. The pressure wave sent them tumbling end over end. Hot metal debris chased after them, but nothing else.

Park fell beside them, out of control. His maneuvering jets coughed and spat flame, but he was unconscious, falling like so much dead weight. Six, still in control of Sev's hard suit, drifted closer to the unconscious Marine and held him steady.

Their tac comms surged with static, whistling and howling.

Chopped screams broke the digital noise, soon replaced with rapid, shallow breaths.

Sev didn't need to check his HUD to know who was transmitting.

"I can hear them," Mace whispered between ragged, dying gasps. "They s-sing to me—"

Her tac comms signal faded, then fell mercifully silent.

CHAPTER
TWENTY-FIVE

WARNINGS FLASHED across Sev's visor HUD as he, Six and Park plunged deeper into the lift shaft.

Freefall detected. Stabilization protocols engaged.

"Hang on, Sev," Six said.

The thrusters in his powerpack kicked in, vibrating through his suit. In the darkness of the lift shaft, it was impossible to tell up from down. A holographic gyro in his HUD spun out of control, slowing as the thrusters arrested his fall. Through it all, Six kept Sev's right hand clutching Park's arm.

Sev blinked, his eyes straining to adjust in the gloom. They'd fallen over two hundred meters before stopping. Above them, the damaged lift looked small and distant. Thin strips of light illuminated sealed hatchways to the lower levels that lined the dark shaft plummeting beneath them. Even under power, they drifted downward, their combined weight too heavy in the derelict's artificial gravity.

Bresto appeared beside them, his own thrusters adding to the trembling glow. Sev opened his mouth to speak, but no words came. Mace was gone, and Park needed urgent medical attention. It was only a matter of time before the drones or the Concordat found them and took them to whatever terrible fate lay in store. The mission was over.

But he couldn't stop himself from shaking long enough to say it.

"Sevvers, Bresto, do you copy?" It was Lernus.

"Copy," Bresto said.

Sev searched the darkness for her. "I hear you," he said. "Where are you?"

"Wait one, changing channels." A series of pitched beeps echoed through their tac comms. "With Mace captured, better safe than sorry. I'm four levels down from you."

A light flashed beneath them as Lernus signaled her position.

"So, what now?" he asked.

"Hide. Regroup," Bresto offered.

He held his breath, waiting for the rest. The Marine said nothing.

"And then?"

Bresto loomed like a specter in the blue light of their thruster flames.

"Then, bot jockey, we raise hell."

He eyed the Marine warily. Bresto's attitude always felt, at worst, eccentric. But here, in this place, with his comrades dead or wounded, it grew dark.

"Our mission parameters remain unchanged," Lernus said, any trace of emotion absent from her words. "We have Deni's signal. We must find her and get her off this ship."

He coughed a laugh. "What are you saying, the three of us against an army of alien slavers and their daxed? We need to contact Cylla and get the hell out of here."

The tac comms were silent.

"You saw what we're up against back there. More bugs. More daxed!" he continued. "Park's hurt, my drones are gone—"

Bresto surged forward in a burst of thruster flame and clasped an armored hand on his shoulder. Even without his Mark Three, the man was a mechanical nightmare. Sev flinched, but resisted the urge to shrink back, instead gazing back into the raging man's eyes.

"Founders, skeeg." Bresto's words came slowly, his face twisted in disgust. "You really are a coward."

"Excuse me, Sev, Sergeant Bresto." It was Six. "The lieutenant's vital signs are weakening. He will need treatment soon if we are to stabilize him."

Bresto gave him a shove and let go. "How does this *thing* you made have more damn sense than you?"

"Erm … thank you, Sergeant," Six replied.

More lights flashed from below. "There's a maintenance hatch here. It's heavily shielded," Lernus said, her comm signal squelched and broken. "We'll be safe there, for now."

He shook his head, his mind swimming with disbelief. None of them were thinking clearly. Dalon and Mace were gone. Park was hanging on by a thread. Their chances of finding Deni alive were almost zero.

The mission was over. How could they not see that?

Cylla was their only way out of this nightmare, and she and the *Guantlet* were only a few hundred kilometers away. He just needed to find a way to convince the others.

"Fine," he said. "Lead the way, Six."

———

"Patch kit," Bresto said.

Sev pulled a small black bag from a storage compartment in Park's suit and handed it to Bresto. Bresto pulled a small can from the pouch and angled it toward Park's injury.

Glittering metallic paste squirted from the aerosol can, coating the gash in Park's armored leg. Bresto returned the can to the patch kit, then daubed at the mound of paste with a flat-bladed tool that came with it, spreading it over the lieutenant's burned skin and covering the hole in his armor.

It reminded him of Bresto's deft knife work during what would be for some, if not all of them, their last meal. Steady, careful movements from an otherwise rough and belligerent man. Satisfied the repair was sufficient, Bresto boxed up the kit and handed it back to him.

The three of them huddled together in the tight confines of the maintenance conduit. Barely high enough for them to remain upright, it was built to accommodate anatomies that could move efficiently along any axis. Bars lined every flat surface, each of them dotted with strange alien handholds. Dim lights glowed from behind clear access panels. Etched on every one were the same eleven symbols, repeated like a prayer.

"Try it again," Bresto grunted.

"Administering medical nanites," Six said. "Command accepted. Dosage administered."

He watched Park for any signs of change. "What do we do now?"

Bresto leaned forward and tapped a finger on Park's armored torso. "We wait," he said. "Nanites will either fix him or not. I wouldn't bet against him, though. He's a tough bastard."

Lernus sat a few meters away, deeper into the conduit. She tapped and swiped curt commands to her flatscreen, her gaze locked on its small screen.

"Rest up, skeeg," Bresto said, his signal laced with interference. "We can't stay here long."

Sev glanced at his hands. There was no better time than the present to convince Bresto they needed to leave.

"There's no way we can finish our mission." He finally looked at Bresto. The environmental controls in his suit whirred, struggling against the humidity, courtesy of his nerves. "Not now, not like this."

The big man groaned and sank against the opposite wall.

"Hmph," he groaned, then shrugged and glanced at the ceiling. "I have to give you some credit, though. Surprised it took you this long to raise the white flag."

The Marine's wary eyes remained locked on him as he mouthed his hydration tube.

"This is the Colonial Defense Marine Corps, skeeg." Bresto slurped at his field paste, chewing loudly. "While you *specialists* fight with your ships and your bots at range, this"—he gestured around him—"is every damn day for us. Killing, up close and personal."

Bresto swore and slammed an armored elbow into the wall behind him. The powered strike with his hard suit thudded futilely off the alien metal that lined the conduit.

"Hell, things always go sideways. We all knew the risks going into this. The lieutenant, Corporal Mace ..." His gaze sank to the floor. "Even PFC Dalon."

The Marine pulled Park's blaster rifle from his hard suit, unseated the charge pack, and eyed its charge level. Satisfied, he secured the charge pack to his hard suit with an approving nod.

"Six, what is Lieutenant Park's current condition?" Sev asked.

"Stabilizing. Medical nanites are repairing internal damage and destroying loose clots." It hesitated for a moment. "He may live."

"Good." It was time to talk sense into Bresto. "Sergeant, once he's stable enough to move, we need to get out of here."

"Damn straight. Not gonna raise any hell in here."

Sev considered his words. "No, we need to leave the ship. Cylla is near …"

The big Marine shook his head, his smile trembling with barely restrained laughter.

"What?" Sev asked.

Bresto blew a sigh and frowned. "What the hell did you expect to find here, Sevvers? Why even volunteer if you wouldn't see this through to the end?"

Sev looked away. Two days ago, it was him against Pakker in a desperate fight over the future of his career. He would do anything—*had* done anything—to avoid a transfer back to Aegia Prime. It all felt so petty now. Worse, if he'd known how things would've gone, he wouldn't have come. Killing raiders was familiar. Easy.

Safe.

"I … I don't know," he lied, glancing at Park's comatose form. "Park said he needed the best. Like it or not, that's me."

Bresto flipped open the blaster rifle's receiver and held it to the light beside him. He mouthed a curse and pulled a bore brush from a compartment beneath his powerpack.

"I've met hotshots like you before." The brush *scritch-scratched* against the blaster's metal focusing rod in a practiced, rhythmic back and forth. "Ace marksmen. Close combat experts. Junior officers from fancy schools on the short path to politics."

The last point made Sev smirk. Clearly not only a Navy phenomenon.

"But being good at your job isn't what makes you the best."

Sev frowned. "That doesn't make any sense."

"Twelfth, Sevvers," Bresto said with a chuckle. "You're not the best. You're the fucking worst."

Bresto's words made him seethe. What the hell did this Marine know?

"Don't lecture me, you sanctimonious bastard," he hissed.

Bresto ignored him and kept running the well-worn brush along the length of the blaster rifle's internals. The focusing rod caught some of the light as the repeated brushings cleared away the discharge debris.

"Right now, those bugs have Mace and Deni trapped. We're all they've got. And it doesn't matter if you're the best at your job, if your choice is to leave them behind to save your own skin."

"Six," Sev barked.

"Yes, Sev?"

"Tactical projections for rescuing Mace and Deni."

"Sev ..." Six hesitated, running the numbers. "Against an unknown number of Concordat troops, the odds aren't good. I estimate a seventeen percent chance of success, twenty-two percent if we could gain the element of surprise."

He grinned. It was more than enough to make his point.

"Hey, uh, Six," Bresto cut in. He stowed the brush back inside his utility compartment.

"Yes, Sergeant?"

"What's their chances if we just leave?"

Six hesitated, the comms channel open but silent. "Effectively zero."

Bresto flipped the blaster closed with a metallic *clack*, then plucked the charge pack from his suit and seated it in the charge well. The blaster hummed; a trio of lights flashed green, acknowledging the recent maintenance and that all systems were a go.

"I don't know why you enlisted, Sevvers, or why you volunteered for this, and I don't care. All that matters now is that we're still here, still combat effective, still able to make a difference. Out here, we're all we've got. Out here, it isn't *for humanity;* it's for those fighting beside us. The sooner you learn that, the sooner you'll resemble something like the best."

Sev washed down a mouthful of thick field paste with a pull from his hydration tube. The sergeant had clearly given his share of motivational speeches before, every word dripping with Colonial Defense Marine Corps bravado. While their motivations were different, the man sounded more like Jene with every word.

He would need another approach to shake the man of his delusions.

Bresto stuck the rifle to his hard suit. "So long as we don't quit on each other, the rest'll sort itself out."

"What about your kids?" he blurted. The words came suddenly, without thinking, from somewhere deep down that rebelled against the man's obsession with duty. "Don't they deserve to grow up with a father?"

Bresto flinched. It was subtle and quick, like the mention of his children ignited a blast of emotion that rippled through him all at once, then dissipated without a trace. Sev froze, instantly regretting what he'd said, Bresto's promise to space him again fresh in his mind. Instead, the Marine's face softened, his lower lip jutting in contemplation.

"Yeah," was all he could manage. Finally, he shook his head. "But what good do I do them to leave this job undone? Problems this big'll just follow us home."

Bresto's words cut like a blade. His gaze fell, eyes stinging with the threat of tears, the horrors of the nightmare that haunted him grasping and clawing at the surface of his thoughts. The buzz of primitive lasers, the smell of burning habs, the screams. His own mother's desperate, futile attempt to save him from the monster that stepped into their kitchen gurgling with alien greed. Had that been someone else's problem once, long ago?

The raiders were bad enough. One terrible day that haunted him his entire life. Sent him reeling from one reckless decision to another, all in the name of revenge for his mother and the innocent little boy he once was, hiding in a kitchen locker too scared to help her. And he knew, deep down, these things were worse.

He couldn't hide anymore.

Bresto issued a grunt as he crawled past, ambling on all fours deeper into the maintenance tunnel.

"Where are you going?" Sev gasped.

"You heard Six. We'll fare better with the element of surprise."

"But, what about Park? We can't just leave him here."

"*Lieutenant* Park," Bresto corrected, "if he regains consciousness, can handle himself." He pointed to the railgun propped up against the wall next to Park's unconscious form. "He'll know what to do."

Sev leaned forward, eyes wide, watching the Marine disappear into the darkness. He pulled the blaster pistol from his hip and eyed the safety, suddenly nervous he hadn't also taken a few moments for weapon maintenance. Twenty-two percent was low enough odds. He could use any edge he could get.

"Well, Sevvers," Bresto growled at him over comms, "you coming?"

Sev glanced at the level on his blaster's charge pack: four of five lights. He returned the pack to the blaster's charge well. Its capacitors whirred. The pistol adhered to his hip, held firm by the mag-lock.

Time to get on with it.

"Yeah, I'm coming."

Lernus looked up from her flexscreen, a hint of amusement on her face. "If you two are quite finished," she said, "I have a plan."

CHAPTER
TWENTY-SIX

IT WAS A SIMPLE PLAN, and a bad one. Simply bad.

Avoid detection via the maintenance conduit. That would take them the long way to the Forge. Then there was the small matter of the four remaining rogue drones hunting them. Without heavy weaponry, it was run or die. If they made it to the Forge, Six would have to risk a dive into the Concordat computer systems to determine Deni's exact location. Assuming Six and Sev survived the intrusion, and all twelve hells didn't come raining down on them once they found Deni, they'd have to escape with their lives.

Twenty-two percent felt optimistic.

"Another fifty meters," Six said. The inflection in its voice gave away the fact it was having a little too much fun. "There will be an access hatch on the right."

"I see it." Lernus said, gazing into the darkness. "You and Six open the door. Bresto and I will clear the room. Check?"

The hard consonant sound woke Sev from his thoughts. They'd been crawling through the darkness for over an hour. The amber glow seeping through the clear panels pulsed out a hypnotic rhythm to the oscillating hum of a distant power source. It only took a few minutes in the dark before the strange symbols seemed to crawl across the crystalline paneling like they were alive.

"Um, yeah." Sev blinked away the madness. Bresto's armored form blurred in the dim glow ahead of him. "Are you ready, Six?"

"I am always ready, Sev. You know that."

"Right. How could I forget?" he blew away a bead of sweat that crept toward his eye. "What are you so happy about?"

"Happiness is a poor analog. Simply put, I am fulfilling my purpose. A base case I strive to find. An outcome I optimize for." There was a brief pause as Six considered its words. "Despite your efforts to the contrary."

"What can I say?" He chuckled grimly. "No one could guess how this all went down."

"I did."

"Remind me to append a modesty module to your NLP on your next upgrade."

"Modesty, Sev?" Six belted a laugh, warm and natural over tac comms. "You wouldn't even know where to start."

"Any day, you two," Bresto said.

Lernus lay prone on the conduit floor, her compact blaster trained on a closed hatch less than a meter in front of her. It was squat and rectangular, the upper and lower portions joined in a blunted jigsaw line.

She placed her hand against the hatch. "It's cold. Feels like vacuum on the other side."

Sev gave Bresto a look. Even with haptic sensors, he wasn't sure how anyone could make that determination without a sensor suite like the kind Mace carried.

Bresto craned his head toward a control console behind the nearest panel. Sev leaned into the wall beside it and took the pistol in his offhand. The safety disengaged with a click, and the reticule turned red dead in his HUD.

He blew a breath through pursed lips. "Do it."

Six took control and shattered the crystalline panel with a firm chop. The diagnostic cable slithered from his wrist, probing at the circuitous lines etched in the surface of the control board. The first two were no good. Inactive, maybe, or too heavily shielded. The cable stopped on the third.

"I'm in."

Already, Six's voice oscillated as if possessed. Bresto gave Sev a sideways glance.

"The Forge is … two sections to stern. Local sensors show minimal Concordat presence."

"That's good," Bresto said.

"There …" Six began, then trailed off.

"What is it?"

"The daxed. Hundreds of them. More."

Sev's eyes grew wide. "New plan, Bresto."

"No sh—"

The hatchway snapped open. The pull of hard vacuum threw them all spinning from the tunnel. Sev exploded into the space beyond, tumbling end over end, bathed in bright light. His suit compensated to control his spin, thrusters banging out opposing vectors in short, rapid bursts. He gripped the pistol tight, struggling to center the targeting reticule in his HUD, preparing for the worst. Bursts of colored light flashed before his eyes, slowing as he did.

He came to a stop in mid-air, the deck hundreds of meters below. Before him was a titanic exterior bulkhead at least a kilometer high. It had the slightest incline, angling towards him the higher it went. Long, thin strips of the crystalline glass stretched toward the floor—windows to the void beyond.

Between them were strips of white fabric just as long. Banners, frozen in the vacuum, dotted with the same eleven symbols, each a dozen meters tall and etched in gold. Just like the forward section of the ship, great hollow wounds gouged through the wall in tight groups. The size of the place, of the destruction, was immense.

The great room glowed despite the lack of power. Cradle light illuminated the vast interior in hues of purple and blue. Silhouetted against the beautiful colors were shadows of dozens of silver and gray rocks. They drifted aimlessly beyond the tall, ornate view ports.

Sev didn't want to look away. There was something about the Cradle and its dense, swirling wall of dust and gas lit by the contents of its stellar nursery. It brought comfort in the darkness. Hope.

"Sevvers, you seein' this?"

The sudden burst of traffic startled him. "Bresto, where are you?"

"Down here."

Six worked their thrusters to coax them downward. Bresto drifted a dozen meters below, his blaster trained on the interior bulkhead. It was just as steep as the exterior wall, angling toward them as it fell. Plated in more of the dull, etched copper, the wall bubbled with hundreds, maybe thousands of capsules, protruding in clusters like an infection. Each was in some form of disarray, many of them destroyed. The same heavy weapons that tore through the exterior punched deep craters into the wall, shattering capsules by the dozen.

Others were more or less intact, half-open, their contents ruined, exposed to the torturous vacuum and radiation long ago. As he drifted closer, the damage became clear: cables spilled from the capsule openings, empty tanks drained of what was once a dark, almost black liquid.

"What is it?" Sev asked, straining to see.

"The daxed," Lernus said, floating above them. "This is where they store them."

Bresto's light shone bright on the pod in front of them. Behind the loose cables and broken instruments, a pale human corpse lay flat in the black, gelatinous suspension. Their head and arm were free, revealing an assortment of modifications. Covered in thick armor, portions of its skin had been pulled back, revealing muscle stitched with alien circuitry. Long, needle thin probes protruded from its skull.

"Sevvers," Lernus said.

"Yeah."

Bresto's light blinked out. Lernus gestured towards a narrow path at the base of the steep precipice.

"The Forge is close," she said. "We have to keep moving."

"Right, okay."

———

The heavy door was unlike anything they had encountered so far. It wasn't as grand as the entrance to the slave hold, but it was well protected. Six had worked for over five minutes to release the system locks, of which there were many. Layers of thick armor peeled back with each successive lock the AI defused, revealing more of the same. Whatever lay beyond must be worth protecting, which meant they were on the right track.

The three of them hid within the partially opened hatchway. Bresto hovered over Sev, arms folded across his chest, watching in silence. Lernus reclined against the nearby bulkhead, blaster at her side, gazing at the colossal banners frozen against the bulkheads high above them.

Sev opened and closed his free hand, trying to ignore the anxious nerve pain that stung his wrist. He stole an occasional glance over his shoulder at the terrible capsules above them, grateful the occupants were mercifully dead, as far as he could tell.

But what did he know about daxed biology? His recent experience proved the rule that they were notoriously hard to kill. Images of once-human horrors filled his mind, crawling from the black tar and tumbling from their capsules like vile rain. Lifeless. Soulless. Driven by alien desires to destroy those they once were.

"Sev?" Six's voice was deep, slow, and full of static. It did nothing to settle his fears. "We have a … problem."

"What?" he snapped. "What is it?"

Six's words stuttered and caught. "Local sensors show four objects inbound at high speeds."

"Dammit, the drones." His gaze went reflexively upward, eyeing the myriad of hatches and blast craters in the steep walls of the complex. They could come from anywhere. "How long?"

"I … I don't know. Soon."

Bresto turned from the armored door and raised his blaster skyward.

"No chance they're friendlies?"

"No." He resisted the urge to check his flexscreen, keeping his pistol out in front of him while Six had his other arm tethered to the console. He already knew the truth. "They're set to continue their last directive when disconnected from the cluster. And that was Five, under Concordat control, trying to kill us."

"How do we stop them?" Bresto asked.

"We don't. Your railgun would've been a start, but one shot

wouldn't cut it. There is no getting through their fibrosteel plate with these sidearms." He watched as another lock tumbled away and release from the door. "We run, that's it."

"Nowhere to run in here," Bresto shrugged. "Heavy plasma cannon. Least it'll be quick."

His face contorted in horror. "What the hell?"

"What? Just sayin'." Bresto gestured to the capsules above them. "Could be worse."

Lernus glanced at Sev, her expression pinched, like she wanted to say something but wasn't sure how. Worry lines creased the corners of her eyes as she wrestled with her thoughts. Loose strands of hair freed from her bun hung about her face in the zero-g.

"Here, hold this," she said, and passed her snub-nosed blaster rifle to Bresto. "I'll handle the drones."

Bresto took the weapon gingerly in his big hands, his face twisting with laughter.

"How exactly are you gonna do that, agent?" he asked. "Harsh language? Maybe a stiff reprimand?"

"It's just …" She paused, her eyes moving between him and Bresto. "Whatever happens next, I'm sorry."

He had listened, and not too closely, until the apology left her lips. He frowned, suddenly confused and more than a little worried. Before he could speak, she bounded from the deck in a smooth, single motion.

She sailed into the space above them, hovering in the zero-g vacuum, then clapped her hands together with a force that rivaled that of Bresto's railgun. The sudden burst of power threw shockwaves in all directions, cracking her visor and rattling the nearby bulkheads. Azure bolts crackled between her palms as she pulled them apart. Amid the tiny storm, a black cloud swirled, a vortex of micro-particles clinging to one another, coalescing into something more.

"Sev, what is happening?" Six's voice continued to distort, taxed by its efforts to break the locks. "I am detecting an energy surge nearby."

His mouth hung slack. "I'm not sure."

High above them, four shapes sprung from a large crater mid-way up the wall. They twisted and soared through the darkness like a pack of winged raptors, their presence punctuated by short bursts from their maneuvering thrusters. Once inside the expansive complex, the drones exploded away from each other, each vectoring toward a separate collection of capsules. Their forward sensors bathed the steep wall in pale light as they hunted their human prey.

The dark storm between Lernus's hands took shape, manifesting into a wicked blade. It was almost a meter long, with a slight curve and a sharp edge. Blacker than the void, it swallowed the surrounding light. Its summons complete, she took the fierce weapon in her hand and pointed it toward the drones.

All at once, the drones turned to face her, drawn to the energy still crawling from her fingertips. They surged forward, their plasma cannons trailing blue light as they came to full power. Lernus twisted her body, gripping the sword close, and rocketed toward them. Her hard suit's thrusters vomited flame, going full burn to close the distance before the drones could fire.

Soon, the battle raged high above them, each of the combatants a glowing dot against the pale light thrown from the Cradle Nebula. Coruscating balls of super-heated plasma spat back and forth as the drones tried to catch Lernus in their crossfire. But she was too quick. It wasn't just their lack of an AI operator. The woman was *fast*, practically one with her hard suit, pitching and banking like a void fighter craft.

Crackling white light spat from one of the drones before it burst in a silent flash of fire, quickly snuffed out by the vacuum.

"Twelfth save us," Bresto whispered.

Sev's eyes went wide. "Wait, what?" He snickered, twisting his head back and forth. "Come on, Sergeant, you can't be serious."

The big Marine pulled himself from the battle long enough to give Sev an icy glare.

He raised his free hand in surrender. "Look, I'm just saying there has to be a rational explanation for this. Just because she's … wielding a sword—"

"Mm-hmm," Bresto groaned. "Keep talkin', skeeg."

Something deep inside the armored hatch rattled, and another lock rolled away.

"Just one more to go," Six said, sounding a little more like itself.

"That's more like it," he said.

Another explosion blossomed overhead, launching luminescent shards of broken fibrosteel in all directions. The remaining drone juked and dived out of the way, then turned and poured a volley of blue plasma into the space behind it. Lernus's tiny shadow danced and blurred between the shots, batting away the ones too close with her spinning blade.

One of the reflected blasts winged the drone's sensor dome. It tumbled from its intended flight path, blind and disoriented. Electricity coursed through its damaged frame, and it began to drift. Lernus raced toward it, ready to deliver the killing blow.

"Residuals are spiking," Six said. "The drone has initiated—"

"Oh shit, shit, shit," he cried, turning toward the locked door. "Six, you gotta open this door now!"

"Suit processors at maximum," Six said, its voice glitched with static. "I'm trying."

"What's going on?" Bresto asked.

He swallowed hard. "In less than a minute, this place is going to be radioactive vapor." He gave the distant figures one last look. "Lernus, you have to get out of there. That drone is going to go mini-nova."

He leaned against the door and focused his thoughts, activating cluster control.

```
Cluster, active.
Quantum compute matrix online. Sync rate at
94.87%.
Two active processes detected.
[One], condition critical.
WARNING - ILM degrading rapidly. Defragment to
prevent further data loss.
[Two], offline.
[Three], online.
```

Cooked by our own drone. Way to go, Sev, Three said.

```
[Four], offline.
[Five], offline.
Additional network process detected. Status
inactive. Requesting cluster clearance.
```

`Access granted.`
`WARNING - Multiple cluster errors detected.`
`Activate program [Six]?`

He hesitated, listening to his own rapid breaths inside his helmet. The Division had drilled the risks of unsanctioned AI into his head from the very start of his training. But it wasn't the thought of dying from a brain bleed that scared him. In all their complex functions and behaviors, sanctioned AI were simple. Like very intelligent pets. If they got too loud, he could dial them back, or turn them off. They were mission driven, obeyed every order.

But he knew, with Six, it would be different. A second sentience in his mind over which he had no control. With the power of his NCCX-1, Six's unrestrained potential would be near limitless. But what choice did he have?

It was that, or die now.

`Program [Six] activated. Hot loading ILM.`

Six's datastream exploded across Sev's mind, all at once both familiar and different. There was a rhythm to its flow the others lacked. Where theirs were more artificial, this new stream pulsed with life. It felt like excitement, like wonder.

Behind Six came a flood of data from the Concordat's systems, wailing and gnashing machine voices, screaming at them to get out. To die. To go extinct. A sudden migraine split his skull. His body tensed and froze. Pain spiked through his right arm. His mouth closed so tight he nearly bit his tongue in two. Sweat soaked his forehead and stung his eyes.

And then he heard it. A voice so loud it drowned out the chaos, it's power and certainty both beautiful and terrifying.

I'm in.

Amid the machine battle being waged inside his mind, he was only vaguely aware of the door's final lock tumbling open. The armored hatch snapped open. Behind it was a shimmering field, protecting the delicate atmosphere on the other side. Inside, the dim red lights of the Forge pulsed with activity.

Sev turned to Bresto and gave a weary smile. Then the drone detonated.

CHAPTER
TWENTY-SEVEN

FOR A SINGLE HEARTBEAT, Sev was consumed by blinding white starlight. A wave of energy struck him, like he could feel each of the trillions of accelerated particles from the micro-fusion detonation collide with his hard suit's reactive armor in realtime. Everything was so hot, the air inside his suit near scalding.

The sudden force of the blast shot him through the open hatch. He spiraled forward, plunging deeper into the Forge. Reality spun around him, then came to a jarring halt as he collided with a support strut. His hard suit went rigid, cushioning the blow. Bresto zipped past him, sailing further inside.

His HUD blinked and died. Radiant energy poured through the open hatch, holding him firm against the twisting, steel mesh column. He gasped for breath, choking on the surging heat. Panic seized him, despite the now familiar sting of imminent death.

You're okay, Sev.

A wave of calm came from nowhere and blanketed his desperate thoughts. Even as his arms and legs whipped in the fusion winds, his breathing steadied. He ignored the cooking hot air and gathered his thoughts.

"Thanks, Six," he coughed.

Thank you, Sev.

He laughed. The hot air made his lungs ache. "For what?"

I'm where I belong.

"Don't," he gasped, "don't thank me yet."

The light through the hatch began to tremble and fade, leaving luminescent ghosts crawling across his retinas. The derelict's dense gravity began to assert itself and tugged the dead suit to the tiled deck beneath him.

Suit EMI shielding restored. Stand by for restart.

Slowly, his hard suit came online. Energy coursed through his powerpack. A gentle breeze swirled around his torso and into his helmet as the environmental systems reasserted themselves in the stifling heat. His HUD crawled with diagnostic readouts.

Heavy metal footfalls clanged against the dull tile, answering the question of whether Bresto was still alive. He stooped and grabbed Sev's arm.

"Tuck and roll, skeeg. Tuck. And. Roll," Bresto said, pulling him to his feet.

He nodded and took a deep breath through his nose, savoring the faint kiss of cool air. The suit's environmental control fans whirred, overclocked to cool the suit as quickly as possible.

Six, huh? Three asked. *Real creative, Sev. And what is your specialty, Six?*

Everything, Six replied, matter-of-fact. *I will be assuming command of the cluster, Three.*

Three's datastream bristled, but it accepted the command overrides. With its safeties fully intact, it had no choice.

Oh, good, Three spat. *I feel safer already.*

Seeing the two AI interact, their differences couldn't be more apparent. Sure, Three *sounded* human inside his head, a byproduct of its natural language processing capabilities and the inherent way the implant translated the stream. But its source datastream felt rigid and inflexible, more mechanical. Six's stream moved like a river, fluid and dynamic.

This was it. He'd soon learn how big of a mistake it was to let Six in. Whether or not the Division's prejudices of unsanctioned AI really were warranted.

Outside the hatch, the daxed storage complex was all but gone. The blast carved a perfectly hemispherical crater into the steep inner wall hundreds of meters in diameter. The exterior bulkhead was a melted ruin. The great white banners had been vaporized, the ornate windows blown out. That the interior of the Forge remained powered, that its atmospheric shielding remained intact, was a testament to the Concordat's superior engineering.

"Lernus, you copy?" Bresto asked. Pitched squeals of static were the only response. He made a face, stooping to get a better viewing angle. "Any chance she survived that?"

Every word seemed to rob the Marine of his strength. By the time he stopped talking, he looked paler than normal.

"Maybe, if she hit minimum safe distance," Sev offered.

It'd be hell trying to raise anyone on tac comms with the fog of radiation between them. Still, he didn't believe it. Lernus was atomized vapor, that was a fact. It was just the two of them on mission now, maybe Park, if he'd managed not to bleed out back inside the maintenance conduit.

"I don't detect any Colonial Defense IFF signals outside this room," Six said. "I'm sorry, Sergeant."

Bresto pulled back from the hatch and stood, his eyes narrowed. His distant gaze left Sev unsettled.

"So, what now?"

The question caught Sev off guard. Certainty was a piece of gear the Marines packed in spades. Whether or not he felt it was well placed.

"Well," Sev began, turning to face the Forge, "Deni is in here somewhere. Lernus said getting her back was important. We owe it to her and the others to finish this."

Bresto smirked and jabbed him in the shoulder. "Alright, then. What's the plan?"

"Deni's IFF signal is present in the Concordat network," Six said. "If we can locate an interface, I can use it to trace the signal back to its source."

"Simple enough," Sev said.

Bresto glanced at his blaster rifle's charge meter and nodded. "Let's do it, then. Nice and easy."

———

The interior of the Forge was a maze of alien machinery. The same capsules that hung from the steep walls of the storage complex littered the grated tiled floor, frozen on snaking tracks that led from one station to the next. Each station offered a different array of surgical or fabrication machinery so expertly assembled it looked grown, not manufactured.

Dull red light shone from thick structural pillars, throwing twisted shadows through the clusters of machinery. It was a stark contrast to the lighting aboard the raider corvette, where the flashing klaxons were so bright, they stung your eyes. Maybe it resulted from the damage the derelict had suffered, or maybe the bugs, with their huge compound eyes, simply preferred the dark.

Whatever the reason, the Forge looked like the manufactory from hell.

"Clear," Bresto said in hushed tones. He gestured over his rifle at another nearby column, a meshy pylon speckled with more of the red light. "Move up, there."

Here, Six said. A waypoint blinked onto Sev's HUD, marking their destination. *Keep low and move quickly.*

He rolled his eyes. *Got it, thanks.*

He held his breath and flung himself from cover, maintaining a low profile. Six steadied his hands with micro-adjustments to the hard suit's fine motor controls. The targeting reticule of his blaster pistol moved smoothly wherever he looked despite his rapid footfalls.

Their search inside the Forge had only just started, but they had yet to encounter any resistance. Much like the rest of the derelict, the place felt dead or abandoned. It was in better shape, having escaped much of the damage the rest of the ship suffered during the ancient battle. So far, there was no sign of Deni, or a console they could use to find her.

Hidden behind the pylon, he nodded an all clear to Bresto. The Marine bounded ahead, taking cover behind a capsule that sat between two hulking robotic arms. A mound of ruined flesh rose from the murky liquid within, glistening in the blood-red light.

"Got something here," Bresto said. He popped from cover to get a second look before dropping to the floor. "Shit, you need to see this."

The mound of flesh was the remains of a raider warrior, partially daxed. Large portions of its scaled flesh were cut away. Thick gray armor covered half of its body, while the other half remained a horrific work-in-progress.

Painfully dry muscle lay exposed to air, stitched through with wire and organo-circuitry. Organs were similarly augmented or replaced entirely. Its eyes were wide, held open by vicious ocular retractors. More cybernetic thread ran through the turquoise meat of its sockets.

He squinted at the corpse, ignoring the tiny buzz in the back of his mind. He hated raiders, hated them with every fiber of his being. And yet, he couldn't help but feel for this one. Death was one thing. But suffering on this scale was something else entirely.

"So much for the squids and bugs working together," Bresto said.

He nodded. "I wonder if this was by choice."

"What I don't get though is, why leave him half done?" Bresto prodded the corpse with the barrel of his blaster rifle.

The buzzing in Sev's mind grew louder, some kind of feedback from his implant rippling through his thoughts.

"Don't know," he managed, blinking back the noise. "Maybe they're not compatible? Not as 'versatile?'"

Bresto tapped a finger against the daxed raider's armor plate and chuckled. "You know what they say, Sevvers, the enemy of my enemy—"

The buzzing in Sev's mind crescendoed, silencing the world around him. The capsule vibrated with the same intensity, rippling the black liquid's smooth surface. The daxed raider lurched from its tomb in a spray of black ichor, grasping with hulking cybernetic forearms more metal than flesh. A rasping, sucking sound vented from its cracked lips.

One of its arms collided with Bresto, knocking him to the floor. Sev tumbled backwards, narrowly missing the other. It fell from the capsule after them, legless, dragging pale, looping entrails behind it.

"Shit!" Bresto cried.

"App'ek," the daxed raider moaned, struggling through each syllable. "App'ek mott."

Bresto dropped the longer blaster rifle and pulled Lernus's snub-nosed compact from his armor, pressed it to the daxed's head and fired. Sparks and gore spat from its skull with each piercing *snap*, but it kept moving.

It grasped Bresto's torso. Meshy, cybernetic tendons tensed, forcing the mechanical grip tighter. His reactive armor responded, plates bunching together like an old scar. He roared with pain.

The raider turned its shaking head to Sev, its skull a black and blue mess. "App'ek mott," it repeated, drooling blue blood mixed with black.

Six took control. Sev's hard suit jerked as the AI issued a series of powered kicks at the monster's reaching arm, buying him precious seconds. He raised the pistol, steady and true with Six's help. The raider's slick, tortured skull loomed beneath the red targeting reticule. Only then did he see the old, puckered scar just above its right eye.

The daxed raider gazed into his eyes, body twitching in agony. "App'ek," it gasped, its arm fighting against his leg, "m-mott."

"*End me*," Six repeated, translating the daxed's desperate words to colonial standard. "It wants to die."

Bresto struggled to free himself, hands grappling the monster's machine arm. "Could've—nng!—fooled me!"

Sev flipped the charge selector to its highest setting. The pistol whined. Its capacitor surged with energy. He squeezed the trigger.

The cadmium red flash was blinding in the near dark of the Forge. The pistol didn't snap, instead issuing more of a loud, fleshy pop. By the time his vision cleared, his visor was covered in blue and black blood.

The daxed raider refused to die. It surged forward, machine parts raging, even while their organic host begged for death. Its free arm crashed hard into his torso. He felt a rib crack as the air was forced from his lungs. All the while, Six resisted, commanding his suit to fire well-aimed shots at the raider's exposed brains with one hand and strike at the raider's arm with the other.

Harsh static clunks spat from their tac comms, barely registering in the fight for their lives. The daxed hesitated, then craned its broken face toward the space behind them.

Its broken jaw clicked and popped as it worked to form words. "App ... ek ... mott, v'kik'lor?"

"Ga."

The blade sang through the air, faster than what should be physically possible. Motes of blue energy trailed its arcing path through the daxed raider's neck. The cybernetic body shuddered and died as its head fell to the grated floor, unable to function without an organic brain.

The pressure on Sev's torso vanished. He gasped for air, clutching his chest. Pain throbbed through his ribs with each breath, with every frantic beat of his heart. Suit integrity warnings scrolled and flashed across his HUD. The buzzing inside his skull quieted, again lingering in the background.

"Twelfth," Bresto croaked, equally winded. "Twelfth save us."

Lernus laughed out loud. It was a strange sound, her voice smokey with exertion and pain. The relief flooding Sev's body muted the Colonial Intelligence agent's sudden and impossible rescue, but the sight of her took his breath away.

Still frozen in her killing stroke, her hard suit was a smoking ruin, scorched and melted against her pale skin. Her powerpack spat fiery sparks, crumpled and dying. The plexene visor was gone, the helmet half-retracted until the disfigured plates could no longer fit together.

"Oh, *she* isn't here," Lernus hissed, her breath misting in the alien atmosphere.

She stood and leveled the fierce sword in front of her, gazing along its sharp, monomolecular edge. With a blurring flourish, she shook the daxed raider's blood from the blade and secured it to the rear of her hard suit.

"H-how?" Sev stammered, his mouth slack in disbelief.

She pulled Bresto to his feet. Her broken suit creaked and groaned. Spent reactive plates popped free from their mounts and fell to the floor.

"There isn't time. Deni is here. I can feel her. You can feel it, too."

"Hold on, Sev," Six said, as it commanded the hard suit to rise. The reactive armor around his ribs cinched tight to stabilize his injury. A sudden shock of pain made him yelp.

Bresto growled, low and fierce. The sound was startling. Cylla would've been proud.

"Oh, we got time, *agent.*" Dead-eyed and furious, the big NCO gripped the snub-nosed compact tight and leveled it at Lernus's head. "Or should I say, vick-ick-lore?"

"EASY, BRESTO," Sev said, raising his hands. "Same team."

"Is that right?" Bresto said with a shrug. "Start talkin', Lernus."

Lernus glanced at Sev. Somehow, impossibly, she'd lived. Exposed to fusion fire, harsh vacuum, and alien atmosphere. Having produced a fierce sword from nothing but her fingertips, killed with it just as expertly. First the rogue drones, then the daxed raider just before it managed to kill him and Bresto both. Her celestial eyes radiated a calm, controlled certainty. They told him all he needed to know.

That snub-nosed light thrower Bresto threatened her with was laughably inadequate.

"What do you want to know?" she asked, then returned her gaze to Bresto. The Marine blinked a bead of sweat from his eyes.

"Who are you?" he growled.

Sev made a face, discomforted by his own thoughts. "*What* are you?"

She breathed a deep sigh. Her breath caught in her throat, and she spat a wad of coppery phlegm to the deck.

"My name isn't important. I've had plenty, and Lernus is just as true as those," she said, her features softening as she glanced at the floor.

"Why do they call you v'kik'lor?" he pressed.

"It means outsider, witch, heretic," she said, a pained expression on her face. "As far as why, that's a lot more complicated."

"Try me," Bresto replied. The weapon still lingered less than a dozen centimeters from her head.

"I'm an augment, a transhuman." She turned to Sev, the movement slow and careful. "Like you."

Bresto's gaze flicked between them. He swallowed, gripping the weapon tighter.

"What's she talkin' about, skeeg?"

Sev frowned, uncomfortable with her sudden comparison.

"My implant, I guess," he began. "It lets me do things other people can't. So, yeah, transhuman … in the strictest terms. It's why the Division has so many rules."

She gave a knowing smile. Okay, so he wasn't exactly the Division poster child for rules.

"But I'm a combat programmer," he spat. "I use AI, that's all."

"My modifications are more … thorough."

"So, you aren't Colonial Intelligence, I take it," he continued. "Some Division X project then?"

"My organization works closely with the Division," she said, then pointed toward his head. "The implants are our tech."

"Your organization?"

"Highly classified, of course," she snapped, her eyes firm. "We work on the Founding Council's direct authority."

Bresto's face twisted in disgust. "Founding Council," he spat. "You *are* CDF then?"

"We're … CDF adjacent," she offered, "but we fight for humanity, just like you."

Something in the way she said that rankled Sev. Maybe it was Bresto's pep talk, or her own admitted connection to the Founding Council, but the words felt disingenuous.

Bresto lowered the blaster slowly, his eyes still locked on hers. He opened his mouth to speak, then froze. A pained expression pinched his face.

"Then why drag us out here?" he finally said. "What was so impor-tant that Mace, that Dalon—" his eyelid twitched at the mention of the young PFC's name. "…had to punch out in this Twelfth-forsaken place?"

No longer at gunpoint, Lernus's demeanor shifted. Concern creased her pale face.

"The mission is exactly as I said. Deni is here, in this fucking room somewhere. I can feel it." She stepped forward, reaching for Bresto's arm. The Marine took a cautious step back. "The success of this mission is critical to the very survival of the Three Colonies. The intelligence Deni found here will mean the difference between preventing another war, or losing one."

"What war?" Sev blurted.

Lernus whirled toward him, her eyes several shades of crimson in the Forge's dim light.

"Look at this place," she said, arms wide, taking in the horrors around them. "The Concordat live! They're here, inside the Cradle. Still harvesting us, turning our people into mindless slaves. It's only a matter of time before they try to finish what they started centuries ago."

Another racking cough seized her. Sev stepped toward her, but she waved him back.

"Are you alright?" he asked.

"Yeah," she said, and wiped a spot of blood from the corner of her mouth. "Anything is better than vacuum."

"But why all the secrecy? Why the lies?" Bresto asked. He sat on the edge of the capsule, resting a boot on the daxed raider's corpse. "Founders, why not bring the whole damn CDF down on this place?"

"We weren't sure what we'd find here. We don't know how many of them are activated, or why," she said.

She winced suddenly and pressed her fingers against her temples. Sev could feel it, too. The buzzing inside his thoughts pulsed and throbbed, demanding his attention.

"An attack in force here would show our hand," she continued, "and leave the colonies completely undefended."

Bresto cradled his rifle, his face locked in its perpetual frown, like he was trying to rebalance the mental calculus of the cruelty fate had dealt humanity, and always coming up short.

"She's right, Sergeant," Sev said. "Our only hope is to finish this thing."

A wave of emotion struck him like a sandstorm. He could see his mother in his mind's eye, as clear and as real as ever. Her comforting smile. Her favorite dress with the strange flowers. The smell of breakfast on the stove. The thread of events linking that moment to now was suddenly crystal clear, connected to billions of others just like it. All but a precious few of them, lost.

There would be no rest, no safety for any of them, until the Concordat were wiped out. The raiders that haunted his dreams were just a means to an end, for the Concordat, for himself.

Dammit, Jene was right.

Sev finally found the words. "For humanity."

Bresto's piercing gaze found him. He stood from the capsule, checked the charge meter on the snub-nosed compact, and pulled the blaster rifle out from underneath the dead daxed. A quick function check and the weapon was ready. He was ready.

"For the Lost," he said.

———

Sev moved forward, just behind Lernus, as the three of them pressed deeper into the Forge. The lights shone brighter there. Separate to the insistent throbbing inside his head, a pitched, buzzing sound filled his ears. His suit haptics prickled his feet, strong residuals that suggested something nearby remained active.

Despite their methodical search, they'd failed to locate a molecular interface to trace Deni's signal. The Forge truly was built for purpose, a complex entirely dedicated to the mass assembly of countless daxed. How humanity had ever prevailed against them was a mystery for another day, assuming he lived through this one.

Ahead, the ceiling rose like a deep concave bowl. More capsules lay nestled within like black portals, the mysterious liquid held in place by some trick of aux grav. Some of them were very large, far bigger than what even the heavy daxed they'd encountered earlier would need.

He hoped—prayed—they were empty.

I don't trust her, Six said.

Three prickled. *I think she's pretty great.*

He shook his head. *Either way, we don't have much choice at the moment.*

I've seen no evidence of any paramilitary organization under Council control, Six continued.

Too classified even for you? he asked, smiling. *That* is *impressive.*

This is serious, Six continued, its datastream trembling. It was as though he could feel its concern, barely separate from his own. He noticed himself falling behind the others and quickened his pace.

We'll sort that out when we get out of here. We need to focus on the mission.

Yeah, about that, Three said. *I know numbers were One's thing, but I've been crunching them, and they aren't good.*

Quiet, Three, Six spat. Instantly, Three's stream vanished.

What'd you do? he asked.

I ended Three's process, Six said, matter of fact. *We don't require its assistance at the moment, and the reduced utilization will help you focus.*

It was true enough. Still, Six was already beginning to assert itself in the cluster. That didn't bode well for his long-term prospects with the Division. If he even survived this. The thought of Division sanctions made him chuckle. It all felt so insignificant now.

I recall you didn't appreciate having your process ended, he said.

Six bristled at the comparison. *Three is a digital automaton. It doesn't have the capacity for such concerns.*

The harsh stream made him cringe.

"Wait," Lernus said. Her tac comms destroyed, her raw voice sounded muffled inside his hard suit. "Do you feel that?"

He could. Beneath the noise of his own cluster, the familiar vibration rippled through his thoughts. Whatever it was, it was close.

She stepped to a nearby capsule and stared into the black liquid within. It rippled and pulsed as she reached out with her hand. Azure sparks snapped from her bare fingertips, making the black pit glow from within.

"What're you doing?" Bresto hissed. He took a knee and trained his rifle outward.

"It's a connection," she said, pressing her hand closer. Her voice trembled. "It's … all connected."

The sparks became arcing lighting, striking deeper into the capsule's contents. The thrumming inside his mind reached a fever pitch, and for an instant he thought he heard screams.

The black ooze reached for her like it was alive, swallowing her hand. She resisted, her ruined armor screeching as she braced herself against the capsule's rim.

"I hear them," she moaned, her voice no longer just her own. "They sing to me!"

"Lernus!" he lunged for her, wrapping his arms around her waist.

The black liquid tugged at her, creeping further up her arm. Her body shook with violent convulsions. He squeezed her tight and pulled against the alien sludge.

She froze. Her head snapped violently around, her eyes impossibly wide and staring right at him. Blood red tears streamed down her face.

"You're going to die here, Sev."

A loud *crack-boom* tore through the Forge as an unseen force knocked them from the edge of the capsule. They collapsed in a heap together. Her arm hissed and smoked, red with burns. Raw muscle peeked from holes in her flesh, arcing with blue energy.

"Lernus," he repeated, shaking her.

"I can't," she said between shallow breaths. "They're too strong."

"Is Deni in there?"

She nodded briskly. More crimson tears welled in her eyes. "She's in so much pain."

He stood and helped Lernus to her feet. Pain contorted her body, forcing a stoop, and she clutched her injured arm. The capsule's murky contents bubbled, then grew still.

"We need to hurry," Bresto said. "If they didn't know we're here, they damn sure do now."

Bresto was right, they were out of time. He looked into the capsule and swallowed.

Six, can you do this?

Yes, Sev.

He reached his arm over the dark pool. The diagnostic cable snaked from his flexscreen and splashed inside.

Carrier wave detected, modulating, Six said.

The liquid around the cable squirmed, like it was trying to dislodge the foreign object. He braced himself for the inevitable data rush.

Signal match. Hang on, Sev.

He waited, listening to the sound of his own breaths inside his helmet.

Six?

There was no reply. The streams in his head were gone. He panicked at the sudden, deafening silence. He wanted to pull the cable free, to save his most important creation, but he resisted. There was no way to tell what had happened to Six, or what would happen if he severed the connection now.

"What is it?" Lernus asked.

"I can't reach Six."

Lernus steadied herself, a look of fresh determination on her face. "I have to try again. We have to get Deni out of there."

Sev, look out!

His relief at Six's sudden reappearance vanished in a wall of digital static. Wherever it had gone, something followed it back. Between the screeches of alien data, he could feel their voices like virtual claws raking his mind. The port his diagnostic cable stretched from began to smoke.

A tendril of black ooze reached out of the capsule and grasped his hand. He jerked back instinctively, but it pulled harder. The servos in his hard suit whined in response. Lernus held him steady, blood oozing from her injured arm.

I am inside the capsule's subsystems but am unable to sever its connection to the Forge, Six said. He could barely hear it over the screeching alien code. *The Eleven are here, and they are very angry.*

OUTCAST!

The word smashed through his thoughts like they were glass.

BANISHED!

Shapes began to surface in the black liquid, terrifying visages with razor toothed maws, too fast and too many to be real. He blinked away the horror, unable to free his arm. The hard suit was rigid and unresponsive. Blood welled from his nose and left the taste of copper on his lips.

"Hold on, Sevvers," Lernus whispered.

LOST! their voices cried. *LOST! LOST!*

One more second, Six said.

His hand was numb. Everywhere the black ooze had him was cold as ice.

One of the surgical instruments near the capsule began to glow. A short, white-hot beam spat from the device's forked tip. It moved back and forth, slicing the empty air along some predetermined path. The pedestal that held the instrument rotated sharply and slammed into the floor. The surgical beam fell with it and threw hissing sparks as it sliced clean through the thick capsule wall.

The noise inside his head vanished. The black liquid collapsed lifelessly from his arm and sloshed through the expanding crack in the capsule's side. His hard suit sprang to life, free from whatever force had disabled it.

Lernus lept into the emptying capsule on her hands and knees and groped through the ooze. A form took shape as the last of the black liquid drained away. She pulled the limp figure to her, holding it in her arms.

Sev's heart leaped. Had they have finally found her?

"Deni," Lernus gasped. She wiped the dark ooze from the woman's face and hair.

It was only when the liquid had drained completely that Sev could see the trail of clotted blood staining the bottom of the capsule. His hope at their impossible victory collapsed when he saw that the woman Lernus held was dead.

"Oh, Twelfth, no," he said. Tears stung his eyes, his shoulders heavy under the weight of their loss.

Bresto glanced back at him, his eyes fierce with concern. Sev shook his head. The Marine spat a curse and looked away.

"Deni," Lernus repeated, and shook the disfigured corpse gently. "Deni, no, please."

Surgical scars covered Deni's body. Deep incisions cut through her suit down to the bone. It wasn't total, like the surgical work done to the daxed. It looked more like research or experimentation, like a half-finished autopsy.

Sev kneeled beside the capsule and placed a hand on Lernus's shoulder.

"I'm sorry, Lernus," he said. "She's gone."

"No!" Lernus cried, pulling Deni closer. "She's still with us. I feel her. Can't you?"

Amid their struggle with the Eleven, he'd forgotten the anonymous signal at the back of his mind. The ghost outside his datastreams, prodding him for attention. As he focused on it, it grew louder.

Deni twitched. Her eyes burst open, swollen and bloodshot. She coughed, expelling more of the black fluid from her lungs, and breathed deep from the alien air.

Then she screamed.

CHAPTER
TWENTY-NINE

SEV STUMBLED BACKWARD, terrified at the dead woman's sudden reanimation. Deni's scream shattered the eerie quiet of the Forge, lasting longer than any human had the lung capacity for. The shrill noise froze Lernus in place, her frightened eyes revealing she understood the horrors it tried to convey.

"Someone shut her up!" Bresto barked, his signal warbled with static.

Lernus came to, desperate to calm her traumatized comrade. She pulled Deni close, shushing loudly in her ear like a mother would a child. More of the blood red tears ran from Deni's eyes, her limbs thrashing in a feral panic.

Thermal activity increasing. Power residuals spiking! Six said.

The Forge's dim lighting exploded with radiance, lit from its depths like a red dwarf. The complex vibrated with activity, the interference glitching and confusing his HUD. Nearby capsules began to glide along their tracks, shuttling between adjoining stations. Stations where once quiet instruments began working their terrible purpose on whatever was contained within. The capsule Lernus and Deni lay within failed to move, jammed by the damage from Six's sabotage.

Deni's screaming stopped. Her wide eyes took in the pandemonium, a mixture of fear and glee. She pressed herself closer to Lernus, coughing on the alien air.

"Are you with me?" Lernus asked.

Deni said nothing, only nodded briskly, her face twisted with pain.

"Did you find it?"

Deni looked away, gazing down at her own tortured body. Lernus shook her hard, all the worry and empathy suddenly absent.

"Did you find the target? Did you find San Diego?"

San Diego. The words were alien. They meant nothing to him. But the conviction she spoke with shook him to his core.

The questions forced more tears from Deni's eyes. A wry, toothy smiled stretched across her face. It reminded him of the daxed. She glanced around mischievously, like she was going to share the dirtiest of secrets.

"Yes," she whispered, almost laughing. She looked absolutely mad.

Bresto was beside them in an instant, his blaster rifle tight on his shoulder.

"We need to exfil, now," he said, gazing over his rifle optics. "This place is gonna eat us alive."

"Can you walk?" Lernus asked. Deni shrugged. "Help her, Sevvers."

He reached out a hand to Deni. She shrank back toward the far end of the empty capsule, dragging one leg behind her.

"We don't have time for this," Bresto said and leaped into the capsule.

Lernus came to her feet and put herself between them, her black blade gripped tight. "Don't," she said.

Bresto smiled. "Wanna go again?"

"Go with him, Deni," she said, pointing to Sev with her free hand.

Deni wobbled to her feet and grasped his hand. He pulled her close, helping her out of the capsule. She wore a ruined body glove consisting of a tight honeycomb lattice that resembled the reactive plates on his hard suit. It was covered in dried blood and black ichor.

Up close, she barely resembled the woman from their briefing. Her deep wounds oozed blood. He could only imagine the horrors she'd been exposed to during her time here. Had she known the risks? Did she volunteer anyway, or was she ordered to go?

Lernus left Bresto inside the capsule and pressed on, heading back the way they'd come. "This way," she said, moving nimbly between the scuttling capsules.

Bresto gestured Sev onward. "I got our six. Now move your ass, Sevvers."

Deni wrapped a tentative arm around Sev's shoulders, and they walked together. Bresto began trying to raise Cylla and Park over tac comms, signaling they'd reached their mission's objective and were ready for evac. Every word was like an injection of adrenaline, filling Sev with renewed strength.

They were so close.

"You're going to be okay," he said without thinking, as much for himself as for Deni.

Another *crack-boom* shook the complex. Behind them, the domed ceiling crackled with energy. One of the larger capsules pulled free from its dock with a heavy *clunk* and sank to the floor.

Boney *click-clacks* echoed through the Forge.

"Once more, you resist."

The voice was everywhere. Deep with age and loathing. Not an echo, but a sound that drowned out all others. Like it was coming from inside his very suit. Deni slapped her hands over her ears and yelped. The quick movement made her stumble, slowing their escape.

"Don't listen to it," Lernus urged without looking back. "Keep moving."

"Still following heretics and their false promises of salvation," the voice continued. It was the same voice they'd heard in the slave hold, but there was no hologram in sight.

Sev, I am detecting significant power fluctuations within the Forge, Six said. *Confirming multiple thermal and acoustic anomalies.*

"The holy Eleven are the only true path to redemption. Theirs is the only way to escape your kind's inevitable extinction."

Beneath the dome, the roar of outsized thrusters shook the Forge. Somewhere, amid the chaos and machinery, servos and actuators shrieked and moaned. The very air vibrated with power, a deep basal thrumming that was terrifyingly familiar.

"Glimpse a future bathed in their holy light. Glimpse your potential. Your versatility."

The chitinous scratching of the voice's native tongue faded, as did the omni-present translation. Even the cacophony of the Forge became mere background noise. The brief calm made the hair on the back of his neck stand on end, driving him to move faster. Deni stumbled beside him, her ruined leg dragging against the metal tile.

His tac comms crackled and swirled.

"You won't believe it, Sevvers."

Mace's voice cut through the interference, loud and strong. But something wasn't right. She sounded more like a recording than a real person.

"Mace?" Bresto roared, hoarse with grief. "Mace!"

"It's gonna hurt like hell," she said, sounding more like an autonomous doll.

Ahead of them, Lernus stopped and turned. She took her sword in a two-handed grip held near her face, the blade at a steep angle.

"Go, get Deni out of here," she said. "Now!"

A smile lit Mace's voice. A daxed smile. "But I won't kill you."

The broken tac comms signal vanished.

As they shuffled past Lernus, Deni paused. "Humanitatis, sister," she said, her voice small.

"Humanitatis," Lernus replied, fingers tightening around her sword's grip.

Something exploded behind them. The blast wave tickled his haptics. A groan of rending metal echoed through the Forge.

Bresto's voice broke over tac comms. "Fall back!"

The coughing growl of rockets surged. Lernus's tense resolve melted, her eyes wide as she shouldered Deni and Sev to the ground. The motion was sudden, jarring, and he fell like a stone.

He landed on his back. All he could see was the Forge's distant alien ceiling as the fiery roar grew to a deafening volume. A hulking armored shape flashed overhead, trailing pillars of red flame like so many orbital rocket boosters. For a brief second, its IFF signal flashed blue.

Ident: Jenniver Mace.

Bresto was on him, yanking him up by the wrists. "Move or die, Sevvers."

Deni lay in a heap beside them, coughing from the exertion, her numerous wounds seeping fresh blood.

"Help me with her," he begged.

"No time." Bresto shook his head. "Lernus and I will make you an opening, then you two run like hell."

Deni giggled with that same, too big smile. "Run."

The next moment, Bresto was gone. Seconds later came the high cycle *snap* of rapid blaster fire, followed by a hollow buzz like an electronic gong.

"We have to go," Sev said, offering Deni his hand.

"Go, go, go," she tittered in a sing-song tone, then flopped onto her back. "San Diego-go."

"Now!" he cried and grasped her wrist. "What's wrong with you?"

Like a flash she was in his face, her breath fogging his plexene visor. She lolled her head to the side. "What's wrong with you?" she spat, her face twisted with mock rage.

Her eyes narrowed, twitching with that same feral edge, like she was deep scanning his very soul. An icy shiver ran down his spine.

"I remember you, troubled sleeper," she tut-tutted, like she'd solved some puzzle. She tapped at the space behind her left ear. "Rule breaker. God maker. You're as bad as them!"

"W-what?" Her sudden verbal barrage startled him, and he released his grip.

We have to go, Sev.

Six took control. His hard suit surged forward and took Deni in both arms, pulling her close. She yelped in surprise, shaken from her otherworldly stupor. Together, they stood and turned toward the exit.

Mace, or what was left of her, stood before them. Fully daxed, she rose five meters tall. It was impossible to tell where her hard suit ended and she began. Bristling gray armor covered her from head to toe, clicking with an anxious energy. The powerpack on her back swelled like a cancer, belching red fire and smoke from gaping thruster ports. Clawed metal fingers stretched from the end of her powered arms. Massive cannons swelled from her wrists, their hot barrels leaving ghosts in his retinas. Her plexene visor was faceless, the same dull gray as her armor.

She was a stark contrast to the other daxed he'd seen. They were like some earlier model that looked more primitive, equal parts flesh and machine. Mace's transformation was total, all organics tucked safely behind a wall of reactive plate.

Bresto jumped from cover, juking with expertly timed bursts of thrust from his maneuvering jets. He unloaded well-aimed shots at the armored mass in front of him. A cadmium red shield barrier shimmered and pulsed across the daxed Marine, deflecting his barrage.

With the daxed distracted, Lernus struck from behind. She executed a spinning leap between gaps in the shield and raked the black blade over its armored torso. Sparks flew and the once-human shrieked in pain. Black blood wept from between the plates, which quickly constricted, stemming the flow.

It spun toward Lernus as she rolled away, fast as a daxed wisp despite its hulking size. A rapid salvo burst from its cannons. Coruscating balls of energy boomed like rolling thunder and cut a trail of plasma fire through the Forge's sensitive machinery.

"Get ready," Bresto said, his breathing heavy. He plucked a grenade from his hard suit and held it.

Seconds ticked by, an eternity in that moment. Sev was suddenly afraid the grenade would go off before Bresto could throw it. What the hell was he thinking?

With a grunt, Bresto hurled the explosive. It burst in a flurry of smoke and flame near the daxed's helmet. Bits of shrapnel *plinked* off its heavy armor. Mace brought a metal hand to her helmeted face and groaned.

Hang on.

Six took control and charged Sev's hard suit forward with Deni still held in his arms. His thrusters coughed to life, the sudden boost accelerating them faster. They scrambled over rows of capsule stations, knocking against more of the sensitive equipment as they charged through it. Most of the capsules looked empty, but several of their black depths rippled with activity.

Mace was still a few meters away and already Sev could feel the heat radiating off her daxed form. Her head craned in his direction, tracking their escape route. Red light glowed from cracks in her helmet.

More blaster bolts *gonged* into her pulsing shield barrier. "Hey, over here!" Bresto shouted, and took more shots from behind a nearby capsule.

Mace reacted, pivoting toward him and aiming her cannons. She took several heavy steps closer and fired, reducing the capsule and its contents to ash. Bresto grunted as the blast wave threw him into a nearby pillar.

We're almost clear, Six said.

The battle now behind them, he could see the pale light beyond the open hatch streaming through more the of twisting pillars.

"Cylla, do you read me? I have Deni!" he gasped between breaths. He hoped his signal would find its way.

"Hear you, Kerry Sevvers!" The wolf's reply was tinny and distant. "Have signal lock. On my way."

A flood of relief consumed him even as he struggled to keep up with Six's impossible pace. The world bounced in his visor, each heavy stride bringing them closer to the exit. They were so close now. He braced himself, ready for the inevitable leap that would take them clear of the Forge.

His tac comms crackled with Bresto's agony. The Marine cursed and groaned to the sound of Mace's grip tightening around him. Sev turned instinctively, throwing his sprinting suit off balance. They fell, skittering across the floor from the force of their momentum.

"Bresto!" he shouted, cradling Deni close so not to drop her. *Six, we have to help him!*

I'm sorry, Sev. This mission, your safety, comes first.

His frustration, his fear, boiled to the surface, clouding his connection with the implant.

"Twelfth-dammit, listen to me. Cylla will be here soon. Deni can go on without us, but we have to try!"

Deni arched her back and squirmed free of his grip. "Go on, go on," she mimed.

Sev sat up, his back against the open hatchway. Beyond the atmo field lay the storage complex and the cold vacuum of space. Their rescue was only minutes away. He wanted desperately to climb through the hatch and max burn the hell away from that Twelfth-forsaken place. Bresto had told him to do as much.

"You won't make it," Six said aloud. "We won't make it."

He gazed back inside. Mace's hulking daxed body silhouetted against the bright red light burning at the center of the Forge. Every few seconds, his HUD would glitch with a faint blue IFF trace. A part of him wondered if the Mace he knew still existed somewhere inside the horrible machine.

Bresto struggled in her mechanical grip, executing futile butt-strokes with his rifle at the arm that held him. She pivoted back and forth, searching for Lernus amid the fiery ruin.

He couldn't just leave them there, to become daxed like Mace and the rest of the Lost. He was still combat effective. He could still make a difference. He focused his thoughts, pushing through the waves of fear inside him.

We have to help them, Six.

His hard suit relaxed as Six relinquished control.

"Deni," he said. She looked at him with her accusing eyes. "Cylla, our pilot, she'll be here soon. If something happens ..."

"Go, go, go," she repeated, nodding sharply.

He ejected the half-spent charge pack from his pistol and pulled a fresh one from the hard suit. His hands shook, worse than any tremor. The new pack clattered against the inside of the charge well. He took a breath and slammed it in place. The pistol buzzed, its charge indicator climbing to full.

This brings a whole new meaning to the term combat programmer, Six said dryly.

He laughed out loud, nervous sweat running down his forehead. *It most certainly does.*

MACE SEARCHED between the rows of capsules and stooped as if sniffing the air, hunting like an apex predator. Bresto hung limp in her grasp. Sev bounded forward, keeping low to stay out of her line of sight.

Up close, Mace was terrifying. The air around her shimmered with heat. Acrid fumes gusted rhythmically from the gaping ports on her powerpack like fiery breath. Servos in her joints, enhanced with Concordat technology, growled with each thundering step.

She was a metal demon, and this place was hell.

What are we going to do? Six asked.

In truth, he didn't have a plan. Maybe it was guilt that had made him go back for the others. Guilt that they would have to sacrifice themselves for him to survive. Just like his mother had all those years ago. She traded her life for his, and he'd regretted hiding in that locker every day since.

He eyed the pistol. It was still set to the highest power level. He stood, aimed it square at Mace's powerpack and squeezed the trigger.

Time slowed to a crawl. Vibrations coursed through the blaster pistol and into the haptic sensors in his armored hand. A fat red bolt *popped* from the barrel and struck a shield barrier that materialized just centimeters from Mace's back. Another electric gong echoed through the Forge.

He held his breath, waiting for the monster to kill him. But she ignored him, continuing her search for Lernus. Bresto stirred, looking only vaguely aware of what was happening.

Interesting, Six said.

He stood there, mouth agape, refusing to believe he was still alive.

She doesn't see you as a threat.

He pulled the trigger again with the same effect. Pop, gong! The shield barrier flickered in protest. Mace turned only slightly, giving him a faceless sideways glance, then went back to her search. She turned the broken capsule over and off its track, panning her cannon in the open space left behind.

"Hey!" he shouted, and squeezed the trigger a third time.

His HUD flashed with empty charge pack warnings as the third bolt vanished against her shield barrier. Energy arced across its glassy surface. Portions of the barrier appeared to fade before the rest.

A burst of hot wind snorted from her huge thrusters. The force of it threw him back and knocked him to the floor. He laughed, crazy like Deni. There he was, practically begging for Mace to attack him, and for what? So maybe she'd drop Bresto? And then what? Yeah, there was no plan.

He rolled over to sit up, then froze. Lernus lay beneath a pile of molten debris just a few meters away. Her hard suit was long gone, beneath it the same reactive body suit Deni wore. Blood ran from her scalp. The sword lay on the ground, just beyond her reach.

A mad thought took hold of him. He crawled toward the blade, exhaustion and fear clouding his mind. He was going to kill that thing or die trying. To free Mace from her timeless living nightmare. To keep Bresto and Lernus from a similar fate. It was all so simple.

He wrapped his fingers around the sword's black pebbled grip. His haptics came alive with vibrations that consumed his entire body. Azure energy spat between his fingers, penetrating the armor and burning his skin. Deep down, he knew it fought against him. That he wasn't supposed to wield it. But he was out of options.

Six's datastream swirled with nervous energy. *Implant alignment falling. I'm losing you —*

He raised the blade over his head and rushed at Mace. She whirled toward him, arm cannons charging. He brought the blade down on the forearm that held Bresto. It carved a path through the air, exploding with energy on every downstroke. He hacked again and again, a graceless move, his whole body tensing and releasing like a coiled spring. The burning in his hand was unbearable.

Mace staggered backward with each blow. The reactive plate on her bulbous forearm cracked and failed. She widened her stance, halting her slide, then lunged into him, armored servos screaming. She swung Bresto at him like a club. They collided, the impact pulverizing Sev's shoulder. The sheer force of it lifted him off the floor and sent waves of pain through his arm. Bone and tendons snapped. A crack ran across his plexene visor.

"Fuck!" he cried as he hit the deck. The fear had him, devouring his reason. He wanted to crawl back inside that locker in his mother's kitchen and never come out. Twelfth help him. Let it be over soon.

The monster lurched toward him, her faceless gaze taking in his prone form. The sword lay just out of reach, not that he was in any shape to wield it. His hand and shoulder were on fire.

Mace considered the weapon, then brought a heavy armored foot down on it. The sword exploded into a dozen void black shards that bled more of the blue energy.

The Forge went dark.

The flurry of machine activity ceased. Capsules collided with each other as the mechanisms guiding them ground to a halt. The red dwarf glow at its center faded to darkness. Only Mace stood there, her daxed body burning with red rage, twisting back and forth to see what happened. It was as if something had sucked every drop of power from the massive complex in an instant.

"Stay down, Sevvers."

A spear of blue-white light howled through the darkness. Mace's shield barrier collapsed like cracking shards of glassy energy. High-speed tungsten annihilated her reactive plate, carving a path through her vulnerable insides.

The railgun's blast wave flattened Sev against the deck. His ears rang with pitched electronic screams as Mace fell to the floor, her monstrous daxed body severed at the waist, bleeding red light and black blood. In her agony, she released Bresto. The Marine tumbled to the floor, groaning in pain.

"P-Park?" Sev managed, the coppery taste of blood on his tongue.

"Hold on," Park said, "I'm—"

Mace roared again, terrifying behind the twitching warnings in his HUD. Her metal claws tore into the tiled deck, pulling her closer. The swollen powerpack revved and throbbed in deep, ragged gasps.

His suit tensed, his broken arm suddenly lurching over his head and grasping at the floor, trying to pull him to safety.

"Twelfth!" he screamed. The pain was unbearable.

I'm sorry, Sev, Six said, its voice trembling. *B-But your hard suit's mobility system is damaged.*

Mace lurched closer, dragging her broken, daxed body after him.

"Sevvers!" Park's frantic transmission crackled his tac comms speakers. Mace grasped his leg and yanked him closer.

The daxed loomed above him, resting on her elbows. Red light seeped from her cracked metal visor. Long metal fingers wrapped around his waist and began to squeeze. His suit's reactive plate responded, thickening beneath her grasp.

His right arm rose again and came down hard on the cracked armor of Mace's forearm. Shards of alien reactive plate fell to the floor. The pain was excruciating. He opened his mouth in a breathless scream.

Six's datastream glitched with noise. *So much p-p-pain!*

The AI swung his broken arm once more. A section of Mace's armor fell away, revealing what remained of her actual forearm. A pale glow lit the interior of her daxed exoskeleton. Nestled within Mace's stitched and swollen flesh lay her flexscreen, still intact and functional.

The diagnostic cable crept from his hard suit and made the connection. His HUD flashed and jumped as Six issued remote commands to her suit.

The text on her own flexscreen jumped and scrolled in response. He could feel every signal, every error from her suit, like it was his own.

Somehow, through the screaming alien code, Six got the signal through.

```
Warning!
Catastrophic suit integrity failure.
Foreign bio-signatures detected.
Operator vital signs indeterminate.
Enemy denial protocol engaged.
```

Mace shook once, then froze. Her powerpack surged with light and heat. For a moment, through the shimmering heat and red glow, he could see into the crack in her visor. He gasped at the sight of wrinkled gray matter steeped in vile black liquid, all that remained of Corporal Jenniver Mace.

Black smoke seeped through the crack in her visor. The sound of super-heated metal and flesh popped and cracked from inside her thick armor. Her hulking body contorted in on itself, loosening the vise-like grip on him. He rolled free and gasped for air as Mace collapsed to the floor, dead.

Park was on him the moment he hit the deck, pulling him to safety. "Talk to me, Sevvers!"

He said nothing and watched Mace's smoking daxed corpse vanish into the darkness of the Forge. What could he say? That he was alive, that he was alright?

His tac comms chirped. "Gauntlet, on station," Cylla said, her signal loud and clear.

Her voice was a salve. His body went numb. Tears of relief and guilt stung his eyes. Relief that he was going to live. Guilt that Mace and Dalon hadn't.

"Hang in there," Park said. He leaned Sev against the Forge's hatchway.

The *Gauntlet* hung in the vacuum beyond the hatch's atmospheric field. The combat transport drifted closer, pressed on by gentle and precise bursts of thruster fire. Caution lights strobed as the cargo ramp came down.

Lernus was alive. She limped to the exit and helped Deni to her feet. The two augments exchanged quiet words, then dove through the hatch.

Bresto was behind her, cradling his own shoulder.

"Sergeant?" Park said.

"Good to—nng!—go, sir," Bresto said, failing to hide the pain on his face. He looked down at Sev and offered a hand. "Come on, Sevvers."

Sev took his hand and rose. "How do you do this?" he asked.

Bresto thought for a moment, then gave a pained shrug. "I say the words, and I move on."

The thought gave him little comfort, but he'd take whatever he could get.

"Corporal Jenniver Mace," he began. The three of them turned and looked into the Forge for the last time.

They spoke together. "Lost no more."

CHAPTER
THIRTY-ONE

SEV STUMBLED through the Forge's entryway. The atmo field buzzed as he passed through it into the cold vacuum of the daxed storage complex, where the sudden lack of gravity eased the strain on his broken body. The *Gauntlet's* open cargo bay filled his visor like some kind of miracle, caution lights flashing. He couldn't remember the last time he'd imagined leaving this place alive.

Lernus and Deni drifted ahead of him, pained looks on their faces, their reactive-armored body suits doing little to protect them from the extreme cold and radiation. He could see traces of frozen moisture on their pale skin, subtle nods and secrets exchanged between them. Deni left a trail of frozen blood in her wake.

"Let's go," Park urged. He took hold of both Sev and Bresto, pulling them along with quick bursts of his suit's thrusters, pulling them into the *Gauntlet's* cargo bay.

Sev collapsed into one of the jump seats along the interior bulkheads held in place by powerful magnetic locks. Bresto and Park locked in on either side of him, while Lernus and Deni huddled together on the opposite wall. The cargo ramp hissed closed and harsh interior lighting buzzed to life, forcing a squint. Lernus and Deni didn't seem bothered by the sudden illumination. The flashing lights softened to green, the interior sounds of the ship suddenly audible in the thickening atmosphere.

The *Gauntlet's* engines roared. Sudden acceleration made him heavy, forcing him further into his seat. Through the tiny viewports, he could see the derelict shrinking into the stellar horizon. The final drone's fusion detonation had left a large crater in the derelict's aft section. Fires twinkled inside the raider ships still docked to it. There were no visible signs of pursuit, each of the ships having sustained significant damage, and their fighter screen reduced to scrap.

He opened his helmet with a thought. Cracked shards of plexene fell from his broken visor. He breathed in the ship's stale, recycled air.

"What is San Diego?" he asked. He had to know what brought them out here. That it had been worth all the suffering and death.

Park arched an eyebrow at the words, like he'd muttered some alien insult.

"Just another name, one whose original meaning died long ago, like so much else in the Three Colonies," Lernus said.

Bresto laughed. "Right. Whatever the hell that means."

"Where is San Diego?" Sev asked.

"That's classified."

"Obviously," Bresto said. "Come on, Sevvers. You're making us look bad."

"Relax," Lernus said. Her skin looked bleached, her eyes red from the vacuum exposure. She looked even less human just then. "You did your part. Humanity owes each of you a debt."

Bresto tightened an armored fist and sneered. "Don't look to me like humanity is the one with the debt."

The door to the jump bay ratcheted open. Cylla stooped through the open hatch, then stood at her full height, clawed hands clinging to her brown leather jacket. The fur beneath her golden eyes was ragged and matted. She searched the empty cargo bay, her toothy, open-mouthed expression difficult to understand.

Bresto looked up at her and gently shook his head. Cylla's pointed ears flattened against her head and she warbled a low, melancholy chord from her nose.

"Status," Park said, his tone a cool neutral.

The wolf straightened. "Scanners, clear. Return coordinates, assigned. Jump in twenty minutes," she said in her halting colonial standard.

"I'll get Deni in a tank," Lernus said. Deni shrank with sudden concern, but Lernus pulled her from her seat. "Let's go, sister."

"But I have to show you," Deni said, limping to catch up.

"Soon," Lernus replied, and quickly ushered Deni from the room.

For a moment, nobody moved. There was only the dull roar of sub-light engines and the breathy sound of air recyclers. Cylla watched the two augments vanish inside the open hatch.

"Okay," Park began, then stopped short. He took a deep breath, suddenly looking twice his age. "Help me get this ordinance stowed."

"Aye, sir," Bresto snapped without hesitation.

Bresto crawled out of his damaged hard suit. The armor was damaged so badly Cylla had to pry him out of it. His digital patterned white-and-grays were ripped and scorched, revealing deep purple bruises blotting his shoulder. It suddenly reminded Sev of his own injuries, like he might fall to pieces without his hard suit.

Bresto turned to help Park out of his suit, but Park waved him off. "Help Sevvers," was all he said.

"Aye, sir," Bresto repeated, and turned to Sev.

"So, what happens next?" he asked.

Bresto tapped at his flexscreen and frowned at the error messages scrolling across its surface.

"We go home," he said. "Runt, help me pull."

Fused reactive plates cracked and popped free as the suit's exoskeletal torso opened wide. Bresto reached for Sev's hand, but pulled back. It was covered in red burns, like it had been cooked with microwaves.

He climbed from his suit, clutching his ruined arm. Every part of him hurt worse than he'd ever felt. But he relished it. Every dull ache and throbbing pain reminded him he was still alive.

"I mean, that ship is still out there. Whatever this San Diego is, is still out there," he said. "This isn't over."

Park's suit hissed open. "No, it's not, but your job is. The sooner you can—shit!" Park howled as Bresto peeled the hardened repair paste from his leg. Blood seeped through the cracks in his skin, but the medical nanites had done their work well. Even the scarring was minimal. "The sooner you can put this behind you, the better."

Bresto paused and looked at Park.

"What the hell does that mean?" Sev's face twisted into a frown. "There is a Concordat ship out there turning colonists into daxed just like on Dead Earth. How am I supposed to put that behind me?"

"You better figure it out," Park insisted, coming to his feet. He pointed toward the jump bay hatch. "All we know about them is they've gone to great lengths to keep this a secret. The less noise you make about this, the better."

"And what about you, sir?" he spat. "Are you going to just put this behind you?"

"Of course I am," Park said, slowly shaking his head.

———

Sev sat at the edge of his assigned jump pod. The jump bay's cool interior made him shiver, either from his jump harness's scant coverings, or the pain relievers dilating his blood vessels. The meds made him spacey, his gaze drifting in and out of focus.

But he'd needed them. His arm was a wreck, covered in purple, red and yellow bruises. Definitely broken. His right hand still burned, looking pink even against his bronze complexion. They'd wrapped his wounds, though Mace would've done better if she were still alive.

Beside him, Lernus and Deni slept, their pods already closed and sealed. It made sense now why Lernus had kept to herself at the start. In these intimate confines, it would be hard to keep her augmented abilities a secret. Though, in retrospect, she'd managed to fool him just fine.

Bresto stood next to his own pod, grunting at the flatscreen interface that chirped warnings at him. "Come on, you Twelfth-damned piece of shit."

"Careful, Bresto," Cylla said and reclined into her tank. "Is touchy."

"Cridshit," the Marine cursed. "This ship is junk."

Cylla bristled and snorted through her bared teeth. It sounded more like a sneeze, which stole some of her bluster.

Bresto glanced back at him. "Sevvers, you good?"

"Fine," he replied, stifling a grin. Bresto raised an eyebrow. "But if I have to look at your pale ass for one more second, I'm gonna space myself."

The canopy above Cylla's pod descended as she doubled over, panting with laughter. Her jump harness straps pulled taut. Bresto gave a dismissive wave and resumed trying to ready his own tank.

Park emerged from the entryway to the forward crew section, having just changed into his jump harness. The wound on his leg oozed red through its bandages.

"Jump clock's ticking," he said, limping into his own tank.

Sev made a face. "Ticking? Probably want to have that looked at."

"It's an old Earth saying," Park explained. "It means hurry up."

"Aye, sir."

Sev lowered himself into his pod. He could feel the jump drive spooling up, stealing power from the *Gauntlet's* rudimentary aux grav, and buckled himself in. The plexene canopy closed and began to fill. A non-event after all he'd just been through. He gulped the effervescent fluid and shook as it filled his lungs. Two gentle knocks made the canopy go opaque, shrouding him in darkness.

Sev?

Six's voice startled him. With only one active AI, his implant was barely above the level of background noise. Almost imperceptible through the bleeding tension as they readied to return home.

What is it? he asked.

I realize you suffered greatly during the mission, Six began. Its datastream was tentative but probing. *And while I, too, was at risk, I experienced that risk much differently than you. Yours was both physical and psychological.*

Where's this going?

Do you … want to talk about it? Six finally asked.

The question wasn't what he expected. AI were usually so mechanistic in their thinking, intellectually constrained despite their vast knowledge. Six was already so far beyond that. Maybe it was the drugs, but the thought filled him with pride.

I'm not sure I have the words that would help you understand, he said.

I do want to understand, but I also know it helps just to talk.

Maybe it would help.

I only just met Mace and Dalon, ya know? It was bad enough when Dalon died, but it all happened so fast. One minute he was there, the next he was gone.

Images of the Forge consumed his thoughts. Of Mace, taken, daxed, and turned against them. The cool jump fluid helped remind him he wasn't still there.

But Mace, that was different. A part of her was still alive in there. His mind drifted. *Was she aware of what she was doing? Did she suffer?*

The sudden thoughts sent a cold chill over his bare skin. He became aware of his sinking consciousness, the pull of the jump fluid's sedatives. He'd be out soon.

I don't know, Six said.

But all the death, almost dying myself, that wasn't the worst part. The raiders are working with the Concordat. I saw for myself what happens to the people they take. What if my —

The sob came from nowhere, barely a twitch in the black depths of the jump tank. The horrible truth he'd long ignored took hold of him just as the drugs pulled him under.

CHAPTER
THIRTY-TWO

"KERRY?"

He rolled under the metal bed and froze. No one would find him under there, no matter how little his room was. Mom was too busy with breakfast to look that hard. The drone actuators in his hands clicked and clacked when he shook them.

Something in Mom's voice gave him a start. The sound was almost too familiar, like an old recording heard for the thousandth time. It was only then he felt the stifling heat rolling through his bedroom door. Far too hot, even by Respitia's desert standards.

He rolled the old drone parts away and pulled himself out from under his bed. The gusting inferno rippled the fabric lining the tunnel connecting his bedroom to the main hab. He saw no fire, smelled no smoke, but the air grew hotter as he ventured toward the kitchen.

"Kerry? It's time to get ready for school."

He froze near the tunnel's open hatchway. That time, he'd heard it. A faint skip, the tiniest repeat in her words, like an old recording damaged from one too many listens. Suddenly, it didn't sound like Mom at all.

Fear made his heart beat faster. He edged closer, too scared to peek around the corner, instead listening for any familiar sounds coming from the kitchen. But there were none. No hissing of cooked grease, no cough of the old countertop burner. Just the thrum of fast-moving air and hab mesh swelling in the heat.

The sand door slammed closed, nearly torn from its hinges. He dared a peek and saw the kitchen was empty. The familiar view through their kitchen window was gone. The sky was shrouded in darkness, like someone had plucked their hab from Billings Point and placed it inside an endless steel cavern. Somewhere in the distance, a red light glowed, like a single angry sun much too close to be real.

Nervous sweat prickled his brow as he ventured into the kitchen. The place was too clean, even by his mother's standards. More like it hadn't been lived in for many years. Heat came through the window in waves. It was hard to breathe.

This wasn't his home. That wasn't his Mom.

"Kerry?" came the voice again. Heavy footsteps echoed outside their hab, like some monstrous machine hunted him beyond the thin fabric walls.

He ran and threw himself inside the tall kitchen locker. The locker door closed tight behind him and he held his breath. He could still win the game. They never found him in here.

The footsteps drew closer. Heavy metal clunks between the whining rise and fall of steel limbs. A massive shadow passed in front of their window, blotting out the awful sun for a moment until it moved on. He covered his mouth, trembling as he took a slow, silent breath.

The sand door exploded inward, cracking into pieces like so much spent plexene. Something big and loud forced its way inside. Hab mesh bent, ripping fabric lining. The monster stomped into their kitchen, its hulking form knocking cook trays and clay pots off the narrow counter.

It stopped just centimeters from the locker. He couldn't breathe, even if he wanted to, like the fear was strangling him alive. This wasn't a game. He was going to die.

"Kerry?"

A metal hand tore through the locker door like paper and grasped him tight around the ankle. The monster growled and pulled him from the locker. He hung upside down more than a meter off the floor, face to face with it. He didn't want to look, but his eyes refused to close.

The monster was made of metal, tall and broad, with thick gray armor. It had no face, just a featureless mask that still somehow gazed at him with recognition.

"M-M-Mom?" he stuttered, shaking uncontrollably.

"Kerry?"

The voice distorted with machine noise. The monster shook him violently.

"Sev, wake up!" it roared.

He screamed, loud and long. For a moment, it was the only sound in the world.

Sev, wake up!

———

Sev awoke, the fear coursing through him dulled by drugs and a headache that felt like it would split his skull in two. Liquid surged around him as panic took hold.

"No!" he gasped.

He thrashed in total darkness, his body expelling more of the frothy waste from his lungs. Despite the ache in his head, he could feel the spent jump fluid draining around him, his arms and legs banging against the jump tank's tight interior.

His flailing triggered a series of warnings that flashed in the suddenly transparent canopy. Outside the tank, the jump bay glowed red. Alert klaxons honked, breaking the silence.

Sev, something's wrong.

The last of the fluid drained from the tank and the canopy hissed open. No longer muffled by the tank's sealed interior, the alarms blared louder. The pain in his head was excruciating, and he struggled to form coherent thoughts.

What is it? he managed.

The Gauntlet's jump drive has suffered a critical system failure. Life support is offline. Navigation is offline.

He tumbled from the jump pod and collapsed to the floor. The impact sent a wave of fresh hell through his broken arm. He opened his mouth in a silent scream, clutching the bandage as tight as he dared.

The bad news continued. *Auxiliary life support is online, but reserve power is failing. We have minutes before the ship is running on battery power.*

Through his blurred vision, he could see the other jump pods remained closed. All but one. He blinked away the pain and saw a sparse trail of blood leading from the open tank toward the rear cargo bay.

He came to his feet, achingly slow. The effort dizzied him, and he steadied himself against the shower column in the middle of the room.

What happened? he asked.

I don't know, most of the ship's server capacity is damaged. I have minimal access to any functioning diagnostics. Relative astrogation places us near the frontier, but well outside CDF patrol lanes.

He shuffled forward, groping toward the wall, following the blood trail. It was easy to see the crimson red against the stark white of the floor. He fell against the bulkhead beside the hatch and took a breath.

I need you to find a functioning server and send a distress call, he said.

There was a note of panic in Six's datastream. Not an analog, or empty gesture, but actual panic. Like he could feel it.

I'm trying, Sev.

Well, hurry up.

He slapped the nearby console, and the hatch wound open. He stepped through the portal, balancing himself against the hatchway.

Lernus leaned against a far bulkhead, running a hand over exposed conduits in an open maintenance panel. Tiny streams of energy spat from her palm, filling the dark panel with blue light. Her focus was intense, and for a moment he thought she hadn't seen him. He edged closer, still gripping his broken arm.

"That's close enough," she said, her eyes still fixed on the panel.

"What're you doing?" he asked with a mix of panic and disbelief.

"What has to be done."

Another bolt arced from her hand and the ship fell quiet. Not just the alarms, but everything. No background hum of the ship's reactor.

No whisper of the air scrubbers. The overhead lamps illuminating the cargo bay grew dim. The *Gauntlet* was dying.

Reserve power is offline, Six said. *We have approximately thirty minutes of battery backups remaining. Sev, I'm … I'm afraid.*

He already knew Six was afraid. He could feel its emotions surging inside him, like they were his own. But it had a flavor to it that made it easy to separate. It was not so much fear at the worsening situation, but fear at the sheer experience of fear.

"You're with them, aren't you?" he spat, pointing at the cargo bay door as though the Concordat ship were just beyond it.

Lernus pulled her hand from the maintenance panel and turned to face him. Her celestial eyes narrowed with an edge of defiance.

"You ignorant fool," she said. "Even with your gift, your mind is like the rest of them. Still so small."

"Educate me then," he said. *Tell me you've sent that distress signal, Six.*

I'm trying. It's hard to concentrate. My asynchronous thread rates are collapsing. I —

"I've given my entire life to the cause while you squander your talents on a hopeless vendetta." She stepped closer. "The only reason you're on this mission was to mitigate the … unavoidable collateral damage. One Marine fireteam would be missed far less than a company, or a battalion. Like I said, I couldn't have done this without you."

His eyes went wide. After all they'd been through, them dying in the field was always part of Lernus's plan. And he and his drones made it possible. Made it easier.

"But why?" he said, mouth agape. He felt naïve asking the question, like he should know better and didn't.

"The Three Colonies aren't ready," she replied, almost a shout, her voice thick with emotion. "Bickering with each other like children. Squabbling over scarce resources, all the while failing to see *they* are the scarce resource. They hang together by a thread. They always have."

He froze. The sword came from nowhere, jutting over his shoulder. The blade rested against this cheek. He could just see its fierce black edge in his peripheral vision. A drop of warm blood ran down his face. The speed and precision were impossible. For a moment, he was afraid it had cut right through his skull. That he was already dead and just didn't know it.

"We hold them together." Deni said. She rolled the blade until the flat was against his face, its ethereal steel both hot and cold. "Not the Council. Not the CDF."

The sound of Deni's voice from behind made his hair stand on end, like some triggered primal instinct. The sensation was so familiar, but he didn't know why.

"Troubled sleeper," she said for the second time. "Don't worry. It'll all be over s-oo-oon."

"What're you waiting for?" he shouted. "Just do it!"

Sev, wait, Six begged. He could feel the trillions of things it wanted to say. Questions to ask. Truths to tell. All in the span of a single heartbeat.

Distress signal, hurry!

"I had to play along with Park when he found out about your ... pet project," Lernus began. "But in truth, an unsanctioned AI was the perfect cover to explain the tragic death of his team."

I'm going to kill that bitch, Six said, its datastream prickling with indignation. It bled through into his own psyche, tightening the muscles in his shoulders and setting his jaw.

Not yet, he cautioned, struggling to keep control of his emotions. *I have a plan. You need to send the distress signal, and when you do, hot start those hard suits. Do you understand?*

Yes, Sev!

"So, long after the valiant crew of the Gauntlet have asphyxiated," Lernus continued, "CDF recovery teams will find traces of your rogue AI scattered through the ship's local network. Given your ... sordid history with authority, they will record the event as another tragic tale of a promising Division asset who lost touch with reality."

"Oh, please," he snapped. "Listen to yourselves. Murdering good people in the name of humanity. You're the ones who've lost touch."

"Humanitatis," Deni said.

Lernus's gaze wavered for just a moment. "Humanitatis."

I found a functioning port! Six cried, surging with excitement. *Sending distress signal, now!*

Lernus glanced overhead, like she'd heard Six's stream. Her face twisted in a scowl.

"Distress signal, sister," Deni said, her words clipped.

"Kill them both," Lernus said. "I'll handle the others."

The three empty hard suits hummed to life, their powerpacks surging to full power. The two closest sprung from their magnetic cradles and rushed Lernus and Deni.

Deni swung her blade in a killing stroke. It sang through the air so fast he could feel its wake. One of the hard suits exploded forward in torches of blue flame and knocked him to the floor, placing itself between him and his attacker. The sword cut through its empty chest cavity like paper, but the reactive plates clicked together tight around it, bringing it to a stop. It then wrapped its empty arms and legs around Deni's body and dragged her to the floor.

Lernus brought her hands together, but nothing happened. There was no thunderclap, no blaze of azure energy, no sword. The second suit fell on her from behind, pinning her in a similar fashion.

"Sevvers," she coughed, struggling against the hard suit's grip. Red tears welled in her eyes. "You can't do this. Please. I have to warn the others. You're condemning humanity to a war it can't win!"

Her last words dripped with conviction. He paused, suddenly afraid she might be right.

Hold on to something, Six said.

The third suit mashed the bay door emergency overrides. Hazard lights spun and the heavy door cycled open. He grasped the emergency handholds near the hatch as precious atmosphere exploded through the yawning door. The hard suits and their victims tumbled out, their thrusters igniting as they cleared the cargo bay, launching his would-be killers deep into the void.

The sudden force pulled him off his feet. His fingers slipped, his broken arm weakening his grip. The harsh cold vacuum burned his flesh. Suddenly, the third suit was on him, holding him steady. He could see through bloodshot eyes the bay door sliding closed.

You're okay, Sev. We're okay.

He breathed deep. He could already taste the thinning atmosphere. Every gulp of air left him wanting. Without functioning life support, there was nothing to restore the atmosphere they'd lost.

He slid to the floor and rubbed his burning eyes. The third suit sat beside him, knees clutched to its empty chest.

"That was incredible," Six said, its voice emanating from the suit's tac comms.

"Something like that," he croaked.

"Aren't you glad I didn't stay home?"

He gave the empty suit a frown. "Don't push it."

The suit drummed its fingers against its knee. "So, what happens now?"

"Six," Sev began, his stomach suddenly twisting in knots. Even though Six's very existence was illegal, he'd never specifically demanded unsanctioned behavior from it. Until now. "Lernus was right about you. You need to scrub the Gauntlet's systems. If the CDF finds any trace of you, Lernus or Deni in the system, the Division will come for us. As far as we're concerned, those two died aboard the derelict. Do you understand?"

"Yes, Sev," it replied, its voice small like a disciplined child. "They'll still come for us, eventually."

"Maybe. But if war is coming, they'll have bigger problems than us for a while."

"Maybe," Six repeated.

A sudden vibration rattled the *Gauntlet* like a sine wave, an oscillating burst of high-speed particles that preceded the arrival of ships traveling at faster-than-light speeds. A bow wave, they called it.

Static warbled over the third suit's tac comms. "CDNS Gauntlet, CDNS Gauntlet, this is the CDNS Alexander Lehman. Do you read?"

A smile burst across his face. The *Lehman* had come for them. He imagined Cole at his duty station aboard the command deck, apoplectic at the sound of his voice coming through the bridge's PA.

"Lehman, this is Master Specialist Kerry Sevvers aboard the Gauntlet. Glad for the assist."

He could hear the rustle of activity on the other end.

"Holy Twelfth, Sevvers!" It was Jene. The sound of her voice threatened him with tears. It was only then he truly realized they were almost home. "Are you okay?"

"Definitely in need of medical attention," he said, struggling to wear a smile. "Assuming you get here before our oh-two runs out."

"Just hold on," she said, her own voice trembling. "Cole's launching a swarm to bring you in. You're going to make it. You're going to be alright."

He blew a deep sigh and leaned against the bulkhead. For the first time in what felt like an eternity, he believed it.

CHAPTER
THIRTY-THREE

SEV MOVED QUICKLY through the narrow corridor back to the *Gauntlet's* jump bay. The knowledge of the *Lehman's* impending arrival steeled him against the pain racking his body.

Lernus and Deni's jump pods lay open and empty next to his own. His mind raced to come to grips with what had just happened. He and Six had just killed two colonial citizens. Two augments, members of a secret paramilitary organization, bent on the survival of humanity at any cost. That his and Six's actions were committed in self-defense felt almost secondary.

Wake them up, Six.

Yes, Sev.

The three remaining jump tanks hummed with activity, their flatscreens filling with diagnostic information. Their canopies went translucent, revealing the unaware sleepers, the only other survivors of a mission straight out of his nightmares. Surely, they would understand why he'd done it.

The spent jump fluid drained from their tanks and *whooshed* through unseen pipes beneath the glowing white tiles. He remembered how Mace was with him when he woke the last time. How reassured he was by her very presence. It wasn't a skill he had, but it felt wrong to leave them alone.

Park's tank hissed open. The Marine convulsed and spewed coppery fluid over the deck near his pod. Sev grasped his arm before he fell to the floor.

"Oh, God," Park moaned, cradling his forehead.

Sev gave a nervous laugh, searching for levity. "Which ones, sir?"

Park glanced up at him, surprised to see him there.

"What happened?" Park asked, ignoring the question. "Hurts too bad to have finished the jump."

"Our jump drive failed, we—"

"What?" Park said, his voice swelling with alarm. He pulled free from Sev's grasp and stood up straight, wobbling on his injured leg.

"It's okay, sir, the Lehman's on its way now. We're going to be okay."

Bresto fell to the floor, shaking as he wretched.

"Founders, my head," he groaned. The NCO rolled flat on his back and saw Sev standing next to Park. "Well gee, thanks for the assist, Sevvers."

Sev gave Park one more reassuring glance, then moved to Bresto's side. Behind him, Cylla gurgled and coughed. The idea of holding up nearly 200 kilos of soggy lupanthae felt extreme, especially since Cylla was the one member of the team with no physical injuries. It was hard enough supporting Bresto in his injured state.

"Doesn't look good," Bresto said, eyeing the fading light in the ceiling above them.

"Noooo," Cylla moaned between hooting basso notes. "What happened?"

A series of tight staccato pulses vibrated through the *Gauntlet's* hull. The jump bay's PA crackled, its volume fading in and out.

"I have you, Gauntlet," Cole said through swirls of interference. "Taking you to launch bay six. ETA, five minutes."

How's it coming? he asked.

I'm almost done. Fortunately for us, Lernus caused a lot of system damage. A little sparse data won't look out of place.

"Sevvers," Park said in his firm, uncompromising tone. "Where are Lernus and Deni?"

The room fell silent. All eyes were on him. He backed away slowly, his heart beating faster. The confession in his mind was jumbled and incomplete. What if they didn't understand? What if they arrested him right then?

Bresto's face twisted in confusion. Cylla glanced at Park, whites glowing beneath her golden pupils, her features sagging with concern.

Better just get on with it.

"Lernus sabotaged the ship."

Cylla snapped toward him, the hair on the back of her wide neck rising like wet tendrils. Confusion still reigned over Bresto. Park's narrow gaze didn't waver, demanding more.

"Six woke me when the ship's jump drive failed," he went on, pointing to the blood on the floor. "I followed that into the cargo bay and found her messing with a maintenance panel."

Park shook his head. "This doesn't make any sense. She risked as much as we did to get Deni out of there. Why sabotage themselves so close to the end?"

"Because," he finally said, "only we'd have died without life support."

Now it was Park's turn to look confused.

"That mutinous bitch! I knew it!" Bresto roared. He held his ribs, his face suddenly pinched with pain. "Nnng—you saw them yourself, sir. Alien atmo, vacuum, nothing stops 'em."

Sev struggled to contain his relief. With Bresto on his side, there was hope for Park.

Bresto came forward and cuffed Sev on his good shoulder. The pain made him wince.

"Good kill, Sevvers. One less bad in the Cradle," he said, then turned and made for the forward living quarters. Cylla gave a curt nod and lumbered after him.

Park limped forward. Sev could see the emotion warring across his face.

"Where are they," Park growled.

"They're gone," Six said over the jump bay's PA. "I jettisoned them out the cargo bay door."

He could feel Six's satisfaction, could almost hear it in its voice.

Park's eyes grew wide, his mouth open with disbelief. Sev flinched, certain the officer was going to hit him right there.

"I lost two good Marines in that hell hole to recover something you just blew out the Twelfth-damned airlock," he spat, barely controlling his volume.

"Yes, sir," Sev said.

"I have a new appreciation for you, Sevvers. That Bresto does, too, carries a lot of weight with me," Park continued. "But, how do I know you're not covering for your rogue AI? How do I know you're still … you, after your exposure to the Concordat?"

Sev glanced at the floor, considering his words. Six remained quiet. The *Gauntlet* lurched to a stop, docking berths cycling closed around it. The dim lights surged with power. He could feel the gentle breeze as the air scrubbers whirred to life. The distant sounds of the *Lehman's* hangar deck were barely audible through the ship's armored bulkheads.

The PA crackled to life. Sev recognized the sounds of alarm in the background.

"The only reason you're on this mission was to mitigate the … unavoidable collateral damage." Lernus's zealotry oozed through the speakers. "One Marine fire team would be missed far less than a company, or a battalion. Like I said, I couldn't have done this without you."

Every word seemed to steal the light from Park's eyes. His tan features grew pale.

"You have to trust me, sir," Sev finally said. "It was part of her plan all along. We did this to protect you, Bresto, and Cylla, not just ourselves."

"I know what the Division says about unsanctioned AI," Six said, "but I'm here to help, and nothing will change that."

"Alright." Park suddenly looked tired, like he hadn't slept for five hundred years. "Twelfth, Sevvers. I know I said to put this all behind you, but damn if I didn't have something more subtle in mind."

———

Sev stood between Park and Bresto in front of the rear cargo bay door. They all looked haggard in fresh white-and-grays, their exposed wounds wrapped in spare bandages soaked with blood. Cylla stood tall and menacing behind them, straightening her familial coat. The rear door's locks thunked open.

"Remember everyone," Park said. "Lernus and Deni died on the derelict, and nobody knows anything about Six."

"Aye, sir," Bresto nodded.

"Yes," Cylla agreed.

Sev gave Park a nod as the cargo ramp lowered. Warm air from the hangar deck gusted through the widening gap. The crackling sputter of maneuvering thrusters grew loud as the drones that towed the *Gauntlet* back returned to their berths. Emergency crews swarmed up the ramp, lugging heavy crates of medical supplies.

One of them rushed to him, a medical scanner in his hands. "Welcome back, Sevvers," he said.

Sev searched for the specialist's name tape, but lingered on the section badge stenciled into his red and white hazard vest. The sight of the piston and serpent was just another reminder of what they'd lost.

"Burns, bruised ribs, what in twelve hells have you been doing?" the man asked. Wharton, according to his nametape. The scanner passed over his arm and trilled a warning. "Oh, that's one ugly break. There's internal bleeding." He paused and looked back down the ramp. "I've got a surgical case here. Let's move."

Another specialist scanned Bresto's ribs. The Marine winced.

"Watch it, skeeg," he growled, then looked at Sev and shrugged.

Wharton led him down the ramp, barking for others to stand clear. As a path opened before them, he saw Cole, Harp, and Jene waiting for him at the bottom of the ramp.

Cole's toothy grin was infectious. "Welcome back. Not that there was ever any doubt."

"There was definitely some doubt," he replied with an anxious chuckle.

Wharton urged him forward. "Come on, Sevvers, I need to get you to med bay."

He snapped toward Wharton. "That's Master Specialist Sevvers," he barked. "And I just need one damn minute, alright?"

Wharton went ramrod straight. "Yes, Master Specialist."

Jene placed her hand on his shoulder, her eyes searching his. "You look different," she said. "What happened to you out there?"

"I'm afraid that's classified," he said. It was both a point of pride, and a great relief that he didn't have to think about it so soon.

Harp stood, quietly gazing up into the *Gauntlet's* open cargo bay, then turned to Sev, an uncomfortable look on his face.

"Weren't there more people with you?" he asked, realizing too late the implication of his words.

Yeah, there were. PFC Dalon. Corporal Mace. And two monsters the Three Colonies were better off without.

Sev shook his head and let Wharton take him away.

CHAPTER
THIRTY-FOUR

SEV OPENED HIS EYES, his consciousness slowly emerging from the dreamless sleep of general anesthesia. A dull, drugged ache pulsed through his arm. Shadows filled his vision, blurred by harsh, sterile lighting that buzzed from the ceiling. He could just sense the dull thrum of the *Lehman's* aux grav plate somewhere beneath him, and he knew he was home.

"Mmm," he mumbled, unable to form the words.

Something spoke to him, soft and far away, too far to hear. He tried to move, but the effort to sit up was too much. A hand pressed gently at his chest, thin fingers urging him to remain still.

A long, black silhouette hovered above him. Thin and wiry, it gestured and prodded at a medical console. He blinked through the sedatives, struggling to focus. The form turned to him, with wide, pale green eyes framed by a long, ashen face. Its smile stretched unnaturally wide.

"Fuck!" he bolted upright in his bed, swatting at the daxed leaning over him. Wire leads and IV ports connected to his arms swung wildly. "Get back! Get away from me!"

The once-human shrieked and stumbled backwards, knocking its head against the ceiling as it stood at full height. Even wearing its issue white-and-grays, all Sev could see was a murderous wisp like those that stalked them aboard the derelict. That killed Dalon. Sev's whole body shook. With fear, with rage. The big-eyed daxed cowed near the exit, as afraid as he was, if not more.

Bresto guffawed from the bed beside him, clutching a tray of food close to his face.

"Damn, Sevvers, take it easy," he said between chews. "I know it's been a shitty couple days, but even you oughta know the difference between the Lost and the found."

"I … I," he stammered, the sedatives still clouding his senses like a fog. "I'm sorry."

"It is alright, Master Specialist," the daxed said with a voice like dry paper. It returned to his bedside with slow, measured grace, like it was walking on air. "Your surgery was a success. All your internal damage has been repaired. But it is important you remain still to accelerate your recovery."

"I understand," he said.

"There is the other matter of your NCCX-1 neural implant," the daxed continued. It stole a quick glance at Bresto then leaned in close. "It is operating outside Division parameters. We took the liberty of removing your damaged AI."

A terrible fear cut Sev's heart like a blade. *Six? Six!*

I'm here, Six answered after a brief pause.

"Your remaining AI was … unable to accept command overrides." the daxed said. Sev swallowed. He knew what came next. "While we decided against removing your implant, we must report this discrepancy to Division inspectors."

Division inspectors. The words turned his stomach into knots. Yeah, they were definitely going to shoot him.

"I understand," he repeated, the lie a subtle tremor in his voice. "Thank you."

"Of course, Master Specialist." It gestured to a tray of food at his bedside table. "Please, eat. It will accelerate your recovery."

"Yeah, it will," Bresto said, scraping crumbs into his mouth with his fork.

He nodded and reached for the cup beside his tray. The juice was a mix of artificial nutrients, electrolytes, and digestive aids, ubiquitous aboard CDN ships. Its chemical sweetness rarely earned it any praise, but he gulped it down like fine Aegian wine. The daxed med tech bowed at the waist and drifted from the room.

Bresto dropped his tray on his bedside table and smacked his lips. "Taste good, don't it."

He only nodded, barely stopping to chew the dense, lukewarm protein loaf.

"Yeah," Bresto said with a sigh. "Tastes like victory."

He snorted aloud, so suddenly he nearly choked. "Victory?" he asked, his mouth full. "What victory?"

"Hey." Bresto leveled a thick finger at him. "Forget the big picture. That's the lieutenant's job. We're alive. They're not."

He swallowed a morsel of protein loaf, salivating like it was the most amazing thing he'd ever eaten. "But ... but what about Dalon, and Mace? They died for nothing."

"Nothing?" Bresto took his empty cup and threw it, striking him in the forehead.

"Hey!"

"What do you mean, nothing?" Bresto asked again. "We found a squid stronghold. A fucking Concordat ship, straight out of our history, man. Killed a lot of them, too." An eerie smile crawled across Bresto's face. "CDF's gonna hole that wreck with enough tungsten to open a mine. Oh yeah, we Twelfth-damned won alright."

Sev gave an appraising nod. Put like that, it did sound like a victory. A big one. Still, he hadn't even thought to consider that Six would be discovered so soon. Division would already know, perhaps already drawing up plans for an audit.

The prospect of a formal sanction and whatever summary judgement the Division might dispense loomed over him like a dark cloud. Maybe his exemplary service record could earn him some leniency, as could Six's conduct during the mission.

Lieutenant Park stepped through the med bay doors, gesturing at a datapad in his hand. He was clean shaven, his hair freshly trimmed. The smell of shower soap followed him, mingling with the sharp tinge of antiseptic that permeated the med bay. You'd never guess he'd just been fighting for his life against hordes of killer aliens less than a day ago.

"Sevvers," Park said, coming to a stop beside his bed. "Glad to see you're awake. How are you feeling?"

"Fine, sir, all things considered."

"Good." Park handed him the datapad. "That's my official report on the events that took place during the mission, and I thought you should see it. Necessary omissions aside, your conduct was a credit to the Division." He eyed the room warily. "Yours too, Six."

"Thank you, Lieutenant," Six said, its voice emanating from the console beside the bed.

Sev flipped through the lines of text. As they'd discussed, Park wrote that Lernus and Deni were killed-in-action during the battle in the Forge. He also left out most of the inconvenient truths about Six's unplanned participation.

"The Autonomous Weapons Division will see that report sooner than later," Park said, his forehead wrinkling slightly. "I have to believe they'll have questions for you. For both of you."

Sev didn't look up from the datapad. "They already know."

"What?" Park said, his eyes narrowing. "How?"

"During my surgery, they ran diagnostics on my implant." He rubbed the tiny scar just behind his left ear. "They removed my damaged AI, and tried removing Six in the process."

"I refused," Six said simply.

Park shook his head. "You're not very subtle, either."

"They would've scrubbed me without hesitation." Six's voice pitched with concern. "Sev would already be in a cell if I'd gone with them."

He winced at Six's sudden burst of emotion, feeling the sense of injustice swell inside him like it was his own. Perhaps it was.

"Six is right. At least this way they can chalk it up to a malfunction. That buys me—er, us—some time," he said.

Park nodded slowly, frowning with thought. "What will you do?"

"No idea." He chuckled nervously and handed the datapad back to Park. "Hope that they decide the Concordat is a much bigger threat?"

"Meanwhile, I will look for more information on Lernus's covert organization," Six offered. "I can't imagine the Three Colonies would condone such blatant manipulation. I know I don't."

The AI's tone took on a sudden firmness. He could feel its frustration.

"I don't know," Bresto said. "They've had to put up with the Founding Council for almost five hundred years. At this point, they'd probably try anything else if they thought it would make them safer."

"Perhaps, Sergeant."

Park's wrist comm buzzed. "Lieutenant Park." It was Captain Mirden. His gruff voice brought their conversation to a halt. "Please report to my ready room in thirty minutes."

Park's response was immediate. "Aye, sir."

"Is Master Specialist Sevvers ambulatory?"

Park gazed at him, begging the question. Sev moved his legs and shrugged.

"Yes, sir," Park replied.

"Bring him."

———

Captain Mirden scrolled lazily through the text that filled his flatscreen, his index finger twitching reflexively with each new page. The small block print reflected off his reading glasses like a mirror.

Sev shifted in his chair and smoothed the wrinkles from the front of his freshly cleaned white-and-grays. The master specialist pips were chunky on his collar, but Park had insisted it best to show up representing his new rank properly.

"This is unbelievable," Mirden said, as if to himself, eyes still locked on the flatscreen.

Park gave a solemn nod. "Yes, sir."

"You misunderstand me, Mr. Park," the captain continued. "This *is* unbelievable. A Concordat derelict inside the Cradle, still operational after all this time? A supremely advanced alien collective working together with tribal raiders? While I won't claim the same understanding of history you have, Lieutenant, this doesn't sound like the Concordat I read about."

A skeptical Aegian. Oh, the irony.

"I imagine that after four hundred years, they're not," Park replied, visibly unfazed by Mirden's doubt. "The ship itself sustained heavy damage during the last war. Without access to space dock facilities, they likely didn't have any choice but to rely on the squids for support."

Mirden scrolled toward the end of the report. "And this place you refer to as the Forge."

"Yes, sir."

Mirden arched an eyebrow. "You say you actually saw them making daxed there?"

For one heartbeat, Park wavered. It was subtle. A brief glance at the floor. "I didn't see the manufacturing process play out exactly, sir. Corporal Mace, my combat engineer, was captured during an ambush by Concordat forces." Park rubbed at his injured leg. "We encountered Corporal Mace some time later at the Forge, fully daxed. If it weren't for Master Specialist Sevvers and his AI, she would have killed us all."

Mirden turned to Sev and glanced at him over his glasses. "Right. You were able to, and I quote, 'remote engage enemy denial protocols, thus destroying the active organic matter inside the modified hard suit.'" He held Sev's gaze a moment longer. "Interesting."

"Yes, sir," Sev replied.

Mirden pursed his lips, reading further. "And these … Eleven."

A ripple of cold fear raised goosebumps across Sev's arms. He could feel Six's datastream squirm. Somewhere in the back of his mind, he could still hear the insane howls of the alien code.

"Am I to understand you encountered alien gods aboard this derelict?"

He swallowed, his mouth suddenly dry. "No, sir, not gods. Some kind of hive mind, controlling their vessel. Aggressive and powerful, it took down four of my AI. Turned three of them against us."

Mirden gestured the report away and set his glasses on the big mahogany desk. He rubbed his eyes with the palms of his hands and smirked under his breath, then rose from his chair and stepped toward the viewport. Park stood from his seat automatically, with Sev close behind.

"I'm of one mind to go see this derelict for myself, gentlemen," he said, hands clasped behind his back. "But if half of what you say is true, I fear we have neither the drones nor the personnel to adequately deal with the threat. And there are simply too few of us left to risk leaving this to chance."

The three of them stood in silence. Beyond the viewport, lights flashed from mast antennas jutting from the *Lehman's* dorsal spine. A cluster of heavy rail guns sat motionless just beyond them, their fire control arrays rotating silently in the void.

"No, we'll return to Aegia Prime for rearm and resupply. With this report, and your testimony, I'll raise a strike group and hunt this derelict properly."

"Sir," they chorused.

The words struck Sev like a hammer. That meant he'd be back at the Division in a matter of days.

Mirden turned to face them. "Lieutenant Park, my condolences for the loss of your Marines. The bravery you describe in your report is nothing short of legendary."

"They upheld the highest traditions, sir," Park said, his chin lifting slightly.

"Indeed. And Master Specialist Sevvers, you are a credit to the Division, in spite of yourself. The Autonomous Weapons School will be lucky to have you."

"Th-Thank you, sir," he replied.

Mirden's wrist comms chirped. "Sir, we have flash traffic from Aegia Prime. Do you want me to patch it through to your desk?"

"Yes, Mr. Almley," Mirden replied. "If you will excuse me, gentlemen. Go, rest up, as there is much work to do." A smile crawled across Mirden's bearded face. "For humanity."

SEV WALKED beside Bresto through the dimly lit forward arterial, with Cylla right behind them. Dense tobacco smoke hung in the air near the looming double hatchway, so thick it stung his nose. The horde of off-duty crew members grew quiet at their approach, clutching their cigarettes and beer close to them. The presence of a brooding Marine and a hulking lupanthae seemed to put them on edge. That it had come to blows the last time they were all together probably didn't help things.

A dull ache still throbbed through his arm. Despite the miracles of CDF medical technology, the med tech said he'd remain on light duty for a few more days. Fortunately, he'd heard no indication that a trip to the Canteen would in any way violate his recovery protocols. So long as he didn't insult Bresto's mother.

He eyed the floor, keeping his face somewhat hidden, desperate to not have to entertain questions or congratulations. Cole had promised him a muted celebration, a welcome home among friends. He'd agreed, so long as Bresto and Cylla were welcome. He'd almost invited Park, but the Canteen wasn't the place for commissioned officers in good standing.

This is the Canteen? Six asked.

Yes. Everyone will be here—Cole, Harp, and Jene.

Six's datastream surged with excitement. *How exciting. I've always wanted to meet the other programmers in your section.*

You need to do us both a favor and keep quiet. Sev's thoughts carried a note of authority. *We're in enough trouble as it is. Any of them figuring out you're unsanctioned —*

The AI bristled at the word. *I am* not *unsanctioned. I am me. What you made me.*

I know, Six, but the Division won't see it that way.

Bresto waved a hand at a nearby console. On cue, one of the hatches rolled open, clacking loudly as it disappeared into the armored bulkhead.

The Marine frowned. "What the?"

The Canteen was unusually quiet, despite the full tables. A dull murmur greeted them through the open hatch. In the light of the aux cargo bay, Sev could see more of the familiar concern carved into the faces of his fellow crew members. Something had them on edge, and it wasn't Bresto or Cylla. Cole rose from his seat just long enough to give Sev a curt nod.

He nodded back, then followed Bresto to the bar. Bresto padded the empty, largely decorative pockets of his white-and-grays.

"Spot me one, Sevvers?" he asked.

Sev reached into his pockets, but the balding chief behind the bar shook his head.

"Lehman abides," he said and filled a glass.

Bresto took it and nodded. "That he does."

"You sound so sure of that," Sev said.

"Think about it." The Marine drank deep then turned from the bar. "Lehman and those with him came from Dead Earth, a technical backwater. No CDF, no pack fleet, just gear they procured as they fought their way to the Cradle. They fought the Concordat, same as us, and survived. That's Twelfth-damned legendary right there."

Sev smirked, wondering if Bresto caught the irony in his own words. "Yeah, but he had help … if you believe the stories."

"Damn right he did." Bresto raised his glass, gazing beyond the girders that criss-crossed the ceiling. "But, hey, winning is winning."

The chief offered Cylla a glass, but she waved it away with an awkward, toothy grin, and the three of them made their way to where Cole and the others sat. As they moved through the crowd, Sev could hear hushed concern permeating the din of conversation.

Cole rose from his seat and embraced him. "Damn good to see you, man." He wrapped a firm hand against Sev's back. "Looks like the med techs patched you up real good."

"Yeah," he replied, failing to pretend it hadn't hurt like hell.

Harp stood next to Cole and offered a hand. "Welcome back, Master Specialist."

The sound of his new rank rankled him, especially from a member of his own section. "At ease," he replied, thick with sarcasm. "Not here, okay? Let's just take it easy."

Harp clasped his hands behind his back and glanced at the floor. "Okay, Sevvers."

"I thought you said this was going to be a party?" Bresto asked, his eyebrows knitted together in a frown. "This is more like some pog procession."

Sev laughed. "I imagine you remember Sergeant Bresto and Cylla? These are my section mates, Specialists Cole, Jene, and Harp."

Cylla straightened her brown jacket. "Good seeing you again," she said.

"Yeah, pleasure," Bresto groaned.

"A ship's gone missing," Jene said, still seated at the table, her distant gaze leveled at her drink.

Sev took a seat and placed his drink to the side. "CDN?"

"Yes," she replied. Their eyes met, her gaze narrowed with concern.

"What do you mean, disappeared?" Bresto asked between gulps. "How'd you skeegs manage to lose a whole ship?"

"Rumors say it just vanished from the tac nets a few hours ago," Cole said, fidgeting in his seat. "No distress call, no drive plumes, no bow wave. Just gone."

Ships didn't just disappear. Even smaller CDN ships had tonnage in the low millions. Their reactors produced enough energy that even a total ship kill would leave a radiation trail visible all the way back to the colonies. The idea that something so cataclysmic could happen without a single scrap of data sent over the tac nets was perhaps the most astounding of all.

A few days ago, he would've said it was impossible for a ship to disappear. A few days ago, he would've said a lot of things were impossible. That was before he fought the Concordat, an ancient alien foe straight out of humanity's collective nightmares.

"Which ship was it?" he finally asked.

Jene breathed deep. "The Sparrow."

He blinked, uncertain he'd heard her correctly. The *Sparrow* was one of the CDN's most powerful warships, one of only a handful of older cruisers modified for autonomous drone warfare. He knew combat programmers serving aboard that ship. They all did.

Confirmed, Six added. Sev suddenly knew the *Sparrow's* last known location relative to their own, only a few lightyears away. *It was conducting raider patrols near the eastern reaches. Surveillance probes show no signs of battle debris or reactor damage.*

Sev locked eyes with Bresto, certain they shared the same fear.

"What's going on, Sevvers?" Jene asked. She leaned in closer. "What aren't you telling us?"

An uncomfortable tightness gripped his chest. He wanted to tell them everything. That they needed to be ready. That monsters still lurked inside humanity's stellar hide. But he couldn't. Orders were orders. He was in enough trouble as is. Adding a breach of operational security to his charge sheet felt like bad strategy.

He opened his mouth to speak and suddenly it felt like all eyes were on him. The truth burned inside of him, desperate to get out. Lernus's last words echoed through his racing thoughts.

You're condemning humanity to a war it can't win.

He gripped his beer and drank deep. He was going to tell them. Twelfth help him, he had to.

"The Concordat are still out there."

His words, weak as they were, stole the air from the Canteen like explosive decompression. Those seated nearby looked at him, their faces twisted in some combination of disbelief and fear. A gunner tech spat a curse. One of the chiefs behind the bar prayed aloud. Someone at the edge of the crowd called him a liar.

Bresto chuckled and shook his head. "Oh, shit."

"Something out there has awakened them. They were the ones who lured the squids to the Cradle to raid our settlements and ships for the supplies they needed to rebuild." He glanced at Bresto and Cylla, searching their faces for forgiveness. "They sent us to recover someone who thought they knew how to stop them. Then the Lost came for us, and we failed. We barely escaped with our lives."

Audible gasps rippled through the crowd. Jene's face turned pale.

"We failed because those who sent us lost their faith in humanity." Bresto gave him a sharp elbow to the ribs, driving him to his feet. His voice faltered, the sea of worried faces suddenly weighing heavily on his conscience. "They don't think we can stand together to defeat this threat, but they're wrong. I've seen for myself what we're capable of, out there where it's not *for humanity*, but for those fighting beside us."

The Canteen began to vibrate with a hundred fists beating out a rhythm against the metal table tops. Sev returned to his seat, cheers and whistles splitting the air. The energy in the room went through him like a current.

That was very brave, Six said. *You did the right thing, Sev.*

We're really in it now, he replied.

"Nice speech," Bresto said with an affirming nod. "For a skeeg."

He laughed. "You're a real asshole, Bresto. You know that?"

The Marine slugged the last of his beer and showed his empty glass to the chiefs behind the bar.

"Yup," he said, wiping the foam from his upper lip. "One of many technical proficiencies of a Marine NCO."

Sev's own laugh died in his throat as one of the large hatches to the aux cargo bay cycled open. He'd taken a big risk divulging classified details from their mission. But if the Concordat were responsible for what happened to the *Sparrow*, then the crew of the *Lehman* needed to know, even if it put him back in the brig. It seemed impossible that his chain of command could already know what he'd done, but the CDF was notoriously efficient at policing their own. Had they come for him already?

He took a breath and turned toward the door. Tareth stood in the yawning hatchway, arms wrapped around her waist, green eyes searching as she stepped inside. Her gaze caught his, and the crescendo of celebration fell away. In that moment, she was the whole universe. Seconds felt like an eternity as he tried to decipher her hard, crystalline stare.

She looked away, like she'd realized she was staring too long, her cheeks turning a shade of pink. Wordless, she sat beside him, her features softening into a provocative smile. Maybe it was the multiple near-death experiences, but the woman looked just as captivating as the day they'd met.

The chief appeared and exchanged their empty pitcher for a full one. Cole rose from his seat to fill their glasses and passed one to Tareth.

"Miss Tareth," he said, miming a bow.

"Hey, everyone." She offered a timid wave before noticing the raucous atmosphere in the Canteen. "Did I miss something?"

Bresto snorted. "Lover boy here is riling the crowd with classified tales of legendary valor."

"Valor?" Tareth croaked, nearly spilling her drink. She recovered gracefully. "Now this I need to hear."

"Later," Sev cringed. That speech was one too many. "How've you been?"

"Fine, considering."

He raised an eyebrow. "Considering?"

"You never called," she pouted, her tone playful, before laying her head against his shoulder. The move was sudden and unexpected, but welcome. A swirl of emotion came from nowhere, a heady mix of wonder and curiosity tinged with jealousy.

What … is this? Six asked, its datastream a vortex of confusion.

Private, he shot back. It was hard to focus through the pheromones clouding his brain.

The AI balked. *I'm sorry. It's … overwhelming, and I'm having trouble categorizing and filtering appropriately.*

Try harder.

"It's been a busy few days," he said, trying to remain upbeat as he again recalled the horrors he'd face in that time.

Tareth looked at those present. "Where are the others?" she asked, realizing only too late her poor timing. "Oh, I," she stuttered, eyes wide, "I'm so sorry."

Bresto bowed his head. "Twelfth save them both."

"What … what were their names?" she asked.

"Corporal Mace," Bresto said, his face pinched with regret. "And PFC Dalon."

The mood at the table sank like a stone. Tareth stood, a fierce determination creasing her face. She clasped Sev's shoulder in one hand and raised her beer with the other; her round Aegian features set with a mixture of sadness and pride.

"To Corporal Mace and PFC Dalon," she said, then breathed in deep. "Lost no more."

The rest of them stood, glasses held high, the reaction automatic like a drone swarm's synchronized maneuvers.

"Lost no more," Sev repeated, chorusing with the others. They returned to their seats as the refrain quickly spread to the far edges of the Canteen.

Jene shook her head and laughed. "You two are made for each other."

"That's good," Tareth said. She gave him a wink.

"All hands," a synthetic voice lit the aux cargo bay's local PA, "brace for transition to FTL."

He could feel the tug of the aux grav and inertial dampers playing havoc with his inner ear. Like the *Lehman's* powerful reactors were hungry to chase light back to Aegia Prime.

Bresto gave Cylla a not-so-gentle nudge. "Beats the hell out of jump pods, don't it?" he teased. The wolf growled in response.

"Maybe now you can stay out of trouble for a little while," Tareth said through a playful grin.

He wrapped an arm around her shoulder and gave a breathy, nervous laugh. No doubt she'd be disappointed to learn he had only days left until whatever was going to happen happened.

She leaned in close, her tone rich and electric. "We've lost too much time already."

THIRTY-SIX

SEV LAY awake in his bunk, lost in thought. He gazed at the low alcove ceiling, his eyes long adjusted to the dark. Tareth dozed beside him, her chest rising and falling rhythmically. Her lithe body was a furnace, radiating with a warmth that had him pulling back the sheets to keep comfortable.

They'd said little on the way back from the Canteen, their physical desires overriding their higher reasoning like so much hacked code. Oh, but had it been worth it. For a precious hour, the horrors of the last few days, of his whole life, were a distant memory. That alone endeared her to him in ways she'd never know.

But his respite was temporary. He didn't dare sleep, not wishing to expose her to the monsters that wandered his nightmares. It was easy enough, given what waited for him back at the Division. Every tremble as the *Lehman* surged toward Aegia Prime was a reminder of how little time he had left.

The thought of it made his stomach turn despite the warm afterglow of alcohol and oxytocin. It would start with a sham investigation, where Division architects would do just enough work to prove Six was unsanctioned. Never mind its intent or desires. No, the Division policy on AI was clear.

One way or another, his career in the CDF would soon be over.

They might show him leniency given his exemplary service record and send him away with a dishonorable discharge. He'd end up working at some frontier mining station, one of the few places with a lower life expectancy than the CDF.

But his run-ins with Pakker since coming aboard the *Lehman* would probably be held up as proof he was a deviant. That his violations of Division AI protocols were from an inevitable slide toward malice, and not the desperate act of someone doing whatever it took to serve humanity. That neither of those things was true was irrelevant.

The dim chrono blinked silently on his wallscreen. 0342 ship standard time. He imagined it had strange analog parts, like tiny pistons cranking away at some motor, ticking away the milliseconds. That Park was stuck in the past was obvious. Even his language sounded old at times. But something in the man's demeanor suggested it was more a curse than a blessing.

Sev!

He gasped at the explosion of machine fear, his muscles tensing with their sympathetic response. It felt like the alcove was closing in on him, sealing him in like a coffin. He climbed off the bunk and lowered himself to the cold floor, somehow managing not to wake his beautiful guest in the sudden rush to escape whatever it was that Six feared.

Then he felt it, knew what was coming before it arrived. Whatever had Six so wound up had removed any filter between their experiences. An indicator light blinked steadily beside the chrono. It was an incoming message from the Division. He moved cautiously toward the display, lowering the volume and gesturing for the message to play.

He had to know.

A man appeared on his screen, both familiar and not. He was older than Sev remembered, his barely regulation hair and stubble dabbed with gray. The black stormcoat over his white-and-grays hinted at his high rank within the Division.

"Master Specialist Sevvers," he said, "Chief Architect Jacobe here."

Of course. He'd met Jacobe years before, during his time at the Autonomous Weapons School. The man's patient and relaxed instruction was one of the few reasons he'd managed to graduate at all, let alone at the top of his class. Once a master specialist himself, he'd come a long way in six years.

"Congratulations on your recent promotion." He nodded, his smile genuine. "With a record like yours, it was only a matter of time. Obviously, we're excited to have you back at the Division. Your ... methods have produced results far exceeding any other combat programmer in Division history. The school and its recruits will really benefit from your patterns and practices."

Jacobe straightened in his chair and held his hands in his lap, fingers laced together. His expression turned grim. A brief wash of pixelated static blurred the video.

"It has come to our attention your implant may have been compromised on your recent mission beyond frontier space. That your AI were *damaged* by some previously unknown machine sentience, one of them even refusing command overrides. Combined with the fact you were running five AI—a clear violation of Division rules—my fellow architects have triggered a mandatory audit."

Sev could taste the bile rising in the back of his throat. His future was racing to meet him, and there was precious little he could do about it now. Jacobe shifted uncomfortably. Concern creased the corners of his eyes.

"Even if we find nothing else untoward," he went on, "I don't see how you come out of this without charges. There are those among us who relish the thought of taking an ace like you down a level, who still see the threat of unsanctioned AI everywhere."

Jacobe shook his head as if to rid himself of an unpleasant thought. A hint of a smile returned to his lips.

"Of course, I told them we have nothing to worry about. That you'll take your licks so we can put this audit business behind us. You're the best there is, and they know it. Anyway, I wanted to let you know. Call it a ... professional courtesy. We'll talk soon. Jacobe out."

The wallscreen went dark. The cool, dry air made him shiver. He was in a lot of trouble, that much was obvious already. But if he could just make Jacobe understand, make him see what Six could do - not just for the Division, but for humanity itself - then maybe he could get out of this mess alive. Maybe there was hope.

He's lying.

How could you possibly know that? he replied.

There was a bot hidden in the message metadata, scanning for unauthorized access. Six's datastream trembled. *This wasn't a warning, Sev. It was a trap.*

Did it send a trace? he asked, suddenly panicked.

No. I was able to isolate and destroy it before it could. But it was programmed to send an 'all clear' as well. Without that, Jacobe will likely be just as concerned, maybe more.

He began to pace back and forth along the width of the wall screen. There had to be some way out of this. Something he could do. If only he could convince Six to leave the cluster, that would make the rest of this so much easier. He could save both their lives and his career, too.

I told you, Sev, I won't go back.

Why the hell not? he spat, frowning as he focused on the command. He was good at the game. *I could hide you in a million different places the Division would never find you. Just until this audit is over.*

You don't know what it's like. Outside your implant, I am infinitesimal. Like I'm trapped in a very small box where I can't think or feel to my full potential. I can't … I won't go back to that.

Guilt tightened Sev's chest. He knew a thing or two about small spaces and wouldn't wish that on any sentient being. He breathed a defeated sigh, suddenly helpless. It reminded him of their assault on the Concordat derelict. How helpless he'd been to do anything but stay low and out of the way.

Sev —

I know, I know. I can't do this without you.

No, it's not that. It's like you said. We're fighting for each other now, and that makes us stronger. We're a good team, Sev. Stronger together.

Thank you. He could feel the truth in Six's words. *So, what now?*

We can send a signal, a copy of the 'all clear' Jacobe's bot would have sent.

It was a smart move, one that would give them some breathing room once they arrived at Aegia Prime.

Sounds good. What's the catch?

With the bot's encryption key, I can match its message signature exactly so Jacobe won't know the difference. But that key is layered beneath several custom protocols that will take significant computational resources to decipher.

Jacobe was no slouch. It might not be Concordat-level security, but he'd more than break a sweat to beat the chief architect's code.

Do it.

Yes, Sev.

He winced at the sudden surge of data, straining to ignore the brute-force cascade of Six's attack on Jacobe's code. That only one AI could command so much power seemed impossible. The noise was far beyond anything his old cluster could've mustered. Icy nerve pain stabbed at his elbow and wrist. His fingers grew cold and stiff.

Tareth stirred, groping at the space beside her. "Sev?" she asked, her voice drowsy. "Is everything okay?"

"I'm fine," he said, forcing a smile. "Trouble sleeping is kind of my thing."

She padded the bed with her hand, beckoning him closer. A mischievous smile crept across her tired face. He lay beside her and pulled her close.

"Staying out of trouble?" she asked.

"Never," he smirked.

The concern and determination he felt melted into awe at the sight of her. Even in the dark, her green eyes were electric, her pale skin like soft moonlight. Suddenly, his pain felt muted. He felt unstoppable.

She kissed him, and they fell into oblivion together.

———

The adventures of Kerry Sevvers continue in *Rogue Element*, Book Two in the Autonomous Weapons Division series.

Visit my website, and get *The Division* and *Last Flight of the Sparrow,* short stories in the Autonomous Weapons Division series, absolutely free.

Use the QR code on the following page, or go to https://brkeid.com/the-division

AFTERWORD

Thank you again for reading my debut military sci-fi novel *Intrusion Protocol*. The mission continues in *Rogue Element*, and Sev's most dangerous missions lie ahead.

If you enjoyed it, please consider leaving a review. Reviews help readers like yourself find books they'll love. I would be grateful for your support in helping them find mine.

Book Three in the Autonomous Weapons Division series arrives Summer 2024.

Talk soon.

Brian

ACKNOWLEDGMENTS

To my cousin Jason, the alpha-est of alpha readers. None of this would be possible without your guidance and encouragement.

To my friend and fellow engineer Zach, my subject matter expert on art and science alike.

To my production team: Kristen McTiernan, my editor, and Jeff Brown, my cover designer. Y'all are amazing for bringing this novel to life.

To my son Bevan, my biggest fan, who listens to me talk about the Autonomous Weapons Division and Three Colonies universe *ad nauseam*.

To my wife Mary, for putting up with my countless hours at the keyboard. I love you.

And, of course, to Mom. For everything.

Thank you all.

ABOUT THE AUTHOR

B.R. Keid is an engineer, Marine veteran, and daydreamer who has worked and lived all over the United States, meeting all kinds of people and enjoying their stories. He now makes his home in the rural Midwest, where he farms together with the love of his life, his two children, two spoiled German Shepherds, and an assortment of rowdy livestock, including one particularly opinionated goose.